burn your starry crown

by roman leão

illustrations by ryan cicak

Published in the US by Plastic Love Monkey Press

First Edition

ISBN 979-8-88955-979-5

book design by Ray Larsen

for kuku lou

As I went down in the river to pray
Studying about that good ol' way
And who shall wear the starry crown?
Good Lord, show me the way

—Traditional

What if the Star of Bethlehem wasn't a star at all?
—Shakey Deal

Principal Characters

Archangel Sachiel runs a betting scheme on the ability of humanity to spiritually evolve.

Harut and **Marut** are former fallen angels that are trying to game the system.

Jehoel, one of the seraphim, is betting that after two thousand years, the last avatar's teachings have affected mankind in a positive way.

Karabu is a cherub who, after losing big on the Nazarene kid, is betting the parlay.

Kokabiel, having fallen from grace, heads up the Bureau of Nefarious Undertakings.

Ruax is the god of headaches and works for Kokabiel.

Tamiel is Khadae's original name before "going native."

Philomena Fox née Gilliam is the orphaned daughter of the mercantilist and is struggling to understand her place in the world.

Emilia Gilliam is Philomena's mother, possibly Mordikai Fox's lover, and definitely Mortimer's widow.

Mortimer Gilliam is the owner of Fiesta mercantile, a Reverend Fox congregant, and later, a ghost.

Sheriff Christoph Gruffydd is the Tehama County Sheriff.

Águeda María Luisa Iñiguez owns the Fiesta cantina, and is in love with Aaron Urias.

Jose Luís is the half-owner of the Fiesta Livery.

Lucette Narcisse is Philomena's hometown best friend and instigator.

HENRICO COUNTY, VIRGINIA, UNITED STATES OF AMERICA

Mordikai Fox is an itinerant preacher, voluptuary, and impromptu father.

Aaron Urias is Fox's aide-de-camp and partner since the Civil War.

Jeremiah Erasmus Washburn III was a Confederate soldier before he turned decapitated ghost hunter.

MILAKALE, HAWAI'I, KINGDOM OF HAWAI'I

Jonathan Boyle is a member of the Honolulu Rifles and an annexationist.

Allen "Tweed" Colson is a rancher and a member of the Hawaiian League.

Ezra Davis is the bishop of the Reformed Catholic Church of Hawai'i.

Jun Jin is the head chef at Milakale, the Lanthiers' estate on Hawai'i.

Makana Kealoha is a kahuna kupua, a traditional Hawai'ian healer.

Akram Khadae is a fallen angel posing as an Egyptian merchant and opium smuggler.

Alexander Lanthier is a wealthy sugar baron and poor equestrian.

Anias Lanthier is a sugar baroness, hostess, Celtic magic practitioner, and true believer.

Kalani Mahoe is the oldest uncle of Maleko, and works at Milakale.

Kapono Mahoe is the middle Mahoe brother, and also works at Milakale.

Kekoa Mahoe is Maleko's youngest uncle, works at Milakale, and has an eye toward the future.

Maleko Mahoe is the nephew of Noelani and Philomena's partner in crime on the island.

Noelani Mahoe is a cook at Milakale, and is Maleko's aunt and surrogate mother.

Princess Lili'uokalani is the heir apparent to the Hawai'ian throne.

PRIDE OF JEFFERSON, PACIFIC OCEAN

Romo Laurant is a sailor aboard the steamship, *Pride of Jefferson*.

Capt. Kasper Munk is the captain of the *Pride of Jefferson*.

Dr. Coleman Whitaker is the ship's doctor aboard the *Pride of Jefferson*.

SAN FRANCISCO, CALIFORNIA, UNITED STATES OF AMERICA

Saturnino Adão is the majordomo at Edgar Rodolfo's Nob Hill residence.

Niall Hendry is a former London costermonger turned San Francisco haberdasher.

Wei Lei is an opium den mistress with serious connections.

Edgar Bartolmeu "O Elefante" Rodolfo is a robber baron turned swollen kidnapper.

Chapter One: Prolegomenon

1:1   "Place your bets!" Archangel Sachiel called out, his voice rolling like celestial thunder. "Our catalyst approaches Sol system. Our new avatar shall be in play very soon."

The mighty Karabu, a tetramorph with the face of an eagle, bull, lion, or human depending on his mood, strode up to the line of gamblers queued at the bookmaker. He currently wore the face of an eagle, all the better to watch the scrolling odds before placing his bet.

"What is the good word, four-head?" A seraph with the unmarked face of a young child approached the towering cherub, its six red wings folded protectively around itself.

"Feh," Karabu presented his human face in order to spit on the floor. "These monkeys don't have a chance in Hell. I took a bath on the Nazarene kid."

"Come now, mighty Karabu," the seraph cajoled him, a tendency of his kind that drove the larger angel to distraction. "We must have faith that the teachings of the last avatar have had some effect on the native population. They have had nearly two thousand revolutions around their little star. Surely they have made some progress."

Karabu turned to face the profusion of wings, his bull face taking prominence despite a desire to keep his feelings to himself.

"Are you kidding me right now?" He exploded, causing the point spread to fluctuate and a few of the other bettors to turn and watch. "I lost two hundred thousand souls on that match. Do you have any idea how long it takes to save two hundred thousand souls? No, you do not. All you do is fly around emulating dignity and glory. I'm telling you, Jehoel, they do not get it."

"That's not fair," the smaller angel pouted. "Have you ever restrained a leviathan? It's not all hosannas, I can tell you that."

"I am sorry, Jehoel. I shouldn't have said that." Karabu cooled enough for his lion face to take center stage. "This backwater planet drives me crazy. You instill in them one thing, and they do the opposite, all the while swearing that they are doing exactly what you

1

told them. Every day is Upside-Down Day down there. An honest gambler cannot catch a break."

"Do you think they'll get another shot if they shank this one?" Jehoel covered his mouth with one of his wings although everyone had stopped what they were doing to listen in to their conversation.

"Honestly," Karabu leaned his massive leonine head in close. "I am surprised they didn't pull a flood card after that last disaster. I think they may have one more season after this. I may bet the parlay."

"Ooh," the seraph cooed, its red wings rustling, "a long shot!"

"It's the only way I am going to dig myself out," Karabu wagged his shaggy mane. "Plus, I've always had a soft spot for an underdog."

1876

Chapter Two

2:1 The white orb, set in motion by violent force, shot off across a seemingly endless empty expanse before colliding with another, similar sphere. Its momentum skewed but not squandered, the projectile glanced and found a new trajectory—heading toward a final collision.

2:2 The mustachioed cowboy stood across the felt-covered table from Aaron Urias and watched as his opponent calculated the geometry needed to send the white cue ball into his own yellow ball, to the far rail, the side rail, the rail closest to him, and, finally, into the red ball. He then did exactly that.

Urias took the blue cube of chalk from what would have been the riverbank, if the table were a river, and twisted it atop the leather-covered tip of his polished ash wood cue.

"Lucky shot, Urias," the cowboy taunted from across the felt. Unperturbed—the tall former Virginian may have raised a single eyebrow, imperceptible to all but the most vigilant witness—he proceeded to run the table, piling point upon point as the three balls drew elaborate Byzantine patterns within the confined space they were forced to operate.

The cowboy had called the game of straight rail instead of choosing the more restrictive rules of balk line, hoping to take advantage of the specific skill he usually exploited when working a trio of balls against the side.

The name of either game called for the player to hit his opponent's ball where he might find it, bank against the cushioned sides any number of times, and cap it all off by hitting the red ball. A cagey straight rail player could maneuver the triad of balls into close proximity of the rail, or—better yet—into a pocketless corner, to better cycle through the three required movements ad nauseam.

Balk line would have required the two artists to cover the green canvas more completely, the table broken into neighborhoods where one was expected to take care of one's business and move along. Neither option was going to allow the cowboy to keep possession of the newly minted five-dollar half eagles he had foolishly carried into the Bucket of Blood Saloon.

When Urias had finished creating ninety-nine increasingly complex patterns on the felt—none of them any less ephemeral for its mathematical beauty—he paused and brushed back the shock of white that bisected his jet black forelocks; an unruly affair that had begun to slip down and obscure his sightline.

"On the seventh day he rested," Urias intoned, before lining up his final shot.

"What did you say to me?" The cowboy belched, already seeing his gold coins disappear into the pocket of a man who wasn't him; enriching a life that wasn't his.

"We agreed to play to one hundred, right?" Urias asked, either not hearing or choosing to ignore the cowboy's query.

Urias lined up his shot, striking the yellow with his cue ball close to where he stood, and sending it spinning on a long final journey. The orb shot off down the table, glancing the side rail halfway down. Bouncing off the far rail, it began a speedy return to Urias, ricocheting off the opposite side, and striking a point directly below his casual gaze. Undaunted, the wayward ball took a sharp-angled path back into the first side rail and rebounded toward the far end of the table, passing the red ball, and hitting both rays describing the ninety degree corner, before striking the ever-patient red.

"Son of a bitch!" The cowboy exclaimed. "You are a goddamn ringer if I ever saw one." Distraught at the prospect of handing over his hard-found gold, the cowboy reached for the pistol slung low over his hip, only to realize that Urias already had him in the sights of his Union Army-issued Colt.

"There is no need to take the Lord's name in vain," Urias spoke, keeping the cowboy covered. "Matthew 10:9 tells us, 'do not carry any gold or silver or copper in your belts.' As you can see, I only carry cold, hard steel."

The cowboy slowly raised his hands and Urias lowered his gun. "Let's call this a lesson learned. I'd go study on this if I were you."

The mustachioed cowboy left the Bucket of Blood lighter of pocket but wiser of mind, a state that inspired a string of epithets, the force of which propelled him across the room and out onto the dust-covered wooden sidewalks of Virginia City.

2:3   Urias counted his newly won coins, tossing one to the bartender just as the saloon's front door slammed open. Half expecting the cowboy's abrupt return, he slipped his pistol from its leather without thinking and turned to face the entrance.

"Aaron Urias! I should have known I would find you in this den of inequity," the newcomer, who was decidedly not the mustachioed cowboy, called out. "Buy me a drink you scoundrel, I have news."

"Mordikai Fox, I didn't expect to hear from you until the thaw," Urias laughed, parked his Colt, and clasped his friend's kid-gloved hands. "Martim! Set us up with two of those Carson City steam beers."

The bartender drew a pair of draughts and slid them toward the men without spilling a drop.

"It's good to see you up to your old tricks, my friend," Fox said, lifting his beer in salute. "Speaking of Carson City, get your affairs in order, we need to catch a train."

"Slow down, boss. There can't be anything waiting in Carson that we can't procure here," Urias stonewalled. "I know a certain Chinaman, if that's what you're after."

Fox took a long pull from his glass, leaving a shallow scrim of foam clinging to his own black mustache. "We are actually headed out to California. I received a telegram from Fiesta. You remember the Gilliams, the members of our flock who could not conceive?"

Urias raised an eyebrow, this time an outright pantomime of curiosity.

"Emilia has been with child since we were there last, and they have invited us out to witness and bless the miracle."

"That's a nice gesture, Mordikai," Urias prevaricated, "but the passes are sure to still be snowed in. Can we not see the child when we swing through there in the spring?"

"There is something that you need to see," Fox replied, downing the remainder of his beer. "Drink up and follow me." Having sufficiently piqued the curiosity of his friend and part-time aide-de-camp, Fox turned on his heels and walked toward the back of the saloon.

"You are headed the wrong way, my friend." Urias downed his beer and wiped the foam from his closely cropped beard. "There is nothing likely to be back there 'cept empty kegs and tired whores."

"You are forgetting about the back door," Fox answered, not looking back. "As I came in, I noticed a certain unhappy gentleman watching the front of this establishment with a particular interest. You wouldn't happen to know him, would you?"

"Mustachioed?"

"Most impressively."

"Doesn't ring a bell." Urias attempted to pay the bartender but was waived off by Martim's stubby but dexterous fingers. "But why take a chance? Lead on, boss."

The two men made their way through the Bucket of Blood's storeroom and came out in an alley facing east toward the high-mountain desolation of Sevenmile Canyon.

"What is it you need to show me?" Urias prodded, unimpressed by the usual view of desert scrub and mine tailings.

"Skirt this building and look to the west," Fox instructed but elected not to follow. "Watch out for your friend."

"I assure you, Mordikai," Urias spoke back over his shoulder as he walked, "that cowboy is no friend—"

"Do you see it?"

"Holy... wait... What *is* that?" An astonished Urias barely managed to get the question out.

"It appears to be a star," Fox replied.

"Actually, I think that may be a comet," Urias countered, squinting up at the night sky.

"But it could be perceived as star, don't you think?"

"I suppose," Urias admitted, "but that doesn't change what it is. That's a comet. A big one."

"Don't you think that's a sign? A message from the heavens?"

Urias took one last look at the celestial visitor and turned to face Fox.

"Signs and portents are more your purview," he allowed. "What's our play here?"

"Gather your things. As I mentioned, we have a train to catch."

SAN FRANCSICO, CALIFORNIA, UNITED STATES OF AMERICA | 1876

2:4   Niall Hendry hurried past a line of Chinese-operated cigar factories on Jackson Street, his senses attuned to the pungent aroma of tobacco with the fish store across the street adding a dissonant but crucial counterpoint. Hendry was no fan of cigars—or seafood, for that matter—but the familiar farrago of smells always brought his nerves a little closer to his skin. A quick veer into Duncombe Alley and he would soon be reclining on a comfortable pallet in the arms of his one true love: opium.

Born and raised in a damp, smoke-filled warren of outer London, Hendry should have been able to shake off the fog that crept in from San Francisco Bay at night, but the relentless morning drizzle had him chilled to his core.

Entering a dark close like Duncombe was a dicey proposition for the bravest of Anglos that sought out illicit thrills in Chinatown, but Hendry had grown up hard as a costermonger, or street hawker, in London's hardscrabble East End. He still favored the green silk "kingsman" neckerchief that announced his fealty to this rough and ready group, a warning that even the desperate pickpockets and muggers of Marylebone knew well enough to respect and pay heed.

Hendry stopped at an unmarked door at the far end of the alley and rapped on the sill in a secret rhythm known only to regular habitués of the opium den. A Chinese woman dressed in a yellow silk tunic cracked open the door allowing an exotic fragrance to escape into the alley, a smell of dream flowers that pulled Hendry in close to the doorway.

"Mr. Henry, how good to see you," the woman purred and opened the door wide enough for the man to slip in but with a mind to retaining a carefully cultivated darkness in the distant corners of the room. Since arriving in San Francisco—six months... a year... an eternity ago—Hendry had made Madame Wei's joint his home away from home, and yet she still called him Mr. Henry when she recognized him. He wasn't sure if the mispronunciation was a resultant remnant of a Mandarin tongue or if the woman was fucking with him. In the end, he didn't care one way or the other. "We've been expecting you."

Hendry was halfway past the threshold when the woman's words finally broke the pull the solicitous haze had on him.

"'We' whom?" He had time to utter before catching the sight of a familiar phantom sitting tall in a straight-backed chair just past the room's dark meridian. The gaunt figure remained sitting, his shadow drawn even closer to the low ceiling by a silken top hat balanced upon the man's mahogany-colored skull, a sartorial faux pas that for some reason Madame Wei had forgone a long-held superstition against. The man languidly motioned for Hendry to join him. Hendry cursed under his breath and took the only other chair in the room.

"Wotcher, china," the specter spoke. "Taters, innit?"

"You can leave off the patter, the ol' crash and bang," Hendry said, making a point of not taking the man's hand. "For one, I'm not your mate; for two, Madame Wei cares not a wit about our comings and goings; we can speak plainly. To what do I owe this honor, Mr. Khadae?"

"The baked bean sends her regards... regardless," Khadae tittered.

"We've spoken to the Queen, have we?"

"I very well fucking did. And she told me to tell you to start using your fucking loaf, mate. I don't know what you think you're doing down here with the fucking tids, but this is not a fucking holiday."

"Are you here to give me an assignment?" Hendry growled. "If so, give it over; if not, fuck right off back to Wonderland. I've got business."

"Oh, I know what sort of business you've got," Khadae parried. "You listen up, and you listen well, we've got a bit of a situation in the interior. We'd like you to have a look see... if it's not too much trouble."

9

"The interior of what, may I ask?" Hendry let himself imagine what exactly might be contained within Khadae's sallow skin. *Did it hide a black, howling void? Was the man filled with writhing snakes?*

"The interior of fucking California, innit?" Khadae exploded. "My patience with you is about at an end, coster."

The man patted the front of his vest until he found the box of Egyptian cigarettes hidden within. Wordlessly, he glanced toward Madame Wei, whom Hendry had forgotten was still in attendance, and who lit the man's smoke with an economy of movement that betrayed a certain familiarity. Khadae took a deep drag and added yet another layer to the complex atmosphere in the room.

"Do you two practice that act when I'm not around?" Hendry found himself bemused despite the awkward situation.

"Are you, by any chance, a religious man, Hendry?" Khadae finally asked, having regained his almost regal air of detachment.

"You came all the way out here to play the fox hound and run me to ground in a fucking joint to ask if I believe in God?" It was Hendry's turn to lose his cool with the way the conversation was going. "He and I were about to have a nice long rabbit before you showed up. Would you like me to ask 'im anything?"

Hendry could almost hear the snakes shift under Khadae's skin, their smooth bodies slipping past the underside of the dry husk that allowed him to keep his shape.

"We've heard that a child is being born, and there are... extenuating circumstances that have certain parties concerned about what effect it might end up having upon the status quo."

"For fuck's sake!" Hendry physically recoiled. "Are you saying that you want to send me out to the middle of fuck-all to do a baby? Is that what you're asking?"

"Come on, Hendry, we would never ask you to do something like that," Khadae deferred. "You must really have a low opinion of your blessed smoke. We just want you to check it out. What you decide to do about the situation is entirely up to you."

Hendry took a moment and weighed his options. Obviously, Madame Wei was in cahoots with Khadae, which put a serious crimp on what he had planned for the evening. *Fuck it,* he thought.

"Right, then," Hendry rose from his chair, freezing Khadae with a look, "the sooner gone; the sooner back. Madame Wei, until we meet again."

1889

Chapter Three

3:1   *My Dearest Mordikai,*

I hope that this letter finds you well and that my casual use of the familiar does not overstep the bounds of our relationship. You know that Alexander and I both think the world of you. Your rousing discourse at the South San Francisco Opera House was a highlight of our all-too-brief visit to civilization. My husband has spoken of little else since our return to the Kingdom of Hawai'i.

Indeed, it was our talk after your lecture on the need for higher levels of spiritual discourse that inspired Alexander to start a salon for like-minded scholars of the sublime here at our plantation at Milakale. We have already enjoyed visits from several members of the Hawai'ian royal family as well as missionaries of every conceivable denomination and damnation. Apparently, the fertile soil of the tropics is as amenable to growing the human pneuma as it is sugar cane.

I know in my heart, dear Mordikai, that if you were to join us here on the island, you would find a most sympathetic environment for your philosophy to find full flower. Many of the savages—both noble, and less so—who so often find their way to our table would benefit greatly from a bit of guidance toward the light.

Just last night, we had the distinct pleasure of entertaining a Portuguese sea captain who, after consuming a heroic amount of port and brandy, confessed his desperate need of a spiritual lighthouse lest he find his soul dashed upon the rocks of perdition. At least that is what I think he said. Although the Iberian tongues share a common root, I fear the captain's native language has spent too much time in the mouths of sailors, becoming an adulterated lingua franca that everyone pretends to understand a portion of, but no one truly shares.

But there I go, getting unforgivably off track. It is so rare that one meets a person whose soul is immediately recognizable as a kindred spirit that I fear I must unburden myself or burst! That is why you must come join us at Milakale as soon as your busy schedule allows. Alexander has many important business contacts at the Port of San Francisco. All you would have to do is turn up at the shore, mention his name, and your passage will be assured.

Alexander and myself both eagerly anticipate the day that the divine light permits us all to take comfort in each other's company once again.

Your fellow seeker,
Mrs. Alexander Lanthier

3:2 Anias Lanthier put down her fountain pen of brass and koa wood and let her thoughts be carried away by the sound of the surf lapping against the beach far below the manor house. She had been spending the morning catching up on correspondence while the breezes were imua o ka mauna, blowing toward the mountain. This was her favorite time of day, when the gentle trade winds cooled the plantation, and her husband, Alexander, was otherwise engaged—whether busy handling the myriad sticky details of running his sugar enterprise or riding his damnable black stallion like the Devil himself along some overgrown jungle path.

It was mornings such as this when the fiery Irish matron of Milakale could relax and enjoy the exotic life she gained after finally giving into Alexander's repeated proposals of marriage. She respected her husband for being a man who usually got what he wanted, but hadn't fancied the idea of acquiescing too soon, as to let him think he had the upper hand in their relationship. Anias was every bit a match for her headstrong partner and felt that he needed to understand that from the very beginning.

Her father, Augholy Ó Braoin, had fled Roscommon in the Irish Connacht during the Great Hunger and took with him a healthy mistrust of both the British and organized religion, predilections he passed on to his only daughter. Ó Braoin tried to teach young Anias, from the time she could speak, that the only thing that mattered in this world was power—who had it versus who did not—and leave the next world to hang. When she met the dashing young sugar baron with his own ideas on the subject, Anias immediately recognized one of her own kind.

In addition to a healthy mind of her own, Augholy had bequeathed the dazzling young Anias O'Brien a head of hair the color of a cane fire and a complexion to match the finest bone china. Like the tough, nearly translucent, porcelain, her delicate visage belied a strength that surprised many who first came to know her.

Unlike her contemporary, Virginie Gautreau—the mysterious Madame X of the infamous John Singer Sargent painting that had so inflamed the Paris Salon—Anias did not resort to enameling to maintain her pale appearance but rather considered very assiduously how much time she allowed herself to be exposed to the tropical sun.

It was mornings such as this that Anias was certain she had made the right decision to leave her native San Francisco, with all its grubby grandeur, behind. *Who needed the theaters and salons of Market Street,* she often mused, *when she had the sublime spectacle of the entire Pacific Ocean at her feet?* Nor did she miss the false camaraderie of society women. Anias had never been one to accede to the ways other people thought she should behave, and here, in her own private firmament, she wasn't about to start.

The matron's reverie was broken by the sound of riding boots mounting the stairs of the lānai. On cue, the screen door squeaked open and slammed shut.

"Boots off in my house, Alexander," she called out. The rhythmic tattoo of leather heels striking varnished wood came to an abrupt stop. Alexander Lanthier—all six foot, four inches of him, a captain of industry, a friend to kings and presidents alike—knew who was in charge once the threshold of the Big House had been crossed.

Lanthier smiled as he pulled off his polished riding boots, remembering the look on Chester A. Arthur's face—although it had been somewhat disguised under formidable muttonchops—when his blushing bride once ordered the American president to do the same.

"Tweed Colson sends his regards, dear," Lanthier relayed as he padded up behind his wife in his stocking feet.

"That rapscallion?" Anias questioned. "Why doesn't he come pay his respects himself? He is a grown man. He should know his manners."

"Now, my love," Lanthier laughed, "I am afraid that Allen doesn't have the constant prompting toward civility that I enjoy. You know that he is still a bachelor. Men tend to trend toward the bestial unless motivated otherwise. Besides, he is still smarting from the tongue lashing that you gave him when he tracked mud onto your Persian carpet. He is afraid to set foot in this house."

"Oh, balderdash," Anias exclaimed. "I don't know how your friend ever expects to find a wife if he is so easily intimidated by the fairer sex."

"No one has ever accused you of being fair, my dear," Lanthier parried. "I think most of our cohort see you somewhat as a benevolent dictator, someone to be respected yet watched closely for sudden changes of policy."

"Come now, since when have good manners been subject to any whims of fashion?"

"What are you doing, my love?" Lanthier sought to change the subject.

"I was just writing to Reverend Fox in California," she said, turning to address her partner in love, business, and faith. "I've invited him to come visit Milakale if he ever has the time."

"What a blessing that would be, but I'm sure Mordikai Fox has his hands full out there. You of all people are familiar with the state of your state," Lanthier joked.

"Indeed," Anias allowed. "That's why I don't know why you comport with those who would drag this paradise into that bed of vipers."

"It is merely business, my dear," Lanthier went on a gentle defense. "America needs sugar, and sugar it shall have. Besides, I believe it is our duty to protect this nation from the lesser God-fearing nations that might have designs on her."

Anias' husband waited a beat before seeing a tender spot in which to stick a barb, and against his better judgment, did so. "You know as well as I do the Union Jack sullies a corner of the Hawai'ian flag that flies right now over King Kalākaua's palace in Honolulu. And we sure as blazes can not allow ourselves to be held hostage by another half-mad foreign opportunist like Tromelin again."

"Alexander Lanthier," Anias responded, not giving the man the benefit of detecting a decibel of distress in her voice, "I know you are not trying to justify your schemes to me by bringing up an incident that happened fifty years ago. I imagine if *un espèce de rat* like Tromelin were to try sailing into Honolulu today, while demanding that we all speak French, he would find quite a different welcome waiting for him. Besides, you ought to know better than to try and goad me into buying into your politics by waving the Union flag in front of me. While I am no bulldog, you will not find me a willing bull either."

"Forgive me, dear heart," Lanthier acquiesced and moved once more to change the subject. "Is that the program from the Opera House where we saw the reverend? What do you have written there?"

Anias let her husband think about his indiscretion a moment longer before following his lead. "It is a bit of his sermon," she said, handing him the paper. "I can't seem find a reference to it in our Bible anywhere."

Lanthier took the program and read aloud from his wife's elegant script.

"'What fiery creation / Streaking 'cross the skies / Brings light onto the darkness / Holds a mirror up to our eyes? / Who illuminates our wants / Shines on our desire / With a burning starry crown / And a [...] of blazing fire?'

"I can't quite make out that word," Lanthier pointed at the sheet. "Could it be a sword? The Archangel Michael wields a flaming sword."

"For the life of me, I can't recall," Anias bemoaned. "What else could it be?"

"I guess we will just have to ask the good Reverend Fox when we see him next," Lanthier kissed the top of his wife's head and turned to leave. "I'm headed out to the fields, my dear."

"Am I to expect the usual rabble to join us for supper this evening?"

"Who can say what might wash up on our beautiful shores, my sweet? Perhaps Reverend Fox himself might walk across the water and pull up a chair at our table. Stranger things have happened."

"That is of absolutely no help," Anias protested. "Be gone with you, then, scalawag!"

Chapter Four

4:1　Emilia Gilliam gazed out the window of her second-floor bedroom at the dry, flat expanse of the Central Valley town of Fiesta. Her home was one of the few buildings in the agricultural community that bothered to raise itself as far off the ground. It seemed to her that most folks were content to sleep close to where they worked in the sylvan soil.

You have to admit, she thought as she looked out at the scrub oak foothills that rolled endlessly toward the Sierras, *that is one hell of a view.*

Emilia left further contemplation of the scenery to a delicate pair of Irish lace curtains as she sat down before the mirror above her carved wooden vanity. She piled her long white hair upon itself before achieving a suitable elevation and locking it into place with a clasp of ebony and gold.

A bottle of Dr. Kilpatrick's Patent Medicine sat on the dressing table between Emilia and her reflection and a silver teaspoon now took residence on a small saucer where a delicate china teacup once lived. The wife of the local merchant took a long look in the silvered glass and wondered where it all went wrong.

She had only been sixteen years old when she met Mortimer Gilliam, merely four years older than her daughter was now. She still thought fondly of the attention the young go-getter had paid her then and the way she quickly imagined a way out from under her strict father's thumb.

Mortimer was never the most dashing figure in the valley, but he had possessed an earnest drive to achieve that Emilia responded to. This was long before the comfort of being the sole proprietor of mercantile goods in the county had encouraged the quickly aging young man's natural tendency toward heaviness.

The young couple had tried for the first two years of their marriage to conceive a child to no avail. It wasn't until Reverend Fox came to their dusty town to spread his uncanny take on the Gospels that Emilia finally was able to become pregnant with their sole child, Philomena.

Mortimer took this miraculous turn of events as proof of Fox's spiritual bona fides. The merchant was convinced that it was Fox's ability to bend God's ear that helped clear whatever spiritual roadblocks had stifled the pair. Although Emilia had joined her husband in becoming intimately involved in Fox's ministry over the ensuing dozen years, it was becoming harder to think of the arrival of their beautiful young baby girl as any sort of miracle beyond the type celebrated by any new parents.

Philomena had grown to inherit a luscious olive complexion and hair as black as onyx stone, characteristics neither Emilia nor Mortimer could claim anywhere in their respective lineages. Her husband considered her Mediterranean features as proof of holy intervention in the girl's conception. *Wasn't the Son of Man himself a Palestinian Jew, after all?* Mortimer would argue, disavowing, as Fox did, any depiction of the Christ as having been of Northern European extraction.

The hardest part of the situation for Emilia was the fact that she could not say one way or the other exactly where her daughter *had* derived her singular beauty from. Reverend Fox himself did appear to come from some sort of swarthy stock. With the revival back in town, Emilia thought that perhaps it was time for her to confront their spiritual leader, a task she was not looking forward to.

4:2 The wooden screen door of the Fiesta Mercantile slammed, drawing a man's voice from back in the storeroom.

"Philomena, is that you?"

"Yes, father," the raven-haired twelve-year-old answered. "I thought I might come down and help you out since tonight's your revival."

Mortimer Gilliam came out to greet his daughter, his wispy blonde hair tied out of his face with a thin leather strap like a native. The undomesticated look he wore from the neck up was out of keeping with his well-fed lower half, where his belly fought to dislodge the very buttons of his woolen vest.

"God bless you, child," the shopkeeper exclaimed, nervously rubbing the honorific knuckles of his right hand where he was missing both a ring and middle finger. "Sometimes I think you are really an angel sent down from heaven."

"Please, father," Philomena chided her father. "Pride *is* one of the seven deadly sins, is it not?"

"Reverend Fox expounds a different take on that, Philomena," the storekeeper expounded. "If we were truly made in God's image, would it not be sacrilegious to do anything less than venerate his perfect likeness? How can we be humble when we have been cast from the holiest of molds?"

The young girl ignored her father's sermonizing and grabbed a well-used gingham apron from behind the wooden counter. She was used to him getting excited when Reverend Fox came to town. It was all he and her mother could talk about a week beforehand and as long again after he was gone.

4:3   Aaron Urias dismounted his horse in front of the store run by one of Reverend Fox's most fervent devotees. In all the years he had accompanied the man on his revival circuit through the hardscrabble towns of California's Central Valley and rugged northern coast, Urias had never met a couple as committed to helping spread the reverend's good word as Gilliam and his wife Emilia.

Urias tied his Arabian mare, black with white rabicano markings on her mane and tail, to a worn hitch and stepped up to the only stretch of wooden sidewalk extant in the dusty town. When their annual itinerary was still being created out of whole cloth, the pair would make the mistake of coming through the area in early spring when Sierra snowmelt inundated the already saturated foothills turning the entire area into one giant mud pit, except for the small dry oasis in front of the mercantile.

Urias walked with the wary bearing of a gunfighter. Underneath his Stetson hat, the distinctive alabaster shock of white split his neck-length hair down the middle, echoing the color of his horse. If there was a story around what turned the center of his hair white, Urias was intent on taking it to his grave, a place he had been courting for as long as he could remember.

Professionally, Urias had been poised to become a Pinkerton detective, but he and Fox had met when they both were young men in the service of the Union during the War Between the States. Fox trusted Urias with his life and respected the fact that his friend was not averse to making a few bucks on the side.

Although he was in no particular hurry, Urias walked with purpose. His heavy boots beat an unrelenting rhythm on the floor of the mercantile, each footfall calling forth a swirling galaxy of dust to dance in the sunbeams streaming through the front windows.

An anxious three-fingered hand appeared from behind the curtain that separated the store's immaculate public space from the crowded stockroom. The disembodied hand waved as if to dismiss its unseen customer.

"We are not open yet," a hidden ventriloquist spoke for the hand. "Come back in an hour."

Having accompanied Fox through all manner of bookings, Urias was well acquainted with the full breadth of theatrical arts. If there was one type of performance he never could stomach it was any sort of puppetry, especially if the poppet in question had the temerity to speak to him.

"Gilliam!" Urias cleared his throat and declared his presence. "This is not the matinee performance. Save your ridiculous gestures for the children."

The hand broke character and pulled the curtain to the side. "Well, if it isn't Brother Urias," the shopkeeper exclaimed. "How fortunate to see you this bright and glowing morning."

"Brother Gilliam," Urias tipped his John B. but didn't go as far to uncover his frosted crown. "I should say you would call it fortunate, given what you charge us for being the middleman for our little package."

Both of Gilliam's hands now performed an exaggerated commedia improvviso using the black vest stretched tight over the clerk's ample belly as a backdrop to better stage their act of innocence.

"Now, brother," Gilliam began his annual performance, waving his disfigured hand toward the cheap seats. "You of all people are well aware of the special... considerations that must be taken regarding said package. It wouldn't do to have the rocket finale touch off on a siding out in Deseret and end up disconnecting the Transcontinental a scant twenty years since they drove that golden spike."

Urias laughed in spite of himself and grasped the fuller of Gilliam's flailing hands in a grip of friendship. "It's good to see you, my friend. How's the family?"

"You just missed Philomena. That girl is growing like a weed," Gilliam sighed. "I need to put up another store of oats just to feed that child. She eats more than my horse."

"That's good to hear," Urias chuckled, a sound he rarely found occasion to make. "And the Missus? I understand she has been to revival this week, but I haven't had the pleasure of seeing her."

"You know Emilia, she wouldn't miss a sermon," Gilliam declared before turning sheepish. "Tragically, it has been hard for me to get away from the store this year."

"I'm sure the reverend understands," Urias said. "We all serve Him in our own way." The two men stood facing each other and let the comment hang in the air, both wondering exactly to which party Urias was referring.

"Yes, well," Gilliam broke the uncomfortable silence. "The fireworks should be here directly. I've telegraphed Rochester and they have guaranteed delivery this morning. I'll tell you what, when the package arrives I will close the store and personally take it out to the site. It will be good to see the reverend in any case."

"Very good," Urias agreed. "I'll leave you to it then, brother." The big man tipped his hat once more and was gone.

Chapter Five

5:1   "Philomena! Wait for me," a gangly twelve-year-old girl tagged with the mismatched appellative elegance of Lucette Narcisse ran after her best friend—elbows, knees, and bare feet all akimbo.

"Hey, Lu," Philomena Gilliam slowed her pace by a fraction but did not stop.

"Why weren't you at school today?" Lucette huffed as she struggled to catch up.

"Today's a holiday," Philomena stated, signaling that any elaboration was going to have to be pried out of her. Unfortunately for the reserved young woman, her friend was more than up to the task.

"Holiday? Today isn't any holiday I've ever heard of," Lucette protested. "How come the rest of us had to go, then?"

"It's a religious holiday, Lu. You wouldn't know about it unless your folks were GLOWers." Philomena didn't even wait for the coming question; the look on Lucette's face was all the interrogation she needed. "The Golden Light of Jehovah's Word; my folks have been followers of the Reverend Fox... well, since before I was born."

"Wouldn't that be GLOJWers? I think you forgot the J," Lucette quipped.

"Silly, you can't write down God's name," Philomena explained. "Don't you know anything? It's bad luck or something. Besides, they do always come back from revival all lit up like a pair of Chinese lanterns."

The girls walked in silence for no more than ten paces, Philomena mistakenly thinking that she was off the hook.

"Have you ever gone to one of those tent meetings?" Lucette finally asked. "I've heard it is quite a show."

"No," Philomena admitted. "My parents always say that I'm too young. I guess there are some pretty intense things going on. I heard that Reverend Fox can speak in tongues, and once he cured an old lady's blindness, clubfoot, and lumbago all at once. Mostly it's just singing and testifying and things like that. Although, I did hear that there was going to be a snake handler this time... for the Pentecostals."

"Snake handler, huh? That sounds like it could be a hoot."

Nine paces.

"How many people go to those things?"

"I don't know," Philomena pondered. "There are people coming from all over the valley. Could be fifty, maybe a hundred. Why?" Philomena finally stopped and gave her friend the full attention that she craved. Looking at her straight, unadorned brown hair, long, plain cotton skirt, and dirt-covered feet, Philomena saw herself reflected in the waif's countenance except that her own long hair was as black as a raven's tail feathers.

"Well, since you ask, I was just thinking with that many people in attendance, who is going to notice two more way in the back?"

"Are you crazy?" Philomena shot back. "If my parents caught us... caught me, it would be the last time I ever saw the likes of you!"

"Come on," Lucette pushed. "What are you, *chicken?*"

Philomena's blood rose up her neck and colored her cheeks. Lucette was her best friend, but if there was one thing that got under her skin, it was the way that she could manipulate her into doing exactly what she wanted by merely calling her afraid.

"What time does the revival start?"

"Seven o'clock. I don't know why I'm telling you, though. We are not going."

"You worry too much, Phil. We'll sneak in, see what it's all about, and then beat the crowd home. They won't know even know we were there."

"..."

"I'll see you at six-thirty," Lucette didn't wait for a rebuttal and skipped off down the dusty street, leaving Philomena to wonder what had just happened.

5:2   Having entrusted the daily maintenance of the revival site to Urias, Fox pulled off his dusty boots and took refuge in his Gypsy wagon. An all-too familiar pull found him on his knees as he removed an ornate black wooden box from its place under his cot. Lifting the lid, inlaid with the motif of a mother of pearl comet soaring over a tropical island, Fox paused as the residual smell of opium lit up the pleasure centers of his brain and made his damaged heart skip a beat.

Fox was first given the drug as Union Army doctors dug out several Confederate slugs from his person, and like many veterans of the War Between the States, had left the conflict with what was often called the "soldier's disease;" an addiction that followed them home. Fox found that in addition to pushing his injuries to the back of his consciousness, using the pipe often helped his mental acuity; his sermons always took on a divine luster after he had indulged in a little smoke.

Inside the box lay a three-foot length of bamboo sheathed in copper and enameled in an intricate motif of white chrysanthemums. Two thirds of the way down, the pipe sprouted a jade bowl the size of a fist and carved into a fecund poppy bulb. The points of the pod's crown curved upwards toward a small hole, blackened from residue and from being held next to the small oil lamp that Fox removed next.

Before Fox had the opportunity to work a small black bead of opium into the proper consistency, a quiet knock at the wagon's door broke his concentration.

"I am deep in preparation for tonight's service," Fox called through the door. "Please see Mr. Urias and he can schedule a personal audience if need be."

"Reverend, it's Emilia. I need to talk."

"Mrs. Gilliam, I would love to speak with you, but now is not a good time. Please see—"

"Brother Urias is not around," Emilia said, "and this is more of a personal matter than I would be comfortable bringing up with him."

"My dear lady, Mr. Urias and I have been though the very flames of hell together. I assure you, there is nothing you can say to me that you could not say to him."

"I think Philomena is your child," Emilia blurted.

Fox was frozen in place for a moment before opening the door to a distraught Emilia.

"Please, Mrs. Gilliam, come in before someone hears you out there," Fox shepherded the woman into the wagon.

As Emilia became accustomed to the darkened confines of the small room, her eyes fell naturally to the open box of paraphernalia. A look of confusion flitted across her shadowed face before it settled into a mask of bittersweet recognition.

"Let me explain," Fox began, having followed her line of vision.

"There is no need, reverend," Emilia said. "I too take comfort in my patent medicines... for my nerves. 'And all who heard should see them there / And all should cry, Beware! Beware!'"

"Ah, Coleridge," Fox picked up the verse. "'His flashing eyes, his floating hair! / Weave a circle round him thrice / And close your eyes with holy dread—'"

"'For he on honey-dew hath fed / And drunk the milk of Paradise,'" the woman finished.

"What can I do for you, Emilia?"

5:3   Mortimer Gilliam locked the front doors of the mercantile and worked his way to the back alley where he had already manhandled the crate containing Fox's big finale into his buckboard wagon. The crate had made it all the way across the country without exploding, but Gilliam was glad to have it out of his store just the same.

Inside the wooden box—nestled in a bed of highly flammable straw—lay a profusion of shells, each one bigger and more colorfully named than the last. America's First Fireworks Company had sent several types of four-pounders to set the stage. A few Willow Tree Showers, followed by several brace of Jeweled Streamers—as well as the famous Cornucopia for good measure—would get the crowd's attention unless they were dead.

The six-pound shells were really the main event. The Rochester factory's Shooting Star and Diamond Shower always helped Fox place an exclamation point at the end of his week long stretch of holy rolling. Fox, however, was uninterested in stopping there, as he loved to go out with a bang, and America's First delivered the goods. Their flagship, and Fox's coup de grâce, was the eight-pound Prize Comet.

Gilliam was well aware how dangerous the crate was and drove his team of powerful Shire dray horses out to the edge of town at a funeral pace. He wasn't at all surprised that Fox was always able to find a local pyromaniac to handle the aerial bombardment. He was, however, amazed that in the past twelve years, no overeager farm boy had been blown to bits. *Just another example of the reverend's good favor with the Master Painter,* he thought.

Fox's revival was always set up in a vacant dirt field just past the Fiesta city limits. To the east of the huge white tent that provided the faithful a place to commune—given sun, rain, or a rare dusting of snow—a seemingly endless succession of low hills climbed toward the Sierra Nevada mountain range.

Gilliam was hoping to quickly find Urias, transfer the crate, and hightail it back to the mercantile before he lost too much business, but if he was honest with himself, there probably weren't going to be that many folks looking for goods, not with God's own circus in town.

Every year he was amazed at the transformation of a lowly patch of cattails, dust, and scrub oak into a little piece of heaven on Earth. By nightfall, practically the entire town of Fiesta would be hanging on every word that fell from Reverend Fox's lips as if they came from Jehovah himself.

He scanned the field looking for Urias, but coming up empty, approached the Gypsy wagon that was Reverend Fox's rolling sanctum sanctorum where he was available for private consultation—not to mention where he finally laid his head when it all was said and done.

The shopkeeper was about to knock, when he heard muffled voices in heated conversation coming from within.

"You can not deny the girl—"

"I assure you—"

"Assure me of what; that you did not take advantage of my faith? That you did not take advantage of me?"

"I did not. I would not, child. Just what are you saying?"

"Were you not listening? Do I have to spell it out again?"

A voice to Gilliam's left nearly startled him into dropping the edge of the crate as he had foolishly let someone approach unnoticed while eavesdropping.

"Sounds like trouble in paradise," a tall man in an ill-fitting silk suit growled in Gilliam's ear.

Embarrassed for being caught listening in on a private conversation, Gilliam sheepishly turned to face the new arrival. He quickly forgot about his social indiscretion when he saw the mismatched pair of men standing behind him.

The Central Valley merchant was used to dealing with the big, rangy men who worked the small farms in and around Fiesta. That sort of work bred a certain raw-boned type and the dangerous jobs associated with agriculture often propagated a tendency toward mutilation of some sort. Gilliam himself had offered up a couple of digits as testament to the perilous tasks to be done on California's rugged frontier. The tall man before him, however, looked as if he had fallen into a grain harvester at some point and had been put back together wrong.

If Gilliam had the time to guess, he might have placed the man as originally being of some sort of Arab extraction. His weathered skin of burnt sienna darkened to almost black around his eyes, while the whites of his eyes paled only as far as yellow-brown before sucking all available light into an unnerving pair of pitch-black corneas and pupils. In his right hand, the man brandished an elegant cane, topped with the mummified head of an unfortunate lizard.

As if chosen to counteract the visceral reaction the first man was sure to elicit, his white-haired partner was a compact paragon of style and carried himself with an unsettling grace, bowing and begging Gilliam's forgiveness for the intrusion.

"Do forgive us," the second man said in a smeary Brazilian accent. "We didn't mean to startle you."

If Gilliam knew one true thing it was that he did not want to be drawn into a conversation with either stranger. His natural tendencies as a salesman betrayed that truth, however, and he found himself telling the man it had been no problem at all. In fact, to his dismay, he found himself asking the pair if there was anything he could do for them.

"Actually, we were hoping to have a word with the good reverend ourselves," the tall man pointed with the dead lizard head. "It appears as if we are all out of luck at the moment. I guess it will just have to wait. I beg you goodnight, shopkeeper."

The slamming of the Gypsy wagon door took his attention away from wondering how the stranger might have known him. Gilliam instinctively looked up only to watch his wife Emilia descend the short staircase.

Chapter Six

6:1 Night came to the valley around six o'clock in the early fall, turning the wide sky a brilliant salmon pink, then purple, then black as the inside of a boot. Lucette showed promptly half an hour later, as punctual as if she owned a pocket watch, which of course, she did not.

Other than the extra story, the Gilliam family home was a typical Central Valley wooden frame house with a large front porch that was a measure of refuge in the heat of the summers and was situated to catch any evening breezes that might have lost their way while searching for the coast.

Philomena's father, as one of the few members of the local business class, had built one of the larger clapboard palaces for his small family. As a result, Philomena was lucky enough to have her own room on the ground floor, a room with a window low enough to climb out of when the mood and opportunity arose.

"Phil!" Lucette called out under her friend's bedroom window, looking around to take note of anyone that might later be called on as a witness for the prosecution, although the entire town of Fiesta looked deserted.

"Quiet," a subdued voice answered back from the darkened interior. "I don't think my mother has left yet. I was sure they would both have been gone by now. We'll have to wait until she goes."

"Darn it," Lucette complained. "I don't want to be missing any hoodoo, especially snake hoodoo."

"I wouldn't worry," Philomena answered. "These things are kind of like a train, slow to get going, but once they're up to steam, they don't stop for anything or anybody."

"Give me a hand up, will you? I'm not going to lurk out here all night. The mosquitoes haven't got the word that summer is over."

"How did you get out, anyway?" Philomena asked as she reached out and hauled her friend up and over the sill.

"Are you kidding?" Lucette asked with genuine incredulity. "You do know that there are six more at home that look exactly like me, right?

My folks couldn't say with any certainty that I'm not there."

6:2   Emilia Gilliam once again sat before the silvered mirror above her vanity. Confronting Mortimer with the idea that Philomena might not be his child did not go well. Her husband had left the house in a rage. The nerves that lay just under her skin felt as if they could burst into flame as a crushing guilt tormented her as it had for some time.

I did nothing wrong, she told herself once again. She hadn't enjoined other lovers. If she had, that might explain the girl's looks and uncanny personality. She just knew, as only a mother could know, that Mortimer Gilliam had no more fathered Philomena than had he sired the mahogany furniture.

In desperation, the woman reached for her bottle of laudanum tincture. If there was one thing that could quench the fire it was Dr. Kilpatrick's Patent Medicine. She was about to fill her silver spoon with the bitter mixture when she heard a quiet knock on the door.

"Mortimer?"

6:3   After playing countless rounds of Reversi, the two girls tired of trying to flip each other's discs from white to black and back again and took to watching dust motes lazily drift through the warm light cast by the gas lamp in Philomena's room as her mother banged around the house in an apparent frenzy.

Why don't we have gas lamps? Lucette remembered thinking before dozing off.

The girls awoke to the sound of two people arguing.

"Darn it, we probably missed the snakes," Lucette protested as she rubbed her eyes.

"Shhh," Philomena hushed her somnolent, yet still eager, friend. "Something's going on." The two girls each held their breath waiting for another round of shouting. Instead, a sharp report echoed down the empty street.

"What was that?" Lucette mouthed, her eyes as round as the full moon rising up over the house.

"What do you think that was?" Philomena hissed. "That was the front door." Her entire being was poised to either fight or flight regardless. She got up and started toward the door as if moving through one of the jars of molasses in her father's store.

"No, Philomena, I think it was a shot!" Lucette's panicked tone stopped her in her tracks. "We have to get out of here."

Philomena hesitated for a second. Every fiber in her body was on full alert as she considered confronting whomever might have had the nerve to fire off a gun in her family's house, but the sight of her best friend making toward the window snapped her out of her panic.

"Maybe you're right," she whispered. "As soon as you hit the ground, start running. We'll go to the revival and get my dad."

"Your dad?" Lucette wheezed as the sash pushed into her abdomen while she lowered herself backward out of the window. "We need to get the police."

"Just go," Philomena resisted the impulse to push her friend the rest of the way out of the window. "Where else do you think we are going to find the police tonight?"

As soon as the two girls hit the dusty street, they both took off running.

Don't look back. Don't look back. Philomena ran and repeated the directive in her head until it crowded out all other thoughts. She did not look back.

6:4 Urias went over the program with the young man he was entrusting with the massive cache of fireworks for the umpteenth time.

"Listen, I am going to tell you one more time," Urias growled. "When the Good Reverend Fox finishes with his story of following the star, that is when you start the launches, small to big. Do you have it?"

The young man, so fresh off the farm that he was still wearing his overalls, nodded and pulled a pack of cigarettes out of his bib pocket.

"What exactly are you thinking of doing right now?" Urias asked, his right eyebrow crawling toward his hairline.

"What?" the boy muttered from around the edges of the cigarette he had stuck between his lips. The boy held the older man's gaze as his hands took it upon themselves to search his myriad pockets for a match.

Urias suppressed the natural impulse to slap the cigarette out of the boy's face. He tried to remember if he had been as stupid at the same age, but came up wanting.

"Look, if you are in a hurry to meet your maker, fine," Urias stepped closer and took the boy's smoke out of his mouth, which remained hanging open. "You are, however, going to have to stop at the Pearly Gates to explain why you took a couple dozen of his favorite people with you."

The boy looked around him and, as if seeing the collection of ordinance for the first time, finally cottoned on to what the man was getting at.

"Look, I'm going to give you this," Urias reached into his pocket and brought out a small silver-finished metal device, half the size of a pack of cigarettes. "It's called a Magic Lamp. I got it off a Dutchman back east. You are looking at the future, here."

The boy stepped in closer, fascinated by the contraption.

Urias pushed the small button on the side and the top of the device sprung open, revealing a wick and the unmistakable smell of kerosene. He then pressed a lever that flipped open the front of the small case revealing a rotating disk that held small charges of gunpowder. Snapping the front closed, Urias again pressed the button, igniting one of the tiny charges within with an audible sizzle. A three-inch flame shot up off of the fuel-soaked wick before he snapped the lid closed and extinguished it.

"This is not a toy," Urias emphasized before handing over the device and turning to leave. "Don't blow up the revival, and it's yours."

6:5 The formerly empty field was packed solid by the time night fell. To the west, back toward town, a sea of faces floated like pink and brown balloons, illuminated by the full moon and firmament of hanging lanterns.

Philomena had wildly underestimated the number of her fellow town folk who must have been feeling the need for a spiritual overhaul. The Good Reverend Mordikai Fox, the evening's guide out of the wastelands of sin and dissolution had contracted for a hundred and fifty chairs to be set up under the large white canvas tent. It was already standing and swaying room only.

Fox had been in business long enough to have built a network of like-minded—that is, anyone with a interest in making a good little piece of change—labor and security types, so that by the time he rolled into town, the show was practically ready to go. Fox reflected back that this year's performance would be the lucky thirteenth time he had stopped into this little knuckle drag town to bring them the glorious Word.

"It's almost show time, boss," Urias knocked on the side of the Gypsy wagon.

"How is the crowd, Aaron?" Fox spoke through the thin wooden door.

Urias glanced back toward the mass of humanity. "What I saw of the opening act wasn't half bad. I think they are going to be ready to be feeling the healing."

"That's what I like to hear. I'm going to let them stew in their own juices for a few more moments, and then we'll throw in the spice."

"I'm ready when you are," Urias answered and turned to meet a solitary shape approaching him at a concerning clip. His right hand automatically fell to his holstered Colt. "Good evening, friend. Is there something I can help you with?"

The figure stepped out of the shadows into the circle of lantern light illuminating Fox's door. Urias immediately recognized the hardware man.

"'Evening, Brother Urias," Gilliam spoke and held out his good hand. "Keeping the good reverend here safe and sound?"

Urias hand hovered naturally above his leather for a moment before clasping the man's own in a friendly shake. "Brother Gilliam, what a treat it is to see you out from behind that counter. I have to thank you for delivering the crate this afternoon. Are we to have the pleasure of your lovely wife's company as well this evening?"

An expert study of human character, Urias noticed a small twitch in the man's countenance before it was quickly and consciously hidden from him.

"Not tonight," the man apologized. "I'm afraid she is feeling a little under the weather. Tell me, is Reverend Fox available for a quick consultation?"

"Sorry to hear about the missus, I hope she recovers soon," Urias shifted his eyes to the Gypsy wagon. "You know how he gets before his sermon, I don't—"

Urias noticed sweat dripping from the man's forehead. "Have you been running this evening?"

Gilliam lifted what he had of both hands in a gesture of full disclosure. "I so wanted to have a word before... I promise, this will only take a minute of his time," he angled. "I know how precious it is."

"Make it quick then, brother. I have got to go make sure that our snake handler is still with us on this mortal coil, so to speak."

"You have my word," Gilliam's eyes flashed in the flickering light. "And please, call me Mortimer."

Urias hesitated before knocking on the wagon. "Reverend Fox, Brother Mortimer would like to have a word with you if it's all right."

"Mortimer!" Fox's disembodied baritone rang the wooden walls of the caravan like a guitar. "Of course; send him in."

Urias motioned for the man to mount the stair, and waited as Gilliam was welcomed inside. *Something doesn't feel quite right*, he thought; still, he knew both men well, and what was the worst that could happen? *Now about that blasted snake handler.*

6:6   The girls were amazed at the size of the crowd amassed on the edge of town. Nearly every adult they had ever met was in attendance, awaiting the Golden Light of Jehovah's Word.

"How are we supposed to find your father in this crowd?" Lucette lamented.

"I have no idea," Philomena shouted to be heard over the sound of excited believers. She scanned the field to find a policeman or someone in charge, but being young had its disadvantages. All she could see was the backs of people's heads, their necks craning to see what was happening on the raised stage.

"Hey, Phil, isn't that your father over there by that wagon?" Lucette motioned through a temporary break in the humanity toward the edge of the lot where a few stunted oak trees threw tortured shadows in the moonlight.

"Father!" Philomena called out. "Heck, he'll never hear us." The girls could see the merchant talking to a tall man wearing a leather duster before the gap in the crowd closed tight. "Come on, Lu, let's go." The pair began to elbow their way through the crowd but their momentum was hardly noticed by the throng and soon they were mired in the crush.

The unmistakable sound of two gunshots put both girls into a panic a quickened heartbeat before the entire gathering exploded into chaos.

PLATE ONE ✳ Mordikai Fox

Chapter Seven

7:1   Anyone in the revival crowd who was tall enough to look back over the sea of eager faithful would have noticed an occasional flash of light as the farm boy entrusted with Fox's fireworks finale played with the Magic Lamp that Urias gave him.

    The general excited murmur coming from the flock drowned out every small pop of gunpowder, as the boy was incapable of not worrying the ingenious mechanism. However, the tall flame that periodically illuminated the low rise where the boy, the device, and the explosive shells all hung fire could have been seen by anyone, but wasn't.

7:2   As soon as Fox let Mortimer Gilliam into his inner sanctum he found himself wishing he had not. It wasn't so much that he didn't ordinarily enjoy the company of one of his oldest and most enthusiastic converts; he did. It was more that the gun the mercantile man had trained on him was making him uncomfortable.

    "What is all this about, Brother Mortimer?" Fox played for time. Perhaps Urias would return and draw the man's attention away. A split second was all he would need to take a gun away from an untrained civilian and then perhaps he could talk some sense into him.

    "Don't call me that, charlatan," Gilliam spat, the barrel of the gun shaking but not changing direction. "Emilia told me everything. Philomena was no blessed miracle, she's a bastard."

    "Hold on there, Mortimer," Fox petitioned, "I don't know what Emilia told you, but I assure you, I had nothing to do—"

    "Liar!" Gilliam steadied his aim and the cessation of shaking was the signal Fox was watching for and hoped he wouldn't see. Time stalled as the distraught man pulled the trigger and Fox lunged to push the barrel away. The slug exited the scene through the thin wall of the Gypsy wagon, as the sound of the shot reverberated within the tight wooden quarters.

On a short rise across a dusty field, a farm boy holding a three-inch flame in his hand fell dead into a crate of fireworks.

In the next split second, in which the entire world seemed to hold its breath, Gilliam fired one final shot, the last thing he would ever do.

7:3　What Philomena would later consider her second life began with a fireball streaking across the night sky, an apt metaphor for the way her adoptive father Mordikai approached the world. Fox hadn't so much adopted the young girl as he had grabbed her as one would snatch a valise before escaping out the window of a burning hotel—although it wasn't a building that had been collapsing down around the itinerant preacher's ears, it was his life. Unfortunately, he was quick to learn that a twelve-year-old child was a lot more trouble to carry than a piece of luggage.

Fox had been more or less entrusted with the pretty black-haired and olive-skinned Philomena by her real father, a man who possessed neither of those traits and seemed quite upset that Fox enjoyed both; a jealousy that Fox felt unwarranted, at least to the degree that Gilliam apparently held it.

Moments after talking his way into the caravan, the distraught man took out the pistol he had hidden in his belt, and subsequently dispatched a bullet through his own head, but not before inadvertently setting fire to the entire revival.

The group of concerned worshippers drawn toward Fox's sanctuary by the pistol's report was understandably distracted by the uncanny sound of the very heavens coming unzipped. Every pious head that had gathered in the field to receive the Word as interpreted by the charismatic and self-indoctrinated Fox, turned toward the ether as a ball of flame plowed spectacularly over a ridge of scrub oak, drawing a smoking furrow in the stars. When the object made impact just over the hillside, the surrounding grasslands spontaneously ignited adding a familiar smell of summer to the tumult and fume.

The late Mortimer Gilliam could not be moved to stir by anything short of the actual hand of God, but Fox, considering himself a curious man in all manner of the word, gathered his considerable wits and stepped over the unfortunate ex-acolyte to see what the commotion was about.

Outside, Fox's flock had been panicked by the repeated self-launch of unaimed shells. In fear for their lives, the faithful scattered like a shattered jar of marbles.

No man alive would ever find fault in Fox's ability to read a situation and quickly and unerringly exploit it for his own good, though perhaps the new corpse behind him had its own feelings on the matter. Fortunately for Fox, Gilliam's opinions were now permanently off the table.

The preacher took a moment to take in the sight of frightened farmers running back and forth before the burning hillside as if hell itself had opened and spilled out upon Jackdaw Junction or whatever the locals called their fallow, weed-choked lot. One thing Fox was sure of—as a student of both the writings and natures of men—was that once the lid was off of hell, it was always a son of a bitch to get it back on again.

He also knew that once their hysteria had subsided to a low simmer, the rabble was bound to remember what had drawn their attention in the first place. A great believer in signs, when a burning chunk of firework fell out of the sky in front of him he took it as just such a portent, grabbed the cooler end of it, and walked back to his wagon.

Philomena and her friend stood perfectly still as the crowd dissolved around them and watched wide-eyed as Fox disappeared into the caravan, and then rematerialized tucking a pistol into his belt while carrying his well-worn bible. Behind him, the meager material trappings of his life took flame and added its own smoke and ash to the soot-filled night sky.

"Hey, reverend!" Philomena called across the distance. "Where did my father go?"

Fox led his elegant black-legged bay away from the smoldering wagon as if he did not hear, or was taking his time to consider an appropriate response. The preacher mounted the bay and finally motioned to the girl, extending his long-fingered hand, an image from that night that would stay with her for the rest of her life. Philomena was drawn toward Fox as if moved by an invisible force.

"Philomena," Lucette hissed. "What are you doing?"

"Where is your mother, child?" The man cooed.

Philomena reached up with her own supple fingers, took the man's hand, and was lifted up behind him on the horse. She merely pointed toward the small town that was the center of the agricultural community currently watching the burning valley as if hypnotized.

Fox set off without a glance back, as was his wont. *If there was one person in the Good Book who got it wrong*, he always said, *besides Pilate, that is—it was Lot's wife. Never bleeding look back.*

"Phil!" Lucette shouted. "Where are you going? You can't leave. We have to find your father!" Behind the girl, shells continued to explode on the ground with shocking ferocity, sending vividly-colored streams of sparks in every direction.

The unfortunate farm boy had placed the eight-pound Prize Comet in its mortar tube before meeting his ignominious end, and it too self-launched once the conflagration reached its lifting charge. For a brief moment, a bright comet dominated the night sky before erupting into a galaxy of new stars.

By the time the dazzling flash faded from Lucette's sight, Fox and Philomena were gone.

7:4   Fox followed Philomena's instructions to a blue clapboard house on the main street of town. The girl jumped down from the horse and ran across the small front yard.

"Hold up!" The preacher shouted. It dawned on him that there might be something in that house that a child shouldn't have to see. "Stop where you are, girl!"

Philomena stopped before reaching the wood-framed screen door hanging from a single hinge. Out of all the crazy things she had already witnessed that evening, perhaps the broken screen disturbed her the most. It wasn't like her father, who took pride in his home— and happened to own the local hardware store—to let something like that stand unrepaired, even for a moment. She was also not used to being shouted at and stood fast with a look of defiance that said at any moment she was going to continue on and nobody was going to stop her.

"I'm going to go in first and I'll give you the all-clear if it is safe." Fox removed Gilliam's instrument of self-destruction from his belt and carefully moved the broken screen. "I am deadly serious, child. Do not come in until I tell you that it is all right."

Philomena nodded her consent and Fox quietly stole inside the house, careful not to bring any attention to himself. After checking to make sure it was still loaded, he held the dead man's gun in front of him, unsure of what he might be walking into.

Although he recognized the trappings of a comfortable merchant-class life, Fox couldn't say that he admired them. On a small, entryway table, a dark, pungent cigarette still smoldered in a cut-glass ashtray. The acquisition of hurricane lamps and white Irish doilies was not anything he had ever been interested in. *Did these people not know material things would merely weigh them down?* He mused. *Did not the Son of Man himself say it was easier for a rich man to pass through the eye of a needle than to enter into his kingdom?*

Fox's reverie was cut short by the discovery of the former Mrs. Gilliam laid out on the parlor floor. Next to her body was an empty bottle of Dr. Kilpatrick's Patent Medicine. Emilia's delicate features were unmarred but for a subtle scrim of foam on her lips. Now released from the ill-fitting disguise of a shopkeeper's wife and harried mother of a precocious young lady, Fox remembered Emilia Gilliam for the beautiful young woman she once was.

On nights not unlike this one in many ways, Fox had been known to entertain an occasional buxom acolyte after an impassioned sermon had driven them both to distraction. Fox was younger then and so filled with the Spirit that it often manifested itself in earthly ways that could be seen as less than divine; but Emilia... Surely he would have remembered an assignation like that.

He thought back to the year that he and Urias came to adore the newborn Philomena. *Maybe the girl was a miracle*, he pondered. The real problem with miracles was that they rarely turned out to be exactly what you were hoping for. *Even the classics, Fox believed, must have had their rough edges worn down by time and retelling.*

"Mother, where are—?" Philomena stopped in her tracks and let out a scream that could be heard for miles.

"I told you to wait outside!" Fox admonished the girl out of pure reflex before going to comfort her as well as shepherd her back into the entryway. He was holding the distraught girl as she shook into his pastoral cravat when voices outside the house reminded him that for the second time that night he was standing over a prostrate body and could possibly be held accountable for the sorry condition of both.

Fox crouched down to better look the distraught girl in the eye. "Listen to me," he searched the girl's panicked face for connection. "Is there anyone I can take you to? An aunt or uncle?"

Philomena's eyes struggled to focus on the lanky preacher's face as her mind struggled to understand what he was asking.

"Anyone?"

"My father," the girl began.

Fox took a deep breath and once again considered his options. He quickly decided the situation, unlike many he found himself in, called for unvarnished truth.

"Listen, my dear, I don't know what exactly happened here tonight, but I do know that your father is not coming back. Is there no one?"

The girl shook her head no.

"What about your little friend, the one you were with tonight?" Fox fished. "Can you stay with her family?"

Philomena shook her head, knowing all too well that the Narcisse household could barely afford to keep food on the table as it was. She didn't need to add to their troubles. The girl began to realize just how alone she was in the world.

"It's settled then," Fox stood. "You can come with me, but we had better get out of here."

The girl was not expecting that sort of offer and it caught her off-guard. "Why can't I stay here?" she exclaimed. "It's my house! My father—"

"Listen, child. Your father is gone, all right?" Philomena's trepidation began to erode his nerves. "Short of some kind of miracle—which, if I could produce, I would—he is not coming home.

Your mother... Your mother cannot help you either. The longer I stand here with this—"

Fox tossed the pistol away into the corner and doing so helped calm him immeasurably. "The longer we stay here, the more likely I will be called upon to answer questions that have no good answers."

"Where can we go?" The reality of the situation became clear for the girl and her natural sense of curiosity came to the fore.

Fox thought for a moment. "We are going to Hawai'i. I have been corresponding with a woman out on one of the islands for some time. I believe she may give us sanctuary."

Philomena, for her part, had only thought of Hawai'i in the most abstract terms, if at all, and a flood of questions came tumbling out of her mouth driven primarily by an inability to deal with the present. "Do they speak English there? Are there headhunters?"

Fox laughed in spite of the gruesome night they were having. "Yes, of course they speak English. The King of Hawai'i is a very cultured man. He would never allow headhunting. I think you are confusing it with Borneo."

Unwittingly providing punctuation to the closing of a chapter of Philomena's young life, Fox reflexively reached over and extinguished the slowly burning cigarette in the entryway ashtray.

"What about monkeys? Are there monkeys?"

"I really don't know. I guess we'll just have to find out."

"I hope there are monkeys."

Chapter Eight

8:1   The Lanthier House at Milakale, which everyone on the Hāmākua Coast simply called the Big House, lounged atop a ridge overlooking a verdant valley sloping all the way down to the ocean. The dazzling white two-story structure was surrounded with expansive lānais, or porches, that provided residents and guests with a shady sanctuary at any time of day. The feature that usually caught the attention of visitors, however, were the two attic windows that shone like the eyes of a predatory cat—also at all times of day—or so it seemed.

What helped the Big House carry off its impression of a jungle feline in repose was the single-story guest wing that seemed to curl along its side like a tail. It wasn't too much of a stretch to imagine the whole structure leaping into action lest unwary prey wandered too close without a proper invitation.

Anias Lanthier, the matron of Milakale, made it her business to rise early enough to watch the sun climb out of the Pacific Ocean in the east every morning. It made her feel less isolated to know that it had just kissed the brown hills of California and inspired the morning birds of the distant country of her girlhood. No matter how early she got out of bed, however, Anias always found her husband Alexander already taking his coffee on the lānai.

"Good morning dear," she said, pulling up one of the wicker chairs beside him to watch the sunrise. "Are you well this morning?"

"Couldn't be better if I was rolled in butter," Alexander stated as a plain fact. "I thought I might take Lucifer out for a ride down to the beach this morning. It'll be good for us both to get some exercise."

"Do be careful, darling," she entreated. "I don't like how spirited that animal still is. I do wish you had named it something else."

"Well, my dear," Alexander laughed, "that is exactly why I love that horse! He keeps me on my toes. It makes me feel young again."

Anias didn't grace her husband's willful injudiciousness with further comment, opting instead to fully take in the dazzling show put on by the dawning Sun.

"I almost forgot," Alexander interrupted his wife's reverie. "There is a Wells Fargo wire from California. We are to have visitors."

"Visitors?" Anias turned her attention from the solar display. "More of your politicians drawn like fruit flies by the rotten talk of annexation?"

"Not this time," Alexander laughed, knowing how tired his wife had become of hearing about all the wonderful things the United States government was itching to bring to the sovereign island nation. "I think you will be delighted by this guest. The Good Reverend Fox has finally answered your invitation. He and a young charge are steaming out of San Francisco as we speak."

"Oh, Alexander!" Anias jumped up and embraced her husband. "That is glorious news! I shall ready some guest rooms today. Tell me, who is traveling with him?"

"A young girl," Alexander grinned. "The wire mentions the reverend is coming out with his daughter."

"His daughter?" Anias practically choked. "Well now, this will be an interesting visit!"

8:2 The strikingly beautiful Anias O'Brien hadn't yet turned twenty when she met her dashing young sugar baron at a society ball on San Francisco's Market Street. The young debutante had been busy making an impression in the rough-and-tumble city with disarmingly attentive eyes the color of the North Sea, seemingly endless waves of red hair, and luminous skin like melted Moon.

Lanthier, for his part, was tall, dark-haired, and comported himself with a bit of grace, something lacking in most of the men Anias had met in the heady days after the gold boom turned her sleepy backwater town into something akin to an ant hill stepped on by a draft horse. All other potential suitors simply faded away upon seeing the two together, ceding the contest to fate itself.

Anias had worked hard to make the distant island of Hawai'i her home and Milakale was the envy of many a ragtag parade of sea captains, missionaries, Hawai'ian royalty, and fellow sugar families that graced, or she should say grazed, her table over the years.

The only people not impressed by the homestead's opulence were the workers who spent their days in the sugar fields and their nights in the shantytown on the edge of the sprawling acreage. As for the native Hawai'ians—the Kānaka Maoli—they considered the low, flat promontory of carefully stacked lava rocks that stuck out like an accusing finger into Milakale's sheltered bay to be kapu. Forbidden.

The Hawai'ians believed the Milakale heiau had been built by Menehune, or the diminutive original inhabitants of the island who worked at night only to disappear with the coming of the dawn, giving the area its name: Miracle.

Before her husband first acquired the property that was to become the Lanthier estate, a Hawai'ian healer, or kahuna lapa'au, lived out on the short, constructed peninsula in a hut built of thatched palm fronds.

The local chief would make his way down the trail from the cliffs surrounding the bay and confer with her whenever matters of a metaphysical nature arose. The path he walked had been traversed by generations of leaders before him and the spirits of those ancestors were said to still walk to the point when the moon and tides were right.

Alexander Lanthier had originally come to the islands as a missionary and, like many, gradually shifted his focus from saving souls to making money. Even after beginning to develop his estate he still retained enough missionary zeal to be able to convince the locals to turn their backs on traditional custom and spend their Sundays in the brand new clapboard church he had built for them. Soon after, an unfortunate "fire of unknown origin" finally cleared the healer's pier for more secular uses, or at least those with more of a Protestant bent.

Most of the locals respected the kapu and would not set foot on the landing. When Lanthier began to unload boats full of lumber and building materials from all over the Pacific islands, he hired the Portuguese who were immigrating to Hawai'i from the Açores. He found the stout men to be hard workers, but also quickly learned that they knew what their toil was worth. Regardless, with the additional help of Chinese workers glad for a respite from the grueling cane fields, a grand mansion soon began to take form on the ridge.

From what would become the Lanthier's parlor—an opulent room paneled in radiant koa wood with rolling walls that could control the intimacy of any gathering—French windows looked out over the reef and gently breaking surf below. A wide, white sand beach marked where the Lanthier's property ended and God's own realty began.

When the house was finished, Anias Lanthier busied herself playing hostess to whoever came to the island that could keep up with the Babel-like profusion of chatter that passing for discourse in her parlor. When talk of annexation by the United States began to take on more of a strident tone, it was often the Lanthier's table that was the setting for such sedition.

While her husband predictably sided with other sugar interests in pushing for the larger nation to subsume the monarchy, Anias remained nonpartisan and would entertain members of the royal family with as much welcome and grace as she would any American opportunist.

The Lanthier's dining room table, set in crystal and the finest bone china, provided a safe place for champions of any cause to meet and attempt to influence the future of the Hawai'ian Islands. Discussions, while often pregnant with portent, rarely became heated at Anias Lanthier's table lest a guest receive a withering glance from the matron herself and lose future access to the inner sanctum, and with it, the endless delights streaming from the kitchen.

Of course, not every guest that sat at the Lanthier table was a politician or carpetbagger at heart. Those with an interest in dining well for its own sake were never disappointed. Anias had interviewed nearly a dozen chefs hailing from all over the globe before deciding on an ageless culinary wizard named Jun Jin.

Jun, a Chinese national originally from Shanghai, ran the Lanthier kitchen with a ruthless efficiency. Although no one would guess it, Jun had already reached his thirties when the British opened the port city up to the West at the end of the First Opium War in '42. Already well established as a kitchen prodigy, the subsequent influx of British, French, and Americans flooding Shanghai's International Settlement allowed a quick study such as Jun to learn how to cook for just about anyone with a mouth.

Since relocating to the Kingdom of Hawai'i, Jun took it upon himself to master the art of kālua—wrapping a pig in taro leaves, burying it in a pit, and slow roasting it until it became so tender that the smoky meat would abandon the bone at the merest touch. He also taught himself how to properly transform the underground corm of the taro plant into the native Hawai'ian staple poi, one of the first non-natives to care to do so.

8:3   Jun was in the small taro patch he had cultivated just out the back door of his kitchen when Maleko Mahoe, the nephew of most of the native staff employed by the Lanthiers, came running up from the direction of the beach.

"Mr. Jun," the breathless boy gasped, "come quick; it's Mr. Lanthier!"

Jun dropped the pitchfork he had been using to pry the large tubers from their swampy purchase and grabbed the boy by the shoulders, anointing his bronze skin with the iron-rich red mud of the island.

"Tell me," Jun commanded with an air of quiet authority that worked to calm the panicked Maleko.

"I was out swimming and saw Mr. Lanthier riding Lucifer along the surf as he does every morning when something spooked the horse. He got throwed pretty bad. I think he might have hit his head."

"Listen, Maleko, go and find your uncles. Tell them to meet me at the beach." The two figures were propelled in opposite directions as if by repellent magnetic force. Maleko flew off toward the center of the compound while Jun turned to run down the well-worn trail to the water.

Emerging from the jungle brush onto an expanse of sand as white and fine as a spilled bag of sugar, Jun saw Lanthier's imposing black steed standing over the prone body of his employer at the water line as if guarding him until help arrived. The horse snorted and shook its massive head as Jun lifted its reins from where they trailed in the surf.

The most cursory look revealed that the master of the house had not done himself a service by falling from such an imposing animal. The man's head lay in the sand, his face licked by gentle waves, as his bony posterior stuck up in the air as if doing an esoteric t'ai chi ch'uan pose. As Jun bent down, a roller filled Lanthier's mouth with salt water and was expelled by an automatic fit of coughing.

At least he's not dead, Jun surmised with relief. *But can he be moved?*

"Jun!" Voices called out from beyond the high-tide mark. "Don't move him! He could have broken his neck." A group of three stout Hawai'ian men ran toward him, their bare feet pounding a triad of tracks into the sand.

"He is still breathing," Jun reported out. "We need to get him out of the surf before he drowns." Jun knelt down by Lanthier's head and gingerly felt along the man's neck checking for an obvious fracture. Maleko's uncles surrounded the pair and awaited Jun's diagnosis.

Jun looked up the beach for a place to move the man as the tide was coming in and soon would cover most of the beach.

"There," Jun pointed toward the abandoned heiau. "We will carry him there."

The three Hawai'ians looked at each other, each willing the other to explain to the foreigner why that shouldn't, or more emphatically, couldn't, be done.

"Now! Help me move the master before he drinks the entire ocean!"

"Jun Jin, we cannot move him there," Kalani Mahoe, the oldest of Maleko's uncles finally spoke. "It is kapu."

"It would be better to let him die in the sea than to bring down a curse on his whole family," Kapono Mahoe explained.

"Jun Jin, we are strong," Kekoa Mahoe, the youngest and tallest of the brothers, broke in. "We can carry him to the Big House without causing him more harm. Let us do that."

"Fools!" Jun exploded. "Enough of your superstition. I will carry him myself if I must." With that, the cook squatted down and cradled Lanthier's head close to his own abdomen. With surprisingly powerful core muscles, he slowly rose to a standing position, holding the supine man in his arms. "Out of my way, if you will not help," he admonished the three men and staggered his way down the beach, his feet sinking into the sand with the extra weight of the unconscious man.

51

Maleko's uncles stood at the edge of the surf and watched as Jun climbed the ancient lava blocks and laid Lanthier out on what was still one of their most sacred places on the island.

"We are doomed," Kalani bemoaned.

"Not us, brother; this will bring sorrow to the house of Lanthier. Should he survive, or not, the Sun has set on the master's family," Kapono surmised.

"He is no master of mine," added Kekoa.

"Nor mine," Kapono agreed, "but he has been a fair man. For a haole."

"Fair or not, he has now earned the wrath of the gods. Being fair will not change things," Kalani lamented.

"Shouldn't it be Jun that has earned the fury of the gods? Kapono pointed out. "He is the one who carried him there."

"Jun Jin is a heathen," Kalani decreed. "He is already damned."

"We are not without blame," Kekoa admitted. "We could have stopped him."

"Indeed, we should have stopped him," Kapono agreed.

"We are doomed," Kalani intoned.

Chapter Nine
SAN FRANCISCO, CALIFORNIA, UNITED STATES OF AMERICA | 1889

9:1   A wet, gray blanket lay over the bustling San Francisco waterfront as Fox and his ersatz daughter rushed to make the steamship that would take them across the Pacific Ocean to Hawai'i. The pair had been traveling day and night, taking the Central Pacific Railroad down from Sacramento where Fox had telegraphed ahead to arrange their passage but not before drawing a considerable amount of cash out of the local Wells Fargo.

The train would only take them so far, and they caught a waiting ferry at the terminus in Vallejo. Fox had plenty of time to ruminate on whether he was doing the right thing. He did not have the opportunity to speak with Urias before leaving and he wondered if his old friend would have tried to talk him out of whatever this plan would prove to be.

Philomena had been fast asleep with her head pressed against the cold window of the ferry and for the first time since the pyrotechnic apocalypse had upstaged her father's suicide, he took a good look at her. Her skin was olive-tinged, like his, and betrayed a Mediterranean ancestry of some sort, although Fox knew next to nothing about his own family tree.

He, too, had been an orphan and knew what it would have meant to leave the girl in the hands of the state, or worse, the church. *What kind of life would she have now?* He wondered, watching the girl's thin chest fill and fall with each exhausted breath.

He carefully reached out to sweep a lock of Philomena's dark hair from her face and found it to be as thick as his own, whereas the late Mortimer Gilliam's hair was as blonde and fine as a hapless child in a fairy tale, and her mother's hair was as white as the tail of the star that had announced the arrival of their child all those years ago.

By the time the ferry put in at its berth in San Francisco, Fox had become more or less comfortable with the idea that he now had a daughter. As comfortable as a man on the run from possible complicity in the deaths of two people could be, that is; as comfortable as a man who was faced with waking a sleeping child who may or may not be in shock from the events of the past few days.

Fox bent down and nudged the girl who stirred not with a start, but with a recognition that ran the danger of warming his soul.

"We are here," he said, tamping down the riot of hair on top of her head.

"Hawaiʻi?" Philomena stretched and looked around.

Fox laughed in spite of himself. "No, child. This is San Francisco. We have to catch a ship. Quickly. Can you do that?"

"Yes... Um, what should I call you?"

Fox thought for a moment. "Philomena, I know you have been through a lot in the past seventy-two hours, but if this has a chance of working... That is, if I can keep what happened to me when I was your age from happening to you... You should probably call me, 'father.'"

Philomena's eyes swam with emotions she was ill-equipped to handle as she looked up at Fox. *Did she love this man as she did her father? No. Did she hate this man for taking her away from the only home she had ever known? That remained to be seen.* She was old enough to recognize that her life was never going to be the same. The girl burst in to tears as Fox stood by uselessly, another feeling he would have to learn to be comfortable with.

"Come on, dear," he soothed, "we have to go."

9:2   Boarding the steamship *Pride of Jefferson* with a tired and emotionally distraught twelve-year-old was easier than Fox imagined. It turned out that every adult he saw traveling with children had the same look of exhaustion and mortal dread that he himself wore. He wondered for a moment if they all were escaping the bloody scene of some equally Shakespearian drama; he hoped not, if simply for the sake of humanity in general.

Once he had the tired child and their meager collective possessions stowed away in a cabin below, Fox took the opportunity to walk the decks as the ship left the Golden Gate. The oppressive marine layer overhead began to dissipate as soon as the Farallon Islands came into sight. Fox wished with all his heart for a cigarette although he had given them up years ago.

"Isn't that a sight, friend?" A husky voice inquired from the shadows.

Fox flinched and turned to face his fellow passenger. A dark-complexioned man in tasteful evening clothes that hung on his gaunt frame stepped into the light. A dapper silk top hat was rakishly balanced atop a head that looked as if it had been hastily assembled from spare steam-engine parts. The man's rubber grommet lips parted to reveal a mouth full of teeth that would put pause to one of the great white sharks that swam below them.

"Isn't what a sight?" Fox asked as he regained his composure.

"Why the islands, friend, just look at them!" The enigmatic gentleman pointed to a break in the fog with a cane topped with what looked like a baby alligator head. Fox followed the man's gaze out to the jagged guano-covered rocks jutting out of the sea.

"I'm sorry, have we met?" Fox asked, the hairs on the back of his neck standing in cold trepidation.

"I'm afraid not," the man conceded, "but I would recognize a man in the business anywhere. Am I right?"

"What business would that be?" Fox caged.

"Why the oldest business there is that doesn't include lying on your back!" The man exclaimed and gave Fox a knowing look. "Or does it? No matter. Oh, hell, do I have to come right out and say it? Belief! We are both in the belief racket, padre. Granted, no matter how sublime the cast, some fish bite and some don't, but in the end, it's all the same. It's the grand game, and you and I are its masters, are we not?"

"No, we are assuredly not, Mr.—"

"I've gone by many names, as I'm sure you have, or will. You can call me Mr. Khadae, or Puddin' Tane, or John Jacob Jingleheimer Schmidt; I don't give a good goddamn, it's not who I really am," he confided. "But let me ask you a question, padre. Who might you really be?"

"That, I'm afraid, is none of your affair," Fox shot back, visibly shaken.

The gentleman took no visible offense to Fox's outburst and merely took advantage of the lull in conversation to reach into a waistcoat pocket and remove a solid gold cigarette case.

"Smoke?" The man asked, snapping the ornate case open with one hand and holding it out to Fox.

"No, thank you," Fox managed, the rich smell of premium tobacco pulling at his will.

"You don't mind if I indulge, do you?" The man did not wait for an answer, but placed a cigarette between his lips and procured a flame seemingly out of thin air. Oddly, Fox caught a whiff of sulfur as his companion lit up and took a single drag before expelling a huge cloud of smoke that obscured the rocks looming before them.

"You know the Indians around these parts thought these islands were haunted," the man abruptly changed tack, pointing out at the night with the glowing cherry at the end of his cigarette. "They called the Farallones, the 'Islands of the Dead.' Quite naturally, they made a point to not paddle out here, all except for one brave. Distraught over the loss of his true love, he made the dangerous trip out to these rocks—it was quite a different undertaking without the benefit of a steamship, I'll tell you that."

"Does your story have a point?" Fox interrupted. "It is getting late."

"Oh, I assure you it does, reverend. You see, the young man made the ultimate sacrifice for the worst reason imaginable—chasing a bit o' wagtail. Of course, once he made it out to the so-called Islands of the Dead, he didn't find his true love waiting to cross over. He found a bunch of seals and rocks covered in bird shit. Understandably disappointed, he paddled his sorry ass back to shore, where his friends—believing he had returned from the Great Beyond—wanted nothing to do with him. I believe they tried to stone him back to death as he slept. You see, nobody wants to die, but even worse, nobody likes to think that someone else can cheat death while they cannot.

"You said, 'tried to stone him to death.'"

"Never underestimate the redemptive powers of bird shit."

"I'm afraid I am going to have to say goodnight, sir." With that, Fox left the man standing at the railing.

"Perhaps you will fare better, padre," Khadae growled, staring up at the darkening sky. "We shall see. Star light, star bright, first star I see tonight—"

Chapter Ten
THE PACIFIC OCEAN | 1889

10:1 Philomena awoke with a start in an opulent stateroom below decks on the *Pride of Jefferson*. A single electric bulb shone brightly under its Bohemian glass shade throwing colored geometric shapes against the cabin's paneling of Hungarian ash and French oak. As one of the first steamships to be equipped with Thomas Edison's recent invention, the company did not yet entrust the operation of the lamps to the passengers, requiring cabin lights to be controlled from outside the door, each switch encased in a locked box of rosewood.

As major stockholders in the steamer line, the Lanthiers had left an open ticket for Fox to join them in Hawai'i, and a place for the preacher and his charge was easily found upon the lavishly appointed liner. However fancy, the portside cabin was still cold and the blanket that Fox had found to cover Philomena as she slept offered meager protection.

Something in her dreams had been disturbing enough for the girl to allow herself to be dragged back to consciousness by the bright lamp, but as she became fully aware, she wondered what could have possibly been worse than her waking life. Philomena only knew that the ornate, but oppressive, cabin was little comfort and the man who wanted her to call him "father" was nowhere in sight.

Driven by restlessness and an irrepressible curiosity, the girl rose from her berth, put on the sole outfit Fox had managed to retrieve from her home, a jacket and fringed skirt—pleated except where she had sewn matching panels of embroidered roses like her hero Annie Oakley—and stole into the passageway. Although she looked ready to take on the world, Philomena quickly realized she had no idea where she was.

Glimmering electric lights ran the length of the seemingly endless hallway with unlit oil lamps at the ready should Edison's folly fail. *Should have paid better attention when we came in,* she chastised herself. *You only have your wits to rely on now, Philomena.*

A young man dressed in a white sailor's uniform stood before an intricately worked panel of polished walnut at the forward bulkhead and she sheepishly called out to him.

"Excuse me, sir? Could you tell me which way I might find some air? It's rather tight in my cabin, and I thought I might like to see the sky to make sure it still exists."

The sailor neither turned nor acknowledged her request, only continued to contemplate the carved likeness of a sailor cavorting with what Philomena took at first to be friendly mermaids, but upon closer inspection turned out to be much more malevolent creatures—a fact that wasn't lost on the chiseled wooden seaman, his face a sculpted mask of dawning horror.

"Excuse me!" Philomena's tone became more emphatic as she moved toward the sailor. "I would like to go up to the deck, could you give—?"

As she reached out to touch the man's shoulder, an unearthly chill rushed the length of the passageway, funneled and magnified by the cold steel hall, and dimming the nascent electric lamps as it came.

The figure finally turned to face her in the half-light and revealed a white, ravaged visage; wrinkled as if brined by the sea. The young man's pale skin hung off the bones of his skull in layers that had started to lose their grip in places.

Philomena was frozen where she stood. *Oh, please don't open your mouth. Oh, please don't open your mouth.* She knew that if the sailor made to speak to her, she would finally lose her tenuous grip on her wavering sanity.

The sound of someone approaching on the stairs adjacent to the dreadful frieze distracted her for a second, and when she turned back to the sailor, he was gone.

"Well, what have we here?" A sandpaper voice inquired. "Why, little Miss Sure Shot, you look like you've seen a ghost." A tall, gaunt gentleman in an ill-fitting suit stepped through the very door Philomena had been looking for. She took the opportunity to skirt around the man and mount the stairs at a dead run.

The figure watched her disappear, a blur of brocaded roses, and chuckled to himself, "Children today."

Moments later, Philomena burst out of the stairwell and into the bright sunlight as if shot from a cannon.

"Hold up there, Bulls-Eye," a young man dressed the same as the phantom stopped her. "What's the rush?"

Philomena stepped forward and poked the sailor hard in the stomach, which to her relief did not deflate, dissolve, or disappear.

"What was that for?" He asked, bemused as he rubbed his abused abdominals.

"I'm sorry," Philomena apologized, realizing just how strange it may have seemed. "I'm... I'm looking for my father."

"Well, I'm afraid you missed the mark, Annie Oakley. You're not going to find him in there," the sailor laughed, his green eyes flashing. "Let's look for him together, shall we? We can't have you going around poking the other passengers."

10:2 The unlikely pair found Fox holding court in a large salon illuminated by immense skylights made up of intricate patterns of cut glass. Several of Edison's lamps hung in matching chandeliers adding to the disorienting kaleidoscopic effect.

Upon noticing his charge enter the room, Fox suspended whatever web of nonsense he had been spinning and rose from his leather swivel chair.

"Ah, Philomena!" He exclaimed. "I trust my daughter has caught up with her sleep." Fox turned to his coterie of ruddy companions and gave an aside. "Ocean travel is so hard on the girl, she has spent most of her short life landlocked, poor dear."

Well cognizant of the game Fox intended to play, Philomena aimed for the back of the room, sensing subtlety would be lost on the lubricated assembly. "Yes, father," she swooned, "the salt air is ever so troublesome."

"Perhaps the poor child needs some nourishment," a pale woman with cheeks painted with the evidence of several gin and tonics offered. "It is almost time for breakfast and I would just love if the two of you would join me at the captain's table." Not waiting for an answer, the woman rose and attempted to straighten her bustled skirt and woolen vest as she led the way.

Before she could react, Philomena found herself sitting before a profusion of silver cutlery—most of which she could imagine no use for—listening to the idle chatter of the idle class.

"So tell me, dear," Mrs. Gin and Tonic probed, "how is it that you have never been to sea? Where has the good reverend been hiding you?"

Philomena let an unnecessary sharp look from Fox glance off her countenance, imagining it hitting and even cracking one of the thousands of glass facets that made up the dining room's light fixtures.

"The Central Valley, ma'am," she purred. "I find that a drier clime better suits my constitution."

"Oh, I know what you mean," the woman took the bait and began to unspool as much line as she could. "My husband and I just returned from the Grand Tour—that's Europe you know—we just *adored* Andalusia, that's in Spain—"

Philomena had been around adults enough to know that they didn't really care what she thought and most of them only liked to hear themselves talk. She kept her contributions to a minimum throughout the rest of the meal, mostly a small, random hodgepodge of "hmmm" and "is that so?"

She couldn't tell if Fox was enjoying putting her through the uncomfortable meal, or was completely oblivious to her clues and cues. In the end, it didn't matter; she was stuck either way.

Just as she was ready to slide out of her chair with boredom, the conversation took a surprising turn and Philomena scrambled to climb out of her fugue.

"I don't want to upset the girl," Mrs. Gin and Tonic slurred, "but I've heard that there's a ghost on board this ship."

For his part, Fox produced the first frown Philomena had witnessed since they began their ocean voyage. "Madam, I must implore you—"

"I saw it!" Philomena exclaimed.

"Saw what?" A lanky Dane in a starched white uniform—perfectly matching his closely cropped hair and beard—inquired as he pulled out a chair for himself. "I must apologize for my tardiness. I had unavoidable business to attend to."

"I saw the ghost!" Philomena exclaimed while Fox noisily cleared his throat. "It was—"

"My dear girl," the man interrupted, "we are not sitting around a campfire telling stories. This very ship, if nothing else, proves that we have finally entered an irrefutable age of science. Thomas Edison himself installed these electric lights so that we might—once and for all—dispel the mysteries that lurk in the shadows."

"But—"

"Please, allow me to introduce myself," the man addressed the table at large, "I am Captain Kasper Munk." The captain then turned toward Philomena. "You, my dear, can call me Captain Kasper."

10:3 Following the overly rich brunch, during which Philomena wisely kept her otherworldly experience to herself, the table dispersed for each party to go figure out how best to digest the meal as they may.

For their part, Fox and Philomena wandered the polished upper decks, finding a crowd of people gathered around a large telescope trained toward the Sun blazing above them. A wiry man in a brown woolen vest and round glasses was holding court next to the delicate instrument.

"This telescope contains the finest lenses available, hand-shaped and polished in Vienna!" He exclaimed. "What a lucky coincidence that I am personally accompanying it to its new home on Mauna Kea during this rarest of cosmic events."

As the man spoke, Philomena noticed a chill in the air and a perceptible dimming of the day. "What is the event?" She asked, searching the faces of the gathered adults to determine if they, too, had noticed anything strange.

"My dear girl, we are about to experience a total eclipse of the Sun, something only visible this time from the middle of the Pacific Ocean!" The gentleman's excitement was infectious and Fox had immediately been drawn in, while Philomena chose to gaze out at the Sun's reflection upon the endless expanse of darkening sea.

Philomena only lost sight of Fox a moment before he excitedly returned to try and draw her over to the contraption. "Come and look at this marvel of modern technology, child! It is things like this that will help us better understand His grand vision."

The girl was slightly taken aback at how quickly Fox could drop into his piety routine. She had been with him for several days now and hadn't heard one peep about God or any plan that He may or may not have for them. If the reverend was privy to any inside information, she truly wished he would let her in on it.

As the bespectacled scientist waved the duo closer, she had to admit that his enthusiasm was contagious. "Right you are, sir! We are making great strides in interpreting the universe around us. Our ancestors would be looking for a handy virgin to toss into a volcano about now."

Philomena shot the astronomer a wary look.

"Not to worry miss, we now recognize that it is merely the mechanics of the cosmos that is spiriting our Sun away, and of course we know with some certainty that it will return. However, the phenomenon is no less astonishing for being better understood. Please, everyone, do not look straight at the Sun on your own until I say so. Come look through the eyepiece instead. I have devised a filter that will make it safe to look at."

Fox, although enjoying the show, knew better to trail anything a showman wanted you to watch. The action was always where they didn't want you to be looking. *You can't fool a fellow professional;* he smirked as he scrutinized the man's every move.

When the astronomer invited the gentlemen and ladies surrounding him to try peering into the eyepiece of the telescope, Fox was sure he was going to catch him lifting a wallet or two, but it never happened; instead the man just dazzled them with explanations about eclipses and their historical context.

After most of the assembled crowd had taken a turn looking through the lens, the astronomer motioned to Fox who had been silently critiquing the man's crowd work on the periphery of the scrum.

"How about you, sir?" He addressed Fox. "Wouldn't you like to take a closer look at one of nature's greatest mysteries? Why, just think of it, what are the odds that we should find ourselves here in the middle of the greatest ocean on Earth just at the right moment to bear witness?"

Fox was drawn in by the man's boundless enthusiasm. "You got me, friend," he conceded. "Let me take a gander through that fine Viennese glass." Fox meandered up through the remaining hangers-on milling about the afterdeck. When the astronomer attempted to explain how to use the telescope, he merely waived him off. "I have heard you give those directions at least twenty times, sir. I would think that even a monkey would have it by now."

The Moon finally finished its slow journey across the face of the Sun, the last meager crescent of flame occluded by its stony mass. All at once, a multitude of stars exploded into view, the day erased and all but forgotten. In the sky, a glowing ring now surrounded a dark void that seemed to still the entire atmosphere. In fact, the uncanny sight had becalmed the very ocean itself.

"Observe now," the astronomer gushed, pointing out the beads of light shining past the Moon's rugged edge, "there are jewels in the Sun's starry crown!"

The preacher bent at the waist and floated his eye above the brass eyepiece. That was the last thing he would remember.

10:4   It was Fox's turn to awake disoriented in his berth, a piercing pain in his head. As he tried to rise, he was gently admonished and held back by a firm hand.

"You gave us quite a scare there, sir," a voice Fox did not recognize came through the haze. "How about you just relax and lie back awhile? I want to make sure there are no residual effects from your spell."

"Spell?" Fox managed to mutter. "What spell? What happened?" As his vision cleared, he saw a very dark-skinned man in uniform hovering over him. Fox gave a start having paid dearly for the wartime lesson that anyone looking at you while you lay prostrate—whether in that position by choice or misfortune—was a potential threat.

"Mr. Fox, I'm Dr. Coleman Whitaker, the ship's physician. I am sorry if I startled you. Tell me, do you have a history of fainting, or perhaps migraine headaches?"

Answering my question with a question, Fox thought. *That is never good.*

"It's *Reverend* Fox, and, no, never," he caged and scrambled for time to get his thoughts together. "Forgive me, doctor, but I have not had the privilege of meeting too many men in your profession with your... complexion. Are you American by chance?"

Whitaker, used to even more inappropriate questions, simply smiled. "No, *Reverend* Fox, this ship flies the Dannebrog, the flag of Denmark. I am originally from the Danish West Indies—St. Croix; have you heard of it?"

"I can't say that I have," Fox admitted, giving in to Whitaker's inquiry. "Are you saying that I fainted, doctor?"

"Not exactly, reverend," Whitaker chewed his bottom lip. "What is the last thing you recall from this afternoon?"

Nice tell there, doctor, Fox thought as he cradled his forehead in his hand. *Too bad we are not together at the poker table. St. Augustine!* Fox entreated the patron saint of drunkards. *Did I drink too much at brunch? No... I did not drink at all.*

"I was with Philomena... Philomena! Where is she?" Fox panicked as the doctor began preparing a shot to calm his nerves.

"The child is fine, reverend. I entrusted my staff to keep an eye on her until we were sure that you were going to come around. Please, you were saying—"

Fox rubbed his temples as he tried to fill in the afternoon's missing blanks, but came up empty. "I was with my daughter on the afterdeck. There was an astronomer there with a telescope pointed at the Sun—at the eclipse. Everyone took a look and I stepped up to take a turn and... I don't remember anything after that."

"You don't remember speaking gibberish before prognosticating that a comet was going to hit Earth, killing everyone?"

"Gibberish? Certainly not," Fox denied. "A comet? That's ludicrous."

"Perhaps it is," Whitaker agreed, "but I assure you, that's what you did do. Several of the other passengers were quite upset."

"Are you telling me that I spoke in tongues?" Fox asked, his headache worsening by the second.

"I suppose you could draw a parallel. I'm not really familiar with the vagaries of the more charismatic religious sects. Is that your *métier*, reverend? Are you usually given to glossolalia?"

When the doctor received nothing but silence from Fox, he continued. "I have to say that I am more concerned that you may have had a seizure of some kind. If you have experienced a history of this— revelations aside—I would start to suspect a brain lesion, perhaps a tumor."

"Stop right there," Fox struggled to speak through gritted teeth as what felt like the mother of all migraines ripped through his skull. "I've never... I've seen men and women filled up with the Golden Light to the point that they made water where they stood. I have seen men handle deadly snakes like babes in arms, and others perform feats of strength that would astonish you; but myself, no. I am but a humble messenger. I can't claim to have the inside track on what God's plan is regarding the future. I truly wish I did."

"Very well, Reverend Fox, I am glad to hear that. It was a pretty grizzly story by all accounts," Whitaker drew back the plunger in his hypodermic needle. "I want to give you a little something to help you relax, if that is all right with you; maybe get rid of the pain you are experiencing in your head."

"I thought you'd never ask," Fox capitulated. "Will you send my daughter in?"

"Of course," Whitaker soothed. "She can keep an eye on you for me. Now lie back and try to relax. This won't hurt a bit."

10:5 Philomena quickly realized there wasn't much involved in watching her narcotized guardian sleep in the darkening cabin. Fox was stretched flat out on the berth still dressed in his morning clothes with only his shoes missing. A barely perceptible snore was the only sign that he was still alive.

She certainly had not had the time to grab any of her favorite books before embarking on this new phase of her life. When she heard a noise in the passageway, she was temped to open the door and ask whomever it was to turn on the electric light and bring her a newspaper or something—anything—to read, but the memory of the drowned sailor lurking at the bulkhead kept her silent, and bored enough to gradually drift off herself.

Philomena awoke with a start and the sudden awareness that something was amiss. As her eyes adjusted to the darkness, she could hear gentle breaths rising and falling like the lapping of waves from the direction of the preacher's berth. *That is not it,* she thought.

The cabin held few places to hide; there were the two berths, a chair, and a small table set up underneath the porthole.

The girl's eyes opened wide as to better exploit any bit of light that might help illuminate what her brain told her she couldn't be seeing. Sitting at the table, as if waiting after dinner for a small glass of port, sat her father—the man she still considered her real father, the recently departed Mortimer Gilliam—only now horribly burned and with a piece of his skull missing.

The screams coming from Cabin 227 brought a small army of ship's attendants. Fox, meanwhile, slept the opiated sleep of the dead.

THE AETHER | The Eternal Now

10:6 *The I that is I remembers fireworks. Not the brightly colored displays that print themselves upon the retinas of the living, but the idea of fireworks. Something I am supposed to do. This feeling of forgetting to have done something has kept me from embracing the I that is All.*

How provincial to have bought into the idea of an afterlife where we remain ourselves. What a sad way to spend eternity. Every bit of whatever is left of the illusion of a singular I yearns to be reunited with the infinite.

I know now that we are but drops of water flung from the crest of a wave. Separate but for an instant, yet still made of ocean, and to ocean we shall return. The ocean is deep and draws me toward itself. Just... Not yet.

PLATE TWO ☀ Philomena Fox née Gilliam

1876

Chapter Eleven

FIESTA, CALIFORNIA, UNITED STATES OF AMERICA | 1876

11:1 It was dark when Mordikai Fox and Aaron Urias stepped off the train at the Fiesta depot with only a single small satchel between them. It was an unremarkable station, indistinguishable from any other that dotted the interior of the burgeoning state of California—a mustard-colored breadbox with a sharply pitched roof as if to avoid the buildup of snow that hadn't touched the dry ground of Fiesta since the last ice age.

What set this particular depot apart, at least for the time being, was the bright celestial body that blazed far above its misplaced mountain geometry and red brick chimney.

"Train travel certainly does have a way of making me thirsty," Urias announced, noticing a busy Mexican tavern that hadn't been there the last time they had been through the hardscrabble agricultural town.

"I'm going to go get a line on a place to stay. You'll probably want to visit the babe."

Fox pulled his watch from his vest pocket and popped open the engraved silver cover. The clock's face reflected as well as explained his exhaustion. It was well past midnight.

"I'll think I'll join you, Aaron," Fox said as he stifled a yawn. "Miracle or not, I know better than to disturb a babe once it is asleep."

As the two men approached the rambunctious cantina, the strains of Mexican son music drew them in from the street and the smell of roasting pork sealed the deal.

In the corner of the bar, four black-haired rancheros stood playing the popular "Cielito Lindo." The copia by Mexico City capitalino Quirino Mendoza y Cortes had been taking the valley by storm and every son jalisciense combo between Fiesta and the ancient ruins of Palenque knew it by heart and wound up playing it several times a night.

One of the musicians, an intense young man holding a Spanish vihuela, threw back his head as Fox and Urias found a table. He sang with a power that belied his compact stature.

"De la Sierra Morena,	*"From the Sierra Morena,*
cielito lindo, vienen bajando.	*pretty heavenly one, they do come down.*
Un par de ojitos negros,	*A pair of lovely black eyes,*
cielito lindo, de contrabando.	*pretty heavenly one, a stolen glance.*
Ay, ay, ay, ay"	*Ay, ay, ay, ay"*

The two violinists and guitarrón player joined in at the chorus, a robust sound that soon swelled to include nearly every full-throated patron in the room. As the crowd erupted into song, a woman in a traditional Oaxacan white cotton blouse embroidered with colorful flowers threaded her way over to the two men. The cut of the garment showed the woman's strong shoulders to magnificent effect.

"Reverend Fox! It's so wonderful that you have come," the woman exclaimed. "Can you believe it—a genuine miracle in our town? ¡La fe mueve montañas! Brother Urias, it's good to see you as well."

"Sister Águeda, this is a pleasure!" Fox exclaimed, recognizing the young beauty from their first revival in Fiesta. "Tell me, have you seen the blessed miracle yet?"

"I have not, reverend," the waitress bemoaned. "Mr. Gilliam has kept everyone away from Emilia and the baby. There are a lot of strange people around these days." Fox and Urias followed her gaze as she cut her eyes toward the bar where a man in a corduroy jacket and green neckerchief sat nursing a beer. Meanwhile, the crowd put everything they had left into their final verse.

"Una flecha en el aire,	*"An arrow in the air,*
cielito lindo, lanzó Cupido,	*heavenly one, Cupid has launched,*
si la tiró jugando,	*and though he was playing,*
cielito lindo, a mí me ha herido.	*heavenly one, he has struck me.*
Ay, ay, ay, ay"	*Ay, ay, ay, ay"*

"Allow me," Urias offered, rising and putting his hand on Fox's shoulder suggesting that he stay in his chair. "Sister, I would kill for some carnitas."

Urias made his way across the crowded cantina. If the man at the bar noticed his arrival, he didn't let on.

"Camarero!" He hailed as took an empty stool next to the stranger. "Cerveza, por favor!" Waiting for the bartender, Urias got a good look at the man reflected in the silvered mirror behind the bar. Again, if the man knew, or cared, that he was being scrutinized, he wasn't showing it, instead, he merely stared into the sorry third of his drink.

"Vierte dos cervezas, por favor!" Urias changed his order.

The stranger decided this turn of events finally merited acknowledgment and turned to face Urias, revealing that the pockets of his jacket were outlined in pearl buttons. A quick glance revealed that similar rows of buttons followed the outer seams of the man's corduroy trousers.

"That's quite some get-up, friend," Urias commented with a surety that even if the gentleman turned surly that he could handle it. To his surprise, however, the man lit up and became quite animated.

"You like the smother suit, do ya?" The man straightened his stance, obviously proud of the display. "I was a Pearly King back home, instead of a fucking errand boy in this sad country."

"A king, you say?" Urias prodded. "We don't get much royalty out this way."

"Well, that's regretful, that is," bemoaned the stranger. "But you've really only got yourselves to blame for that one, what with your mutinous tendencies an' all."

"Guilty as charged," Urias slid the extra beer over and introduced himself. "Aaron Urias, proud descendant of revolutionary scum."

"Niall Hendry, Londoner 'til I die, ex-costermonger, and current lackey for nefarious forces," Hendry held out his hand and Urias took it.

"What is a costermonger?" Urias asked, taking a long pull from his beer.

"Do you not know your Shakespeare in this God-forsaken land?" Hendry asked, aghast. "'Enry the Fourth? *'Virtue is of so little regard in these costermonger times, that true valor is turned bear-herd.'*"

"I'm not familiar—"

"Of course not," Hendry conciliated. "You've been cut off from true civilization through no fault of your own. Made to make your way in the wilderness through the rash actions of your forebears... Forgive me, I don't mean to be rude. I guess I've found myself in my cups this evening. It is still evening, isn't it?"

"I'm afraid not," Urias admitted, his stomach growling despite the beer he had been pouring into it.

"I'll give you the short glory... erm, story, then. Think of a coster as a cross between your veg grocer and a hard man. We aren't gangsters so much as... purveyors of favors, as well as peddlers of Earth's glorious bounty."

"I see," Urias said, not really seeing at all. "So what brings you to Fiesta?"

"Well now, *that* is a sad bit of business," Hendry lamented. "The Devil's work, I'm afraid. And you, Mr. Urias? Which team are you working for?"

"The Lord's, I suppose," Urias prevaricated.

"A toast then! Let the best man win," Hendry drained his glass. "Barkeep!"

11:2 "Oh, my head!" Fox moaned, swinging his legs out of bed and hoping that anchoring his feet to the floor would stop the room from spinning. "Did I drink too much last night?"

"No, I'm afraid that was me," the familiar voice of Urias came from the water closet where he was shaving with a badger-hair brush and straight razor. "Luckily, one of us was drunk enough to talk our way into these accommodations. Apparently, there is a proverbial 'no room at the inn' situation in Fiesta."

"Where are we, then?" Fox struggled to recall the night's events. "The last thing I remember is sitting down at the cantina, and you went to check out the man at the bar."

"Right, interesting fellow, that one. We are guests of the lovely Águeda María Luisa—the woman so nice they named her thrice. We are still at the cantina, actually," Urias explained. "In an apartment around back. They have a thriving little business here."

Fox looked around the small but tastefully appointed room, recognizing nothing.

Urias stepped into the bedroom wiping the residual soap from his neck and hitching his suspenders back over his shoulders. "Are you going to be well enough to visit the Gilliams? Do you need your medicine?"

"No, no," Fox waved off the idea of feeding his dependency. Although it had been fourteen years since he and Urias left the Union Army, their final engagement left them both badly wounded, a situation that still found Fox reaching for a palliative from time to time. "I want to be as clearheaded as possible for this. It is strange, though, ever since we stepped off of that train, I've felt a bit unmoored."

"I have to admit," Urias stepped closer to his friend to check his pallor and the condition of his eyes, "although I lack your sensitivities, there is something strange in the air. I can feel the hair on the back of my neck standing at attention. That is usually not such a good thing."

"Well, let us see what we shall see," Fox rallied. "We didn't come all this way to fiddly fart around."

"That's the spirit," Urias encouraged. "While you make yourself presentable, I'll go in search of coffee. I'm sure there are other sore heads at the cantina. Shall I bring you some?"

"Please," Fox begged as he struggled to his feet. "Black as a Bible."

11:3   "Good day's dawning, gentlemen!" A voice hailed Fox and Urias from behind as they made their way down the dirt street to the Fiesta Mercantile where they hoped to find Mortimer Gilliam and family. Slowly turning, they saw Hendry, resplendent in his corduroy, pearl buttons flashing in the morning sunlight. "It looks like we're not the only ones out this morning."

The two men followed Hendry's gaze to the early spring sky. Above the town, the star the men had followed to Fiesta shone as brightly as it had when they got off the train.

"Well, look at that," Fox mused. "We must be in the right place."

"Niall Hendry, 'costermonger,' I'd like to introduce the Good Reverend Mordikai Fox."

"Reverend," Hendry gave a little bow. Fox couldn't tell if the man was making fun of him or if his Victorian mannerisms were naturally askew.

"What brings you to Fiesta, Mr. Hendry?" Fox opted to believe the man was merely strange.

"Same as the two of you, I'm sure of it," Hendry posited. "'Where is He who has been born King of the Jews? For we saw His star in the east and have come to worship Him.' Matthew 2:2, if I'm not mistaken."

"I am impressed by your knowledge of scripture," Fox granted, "but if you've come to see the babe, you surely can't believe—"

"You've got me sussed," Hendry admitted. "Please do forgive me, reverend. It is a sad fact that I do not believe in much—not beyond what my own cunning and two hands can wrest from this stingy world—but I do represent certain parties that have become... curious."

"Might I ask who your mysterious benefactors are?" Fox inquired.

"Alas, even I don't know where that tangled path might lead," Hendry bemoaned. "I can only tell you that we are all probably better off not knowing. Shall we?"

As the trio made their way down the dusty main street, they began to draw a small crowd following behind at a reasonable distance.

"Is this normal for this town?" Hendry asked once he noticed the throng. "It's a bit unnerving, innit?"

"Perhaps it's a coincidence?" Urias guessed. "There aren't too many directions to go in Fiesta, maybe we've caught them all on a lucky bounce."

"Listen, I've got a shiv in my boot if it comes to it," Hendry said under his breath. "How are you gents fixed?"

"Easy, fellows, they've all come to pay respects to the babe," Fox said as they arrived at the mercantile. "The same as us."

Fox climbed up on the singular stretch of wooden sidewalk that fronted the hardware store and pushed open the door. A small bell alerted Gilliam to his arrival.

"Reverend Fox!" The heavyset mercantilist exclaimed with excitement as he appeared from the stockroom. "We are so honored that you answered our telegram and came all this way." Gilliam looked past the preacher as Urias and Hendry followed in behind him. The crowd out in the street was quickly turning into a mob. "Brother Urias, I see you've brought a friend."

"A recent acquaintance," Urias allowed. "As to the gathering, it is not of our doing."

"I'm afraid that I am to blame for them," Gilliam confessed. "I have told the entire town about the miracle Reverend Fox has bestowed upon us, upon all of Fiesta, really."

"I assure you—" Fox began before Gilliam cut him off.

"Please, reverend, now is not the time for modesty. Emilia and I came to you desperate, as we had tried for years to conceive a child. You said you would pray upon it, and we received a miracle. Look up at the sky if you do not believe it. That star is a sign if there ever was one."

"It's actually a comet," Urias muttered, gaining only a sideways glance from Hendry.

"Mortimer," a melodious voice from the back room called, "are they here? I hear voices."

"Yes, my love!" Gilliam replied. "Reverend Fox has come. The whole town has come. Bring the child for them to behold."

A voluptuous young woman, not yet completely out of her teens, yet moving with the air and confidence of someone completely comfortable in their own skin, appeared from the back of the store. In her arms she carried a swaddling babe showing only a cherubic face topped with a shock of black hair.

"Reverend Fox," the girl cooed as to not awaken the sleeping child, "we'd like you to meet Philomena."

"It means 'Daughter of Light,'" Gilliam explained.

"It's a wee girl!" Hendry declared. "Say, she does look a bit like—"

"She is beautiful," Fox pronounced as he stepped closer to touch the child's head. "May her days be blessed, for in His hand is the life of every creature and the breath of all mankind."

"I've seen enough. You two," Hendry addressed the Gilliams, "good luck with the bricks and mortar." When he received back only stares, he tried again. "The twist and twirl? Blimey, does no one speak the Queen's in this savage nation? The wee one. The baby girl."

Having bestowed his blessing of sorts, the Londoner turned to leave. "Gentlemen, may our paths cross again someday."

1889

Chapter Twelve

12:1 "Excuse, me! Mr. Urias!" The desk clerk at the Union Hotel called after the tall figure dressed in gray sack coat and matching vest. The gentleman's dark trousers were splattered with Bay mud at the cuffs from walking the streets and long piers north of Montgomery Street where the burgeoning city was busy constructing a new seawall.

Urias turned and lowered one of his prominent eyebrows while raising the other, the better to take full measure of the man.

"At your service," Urias lied. "This isn't about my bill, is it?"

"No sir! Your account has been taken care of," the clerk chirped. "Sir."

Urias glanced once at the doors he had been planning to take full advantage of before redirecting his bearing to better give the clerk the pleasure of his full attention. "Excuse me?"

"Paid in full until the end of the week," the clerk began to wither under the man's double-barreled gaze. "You *will* be staying with us for the remainder of the week, won't you?"

"That all depends," Urias loped up to the desk of polished dark walnut. "Are there any messages that accompany that bit of good news?"

"Messages, sir?"

"Am I to simply thank providence for this fortunate turn of events, or is there a string or two attached that you've not yet revealed?"

"There *was* a gentleman here earlier," the clerk took a measured step back from his side of the desk as if the man's long arms could not reach over the mostly symbolic barrier.

"Of course there was," Urias sighed, already tired of playing cat and mouse with the hotel functionary. "And what, may I ask, did this gentleman happen to say; in regards to me, that is."

"He wanted to speak with you—"

"Obviously," Urias growled. "Out with it man!"

The clerk's words fell out of him with a clatter. "The gentleman said that he would wait at the saloon on the corner if you would be so good to meet him for a drink. You can't miss him. He'll be wearing a green plaid suit. He looked as if he had just finished leading the St. Patrick's Day parade."

"Plaid, you say?"

"Yes, sir," the clerk caught his breath. "Plaid."

"Curious," Urias tipped his hat, spun on his heels and hit the front doors with a force that caused the giant chandelier above to shake, its cut crystals tinkling a merry tune out of sync with the violent jolt.

Outside, the fog had moved in off the Bay, wrapping busy Market Street in gauze. Urias felt as if he was moving through an Impressionist painting, the world around him spontaneously faceting and reforming into a colder, damper version of itself as he went. *Maybe a drink isn't such a bad idea after all,* he often thought, and found himself doing so again.

The Baldwin Bar beckoned as bright as a ship's beacon in the gloom. Urias reached the corner at a determined gait and plunged into the gas-lit interior. Above his head, another set of chandeliers did not dare to tinkle, jingle, or chime.

Across the surprisingly empty saloon, given the time and texture of the evening, a man in a green English plaid suit sat at the bar with his back to the door. The heavy Turkish carpet absorbed Urias' footfalls as he approached, but the gentleman apparently had eyes in the back of his head.

"Aaron Urias, what a singular pleasure!" The man exclaimed without turning. "Can I buy you something to help knock back the damp?"

"You may," Urias conceded as he slid onto the stool to the man's left. "If I may ask how you know my name."

"You wound me, sir," the man played at being taken aback. "We have met once before, when the star rose above Fiesta."

"Niall Hendry," Urias exclaimed, surprised. "I didn't recognize you without your pearl buttons. If I may, you seem to have upgraded your wardrobe. No offense."

"None taken," Hendry allowed as he turned to face his guest, revealing a livid scar that ran down his right cheek from his eyebrow before disappearing beneath his prodigious muttonchops.

"I see your outfit isn't the only thing that's undergone a change. May I ask—?"

"*That* is a conversation for another day, I'm afraid," Hendry cut Urias off, introducing him to the experience for one of the few times in his life.

"Forgive me, that was rash," Urias apologized. "What can I do for you, Mr. Hendry?"

"Please, call me Niall," Hendry asked. "After all, we are old acquaintances are we not?"

"I suppose we are at that," Urias allowed. "What can I do for you, Niall?"

Hendry chose to ignore the slight of Urias not extending the same liberty. "Your reputation precedes you, Mr. Urias. I am in need of someone who knows how to find things, and I have been led to understand that you have quite a knack."

"Maybe I do," Urias admitted as he signaled the barman. "Have you lost something, then?"

"I come on behalf of person or persons who have experienced that very misfortune, yes. There is considerable interest in the retrieval of what has been misplaced. Profitable interest as you yourself are concerned."

"I haven't decided that I am all that concerned, Niall," Urias hedged and addressed the bartender. "Double rye, neat. Put it on my plaid companion's tab."

"Let me ask you something, Mr. Urias, as you are sitting to my left. The Bible tells us that the Son of Man has taken his place at the right hand of God. Who do you figure sits at his left?"

"I couldn't say," Urias pondered the question as he took a long, warming pull from his glass. "Why does anybody have to sit there?" He finally posited. "I would guess those two are pretty tight. Three *is* a crowd."

"I think you've hit the proverbial nail on the head! According to an accustomed reading of Scripture, the seat is kept free, but there are some that espouse that place was originally held for Lucifer, the Morning Star, before his ignoble fall from grace."

"I've heard that theory," Urias tensed. "How about you tell me what this is about? I'm done with my drink, and I'm done with these games as well."

"I didn't mean to offend you," the man gestured to have their glasses filled again. "So you are still familiar with the Good Reverend Fox?"

Urias placed his hand atop his empty glass, blocking the attentive bartender from pouring. "I would say you know damn well that I am. Is that why we are sitting here? I'll give you one more chance to state your business, and then I am going to have to say goodnight."

"The girl," the man said.

"The girl. What girl? What are you talking about?"

"My client believes that Reverend Fox survived the recent spectacular events in Fiesta and made off with a young girl. The very one you and I saw together as a wee babe. My client is very interested in getting her back."

"That is ludicrous," Urias exploded. "You are wasting my time as well as your own. After the accident, I identified the body myself. Mordikai Fox had his problems, but I assure you, being alive is no longer one of them."

"I have five thousand dollars that says differently."

"Well, we can't be too quick to judge now, can we?" Urias removed his hand and waved the bartender on.

Hendry bravely reached over and grasped the lapel of Urias' jacket between the thumb and first two fingers of his right hand as if assessing the nature and quality of the material. Before his impropriety lasted long enough to earn a reaction, he slid a small card into the jacket's breast pocket with a deftness that revealed a certain familiarity with small detail work.

"That is where to find me. I am afraid I must take my leave this evening; but I do look forward to doing business with you, Aaron, if I might be so informal—"

Urias wordlessly glanced down at the place on his jacket the man had just molested and then fixed the gentleman's icy blue eyes with his own.

"Very well," the man conceded. "I bid you a good evening, Mr. Urias. Until we might speak again."

Urias watched the plaid pattern move across the room and disappear out the front door. Turning to his own left, he was surprised to see an attractive young woman sitting at his elbow. "Well, now," his eyebrows gave the girl a less severe but no less animated inspection than the desk clerk received. "You wouldn't be the Devil, now, would you, miss?"

"Why don't you buy me a drink and find out?" The woman parried. "Barkeep!"

12:2 Urias awoke in the damp and the dark. It was a good few minutes before he realized the pounding he was hearing was coming from inside his own skull. He reached inside his vest pocket for a match and his fingers closed on Hendry's business card.

My costermonger friend is now a tradesman, then? Urias was familiar enough with the professional classes to realize that the calling card, still out of favor with the American gentry, was becoming ubiquitous among those who worked for a living.

He found and struck a match as he struggled to remember the last bit of conversation he had with the mysterious gentleman in plaid. Urias recalled the man mentioning Fox, five thousand dollars, and then taking his leave. *How did* that *lead to* this? He wondered, holding his head.

Before the match burned down to his fingertips, only partially deadened by the cold, the meager light revealed Urias to be in a dank storage basement. Above his head he could just make out the backlit three-edged outline of a trapdoor, which—if he had to guess—led back up to the Baldwin Bar. *Shanghaied! Blasted crimps!*

Urias was well familiar with the reputation of San Francisco's Barbary Coast. Many an unwary drunken sailor had regained consciousness on a different ship than the one he arrived on. The clippers that plied the trade routes to China often took more men to sail than San Francisco had willing sailors to do so. Crimps like Jim

"Shanghai" Kelly and his ilk made a good living by collecting unwitting but able bodies to help fill out the ships' crews.

Is that what I've become? Urias bemoaned his situation. *No better than a drunken sailor on leave? I think not.* He lit another match and scanned the dank cellar for an exit. A stack of Old Overholt crates caught his eye and he took the time to help himself to a bottle of rye out of an open straw-filled box.

Good enough for Honest Abe is good enough for me, he thought, stashing the bottle in his coat and removing a ring of brass skeleton keys. *Let's see now, there hasn't been a lock made that could hold a son of Mother Urias. The trick is finding... Hello.*

Urias exited into a trash-strewn alleyway awash in hazy sunlight. Once again holding his head to make sure it wasn't coming off, he looked both ways and made his way into the morning throng.

The printed card the man in plaid slipped him read, "Niall Hendry, Men's Haberdasher, 745 Market St., San Francisco." *So, that's where the natty suit came from, perhaps I should see about updating my wardrobe,* Urias spun on his heels and took off down Market in search of answers and, just maybe, a new jacket.

Could Fox really still be alive? He wondered as his boot heels pounded Market Street into mute submission. *Granted, there wasn't much of Fox's body left once the fire was through with it,* Urias thought back to what the two of them had gone through together in '62 as Union soldiers in Virginia. Both men had been part of the Army of the Potomac's offensive against Richmond. By the time the hellish week was over, Maj. Gen. McClellan had lost almost sixteen thousand men. Richmond's defenders under Lee lost twenty thousand.

I should have remembered that Fox is a hard son of a bitch to kill, Urias mused. Lost in reverie, he almost walked past a storefront with painted windows advertising *Shirts, Collars, Gloves, Belts, and Hats.* Piles of said items filled displays on either side of the wooden door.

The pleasing peal of a brass bell announced his arrival, but it needn't have bothered as Hendry sat behind a scarred wooden desk with his one of his many hats in hand as if waiting for him.

"Mr. Urias!" Hendry exclaimed. "You should have mentioned to me last night that you were traveling with only one suit of clothes. We could have ended our business here instead of the bar."

"It looks like you've done all right for yourself, Pearly King," Urias made a quick sweep of the shop and finding it free of crimps—or perhaps even more of an annoyance, dandies—approached the desk. "I'm afraid that I *am* at a bit of a sartorial disadvantage today. I seem to have spent the night in an oubliette. You wouldn't happen to know anything about that would you?"

"Now, Aaron," Hendry put down the hat and spread his hands wide in supplication, "what would it profit me to come to you for help only to see you set sail on a schooner to Shanghai? I have to apologize for the coarseness of my fair city. She sometimes gets carried away."

"Apology accepted," Urias relaxed a bit. "I have been thinking about your offer, and I think I would like to know the truth of the matter as much as you do. Perhaps more."

"Excellent," Hendry grinned and his scar gleamed. "Before we go any further, might I ask you about the nature of your relationship with the Good Reverend Fox?"

"If I might ask you about the nature of the scar on your face."

Hendry broke into deep, husky laughter. "Very well, that only seems fair. I received this beauty mark sometime after we first met while in service of the Crown. The Boer War. Nasty business, that. I was with Colley at Laing's Nek. Four hundred and eighty of us tried to break through the Boer positions, and little more than three hundred men returned."

Urias snorted, drawing Hendry's war story to a premature close. "I'm sorry, I am being horribly uncouth. You want to know about the history Mordikai Fox and I share? I'll tell you. He saved my life. We were both with the Army of the Potomac during the War Between the States. On the fourth day of what has come to be called the Seven Days Battles, we were with Bull Head Sumner's II Corps in full retreat, getting the hell away from Richmond, back toward the James. We were met with three Confederate brigades at a raw hell called Savage's Station.

"I was shot through the leg and the side and evacuated to the field hospital. Our boys fought to a bloody draw that day; then that bastard Lee brought the Devil himself in by train; a naval 32-pounder. That infernal device lobbed shells as far as the hospital where I laid in the mud and the shit, not knowing if I was going to live or die.

"At the end of the day, the Union army left us behind. Twenty-five hundred injured, left to be captured or killed. Despite being wounded himself—gravely so—Fox found me, took me away from there, and patched me up the best he knew how. When we were both strong enough to travel, we left for the West."

"You two are rank deserters, then? I thought I was dealing with a man of honor."

"You hold your tongue, sir," Urias warned, "lest you find it has deserted your mouth. I didn't leave the war, hat man—the war left me. It left me bleeding in the filth with the enemy bringing the very heavens down around my head. Mordikai Fox lifted me up and I have never forgotten it. Do you want to hear about loyalty? I rarely left his side until I found it burned to a crisp. Now you tell me that this man may still be alive? I pledge to you that I will find out the truth or die trying."

Hendry weighed Urias' pledge against indiscretions well past and, if he was honest with himself, perfectly understandable.

"Well, Aaron Urias, you've got the job. Now let us see about those clothes."

Chapter Thirteen
THE PACIFIC OCEAN | 1889

13:1 Giving up the idea of ever closing her eyes again, and having few earthly possessions to be concerned about, Philomena wandered the ship as other passengers readied themselves for arrival in Hawai'i.

A persistent thrumming behind a closed door labeled *Crew Only* finally piqued the interest of the precocious girl. She had always been fascinated by how things worked and an unlocked door possibly leading to the guts of a working steamship was no barrier to her boundless curiosity.

Another peculiar rhythmic sound caught her attention as she mounted the iron staircase leading down into the belly of the ship, an area sparsely lit by a single Edison bulb. Rather than dispelling shadows, the feeble lamp fostered a whole new spate of them.

A quick flash of white linens revealing a surprised cabin stewardess was the first thing Philomena saw as she stepped from the landing into a dim passageway; the second was the bemused face of the very sailor who had helped her find her father in the salon.

The man adjusted his personage—as well as his uniform—as the stewardess gathered her skirts and fled back up the staircase. As the woman climbed, Philomena noticed that she had forgotten to wear bloomers of any kind.

"What are you doing down here, Annie Oakley?" The sailor tried his best to sound stern, but only managed to sound guilty. "This isn't a place for passengers, especially nosy monkeys like yourself."

"I—" Philomena started but quickly realized that she had no good excuse for going where she knew she did not belong.

"Let me take you someplace a little more appropriate," the seaman chided her while making it sound like a golden opportunity. "How would you like to see the bridge?"

Philomena forgot all about the bowels of the steamship and nodded so enthusiastically she almost lost her balance as the ship vibrated beneath her.

"I know the captain is looking forward to talking to you again," the man said, ushering her back up the stairwell.

The *Pride of Jefferson* was the flagship of the Morning Star fleet and, at the length of a new regulation football field, provided a decent hike. As the pair climbed through several decks to the bridge, Philomena's vertigo did not abate.

"Are you all right, scamp?" The sailor noticed the girl's pallid complexion.

Philomena stopped for a moment, held onto the railing, and focused on the black smokestack that towered above them until her lightheadedness faded.

"I don't know what has come over me," she apologized. "I am not usually like this."

The man stood and took stock of his young charge. Although the captain had asked to have her brought in to speak with him, he had all but forgotten about it until Philomena ignominiously found *him* instead. Now he wondered if the girl was up to meeting anyone at the moment. He also wondered if she would mention anything about his dalliance with the stewardess.

This girl could get you put off this ship, a familiar devil on the sailor's shoulder whispered in his ear. As if on cue, another—slightly disheveled—angel leaned into his other ear. *It's not that girl that'll get you put in dry dock, and you know it.*

Unwilling to dash Philomena's hopes, but having second thoughts about the mission, the sailor offered up an easy out. "If you aren't up to this right now, we still have a little time before we reach the islands."

Philomena merely motioned for him to lead on.

13:2 As the sailor opened the hatch to the steamship's enclosed bridge and ushered Philomena inside, Captain Munk turned from a table of charts and smiled.

"Well, Miss Fox, it is a singular pleasure to have such a beautiful young woman on my bridge," he rhapsodized. "I understand that you have already met Mr. Laurant."

Philomena turned before she realized the captain was referring to the man that had brought her to the bridge. She was so used to seeing him around at just the right moment that she had forgotten that they had never been properly introduced.

"Dr. Whitaker told me that we owe you a debt of gratitude for helping him tend to your unfortunate father," the captain continued. "Tell me, how is he feeling?"

Philomena took the offer of the captain's hand and watched helplessly as it swallowed her own in a calloused but friendly grip. "He is feeling much better, Captain Kasper, sir," she ventured, while wondering if she would get her hand back. "Thank you for asking."

"Not many young women your age would have the fortitude to take on such a big responsibility," the captain further piled it on while obviously—or obliviously—intent on keeping Philomena's hand as either memento or hostage. "You must care for him very much."

Philomena wanted to shout, *I don't remember being given a choice*, but thought better of it. She told herself the captain was just being gracious as she wrested her hand from its prison.

The captain gave a small start as if he had forgotten he was holding on to the girl at all. "I am sorry, Miss Fox. I... Can I ask you something?" The captain's eyes shifted to Laurant who remained by the door seemingly ready to bolt at any moment as if there were someplace to escape to.

Philomena saw the men exchange a small nod and wondered just what had been previously discussed. Once again, her curiosity got the better of her.

"Yes, sir, you can ask me anything you like." *What's my name? Puddin' Tane. Ask me again and I'll tell you the same.*

"Miss Fox, Dr. Whitaker also told me that he was sent to your cabin after administering the sedative to your father. There was some sort of a disturbance."

"It was nothing," she caged. "I guess my nerves finally got the best of me. It has been a very stressful couple of weeks."

"I do not doubt it, my dear," the captain sympathized. "I just want you to know that if you saw something... unusual, that you could tell us."

Philomena looked from Captain Munk to Laurant, as they were obviously fishing for something in particular.

"Tell her, captain," Laurant prodded, having finally committed to remaining in the room. "I think she can handle it."

"There have been rumors of strange sightings on the very same deck where your cabin is located. Passengers who may be a little more perceptive than others have seen—"

"Are you talking about the ghost sailor?" Philomena asked, somewhat relived they weren't alluding to her father, her real father, her very dead father.

"You've seen him then?" Laurant stepped up.

"I tried to tell you that I saw him!" She exclaimed. "I saw him right before I met you that first time, Mr. Laurant. That's why I poked you in the belly. I wasn't sure if you were real."

Laurant burped up a single laugh in spite of the charged situation, or perhaps because of it. Either way, it was enough to draw a sharp look from the captain.

"I really don't think this is funny, Laurant, do you?"

"No, of course not, captain," the man straightened up. "Miss Fox, can you tell us what the sailor you saw looked like? Did he say anything?"

Philomena shivered when she thought of what the poor wretch did look like and wondered how badly these two really wanted to know.

"He didn't say anything," she whispered. "He looked... Well, he looked drowned."

The two men looked at each other until Laurant took the opportunity to inspect the shine on his shoes.

"That is all you can tell me, dear?" Captain Munk prodded. "It would mean a lot to the crew if you could positively identify him."

Philomena paused to try and figure out how she was going to describe what she saw without upsetting the two men. *I shouldn't have to do this,* she thought; *I'm supposed to be the child here. Why does no one ever worry about upsetting me?*

"I can only tell you that no one would have been able to positively make that man out," she finally began. "All I can say for sure is that he was a sailor, about Mr. Laurant's height, and had been in too much water for much too long."

The captain looked pained and stared out the window of the bridge at something in the middle distance. "Miss Fox," he began, "in my hubris, I boasted to you about the technical superiority of the *Pride of Jefferson*. As your elder, if I can impart one thing that I've learned the hard way, it is that pride definitely does cometh before a fall."

Laurant and the girl both waited for the captain make his point.

"Miss Fox," he continued, "look out this window and tell me what you see."

"The ocean?"

"Indeed," the captain sighed. "There is plenty of that. I was referring to the mast you see before you. Wouldn't you think it strange that a steamship as fine as this one would deign to employ such archaic technology?"

Philomena looked to Laurant to translate the captain's tangent. The sailor merely shrugged unhelpfully. Unfazed by the girl's inability to answer his question, the captain continued to unburden himself through monologue.

"This ship is rigged with traditional brigantine sails fore and aft, mostly as a precaution against machine failure. My undoing was daring to imagine that if I were lucky enough to catch the trades and employ the sails in consort with the *Pride*'s twin steam engines at full power, I... she just might break the speed record for a Pacific crossing."

The bridge was eerily silent as the captain fought to keep his head above his own tempestuous ocean of guilt.

"The last time we made this route, you see," the captain launched into his explanation as if at an official inquiry, "I decided to try just that very thing."

"We were fully engaged and an unexpected squall appeared out of nowhere. I should have ordered the sails to be fully triced, or closed," he clarified, "but I didn't want to give up the race. I ordered a few seamen to replace our foresails with smaller storm sails that would create less pressure on the masts. We lost a sailor—a young man on his first cruise to the islands—overboard off the top yard. He never surfaced again.

"I sent him up the mast," Captain Munk paused, contrite. "It is folly, I know. He was a grown man, and this is often a dangerous job. He was not the first sailor not to make it home from a cross-Pacific run, and I am certain that he won't be the last."

"If I may, captain," Laurant offered, turning toward Philomena. "What Captain Munk is getting at is that we would all feel a whole lot better if we knew that our unfortunate comrade was not... in turmoil."

Philomena searched the faces of the men for clues as to how she could ease their guilt long enough to get untangled from the uncomfortable situation. She knew for certain that she did not want to be placed in the position of asking a rotting apparition the time of day, let alone how it felt. Luckily, like her adoptive father, she was blessed with a natural ability to read people and think on her feet.

"Sirs," she spoke with as much authority as she could muster, "I can assure you, that your lost friend was not in pain, he was merely... lost. I would be surprised if he is seen again. Now, you will have to excuse me, I should check on my father."

The two men silently watched the young girl take her leave with a lot more bearing than she arrived with.

"What just happened?" Laurant turned to the captain as the bridge was filled with the lack of Philomena.

The captain simply stroked his beard. "Do you think she knows anything?" He finally wondered aloud.

"Captain, if I could read a woman's mind, even one so pequeña, I wouldn't be standing here next to you; I would be a rich man."

Chapter Fourteen

14:1   Urias dismounted and tied his horse's reins to a flame-scarred scrub oak. The acrid smell of burned grass still clung to the site of the aborted revival despite the welcome appearance of quenching rains.

 The uncanny disaster that had cut short Fox's last evening on Earth had blackened the ground as far as Urias could see to the east. The hills were dotted with charred, twisted trees resembling a scene out of the book of Revelations, their misshapen limbs reaching in vain toward the unfeeling heavens in hopeless supplication.

 Urias stood in sharp relief against the monochromatic terrain in a new suit of Breacan Na'n Clerach, the blue tartan the Scots originally designed for their Highland priests. He didn't know, or particularly care, if Hendry was trying to be funny by wrapping him in the colors of the clergy; the pattern of black, lavender, and light blue fit him just fine, the muted colors allowing for freer movement among the shadows when the situation called for it.

 He still struggled with the bombshell the haberdasher had dropped in the Baldwin Bar. *What if Fox was alive somehow?* A pang of guilt shot through the man's chest for possibly mistaking the body he found in the smoldering ruin of the Gypsy wagon for his old friend before leaving the scene to begin drowning his prodigious sorrows.

 The bodies were the same size, he thought. *The man's clothes had all but burned away in the inferno. How else could I have made certain?* A long repressed memory hit Urias with the force of a lead Confederate slug, forcing him to sit down with the horrible revelation of what he would have to do. *Of course.*

 As Urias had writhed in pain, shot to pieces in the nightmare of the Confederacy's siege of Savage's Station, Fox sought to soothe his friend with the story of when he himself had taken a Rebel bullet in the chest. "By all rights, I should be dead," Fox had said. "But look at me now."

 The field surgeons at the time had realized the slug had lodged itself too close to Fox's heart to be removed and sent him on his way to live or die as his luck would have it. A simple nudge in the wrong direction would have meant certain death for him and the formative experience ensured that Fox would live the rest of his days as if they were a gift from God.

How the hell was that story supposed to make me feel any better? Urias mused. At least it had distracted him long enough for his own lead to be removed from within his person.

If the body really is Mordikai, he grimaced as he came to terms with the horrible fact, *he would still be carrying that bullet next to his heart.*

"Goddamn it," Urias swore and spat into drifting ash.

14:2 As one of hundreds of thousands who came to California looking for gold, it hadn't taken Sheriff Christoph Gruffydd long to realize that digging in the Sierra foothills for treasure was not going to make him rich before it killed him or broke him badly enough to ensure he would not fully enjoy the fruits of his labor.

The portly Welch-German immigrant had received some crazy requests in the forty years since he dropped his pickaxe and shovel and put on a star made of the very silver that some other sucker had broken his back to pull out of the ground. What the man standing before him dressed like a Christmas present wanted, however, took the all-time prize.

"Tell me again why you think that the burnt-up body we hauled out of that God-forsaken mess is not Reverend Fox," he squinted up at the shock of white hair cresting the man's head, which—backlit from the window—glowed with a ghostly light.

"I have been retained, by parties that wish to be discrete, who have heard rumors to that very fact. I aim to determine the veracity of that claim before I leave Fiesta," Urias explained.

The silence between the two men lay tortured as the corpse in question as each wondered how far this inquiry was fated to go.

"Fox saved my life and I owe him this much."

Gruffydd sighed before reaching into his desk drawer for a well-loved, and much-needed, bottle of single-malt Scotch whisky and two glasses.

"This sort of business calls for a dram, wouldn't you say, friend?"

"I would at that," Urias admitted.

"Just how do you expect to learn anything you didn't learn before," Gruffydd asked, pouring a desperate amount for both himself and Urias.

Urias told him his plan.

"May Christ forgive you," the sheriff whispered before knocking back his glass in one gulp.

"No sir," Urias lamented as he followed Gruffydd's lead and immediately felt the amber liquid burning in his chest, "I don't believe that He will."

14:3 The presumed body of Reverend Fox had been freshly buried on a low-rising hill in the center of Fiesta's small graveyard. The surviving members of the Golden Light congregation would not hear of having their spiritual leader inhabit a pauper's grave and—as the inconsolable Urias had not yet surfaced from the historic drunk that would finally sputter out in an oubliette in San Francisco's Barbary Coast—they took it upon themselves to enshrine their fallen leader in as much as a place of honor as the shabby cemetery allowed for, a place that Urias now intended to desecrate under the cover of darkness.

Gruffydd declined the offer of cash money to help Urias dig, pointing out that he put on the badge so he wouldn't have to swing a shovel anymore, but was more than willing to accept a generous bribe to look the other way. The sheriff even lent Urias the necessary tools for the job, having kept them close for four decades to remind himself in times of distress just why he shouldered the star's burden.

Under a waxing crescent moon turned bile green, as if sickened by the tableau below, Urias stripped down to his boots and flannel long johns he wore underneath the extravagant plaid. The flickering light from a pair of kerosene lanterns painted him as a Halloween devil as he resigned himself to the unsavory task at hand, his many scars glowing in the eerie light.

"Well, look what we have here," a voice drawled out of the gloom just beyond the lamp's range as his shovel blade first bit the soft dirt. "You look like a hunk of Swiss cheese come to life! Who filled you so full a' holes?"

Startled, Urias dropped the heavy shovel and it bounced off Fox's freshly hewn headstone, hitting him in the shin.

He grimaced as he turned to face his unwelcome guest, trying in vain to materialize his pistols out of thin air while silently cursing himself for getting caught without them.

The feeble moon, while perfect for nefarious nocturnal dealings, offered Urias no help in being able to draw a bead on his unwelcome company.

"Looks like you must a' availed yo'self of some good old southern *hole*spitality," the voice appeared again, this time to the far side of the grave. "If you'll forgive the pun." The voice broke into a gargled consumptive laugh that made the hair on the back of Urias' neck stand up.

"Enough!" Urias exclaimed. "If you have something to say, stranger, step into the light, or go boil your damn shirt."

"Absquatulate? Me? I don't think so, blue belly. I'm afraid I've got unattended business in this here shambles. Same as you."

Urias picked back up the shovel, measuring its heft and marking its aptitude as a weapon in the pinch he found himself in. The stranger's use of the pejorative term for Union soldiers by those in the Confederate south was not lost on him and he choked up on the spade's hickory handle.

"Now, now, Yank," the voice now came from behind Urias as he stood as if ready to knock a fast pitch out of the park. "There is no need to be unfriendly at this juncture. I assure you, the damage has already been done." Having said its piece, the gray apparition of a solider manifested before Urias holding its own disembodied head before it.

Upon seeing Urias' face, the head began to laugh so uproariously that the figure's spectral arms almost dropped it.

Urias had a moment to wonder what would happen if it had. *Would it pass through the earth straight into a grave where it belonged... and what of the body? With no mechanism to steer itself by, would it simply wander around aimlessly for all eternity?*

Urias closed his eyes and began to shake his own head to clear it of the madness that had obviously begun to creep in due to the extraordinary circumstances in which he found himself; and indeed, the figure had disappeared once he reopened his eyes.

"Keep it together, Aaron," he told himself. "You have been through worse and lived to toast or damn them all." He silently wished that he had talked the sheriff out of the rest of his whisky, even if it wasn't rye.

Urias became hyperaware of the sound every shovel of soil made as he wrested it from the cold ground. *Crunch. Sluice. Crunch. Sluice.* The silence of the graveyard seemed to only amplify the noise of the spade grinding into the packed dirt and gravel of Fox's final resting place. *Crunch. Sluice.*

After a while the rhythm and physicality of the act of digging allowed him to begin to think of the visitation by the Confederate apparition as something driven purely by nerves; after all, it wasn't everyday you dug up what you had been led to believe was your best friend's grave. *Crunch.* Urias realized he had been holding his breath for a very long time, and finally let it out in a weary sigh, taking a moment to lean his weight on the shovel.

"Hey, Yank," the ghostly voice returned. "Need a hand?" As Urias strained to sight the phantom soldier, an unarmed skeletal hand flew out of the dark and struck him on the side of the face. Shocked, he bent down into the open grave to pick up the bones, and found them to be no less real than his own. Once again, spectral laughter overfilled the silence.

"Damn your hide, Reb," Urias exploded. "Where did you pick that up? Why do you vex me, fuckhead?"

Once again, the spirit manifested out of the dark, its skull now precariously balanced atop its ragged neck so that it wobbled dangerously from side to side as it spoke. "Now, that's just hurtful, Lincoln lover. You can plainly see that I am currently bereft of both hide and head. You, sir, are less than a gentleman to throw those particular deficits back in my... well, face."

"Who are you?" Urias grunted as he swung the shovel at—and ultimately right through—the ghost's unsteady crown. "What, pray tell, do you want from me?"

"Strike one! Your stance is all cocked up, Yank. You should really plant that front leg. Come up on your back toes and let your trunk rotate... Hopeless. As to who I am, that hardly matters as I am not really myself these days, merely a sad echo of one Jeremiah Erasmus Washburn III, if you must."

"I see what you mean, spirit," Urias surrendered to the fact that he was losing his mind. "That certainly is more name than you have presence."

"You wound me again, sir," the ghost lamented. "If I did not know better, I'd say it might very well have been you who was responsible for my sorry state."

Urias took a closer look at the phantom Confederate and shook his head. "If I had to guess, Reb, I would say a cannonball was the last thing that you didn't see coming. I was no artilleryman; the Devil can take the lot of them."

"Now, see right there," the specter drawled, "who says two old enemies can't someday find common ground? I do notice, however, that you look to have had a better run of luck regarding items of a projectile nature."

"It was no luck," Urias admitted. "It was the man who may or may not be laying in this grave."

"About that," Washburn's head tottered around on the ruin of his neck, "I would get to digging, Yankee. Someone's coming."

PLATE THREE ✳ Aaron Urias

Chapter Fifteen
MILAKALE, HAWAI'I, KINGDOM OF HAWAI'I | 1889

15:1   The *Pride of Jefferson* steamed into Hilo Harbor as a light morning rain watered the volcanic island of Hawai'i. The crowded port was abuzz with activity; north of the boomtown, all along the Hāmākua Coast, sugar plantations were drawing workers from all over the Pacific.

There was such a desperate call for labor that rumors of wanted pirates from the South China Sea hiding out as workers in the cane fields brooked no scrutiny by anyone. The consensus was, if they were willing to do the dangerous and backbreaking job of cutting sugar cane, that was punishment enough for whatever crimes they might have committed.

Recent immigrants from Japan worked the busy docks along with Açoreans, Porto Ricans, and new arrivals from the Spanish Philippines. Company towns like Pepe'ekeo and Honoka'a teemed with the business of providing America and the world its sugar fix.

For a young girl raised in California's Central Valley, Philomena was used to a binary change of season between verdant green to sunbaked brown and back again with little variation. As the steamer maneuvered its way to the passenger dock, she was overwhelmed by the profusion of color surrounding the landing.

The island's heady perfumed air was another welcome surprise as her hometown of Fiesta only ever smelled like dirt and cow dung. Philomena immediately felt she was going to like her new home in the middle of the Pacific Ocean.

Her reverie was interrupted as Fox joined her at the rail.

"I thought I might never see dry land again," she said, not bothering to turn around.

"Boat rides are like operas," Fox remarked, "they sound like fun, but end up lasting twice as long as one wishes them to."

Down on the dock, a native Hawai'ian woman stood out from the bustling crowd dressed in a fashionable box-pleated skirt, and, despite the humidity, a high-necked woolen jersey. As if sensing the girl's gaze, the woman turned to wave.

"Who is that lady?" Philomena asked. "It looks like she is trying to get our attention."

"I'm sure I don't know," Fox admitted, taking a long look at the woman that was returned in kind. "Perhaps our patron has sent a welcoming party." Fox took off his stiff-crowned hat and waved it in the air.

"What's a patron?" Philomena asked.

"Why a patron is a who not a what, my child. Our particular rock and salvation is one Mrs. Anias Lanthier, wife of Alexander Lanthier, a wealthy sugar baron—although he much prefers 'magnate,' I believe. Mrs. Lanthier and I have been in correspondence concerning matters of the spirit. The Lanthiers have some progressive ideas when it comes to spreading the Golden Light. I have faith that we can do great works together."

"Why hasn't she come to meet us instead of sending someone if she is such a rock?"

"I don't know the answer to that either," Fox conceded. "Patrons work in mysterious ways sometimes. Being rich is a full-time job—so I've heard. At least she appears to have sent someone. I would be concerned if you and I were to end up standing on that pier alone."

"Alone? I can barely see the planks for all the people on them."

Fox took a beat to try and determine if his young charge was being insolent or simply specific. "Do try to make an impression, Philomena," he counseled. "We may be here for awhile."

"Does she have any children?" Philomena abruptly changed the topic, having had enough of the world of adults during the long ocean voyage to last her a lifetime.

"Anias? I'm afraid the Good Lord did not see fit to bless Mrs. Lanthier with children, Philomena. Perhaps it will do you both a bit of good to be around each other for awhile."

"What is that supposed to mean?" The girl snapped. "I don't need another mother! I don't even need you!" As the pressure of the long trip and its horrifying visions was finally released upon arrival, Philomena allowed herself to break down in tears.

15:2 On the landing, the pair was welcomed by the Lanthier's housekeeper, Noelani Mahoe, who proved to be a gracious hostess in her own right and placed opulent flower leis on the shoulders of both travelers as they disembarked. After endless days of nothing but open ocean, the humid air—and heady mix of perfumes from fragrant plumeria, carnation, orchid, and pikake flowers—made Philomena's head swim as she followed the sturdy yet graceful woman from the dock.

"Reverend Fox, we are so blessed to have you and little Philomena as our guests," Mahoe gushed.

Once they were free of the crowd, the woman squatted down in her pleats to get a better look at the girl. "And you, my poor dear, this must be some adjustment, yea? Have you ever been to the islands before?"

Philomena couldn't tell if she was making fun of her or not. "No, ma'am," she answered. "I have never been out of Fiesta before—" For the second time that afternoon, Philomena found it impossible to keep from crying.

"Oh, now, it just won't do to have such a beautiful girl weeping in such a public place," Mahoe theatrically waved her hand back at the busy dock. "Let's go home, shall we? You can cry it all out there. Mrs. Lanthier will be so happy to see you both, tear-stained or not."

"Where are the Lanthiers, Miss Mahoe?" Fox inquired. "I expected that Anias would have been loath to pass up a chance to leave the plantation."

"Oh, Mrs. Lanthier is excited to see you, reverend," Mahoe said, glancing sideways at the young girl, "and I'm sure very excited to meet you, little miss. It's just... I'm afraid there has been an accident, sir. Mr. Lanthier—if I might speak frankly in front of the girl—is in a bad way."

"Then you must take us there immediately!" Fox implored.

"What about your trunks?" Mahoe looked around the landing.

"We have no trunks, madam. Please, let us make haste; I feel now that God has delivered me to this island for a reason."

Once again, Philomena was taken aback at how quickly her guardian could slip into what she came to think of as Holy Mode.

"We shall go, then," Mahoe acquiesced. "Afterward, though, you have to let me get some good island food into you. You both look like a couple of stowaways. If Mrs. Lanthier finds time to focus on your bellies instead of her troubles, there will be hell to pay—forgive me, reverend."

"I would listen to her, Philomena," Fox conspiratorially put his arm around the girl as he led her from the dock. "Mrs. Lanthier is a woman who is used to getting what she wants. If she wants us to be fat and sassy, well, I guess we are going to be fat and sassy. I, for one, am fine with that. What say you?"

15:3 The road to the Lanthier's sprawling property was lavishly lined with all manner of citrus trees, where blossoms of lemon, pummelo, and grapefruit all vied to see which could better perfume the soft breeze drifting up the valley.

Fat honeybees buzzed and hummingbird moths flitted from bloom to bloom as Mahoe drove the Lanthiers' barouche carriage past it all with purpose. Pulled by four of their stable's strongest horses, the passengers bounced around, protected from the tropical sun by a collapsible canvas hood.

A carpet of Asian coral jasmine petals that had dropped with the morning's first light was crushed underneath hooves and wooden wheels, releasing even more fragrance as the carriage passed over.

As they rounded a final corner, Philomena was stunned at the opulent beauty of the Lanthier house. When retelling the story of her arrival on Hawai'i, she would always mention that one should think that an ornate Victorian mansion would look out of place on the edge of a tropical forest, but Mrs. Lanthier, her kupuna wahine, or adopted grandmother, somehow managed to infuse the structure with the spirit of the island so well that it looked as if it had grown as sympathetically from the volcanic soil as any fern or acacia koa tree.

A wide lānai surrounded the main house and was outfitted with a small army of wicker couches and rockers set back in the shade. A surprising percentage of the island's important business was done in the cooler evenings out on the Lanthier's porch, where men—and a few native women—could smoke the cigars that Mrs. Lanthier did not allow in her house.

To either side of the Big House in repose, smaller, more traditional plantation bungalows sat as if waiting to fulfill the mansion's needs, and indeed, that is where the house staff and their families lived. On the much smaller lānai of the low, one-story house to her right, Philomena noticed a shirtless boy around her own age sitting on the stair watching their arrival. She waved as the carriage came to a stop and the boy returned the gesture but did not leave his precious shade.

"Who is that, Miss Mahoe?" Philomena asked.

The woman followed the girl's gaze and considered the boy as if noticing him for the first time. "Oh, that is my keiki hanauna Maleko," she tossed. "I should have mentioned him. I can ask him to show you around the grounds if you like. There are plenty of places to explore."

Philomena looked up at Fox for permission. *Just think of the mischief they could get into*, he frowned. While he was less than excited to have his charge run off with an unfamiliar local child just yet, he also realized that he would just as soon not have the girl underfoot as he attended to Alexander.

"Why don't you go introduce yourself?" Fox suggested. "I'll have Miss Mahoe take me to Alexander."

The girl could barely contain her excitement. *Just think of the mischief we could get into!* She thought.

Mahoe dismounted from the driver's seat and handed the reins to a waiting stableman while helping Philomena down from the carriage.

"I'm afraid we must ride mounted from here, reverend. The trail to the beach is too narrow and rugged for the carriage. Do you ride?"

"Miss Mahoe, I was born on horseback. Lead on, for I fear that time may be against us," Fox mounted one of the horses hurriedly brought up for the pair and they charged into the jungle.

"Aloha," Maleko said, leaving his precious shade and approaching the girl who had been unceremoniously left standing alone in the courtyard as the attendants all had scattered back to work.

"Excuse me?"

"Aloha," the boy restated. "It means 'the breath of life.' It's our way of living in harmony and creating positive—"

"Excuse me?"

"It also means, 'hello,'" Maleko sought to clarify, "*and* 'goodbye'... but mostly—"

"You are strange," Philomena's gaze drifted to the opening in the verdant growth where the two riders had disappeared. "Where did they go?"

"I'm not strange, I'm Maleko. They went down to the beach. Would you like to see it? I have a shortcut. We may have to run if we want to catch the action."

"Now you are speaking my language," Philomena brightened. "I'll race you."

15:4   As the Sun began to sink behind Mauna Kea, the ancient volcanic mountain that dominated the view to the west, a small crowd of concerned onlookers covered Milakale Beach. Flaming torches surrounding the stone heiau threw a dancing, infernal light over the scene.

As Fox hurried past worried faces, he imagined they were concerned about the condition of the master of the house, when, in reality, they were concerned about having let their sacred place become the stage for some absurd play.

Alexander Lanthier was still laid out on the lava platform where Jun had placed him as Maleko's uncles had run for help. He was now covered in the woolen Hudson Bay blanket that Anias had carried to the island from foggy San Francisco but found few occasions to use until she found herself running down from the Big House with it.

Jun knelt at the man's side, checking the stricken man's meridians for proof that his qi, or energy force, had not yet abandoned him.

As he tied his horse's reins to a coconut tree and began to run down the beach, Fox was barely aware that Noelani Mahoe had stopped approaching the heiau and, along with most of the house staff, was maintaining a careful distance from the site of the injured man and attendants.

"Mordikai!" Anias leapt up to greet her guest. "This is a blessed miracle! I knew you would come, but I never dreamed we would be so desperate upon your arrival."

Fox embraced the woman and wiped away a telltale tear from her face that belied her usual grace under pressure.

"Tell me exactly what has happened," Fox directed as he in turn knelt down at the stricken man's side.

"Mr. Lanthier fell from his horse," Jun explained. "He is breathing, but he has not awakened. At first I feared he might have broken his neck, and I was loathe to move him, but I could not have left him to drown in the surf. Now, I do not think it is broken, watch." Jun removed a small paring knife from the pocket in his changshan, the traditional long shirt of the Qing dynasty.

Jun had already removed Lanthier's riding boots and wet socks and now gently dragged the dull side of the blade across the arch of man's naked foot. To everyone's relief, the unconscious man's toes flexed automatically. "It is as if his spirit was knocked out of his body and yet the animal continues to function."

No one noticed a pair of winded children appear out of the jungle as Fox knelt down beside his stricken benefactor. The reverend placed one hand on the prostrate man's head and one on his heart.

Hidden behind the heiau, Philomena swooned and almost slipped on a damp patch of pāhoehoe, or smooth lava, which would have alerted all of the adults to their presence.

"What is wrong with you, girl?" Maleko whispered. "You shouldn't have tried to keep up with me."

"It's not that," she protested. "I feel strange."

"You see," Maleko shot back, "*you* are the strange one, not me."

On the platform, Fox played his part for those still standing down the beach. "In the Golden Light of Jehovah's Word," he petitioned. "I command you, wandering spirit, to return to this vessel, so that His name may be illuminated!"

As Philomena liked to say when she retold the story countless times over the long course of her life, "I would be goddamned if it didn't just come back."

Chapter Sixteen

FIESTA, CALIFORNIA, UNITED STATES OF AMERICA | 1889

16:1   Sheriff Gruffydd had been trying to talk himself out of checking on
Urias in an unbroken stream of self-directed conversation since
leaving the comfort of his office, so he was not surprised to hear the
man in question speaking to his own self in the middle of the darkened
graveyard.

The sheriff was wearing both his pistols and carrying a burlap sack
that contained a number of items, not the least of which was the
remnants of the fifth of malt the two men had earlier turned to for
courage, as well as a bottle of Old Overholt rye whose seal had not yet
been cracked.

The resultant racket the quickly assembled collection of supplies
made as Gruffydd huffed and chuffed his way through the maze of
headstones was enough to dissuade any wayward spirits from hanging
around, be they haints or saints. At least that was his hope.

By the time the stout lawman had blustered his way to the
gravesite, Urias was all but finished digging out the hole.

"Ho, there, Urias," the sheriff coughed as to not startle the man
half to death, "I thought better of leaving you to wrestle that box out
alone. It wouldn't do to find you ass over tit down in that hole come
morning."

Urias stood up in the grave and took the measure of his latest
guest. *Graveyards are a lot busier at night than I ever imagined,* he thought
before throwing the shovel down. "Give me a hand out of here, sheriff,
and please tell me there is whiskey in that sack."

While the moon slowly sank back down below the black horizon,
the two men managed to finish the rye as well as the job of disinterring
the pine coffin holding the body they had come to investigate.

"The moment of truth, sheriff," Urias said, looking over his
shoulder for the ghost of J. E. Washburn III. "I would understand,
from a legal aspect, if you didn't want to be present for this next act."

Gruffydd sighted up the neck of the empty bottle of Overholt
before tossing it into the empty grave. "No sir," he resolved. "'In for a

dime, in for a dollar,' as they say. Let's get to it. I will, however, let you do the honors." The sheriff reached into the burlap sack and removed the penultimate items. He handed Urias a crowbar and a cloth bandana. "You might want to put that on, for all the good it will do."

"No, thank you," Urias waved off the offer of the mask. "I assure you, sheriff, this is not my first rendezvous with mortal remains. The smell clobbers your soul with more vigor than it does your nose."

As he pried open the coffin, Urias saw the ghost in his peripheral vision standing behind Gruffydd, its gray flannel body leaning against a tree facing away from the scene, while its head, now on backwards, watched his every move.

The smell that hit Urias was a living, malicious thing, even though the resident of the pine box was as dead as anything the man ever had the misfortune to come across. Gruffydd unconsciously took a step away, as did Washburn, causing his unbalanced head to roll off the back of his ruined neck.

"Jesus, Mary, and Joseph!" Gruffydd exclaimed and promptly threw up the contents of his prodigious stomach, which, in keeping with the tenor of the evening, was mostly spirit.

"Steady on, sheriff," Urias growled though gritted teeth. "The worst bit is still to come."

16:2 The twisted body of the poor wretch in the box had been exposed to flame long enough for its clothes and upper dermis to have been burned away. No one had bothered to try and reclothe the corpse for burial, which was a small relief, as Urias did not relish the idea of undressing it. He knew that he would probably be reliving this scene every sleepless night as it was.

Urias reached around and pulled out his Bowie knife, placing the razor sharp blade against the corpse's blackened sternum. He placed the heel of his gun hand against the butt of the knife and gathered his strength in order to push the blade into the exposed breastbone.

"Hold on, there, Aaron," Gruffydd coughed, reaching into his sack for the final item. "You obviously don't know much about human anatomy. I hate to be the one to tell you, but there's no way you are getting in there with that knife." He handed Urias a small saw and nodded toward the exposed chest. "You're going to have to work for that gold. Or lead. Or whatever."

Urias took the saw, sheathed his Bowie, and threw himself into the procedure. Ordinarily, the bone would not have cleaved as easily, but flame and the time it had spent underground had leached much of the elasticity from the body's natural armor.

"Sheriff, this is where you get to earn your nightmares, if you haven't already," Urias warned once he had finished cutting through the corpse's chest. "Help me spread these ribs apart, I need to see the heart."

The two men each grabbed a side of the body's ribcage and pulled in opposite directions until the interior of the body's chest cavity was exposed.

"Here," Gruffydd grunted and reached for the shovel with one hand while keeping his side of the chest open with the other. "Let me jam this—"

"What have you bad boys found there?" Washburn's ghost leaned in over Gruffydd's shoulder, holding its head like a hat to keep it from falling in.

"Holy mother of God!" The sheriff exclaimed, letting go of both the shovel and his side of the rib cage, causing the cadaver's open chest to slam shut on Urias' hand.

"Damn it all, Reb," Urias berated the spook. "You did that on purpose."

"Come on, Yankee," Washburn grumbled. "My once prodigious capacity for hijinks has been much diminished by my current situation. Let a man find his fun where he might, for God's sake."

"What in the good hell is that?" Gruffydd moaned, backing away equally from the phantom, the corpse, and the grave, his eyes as big as plates.

"Pay that ghost no mind, sheriff," Urias explained. "Washburn there was misguided when he was whole, and, apparently, nothing has changed now that he's gone pellucid."

"And here I thought you and I were getting on, Yank. Very well, then, I've seen what I came for. I will take my leave," Washburn bowed, brandishing his head with a flourish. "Gentlemen."

"Ho' there, specter!" Urias called out. "You never said what it was you've been looking for."

Washburn peered over his own shoulder, a tricky maneuver involving both hands. When he was satisfied they were alone—not counting the sheriff—he leaned in conspiratorially, also a dicey proposition. "We seem to be missing a spirit," he whispered. "One of our own has left the plantation, so to speak."

"Damn your eyes, ghost," Urias lost his patience. "This is no time for riddles. Out with it!"

"Very well," Washburn sighed, a sound that closely echoed the wind through the dry graveyard trees. "That man is not the man you are looking for. He is, however, someone I have been sent to retrieve."

"How do you know that, phantom?" The sheriff finally spoke.

"Oh, fat man," the ghost sighed again. "We know quite a lot. See you soon, by the way."

Animated by Washburn's assertion, Urias tore back into the corpse's chest looking for a piece of Confederate lead.

"What if it melted?" The shaken sheriff asked.

"I hadn't thought of that," Urias stopped for a moment. "It would still be here, though—no matter what shape—and it isn't."

Urias released the body, allowing it to shift in its final resting place, the new angle and rigor mortis conspiring to slowly raise its right arm toward the night sky. The heat of the fire had cooked the meat of the corpse's index and pinky fingers, plumping them out like a pair of sausages, while the lack of interstitial fingers gave the hand the shape of a pair of horns.

"The devil's sign!" Gruffydd gasped and crossed himself, more of a reflex than anything considering the level of damnation the two men had already earned during the course of the night.

"Damn me for a fool for not noticing that before," Urias spat onto the pile of exhumed dirt. "I know exactly who this man is, and it is not Mordikai Fox!"

Chapter Seventeen
MILAKALE, HAWAI'I, KINGDOM OF HAWAI'I | 1889

17:1 A squall roared in from the Pacific and horsewhipped the island as if trying to make it get up and move out of the way. Philomena and the youngest Mahoe sat at the small teak table in the Lanthiers' pantry while Noelani helped Jun cook dinner for the full house.

The dim gas lamps in the kitchen were all but eclipsed by the lightning that periodically washed the entire valley with spectral light. Every time the subsequent peal of thunder shook the kitchen windows, the lamps swayed, flickered, and threatened to go out all together.

A loud banging coming from the stables across the courtyard began in arrhythmic counterpoint to the storm's bombast. Noelani dried her hands on her apron and went to the window to see if she could tell what was coming loose.

"Maleko, go out and check the horses," she turned and leveled her nephew with the steely gaze she had honed helping to raise three younger brothers and now kept in reserve just for him.

"Auntie! I'll blow away out there," Maleko protested.

"*Keiki*, you had better get out to that barn! I don't have time to be playing with you."

"It's OK, Maleko, I'll go with you," Philomena offered. "I'll grab your feet if the storm tries to take you."

Noelani thought to intervene, but given how the dinner hour was approaching even faster than the apparent end of the world, she decided that she didn't have time to babysit some haole preacher's child.

"Maleko, I don't want you two playing around out in that storm," she instructed. "Tie down whatever's loose and get back in here. I'll have a nice hot chocolate for you both."

As soon as the pair sprinted out of the screened porch at the back of the house, the tempest caught hold of them. The two children would not have been wetter if they had been blown into the ocean, but they ran laughing toward the stables regardless.

On the wind, a peculiar rhythmic undercurrent caught Philomena's attention. It was if someone was playing a drum somewhere out in the desperate night.

Since the Lanthier's horse stables looked out over the sloping valley, as soon as the pair turned the corner to check the doors, they were hit with the full fury of the storm. When they dove for cover under the building's overhang, Philomena caught some strange lights out of the corner of her eye, lights that were moving out in the rain. A persistent drumbeat grew louder and harder to ignore.

"Get down!" Maleko shouted as he threw himself on Philomena, driving her to the wet ground.

"Maleko, what are you doing?" She demanded, trying in vain to squirm out of his embrace. "Let me up!"

"Quiet!" Maleko hissed, visibly frightened. "They didn't see you."

"Who didn't see me?" Philomena redoubled her attempts to free herself and see for herself what her new friend was taking about. "Who's crazy enough to be out in this storm? Besides us, I mean."

The drumming became even louder and Philomena could now make out chanting over the sound of the rain and wind. With a final push, she wrestled herself out from under Maleko and was immediately frozen in place by what she saw: a double line of torches moving down the valley carried by an army of ghostly warriors whose bare feet appeared to float above the soggy ground.

The men were outfitted as if for battle with helmets crested with feathers and cloaks slung over their left arms. Their right hands bore the torches, with the biggest and brightest flames bookending the procession. Three large flames also floated in the middle of the marchers and marked the presence of a spirit of obvious importance who was being carried along on a sling.

"Philomena," Maleko whispered, "don't let them see you. It is really bad luck. You or someone you love will die."

Just then one of the warriors turned and caught Maleko in his gaze. "Na'u!" It shouted in an elemental voice that seemed to emanate from the walls of the valley itself, marking the boy as a descendant, and therefore immune from curse. Philomena was not so lucky. The apparition that was being carried in the sling held up his hand and brought the entire procession to a halt.

"Oh, no," Maleko moaned and buried his face down in the wet slurry of mud and sand. "This is bad."

The warrior slowly turned his head with his chin raised as if he detected a strange smell and was trying to ascertain its origin.

"Get down!" Maleko entreated. "You don't understand—"

The warrior pointed at the girl who was powerless to hide from his gaze. His quarry obtained, the phalanx remained still as he deduced the nature of his discovery. The rain itself held its breath and Philomena began to count her heartbeats that somehow continued pounding out their own persistent rhythm. *One. Two. Three. Four.*

A change came over the ghostly countenance as another unearthly "Na'u!" came from nowhere and everywhere at once. Maleko summoned enough courage to peek up from the muck to see if the spirit was again addressing him. It was not.

Philomena, for her part, stood in the rain not comprehending what had just transpired. Somehow satisfied, the night marchers carried on with their push to the sea, their drums and chanting soon drowned out by the redoubled roar of the storm.

"What just happened?" Philomena asked her prostrate companion.

"I have no idea," Maleko admitted. "You aren't Kanaka Maoli— Hawai'ian, are you?"

Philomena had to admit that she wasn't sure exactly what she was anymore, but she was pretty sure it wasn't Polynesian.

17:2 Back at the plantation house, the miraculous recovery of Alexander Lanthier was creating its own tempest. From the head of his imposing dining table, the sugar baron held raucous court.

The word that Lanthier had been struck down had already instigated an influx of concerned neighbors, politicians with attendant agendas, and the merely nosy. The news of his resurrection at the touch of a mysterious preacher from the mainland only multiplied the number of visitors arriving at the mansion despite the storm.

"Thank you, everyone, for coming out in this weather," Lanthier stood and raised his brandy glass. "I am overjoyed that providence has brought us all together to pay witness to a miracle." Lanthier aimed his amber libation toward Fox who was radiating an intoxicating influence of his own, simply by his presence.

"Reverend," Anias Lanthier spoke from the depths of a reverie that had gripped her since her husband accompanied everyone back to the house under his own steam. "I believe that everything happens for a reason. I know now why our paths crossed back in San Francisco. It must have been God's will that befell Alexander, and God's will that brought you to us so that you might prove his mercy for all to witness and recognize."

"I concur," Alexander interrupted. "The scriptures teach us that pride cometh before a fall, and I now see that I have been on a regular path to perdition. I was literally and figuratively riding Lucifer straight to hell, and Reverend Fox here has delivered me."

Fox basked in the accolades for a beat too long to be entirely modest, then stood, raised his own glass, and slowly put it down on the linen tablecloth. He then reached for one of the many low burning candles that helped light the dinner and placed it next to the brandy glass. Every pair of eyes at the table watched the sparkling pattern of candlelight refracted by the glass and its contents as it danced across the starched white expanse.

"There is a light that burns bright and pure as this candle, but by the time it is conveyed by an imperfect lens such as myself—although still illuminating—is often distorted, confused, by our human inability to fully grasp divine intention. I can no more claim credit for Alexander's recovery than I could for creating this flame, this glass, or this brandy.

"I can pledge to everyone at this table, however, that I will make it my vocation to strive to better understand His plan. If you all will join me on this endeavor, together we can make Milakale the glowing candle that helps to guide this world out of the darkness."

The ecstatic response to Fox's oration was cut short by the frantic and soaking wet return of Philomena and Mahoe from the stables.

"Father!" The drenched girl erupted into the dining room, water flying from a tangle of hair that gleamed blacker than ever. "I saw apparitions marching down the valley, or rather they saw me!"

A collective gasp rose from the assembled locals, all of them familiar with the night marchers from either direct experience or legend. Maleko's aunt nearly dropped the platter of kālua pig she had been placing on the table when the pair burst in.

"Keiki, is this true?" Noelani addressed the flummoxed boy who had been caught up in the girl's slipstream but was now visibly reconsidering the wisdom of following her into the mouth of this particular volcano. "If you are playing around, you are going to be wishing that the storm carried you far away."

"'Oia'i'o, it is true, auntie," Maleko counted on the mercy of the truth to keep him out of trouble. "I don't know how, but she was recognized by the kahuna."

A larger gasp came from the opposite side of the table where a shoestring member of the Hawai'ian royal family nearly choked on the large portion of tender pork he had just shoved into his mouth.

"That is impossible!" He spat. "Noelani Mahoe, you had better teach that keiki kāne better. Boy, you had better tell us the gospel about what you saw."

"What is all this, then?" Fox broke in, miffed at how the perfect moment he had so carefully constructed had been co-opted by the pair of half-drowned scamps. "Philomena, tell me exactly what happened out there."

The girl related the entire story from the moment she and Maleko left the pantry until they ran back to the house like they were being chased by the Devil himself.

When she finished, an eerie silence hung over the table, broken only by the royal cousin rising from his chair, dropping his napkin over his plate, and taking his leave.

Two of Maleko's uncles had been standing off to the side of the dinner party for the entire evening, ready, as ever, to attend to the needs of the Lanthiers and their guests.

"I told you," Kalani Mahoe whispered to his brother. "We are doomed."

"Stop talking," Kekoa, the youngest but largest of Maleko's uncles, growled.

"I told you."

"This will be the least of your problems if you don't stop."

"Doomed."

Chapter Eighteen

MILAKALE, HAWAI'I, KINGDOM OF HAWAI'I | 1889

18:1 After Philomena and Maleko's soggy revelation derailed Fox's moment of glory, and Anias finally convinced her exhausted husband to retreat to his bed, the Lanthiers' assembled guests began to disperse out into the night despite the inclement weather. Fox stood under the protection of the covered lānai and watched the lantern-lit procession of horses and wagons trail out into the rain.

"Fickle business, faith," a familiar voice ruminated from a spot in the shadows. "You never know when you're going to lose hold of its tail."

Fox turned to face the speaker but the darkness held his identity close. "I'm sorry, were you speaking to me or about me?"

A flash of light lit up the scene as the reek of sulfur spurred Fox's memory. "I know you, don't I?" Fox chanced as shadow once again swallowed the man, only the glowing cherry on the end of his cigarette betraying where he stood. "We met onboard the *Pride of Jefferson* did we not? Mr. Khadae, I believe."

"At your service, padre," Khadae's bone-dry baritone barked. "Cigarette? No, forgive me, I seem to recall that you have abandoned the habit."

Fox hesitated a moment and then took the man up on his offer. "What could be the harm on a night like this?"

"What is the harm indeed?" Khadae coughed as he produced his gold cigarette case from sodden air. "You'll forgive the theatrics, it is an unfortunate compulsion."

"I have to admit that I have been guilty of the occasional sleight-of-hand in order to better get my point across," Fox conceded before reaching into the darkness to take the offered cheroot.

"We aren't so different, you and I," Khadae rumbled as he took a step out of the shadows, the guttering light from a dying lantern painting his face with diabolic stabs of red and yellow.

Fox, unnerved by the uncanny sight of his companion, took a quick breath and a step backward before regaining his composure.

"Forgive me, padre," Khadae apologized, a hint of amusement tweaking the corner of his mouth. "I only wanted to offer you... a light." Once again, the man seemingly procured a match from another dimension, manifesting and igniting it all in one smooth movement.

Fox leaned in, accepted the flame, and drew the rich smoke into his lungs. His head immediately reeled from the pungent tobacco. "Wow," he coughed as Khadae disappeared the flame as effortlessly as he had called it into being.

"Egyptian," Khadae pointed to Fox's cigarette with his reptile-headed cane by way of explanation. "Only the best."

"I see," Fox managed to say as his blood vessels constricted in response to the long-denied pleasure. "Khadae... is that Egyptian as well?"

"You are a sharp one. I will give you that, reverend. It is a very old name. We've been involved in trade of one sort or another since the days of the pharaohs, but I'm afraid the new landlords have been making it hard for an honest businessman such as myself to make a living. The British have a way of wanting it all for themselves."

"When we spoke before on the ship," Fox queried, "I was led to believe that you were a man of the cloth."

"Cloth? Me? My goodness, no," Khadae laughed like a gallows. "I am truly sorry if I gave that impression. I seem to recall that I said that we were both in the racket. I am certainly not in the business of engendering faith, at least any further than the belief that my goods and services will solve all one's problems. I am merely a humble trader."

Fox extinguished the strong cigarette that had begun to make him feel dizzy and nauseous. "What goods and services can you possibly offer to take the place of faith, pray tell?"

"Well now," Khadae flicked his own cigarette into the rain-saturated yard where it died with a quick hiss. He turned and motioned toward the sky with his cane. "The rain appears to have finally stopped. How about we take a stroll? I have some business to attend to and the night air just might do you some good."

18:2 Khadae led Fox out to the perimeter of the sprawling Lanthier property where the plantation workers' camp defined the ragged edge of what passed for civilization in the wild country. The large encampment was segregated by ethnicity and Fox heard Portuguese, Spanish, Tagalog, and Japanese spoken as they made their way through to the Chinese quarter.

Khadae led Fox past scores of nondescript wooden shacks before stopping before one festooned with glowing paper lanterns in traditional motifs of carp, dragons, and inexplicably, a crocodile.

"Friends of yours?" Fox joked as he ducked under the paper reptile that writhed in the post-storm trade breeze as if it had caught up some intangible being in a death roll.

"Oh, most definitely," Khadae grinned, once again revealing his mouth full of sharpened teeth. "Madame Wei!" He called out once he crossed the threshold. "Wei Lei!"

"Mr. Jackal!" A Chinese dowager appeared—as unaccountably as the cigarette case and attendant flame had—and grasped both of Khadae's hands in an ostensible grip of friendship, although the woman's reticence to let the man's hands go free caused Fox to raise an eyebrow.

Khadae barked something in the woman's native tongue and she dropped his hands at once, giving a slight bow as she did so.

"I'm sorry," Fox interrupted, "did she just call you 'Mr. Jackal?'"

Khadae began to laugh, an abrasive bray like an iron shovel against wet stone. "I'm afraid my reputation precedes me, padre. This fine woman and I have known each other for many, many years. Hang around long enough, my friend, and just see what she ends up calling you!"

Turning away from Fox, Khadae began gesticulating toward the woman while making some emphatic point in Mandarin Chinese. The pair's conversation quickly reached a pitch that apparently called for its removal to another room, leaving Fox to wonder about the possible effectiveness of that strategy considering the size of the house as seen from outside. He kept his mouth shut.

"You will forgive us for a moment, won't you, reverend? I'm afraid I must attend to a pressing matter. Madame Wei wishes me to invite you to make yourself at home. This should not take long at all."

Fox found himself alone in the anteroom of what must have been originally intended as yet another bunkhouse for Chinese cane cutters. A red silk drape featuring a brilliant golden dragon hung over the only other door out of the room and as the moments dripped past, Fox found he was unable to deny his prodigious curiosity.

Pulling aside the sensuous fabric, a darkened chamber—with more low pallets than Fox could count—slowly revealed itself as his eyes adjusted to the shadow. Upon the closest wooden bed, a worker of indeterminate age laid upon his side, a foot-and-a-half length of bamboo and a small oil lamp his only companions.

As Fox watched, a young boy approached the supine cutter and took the length of bamboo from the floor. As it turned, Fox recognized the shape of a small metal stem protruding two-thirds of the way down the tube, ending in a small hollow cap—like a large silver mushroom. The boy kneaded something between his fingers and, upon finally achieving the right pliability, placed it on the top of the mushroom where Fox knew there was a small hole.

The narcoleptic rallied enough to take possession of the pipe and held the metal chamber over the oil flame, all the while poking and prodding its contents with a long silver needle given to him by the boy.

With an effort of breath that Fox would have guessed beyond the man's capacity, the smoker drew all of the vapor the pipe had to offer into his lungs before laying back on his board. The boy took possession of the contraption before it was dashed to pieces on the floor and laid it beside the now sleeping form.

"Opium," Fox whispered. The boy turned and looked at him with no particular interest before leaving him where he stood. As if conjured by incantation, Khadae appeared at the reverend's side.

"There you are," Khadae whispered as he lifted the silk curtain for Fox to leave, the influx of light revealing every one of the pallets holding a wretch similar to the man he had been watching. Before his eyes, the room seemed to stretch on to infinity, the aggregate misery of the human condition causing Fox to moan. He was transported back to the blood-soaked fields of the War Between the States. Every supine dreamer swam in his vision, transforming into a wounded soldier—each opium pipe, a Springfield rifle.

"Come on, padre," Khadae intoned without comment on the scene before them. "Let's you and I get a drink. I have something that belongs to you."

18:3 On their way back to the Big House, the two men skirted the edge of the cane cutter camps, leading Fox to wonder why Khadae had led him through the center of the ad hoc villages in the first place. There was something he was supposed to glean from the short adventure with the Egyptian, but he found himself unable to focus on what it might be. Fox's mind kept drifting back to his vision of the Civil War dead and wounded, laid out in a tableau of torment as far as the eye could see.

"I was hoping you could do me a favor," Khadae grinned as soon as the Lanthier's stables came into view. "I understand that you are quite the accomplished horseman, and I have temporary need of someone who can handle the leather."

"I am that," Fox admitted, relived that the curious stranger was not after any indulgence of a spiritual nature as the weight of the evening was beginning to drag his faculties down to purely physical realms. "It might be good to feel the wind in my hair tonight. What did you have in mind?"

Khadae stopped at the heavy door to the stall that housed Alexander Lanthier's personal steed, Lucifer. The horse, sensing someone there, began to whinny and paw at the straw-strewn floor of its enclosure.

"Kuna shlana wqwyana," Khadae cooed in Arabic. "Be easy, strong one."

"Isn't this the beast that almost killed Alexander?" Fox asked as Khadae opened the door and the horse shook its massive head as if in denial of such a transgression.

Khadae stepped into the pen and up to the nervous animal, reaching out and stroking its powerful neck. "Kun hadi," he soothed the nervous stallion. "Alexander Lanthier is not half the rider he thinks he is, while Lucifer here is easily double the horse he thinks it is. They are, shall we say, mathematically incompatible. If you are up for it, I have been asked by Mrs. Lanthier to temporarily remove the means by which Alexander might be compelled to 'get back up on the horse,' if you follow."

"I follow fine," Fox allowed, "but it all feels a bit disloyal to my benefactor."

Khadae turned from the animal as if to take Fox's full measure.

"Make no mistake, reverend, your sponsor on this island is Anias Lanthier, decidedly not Alexander. Nothing here in paradise happens without the full consent of the matron of Milakale. That goes from the Sun rising in the east, to the passing fish pissing in the ocean. Even you and I, we are not immune from her influence."

Fox thought about just where he stood in the plantation's hierarchy and weighed it against how good it would do his mood to be on horseback once again. He realized that he had not been in the saddle since his last evening in Fiesta, and rescuing young Philomena from that sad situation had not been in any way relaxing.

"I'm no Buffalo Bill Cody," Fox allowed, stepping up to just in front of Lucifer's muscular shoulder, allowing the horse to see him yet staying safely out of the powerful swing of his head. "Compared to Alexander, however, I'll venture that I'm a huckleberry over his persimmon while in the stirrups."

"I did promise you a drink," Khadae admitted. "Honoka'a has both a stable and a saloon that just might fulfill our needs."

"Let us ride, then."

18:4 Fox's mood did lighten once the breathtaking rhythm and power of Lucifer at full gallop underneath him served to focus his immediate priorities. He began to understand why Lanthier gave the animal such a freighted name as the animal ran like the Devil himself.

By the time the pair had reached the small town of Honoka'a, Fox's face had been frozen into a mask of almost idiotic joy by the cold wind and sheer exhilaration of the ride. He was sorry when it was time to dismount and hand the creature's reins over to Khadae who would lead the horse away to its temporary home. Khadae tied his own mount in front of the singular saloon on the muddy track that served as Honoka'a's main thoroughfare. The Egyptian reached into his tunic and pulled out a silver pocket watch.

"It is 10 o' clock now," Khadae said. "Go in and I'll meet you in a half-hour."

"That is a very familiar looking time piece," Fox noticed the striking similarity to his own. "May I ask what you have inscribed in the cover there?"

"I think you already know," Khadae answered cryptically. "It reads, 'A caelo usque—'"

"'—ad centrum,'" Fox finished. "'From the heavens to the center of the Earth!' How is this possible?"

"Come now," Khadae gently chided, "you of all men, Reverend Fox, know that many things, although not probable, are very much possible. Do not get me started."

"It is much too late for riddles," Fox protested. "I must insist that you tell me where you got that watch this instance. I am no longer in the mood for games."

Khadae broke into a hollow, scraping laugh that almost caused Fox to forget his ultimatum. "My dear reverend, the games, as you so indelicately refer to them, have been going on for years. You might better ask yourself where your own keepsake originated."

"I have been in possession of this watch since I was a boy," Fox blurted. "It is the only piece I have to remember my late father by. It was entrusted to me, when I was old enough, in the orphanage where I spent my youth."

Khadae's laugh turned to a choking cough that drew the attention of the saloonkeeper who had come out to sweep broken glass out into the wooden gutter. "Is your friend all right? We can't have any consumptives in here."

Khadae reached out to steady himself against the porch railing. "I am fine, sir; forgive me. My friend here told me a very funny joke and it caught me off-guard. Let me catch my breath.

"Your late father, is that what they told you?" Khadae managed to get out. "I don't know whether to be honored or offended."

"What are you talking about?" Fox demanded. "Speak plainly, man!"

"I gave you that watch," Khadae explained. "It was I all those years ago. And to think, I didn't even receive proper credit."

"That is impossible," Fox spat. "I've had that watch for over forty years. I have carried it into the very mouth of Hell and back out again. Besides, we are about the same age, you and I, are we not?"

"I am older than I seem," Khadae explained. "You know what they say, 'Teak does not creak.' I have been watching you for a very long time. You might say that it's my job to keep an eye on individuals with certain... proclivities."

"Balderdash."

"Perhaps," Khadae admitted. "However, it does pay the bills. You have to admit that you have enjoyed somewhat of a charmed existence, the war not withstanding. If you'll excuse me, I really must get Lucifer put away. It's not a good idea to keep the Devil waiting. I would understand if you may have lost your desire to drink with me for the moment, but please remember that I did mention that I have something for you."

Fox removed his own watch, flipped open the silver cover, and stared at the Latin inscription as he had done ever since his difficult youth. "You spoil me," Fox deadpanned. "Apparently."

"Ha!" Khadae barked and turned to his saddlebag to retrieve a small bundle wound in burlap. "There's the spirit."

Fox took the package and let the rough material fall to the ground as he unwrapped it. Speechless for once in his life, he held his antique opium pipe in a state of shock.

"I think that 'thank you' are the words you are searching for," Khadae offered.

"Where did you get this?" Fox stammered, remembering having left the ornate piece behind in his burning Gypsy wagon.

"Like I said, I've had my eyes on you for sometime," Khadae grinned, showing the sharpened teeth that Fox had once again forgotten about. The sight now turned his blood to ice. "I do love a good fireworks show, and you, my friend, have quite a way with a finale!

"Listen, padre, it has been an evening, hasn't it? If you wish to return to Milakale, please feel free to take my steed. I have a room here in town and can come retrieve her in the morning."

Fox could only stand in front of the saloon holding Khadae's gift in a fugue. Khadae took his silence as complicity, and began leading Lucifer away.

"Now," he turned back and warned with a wry smirk, "do be careful not to get lost."

Chapter Nineteen
MILAKALE, HAWAI'I, KINGDOM OF HAWAI'I | 1889

19:1 Philomena gazed around the well-apportioned room she was just told was hers and hers alone. Exhausted, yet too keyed up to sleep, she doused the delicate hurricane lamp and let the moon cast swaying shadows of the windswept palms outside her window upon the pale papered walls.

"You did good, sweet girl," a familiar voice whispered from the dark corner of the room.

"Father?" Philomena sat straight up in her new feather bed and drew the cool, starched sheets around her.

"Apparently, that's a complicated question," the voice answered. "But, yes, I will always be your father."

Philomena lunged for the lamp.

"No, my dear," the voice entreated. "Leave it off. It's easier to be here in the dark."

"What happened father?" Philomena began to sob. "What are you doing here? What am I doing here?"

"My love."

"How could you let this happen? You were supposed to protect me! You used to tell me all the time that you would never let anything bad happen to me. What happened to your promise?"

"My darling Philomena," the voice moaned. "I failed you. I am so sorry. I wasn't strong enough. You, however, are stronger than you give yourself credit for. You are the strongest of any of us. Your mother—"

"Don't you speak of my mother! Did you kill her? Is that what happened? Then, like a coward, you killed yourself?"

"What? No! I didn't... Your mother isn't—"

"Liar!" Philomena spat, dropping her meager armor of gathered bed sheets. The moonlight charmed her exposed skin to glow with an eerie luminescence. "I saw her with my own eyes. She was dead! And you killed her! I hate you!"

The shadow in the corner wavered as if absorbing the blow. The room became as cool and quiet as a cave.

"There is a lot about yourself that you do not know, Philomena. You know that we always called you our miracle, and nothing will ever change that. As I've watched you grow into the amazing young woman you've become, it has only underscored that fact."

"What are you getting at?"

"Before you arrived, your mother and I tried for years to have a child. It wasn't until we attended the first of Reverend Fox's revivals that we were finally blessed. I knew the Lord moves in mysterious ways, I just never thought... I should have known. The night that you were born, there was a sign, a star. Reverend Fox followed that star and proclaimed it a miracle. I wanted to believe. I do believe."

"What are you saying?" Philomena demanded. "Do you mean to tell me that old hornswoggler is my father?"

"I've made so many mistakes," the voice wailed. "But loving you, and raising you... I don't know if it makes up for them, but I could live—or die—knowing that I've done a legitimate good. I've left the world better than I found it. That has to count for something, right?"

"Father?" Philomena noticed the voice beginning to falter and fade.

"The reverend tries to be a good man," the voice struggled to make itself heard as if it were underwater. "You have to help him overcome his demons. Help him to be righteous."

"Why should I help him do anything?" Philomena cried. "When is it my turn? Who is supposed to help me?"

"Philomena," the voice, now a whisper, declared, "you *are* the miracle."

19:2   It was hours before the girl was able to close her eyes. Once down, however, she slept through the rising of the tropical Sun and the crowing of the plantation's roosters welcoming it. A knock at her door finally brought her back to her new reality.

"Hey, sleepyhead," Maleko called from the other side of the door, "Auntie sent me to get you. It is breakfast time. You don't want to miss it! It is her specialty."

Philomena looked around the brightly lit bedroom that only hours before had been a shifting world of shade and shadow. *Did I dream all of that?* She asked herself before shaking the remnants of slumber from her head.

"Just a moment," she called, suddenly aware of a ravenous hunger. "I'll be right down!"

After a sumptuous feast—where Philomena was given a choice between the plantation worker's meal of fried eggs, small rounds of Portuguese linguiça, and two scoops of steamed rice; or the house breakfast of French toast with cinnamon, bananas, and macadamia nuts, and chose to eat all of it—she and Maleko were sent outside as to not be underfoot when the adults received the day's visitors.

"I've never seen a white girl eat like that," Maleko mused, somewhat astonished at his new friend's appetite.

"Just how many white girls have you met?" Philomena asked in mid-yawn, the combination of the morning Sun, the rising humidity, and the heavy meal combining to have a comfortable soporific effect on her.

"Mostly just older ladies," Maleko admitted. "They seem to only eat malasadas and tea."

"What's a malasada?"

"Oh, white girl, we'll put some meat on you yet," Maleko schemed. "You are like a ghost. I saw you turn even whiter at the beach. You almost faded away."

"I'm fine the way I am," Philomena protested. "And stop calling me that."

"What, 'white girl?'" Maleko pushed his luck. "But that's what you are. You should be happy. You get two breakfasts."

Philomena started to protest, but when she saw the laughing twinkle in her new friend's eyes she realized that he didn't mean anything by the gentle ribbing.

"Can I ask you something, Maleko?

"Of course," the mischievous boy grinned. "Do you need me to explain a pineapple to you?"

"Hold that thought," Philomena said, for the moment not willing to concede that she did. "It's about the ghosts."

"The marchers?" Maleko looked around to make sure that one of his uncles wasn't prowling around within earshot.

"Yes, you said that they weren't supposed to see me, right?"

"Oh, no," Maleko shook his head. "That was not supposed to happen. It is very bad luck."

Philomena laughed wondering how her luck could possibly get any worse. "What if I told you that those weren't the first ghosts that I've seen lately?"

"On the island?" Maleko's eyes widened with a mixture of excitement and dread.

Philomena weighed the idea of telling him about how she had engaged in a whole conversation with her dead father just last night.

"No," she finally said, not yet willing to open that can of worms. "It was on the way here, I saw a drowned sailor on the ship. I even had to talk to the captain about it. What do you think it means? I never saw anything this strange in Fiesta, now I'm seeing dead folks all over the place."

As Maleko mulled over his Philomena's revelation, an idea passed over his face like the Sun's rays dancing out from between clouds.

"I don't know what it means, but I might know someone that does. Let's go back up to the house. We'll have to pack a lunch for where we are going. Or, in your case, two."

Philomena playfully socked Maleko on the shoulder and the two took off running back to the Big House.

19:3　After laying in provisions and stealing a pineapple from Jun's kitchen, the pair hiked for two hours through tangles of sharp elephant grass and phalanxes of mosquitos that sought to suck every drop of blood they could swallow without physically popping.

"Where are we going, again?" Philomena asked for what seemed to her a reasonable number of times. Maleko was running a completely different tally.

"You can stop asking," he said with a sigh. "We are here."

Philomena gazed around at the lush vegetation that looked exactly like all the other lush vegetation they had bushwhacked through. Maleko held back a curtain of green and motioned for her to go ahead, and she stepped into a small clearing of bare volcanic soil. In the middle of the ragged circle a large conch shell missing the top of its spire sat on a round igneous rock that had probably been holding its ground since a volcano had spit it there.

"That is a pū," Maleko explained. "We have to announce our arrival."

"Arrival?" Philomena asked, looking around. "Arrival where? Announce to whom? All I see are mosquitoes, and I'm pretty sure they've got the message."

Without justifying his friend's incredulity, Maleko picked up the conch and held its truncated spiral top to his puckered lips. He gave a short, resonant blast that reminded Philomena of the foghorns she had recently experienced out in San Francisco Bay. The dense jungle quickly swallowed the sound and the pair stood in silence with only the noise of hungry insects for an answer.

"Maybe she is not home," Maleko mused and started to raise the conch for another try. Just then a sonorous tone responded from further in the bush, rising in intensity until it seemed like the very jungle itself was vibrating with the sound. "It sounds like we are welcome. Follow me."

As Maleko led the way even deeper into the verdant overgrowth, Philomena lost all sight of the blue sky and began to feel unmoored as if she was floating on a green ocean toward an unknown terminus. She was shocked out of her reverie when the pair came upon a Hawai'ian woman standing next to the mouth of an open cave.

The striking figure was dressed only in a long wraparound skirt of kapa cloth, covered in intricate geometric patterns. Her cascades of wavy gray hair were thick and long enough to cover her bare breasts, but the remainder of her exposed brown skin shone even in the dappled sunlight filtering through the upper canopy of leaves. To Philomena, she seemed almost to glow from within.

Maleko stepped forward and handed over the pineapple before touching his forehead to the woman's forehead, their flattened Polynesian noses resting against each other as they exchanged breath.

"Makana Kealoha, I would like to introduce Miss Philomena Fox," the boy spoke once the greeting was completed. "Philomena, Makana Kealoha is a kupua, or healer. I think she might be able to help you."

Kealoha stepped up to Philomena and grasped her by the shoulders, causing her to flinch; no one had really touched her since she left Fiesta. The intimate feeling of the kupua's forehead against her own soon soothed her, however; all of the stress of the last few weeks seeming to melt away as she and the woman shared their own breath. As they separated, Philomena was taken in by the woman's striking green eyes, the first she had noticed on a Polynesian since arriving on the island.

"E mālama kakou no ka ho'ola 'ana," Kealoha chanted. "We support each other for healing. You are welcome, Philomena Fox. How can I help you?"

Maleko started to explain, but Kealoha cut him off.

"Keiki, let the kaikamahine speak for herself, yea? Go ahead, dear, tell Makana what troubles you."

"She sees ghosts," Maleko blurted, unable to help himself, "and they see her too!"

"Maleko Mahoe," Kealoha gently chided, "I know that Noelani raised you better than that. Why don't you make yourself useful and cut up this pineapple?" The woman produced a sharp knife out of thin air and handed it to the lightly chastened boy.

"Is that true, Philomena?" Kealoha took a closer look at the girl's face, investigating it from every angle. "How long have you had this gift?"

Philomena was struck by the term. *Gift?* She wanted to shout. *This is nothing but a curse!*

"You are mistaken, Philomena," Kealoha had easily understood the reaction on the girl's face. "Let me guess, you are what, about thirteen?"

Philomena nodded but the woman's attempt to read her put her on the defensive. She had spent as much time as she could get away with at the circus whenever it came through Fiesta. *What's next?* She thought. *Is she going to guess my weight? Will I win a tin whistle if she guesses wrong?*

"I know this is hard," Kealoha sighed. "I was about your age when I began to realize that I was not like everyone else. Tell me, have you started to experience your ka wa haumia, your 'unclean' time? That is when my abilities began to manifest."

Philomena looked to Maleko for help, who merely shrugged with a wedge of bright yellow pineapple flesh in his mouth dripping sticky juice down his chin.

"Your cycle?" Kealoha probed. "No matter. Come with me, my dear, I want to show you something. Maleko, you stay here. And save me some of that pineapple!"

The woman turned and led the way into the cave, talking as she walked. "The Kānaka Maoli—we Hawai'ian people—believe that we are intimately tied to our ancestors. Nā 'aumākua, an endless chain of spirits reaching back into the past, is where we derive our power. We call on the ones who have gone before us to help us in this life. Do you know the names of your ancestors?"

Philomena had to stifle a laugh. "It's complicated," she said.

Kealoha stopped and inspected the girl's face again. "I guess it would be."

As the pair moved deeper into the cave, they began to lose the light streaming in from the mouth. On either side of the tunnel, Philomena began to notice shapes wrapped in material similar to Kealoha's skirt lined up on natural recessed niches in the rock walls.

"What is this place?" Philomena asked, her natural curiosity dispelling any fear she might ordinarily have felt.

"This is a lava tube," Kealoha explained. "When Tutu Pele moves on the land in her fiery form, she creates these tunnels. This is where we bring the ones who have passed on."

"Do you mean those bundles are... people?"

"Not just people," Kealoha stopped before the last bundle in the line, "*the* people. My people. They speak to me. Do they speak to you?"

It wasn't the strangest question Philomena had been asked recently so she answered honestly. "No, I'm afraid not."

"Interesting," Kealoha said, looking from ancestor to ancestor. "Maybe they are being hilahila. Being dead sometimes makes them shy."

"There is something else," Philomena weighed whether or not she wanted to totally open up to this strange woman. "When we first came here, Mr. Lanthier was in a bad way. The reverend thinks that he prayed him back to health, but Maleko and I snuck down to the beach and saw the whole thing."

"The reverend, is he your father?" Kealoha asked innocently enough.

"It's complicated," Philomena snapped without meaning to. "The thing is, when we approached the crowd around Mr. Lanthier, I became so dizzy that I had to sit down. All of a sudden I could see myself sitting there, as if from above, and I saw Mr. Lanthier at the edge of the crowd; but it couldn't have been him because he was laid out on the rocks surrounded by people. Does that make sense?"

"Perfect sense."

"I imagined that I took him by the hand and led him back to himself."

"Through the crowd?" Kealoha asked as if this sort of thing happened everyday.

"Excuse me?" Philomena was momentarily lost in the memory of the incident. "No, it was like they weren't there, and then I snapped out of it. So did he."

Kealoha stood quietly for a moment, as if lost in thought. "Yes, I believe you are right," she said, apparently apropos of nothing.

Philomena looked around to see to whom the woman was taking to if not her.

"Congratulations, complicated girl," Kealoha focused on Philomena. "I seems that you are a kupua as well. Welcome, sister. The veil between this world and the next is very thin with our kind. Often we can lead a spirit who has become lost back to where it belongs. Tell me, has this happened before the incident on the beach?"

Philomena thought for a second and remembered feeling strange as she and Laurant walked the length of the *Pride of Jefferson*.

"Once before," she said, "but nothing happened. There was a ghost on board our ship. Do you think that maybe I helped it find its way without knowing it?"

"It is very possible," Kealoha admitted. "In the end, we are only vessels through which the mana flows. Who can tell a river which way it should find the ocean? It sounds like perhaps you removed an obstacle without being aware of it. Of course, only a kupua of great power can heal only by their presence.

"No, I know she is not Kanaka Maoli," Kealoha once again began to address the cool air. "Stranger things have happened, yea?"

Philomena looked around the lava tube, relieved that the spirits of Kealoha's dead ancestors didn't appear to have anything to say to her, and changed the subject. "How far back does this tube go?"

Kealoha, who was standing quietly listening to the bundles, was surprised by the question.

"I don't know," she admitted. "This is as far as I ever needed to go." She took one last inquisitive look at Philomena in the shade and ushered her back toward the light.

"Let us get some pineapple before that boy eats it all."

PLATE FOUR ❖ Makana Kealoha & Maleko Mahoe

1876

Chapter Twenty

20:1 Niall Hendry had just settled back on his pallet at Madame Wei's hua-yan jian, or "cloud flower room." He was going through the ritual of placing a tarry pea-sized pellet of opium on the ceramic bowl of his long, ornately carved pipe when a chill gripped him from his anus to the back of his neck. It was not the sensation he had been looking forward to.

"Khadae," he spoke without bothering to look behind him. "You certainly do pick your moments, don't you."

"Wotcher, china?" The wraith whispered and wound around to face the supine man.

"I do wish you would dispense with trying to be cute with me," Hendry entreated. "Do you have clever banter ready for every poor sot with the misfortune of knowing you?"

"You wound me, coster," Khadae feigned hurt feelings. "Besides, you know that I only have eyes for you."

"That would make a good song," Hendry parried. "Why don't you scuttle on over to the Barbary and sing it to someone who gives a fig?"

"Oh, how I miss these little *tête-à-têtes*, when you're not around."

"French now, wot?" It was Hendry's turn to affect incredulity. "See, I knew you had more tunes in your repertoire."

"Je mangerai ton âme," Khadae growled.

"There is no reason to be rude," Hendry chastened. "I did what you asked of me."

"You speak French, now?" Khadae asked, genuinely surprised. "My little fruit vendor is coming up in the world."

"First thing, *mon ami diabolique*, I am a salesman by nature, and costermonger by God," Hendry clarified. "It behooves me to understand just what my customers may desire no matter what linguistic shortcomings they may suffer from. Second—and come to think of it, perhaps this should be first—the Vulgar Latin of a Gaul is hardly a step up from the Queen's English. Innit?"

"You English," Khadae bemoaned, "you think you have it all figured out. You give some people an empire and pretty soon they think they own the world."

"We—"

"Know your place, Englishman!" Khadae exploded. "You are nothing but an errand boy. You and your whole island, nothing but the half-simple issue of whatever decent people decided to invade your little mud pit over the centuries. A mongrel, a common fucking cur, that's what you are."

"What crawled up your ass and died today?" Hendry taunted. "Oh, that's right; it was your soul. Is there something I can do to make you fuck off right now?"

"Tell me you did what had to be done," Khadae snapped into focus. "Tell me I can go to my people and tell them not to worry about their precious status quo."

"I see who the real errand boy is in this scenario," Hendry doubled down. "Tell your little cabal that nothing needed to be done. It was a false alarm."

"What are you saying? There is no new Messiah? Was there no miracle?"

Hendry began to chuckle to himself. "No, no miracle," he laughed. "Only a wee girl, and if I were a betting man, I would put a tenner against the odds of divine parentage."

Khadae rose to his full height, standing tall over the supine Hendry. "A betting man is exactly what you are, coster. Don't you forget how you put yourself in this predicament."

"About that," Hendry rose to his feet to meet the man eye-to-eye. "We are done. This little favor is the last I am going to do for you. You need to hook some other sorry fish on your rotten line."

It was Khadae's turn to laugh. "What makes you think it's going to be that easy?"

"I don't give a good goddamn how easy or how hellish you intend to make it," Hendry spat. "All I know is that we are done. You sent me out to do a baby for Christ's sake. Divine or no, that's the line in the fucking sand."

139

Khadae flinched at the mention of the Son of Man but quickly recovered. "Have it your way, English. Only know that you will no longer be under my protection. Go forth and do whatever pops into that little muttonhead of yours, just watch out for the wheel of karma. It can be a bitch, and you, my friend, have been fucking it sideways for years now."

Hendry slumped, knowing the ghoul was right.

"Why don't you go fuck *yourself* sideways."

Khadae broke into a full-throated laugh that would haunt Hendry's sleep for years. "Fair play, Shakespeare. If only that I could."

20:2 Urias woke with a start not recognizing where he was. A quick look around revealed that he was in the bed of Águeda María Luisa Iñiguez, as was Águeda María Luisa. Ordinarily, this turn of events would have brought a satisfied smile to the rogue's face, but something woke him from his slumber and had left him with an uneasy feeling he was all too familiar with.

The pre-dawn chill bit at Urias as he carefully slid out of the warm nest the two bodies had made of a pile of embroidered quilts. The cold brought a focus just as startling as a slap in the face. Urias heard the woman stirring as he made to splash his face and cock—in that order—in her porcelain washbasin.

"What are you doing?" The sleepy proprietor yawned.

"I have to go," Urias stated plainly, though it pained him to do so. "Something is wrong."

"The only thing wrong here is that you are out of bed. Come back in here, it is cold."

Urias turned to see the young woman seductively lift up the quilts to remind him of what he would be missing. Her flawless brown skin and seductive curves acted as a lodestone and he felt his legs take a step toward the bed as if they had a mind of their own. It took a force of will to regain control over his mutinous limbs, but the uncanny feeling that Fox was in danger only intensified the more clearly conscious he became.

"I'm sorry," Urias avowed as he pulled on his dusty trousers and found his Stetson. "I don't think I've been sorrier in my life, but I have to go. Thank you for a wonderful evening."

Iñiguez pulled the quilts over her breasts as she sat up and took a good look at Urias. The look on her face was not anger, but rather the countenance of someone observing an exotic animal they had not seen before; a beast found in some deep distant forest and displayed in the sideshow of a circus midway; a beast out of its environment, out of context, and completely out of its depth.

"Suit yourself," Iñiguez pouted, letting the quilts drop enough to reveal one perfect chocolate brown areola, a sight that nearly reignited the insurrectionary tendencies of Urias' limbs.

Urias left before the rebellion took hold.

20:3 Giving his blessing to Philomena and her parents left Fox in a contemplative mood. After returning to the cantina to retrieve his kit, he abdicated any authority over where his boots should take him next and just walked.

Meanwhile, the comet streamed overhead undiminished in the brightness of the day, its significance even more of a cipher now that he had discovered it pointed to what Hendry had called "a wee girl." He knew better than to ask for a sign, for it was there for all to see, he just couldn't quite grasp at what it meant.

Fox soon found that his boots wanted to be shed of Fiesta and he couldn't muster any argument as to why they should stay. As it turned out, the more space they put between themselves and town, the better he did begin to feel. The open rolling foothills and scrub oak of the eastern Central Valley always calmed his restless spirit. It was close enough to where he came up in the western hills of Virginia that he could cast himself back to a simpler time—before the war, before his calling, before the incessant yearning for an answer, as well as the inevitable disappointment when none came.

The trio—two boots and one man—sooner or later found themselves on the banks of a yet unnamed creek and Fox settled in for some serious mediation. Finding a secluded bend, he removed his contumacious footwear and the gear from his worn leather satchel and administered the sacrament that had calmed his body and soul since he had been dragged half dead from a ravaged Henrico County battlefield.

The bright celestial visitor was reflected in concentric rings on the slow-moving surface of the creek, the light rolling toward Fox in luminous waves as if the comet itself were a pebble that had been cast into the water.

He became aware that he was sitting in the middle of an explosion of California poppies whose fan-shaped petals vibrated at a frequency that Fox could feel down in his spine. All the shades of blue in the attendant forget-me-nots darkened before his gaze, becoming slowly waving mirrors of a night sky not of the California interior.

[01110011 01100101 01100001 01110010 01100011 01101000 01101001 01101110 01100111 00100000... *Identifying receiver... Determining appropriate cultural and linguistic expression*]

"Excuse me?" Fox sat up, struggling to shake off his reverie. Looking around, he was surprised that the day had dimmed and the stars had come out in their profusion. "Is someone there?"

[*Applying apparent/appropriate Judeo-Christian matrices... Initiating 'burning bush' protocol*]

A fragrant sagebrush next to Fox burst into flame, fully waking him from his daydream. Fox sprang to his stocking feet and grabbed one of his empty boots on a pell-mell rush to the creek. Filling the leather boot to the straps with cold water he doused the burning sage before the entire hillside caught fire.

[*He put it out... What do you mean he 'put it out?'... The bush; I ignited it the way it says to in the manual and he poured water on it... Try the direct approach, I guess*]

Fox stood on the creek bank in his wet socks and looked around at the dark, empty countryside. He could swear that he heard voices but as far he could tell there was no one around for miles.

"BEHOLD! YOU THAT HAVE EARS TO HEAR, USE THEM THAT YOU MIGHT... erm, HEAR!"

"Hello? Urias, is that you?" Despite the difficulty of putting on a wet boot, Fox had the distinct feeling that he should be shod for whatever was at play.

"IT IS I, THE ONE WHO IS WHO HE IS, AND THE ONE WHO IS NOT WHOM HE IS NOT!"

"That certainly clears things up," Fox muttered while hopping on one foot, trying to force his heel past where it had bound against the wet leather.

"DO NOT SCORN ME, LEST YOU COME TO WOE! I AM THE ONE WHO COMES ON TIME, AND THE ONE WHO IS LATE! I AM THE ANSWER AND THE QUESTION!"

"OK, Mr. Question, if I may venture a question of mine own," Fox parried, finally standing firmly on both feet. "What can I do for you?"

[*He doesn't seem frightened, what should I do?... I don't know, ask him why not, I suppose*]

"DO YOU NOT TREMBLE BEFORE ME? DO YOU NOT RECOGNISE THE SOUND OF YOUR POSSIBLE ANNIHILATION?"

Fox thought for a moment, mostly about wanting a cigarette, and spat into the dry grass.

"I suppose I *would* recognize that sound," he finally admitted. "I have heard it a few times before. I'm afraid you sound nothing like it. No offense."

"None taken... I mean, WOE TO YOU THAT YOU MIGHT LIVE TO HEAR THE LAMENTATIONS OF YOUR CHILDREN."

"You've hit upon the very reason why I never had any. Now, if there is something I can do for you, come out with it, otherwise, I must be getting back to town," Fox said. "And please stop setting things on fire. It is very dry out here this time of year."

[*Just tell him... You think so? That's not what it says in the book... We can't do this all day*]

"YOU DO... WILL HAVE A CHILD... It's complicated. SHE WILL BECOME THE SAVIOR OF THE—"

"She?"

"WHAT?"

"You said, 'she,'" Fox pointed out.

"TIE THYSELF NOT IN KNOTS. THE DETAILS ARE UNIMPORTANT RIGHT NOW... YOU MADE ME LOSE MY TRAIN OF THOUGHT."

"But you said, 'she,'" Fox reiterated.

[*This fucking guy... Just hit him with the download and close the channel; it's almost quitting time... Are you buying?... Yea, sure, give him the goods and let's go*]

The forget-me-nots at Fox's feet began to oscillate faster and faster, the stars above him spinning in dizzying profusion with his head as the center of rotation. The comet that had burned brightly over Fiesta for weeks began to sizzle with an intensity that Fox could taste in the back of his mouth.

20:4 After checking the room, the cantina, and just to be sure, Gilliam's mercantile, Urias found no trace of Fox, yet a persistent feeling that his partner was in trouble kept him searching the dusty streets of Fiesta. He found himself missing the steed that he had stabled in Carson City when Fox started this wild goose chase.

Perhaps he went to the town livery to borrow a horse, he thought. *But where in blazes would he be riding?* Urias knew from experience that, as small as it was, Fiesta was a booming metropolis compared to the surrounding endless expanse of the Central Valley.

A painted sign on one of the last brick buildings on Main Street advertised *Fiesta Livery, Luís & Castañeda*, although the experienced horseman could have very well followed his nose. Urias was always comforted by the smell of horseflesh. Although the animals could be nervous and skittish, Urias usually found them to be far less so than their human counterparts.

As he entered the stables, he saw a short, dark-haired man brushing a young Arabian mare. The horse shone black except for a white band around its tail and a streak in its dark mane that reminded Urias of his own forelocks.

"Good morning," he called out to the hostler who looked up to see Urias framed by dazzling sunlight. "I was hoping I might ask you a question, and perhaps a favor."

"Boa dia," the man answered, putting down his brush and shading his eyes to better make out the apparent apparition. "Por favor, please come in. Forgive me, I thought for a moment que você era um anjo."

"No," Urais laughed. "No, I assure you, I am no angel.

"Alas, who can truly say they are these days?" The man rose to his full five feet, four inches, and stuck out a calloused hand. "Jose Luís, proprietário, at your service."

"Aaron Urias," he took the man's hand and thought for a moment that he was shaking a leather baseball mitt. "I am looking for a friend of mine who may have come this way looking for a mount."

"I'm sorry, senhor, but no one but yourself has been in all morning. I'm afraid that our fair town is sleeping in today." The man pantomimed someone knocking back a drink, a horsey smile breaking out behind a thicket of dark moustache.

"I see, perhaps a favor then," Urias pivoted. "I need to borrow a horse."

"To find your friend? That should be easy. Unless he stole um cavalo or sprouted wings, this is the only livery in town." Luís took a moment to read his customer and brightened as if on the receiving end of a revelation.

"I have just the horse for you; you look like you were made for each other." Luís patted the haunch of the Arabian mare he had been grooming. "See the white hairs at the top of her tail, she is rabicano, such as yourself."

Urais decided to let the remark slide, as the man did not seem to mean any disrespect by it, and he did have a point.

"I'm afraid we do not rent out our horses, however. This is still rough country. There is too much risk of them coming up lame or being shot out from under an unlucky rider, then where would we be?"

"She *is* a beauty," Urias admitted, beginning to fall under the animal's spell. "How did you come by her?"

"Ah," Luís spread his hands, lifting his cracked palms to the sky. "A very unlucky rider. The two of them rode out one morning, and only esta beleza returned. Forgive me, senhor, for I am sure that your circumstances are different; we searched the surrounding countryside for her owner, but—"

The thought of the horse's original rider lying undiscovered and unburied somewhere out in the vast California wilderness quickened Urias' resolve to find Fox. *This gentleman is a hell of a salesman,* he thought. *Appeal to one's mortal dread, and you can name your price.*

"What do you want for her?" Urias asked, trying hard not to show his impatience.

"A horse like this," Luís began, "could last you twenty-five to thirty years. The Arabians are the best trail horse you can buy. They have resistência, endurance."

"I am very familiar with the breed, Mr. Luís," Urias interrupted. "If you please, I do have pressing business."

"Of course," Luís acquiesced. "I get carried away. Let us say one hundred and fifty, shall we? I could easily get two hundred for a strong horse like this."

Urias thought for a moment, and realized the man was right. It was a fair price. "I will be right back," he said and turned back toward the cantina.

When he returned moments later, he was wearing both his spurs and his guns. Luís retreated to behind what passed for a desk in the stables out of an innate sense of self-preservation.

"You will not have to urge her on, senhor," he said, taking note of the new musical chime to Urias' stride. "I would swear that this horse reads minds."

Urias emptied the burlap sack of gold coins he had won in Virginia City on the counter. "There you are, Mr. Luís. It is all there: thirty five-dollar half-eagles."

Luís made the sign of the cross and pushed one of the gold coins back toward Urias. "Even though they are not silver, I fear that would be a very unlucky start to your long relationship, senhor. Let me get her saddle."

Urias took a good long look at his purchase, inspecting the horse's mouth and hooves. "Tell me, do you know her name, Mr. Luís?"

The man stopped as he took down the Arabian's tack.

"Unfortunately, we didn't keep a record of what she was named, but we have been calling her Cangambá. You might want to change it."

"Is that Portuguese, then?" Urias finished his inspection and cocked an eyebrow toward Luís who had not advanced a single step with the tack. "What does it mean?"

Urias watched as the man weighed his options, catching the very moment that he decided to throw caution to the wind.

"It means 'skunk,' senhor."

Urias was silent for a moment before breaking into raucous laughter.

"I am afraid you may have been right, Mr. Luís," he was finally able to get out, "I think that we may very well have been made for each other. I'm afraid that I can't call her that, however. Perhaps Comet would be a better name."

"É um nome lindo, senhor."

20:5 Águeda María Luisa Iñíguez had just turned down her oil lamps and pulled back the covers to her empty bed when she heard a soft knock at the door. Her pulse quickened as she hoped it might be the handsome cowboy returned to keep her warm, but she resolved to not give in too easily. It was he who chose to leave that morning on some fool's errand, and now that he was cold, tired, and smelly, she was just supposed to welcome him back with open arms? *Yo creo que no,* she resolved.

"Águeda María," Urias whispered, one of the few times in his life he had ever done so. "Open up, I need a favor."

Iñíguez wrapped herself in the top quilt, relit one of her lamps and spoke through the door. "I just bet you do, pendejo," she taunted. "It gets cold out there in the hallway. ¿No es así?

Urias chuckled despite himself. "No, you misunderstand," he began before admitting to himself that he would love more than anything to be back under the warm pile of quilts with the comely woman. "All right, you do understand; but first, a favor, por favor."

"What is it, then?" Iñíguez cracked the door open allowing Urias to see the skeptical look on her face, although the man was distracted by the vision of her smooth neck and shoulders, not to mention her long black hair backlit by the intoxicating yellow light of the single lamp.

"Todavía estoy enojado contigo."

"I know, I know," Urias started to plead his case before remembering why he had knocked in the first place. "Please, I have been out all day searching for Reverend Fox, only to return here and find that he has locked himself in the room. He will not answer and I fear the worst."

"All right, let me get dressed and I can let you in."

"Can I—" Urias took a step toward the threshold.

"No," Iñíguez shut the door in his face, scoring a point for herself. *Deja que el idiota suplique*, she thought. Let the idiot beg, knowing that—in the end—he would not, nor would she want or wait for it.

Iñíguez came out dressed in the embroidered cotton blouse she wore while working in the cantina. The residual smell of fried meats caused Urias' stomach to growl, while the familiar scent of the woman herself began to stir other organs.

"Águeda María—" Urias began.

"Stop right there," Iñíguez shut him down. "Let us check on your partner then I will decide if I am still angry with you for leaving my bed."

Urias' heart responded to the woman's grit and he made a silent decision that whatever the cost, he would get back in her good graces. A moment later he found himself wondering just what it was likely to take and whether he was up to the challenge.

The pair walked in silence down the dark hallway to the room that Iñíguez had rented the two men, although one of them, admittedly, had not spent too much time in it. The woman lifted a large brass ring with several skeleton keys dangling from it.

"Shall I knock?" she asked, poised to open the locked door.

"It will not do any good, Águeda. Believe me, I have tried."

Without taking her eyes off of Urias, Iñíguez placed one of the skeleton keys into the warded lock and turned it, the interior obstructions of the simple mechanism sliding easily past the carved notch in the key's bit. The bolt snapped back and the bedroom door creaked open of its own volition.

"¡La hostia!" Iñíguez exclaimed when the wreck of the rented room came into view. Scraps of paper, pages ripped from unfortunate books, as well as Wanted posters stolen from walls where they had been nailed, littered the floor. The water closet's mirror and washbasin had been smashed and sharp pieces of glass and broken crockery jutted up from a pink-stained puddle from which bloody footprints led toward the bed where Fox lay tangled in ruined sheets. "Is he dead?"

Urias took a knee next to the shambles of his friend and shook him by the shoulder. At once the inert form jerked to a semblance of life with a ragged snore.

"¡Dios mio!" Iñíguez exclaimed. "Is he drunk?"

Urias turned Fox over and slapped the man's cheeks before bending down to sniff at his waxed moustache. "Mordikai's weakness lies elsewhere, and this doesn't look like that either. Hand me one of those papers, there looks to be something written there."

Iñíguez gingerly picked her way over the glittering minefield and grabbed a damp poster. The front was printed with the rough likeness of a morally ambiguous-looking character. Above the scowling visage was written:

Wanted
Al "Gator" Sebek
Dead or Alive*
For Rail Theft, Arson, & General Skullduggery
Reward $500 in Gold Coin

*preferably dead

Glancing at the prize and filing it for when he might have time for a bout of bounty hunting, Urias turned over the flier to read what was scribbled there. In Fox's hurried scrawl was what Urias first took as a bit of scripture he was not familiar with.

Those angels that call themselves holy / And fixers of what has come to pass / This Earth, created then forgot / By God in his firmament / Become, in time, a cess

"What does it say?" Iñíguez moved close and looked over Urias' shoulder at the soggy sheet.

"I think it may be a sermon. I do not recognize—"

Fox's eyes flipped open, staring in horror at some fixed point past the adobe ceiling.

"They will return!" He shouted. "We must nurture these souls or perish. We must—" Apparently exhausted by the effort, the reverend's eyes snapped shut and he recommenced a wall-rattling snore.

"We must what?" Iñíguez asked, her dark pupils swimming in even darker irises.

"Let him sleep off whatever this is. We must clean this mess," Urias looked around at the room and up at his new lover. "Then I must make it up to you."

"Tienes un trato. You have a deal."

Chapter Twenty-One: Entr'acte

21:1 As if sensing trouble, Kokabiel looked up over the moldering piles of work on his desk to see one of his fallen angels appear at his door. The figure was moving so quickly that he outran the sound of his own knock.

"Come," the head of the Bureau of Nefarious Undertakings began—only to find the creature already at his desk. "What is it, Ruax? Can't you see I have a mountain of paperwork here?"

Out of pure reflex, Kokabiel began to massage his temples before the demon began to speak.

"I have news from upstairs," he began, speaking quickly and quietly as if to spare his boss the headache that was sure to come. "Their avatar catalyst is in play."

"Tell me something I don't already know," growled Kokabiel. "I am not concerned. We have wings on the ground to deal with this."

"Do you mean Tamiel?" Ruax raised an eyebrow causing a blood vessel behind his boss's right eye to seize. "He has gone native I'm afraid; calls himself Khadae now."

"The 'hidden power,' eh? Talk about 'hiding in plain sight.' Tamiel has never been half as clever as he thinks he is," Kokabiel pressed on his eye as if holding the nascent migraine down would make it go away. "Is he compromised? The last I heard he was in tight with whatever counts as a ruling class down on that mud ball."

"I am afraid that he may have let his mind wander off of the mission. Their new avatar has been born—"

"Bless it!" Kokabiel roared causing a star somewhere to explode. "Why am I just now hearing of this?"

"That's not all," Ruax mouthed.

"Of course it isn't. What? What can be worse than those blasted cattle gaining spiritual enlightenment? Good Devil!"

"As you know, our ongoing project to corrupt the host upstairs by introducing wagering has been a malicious success."

"There is no need to sweeten the medicine. Out with it."

"I'm afraid that in order to better the odds, someone may have spilled the beans."

The eye that Kokabiel was not actively pressing into his skull bored a hole into the center of Ruax's forehead.

"Gave up the ghost? Let the cat out of the—"

"I am seconds away from smiting the unholy hell out of you."

"All right," Ruax steeled himself knowing full well that his boss was not going to appreciate the news. "It appears that, in seeking to protect the child, two angels made unauthorized contact with the avatar's father."

The migraine that had been threatening to explode now chewed through Kokabiel's forebrain like a ripsaw and he spontaneously vomited a stomach full of black bile on the closest paperwork.

"And told him what, exactly?"

"Everything, apparently," Ruax winced. "It drove him quite mad I understand, but it didn't kill him."

"Who had the balls to invoke His/Her/Their wrath? I can almost admire the cheek."

"I believe it was Harut and Marut."

"Well, that certainly tracks. Did they learn nothing from being hung upside down for millennia? Don't answer that. How did they end up back upstairs anyway? I thought for sure, after that Babylonian business, they would be down here looking for work. Not that I would hire those two halfwits."

"Forgiveness."

"What's that?"

"Forgiveness," Ruax tried to explain. "They said they were sorry."

Kokabiel exploded with laughter. "They said they were sorry? You slay me, Ruax! Look at that, my headache is gone! Please, go away before it comes back."

Ruax made for the door at double the pace with which he arrived.

"And send Wormwood in if you see him," Kokabiel wiped the tears from his face. "We may have to whip up an old fashioned plague if this thing gets out of hand.

"They said they were sorry... Ha!"

1889

Chapter Twenty-Two

22:1 Despite the arrival of the witching hour and the damp cold that lingered upon its passing, Gruffydd and Urias made straight for the creek after finishing their iniquitous business in the graveyard and both stripped down to their birthday suits.

"I don't think I'll ever get that smell off of me," Gruffydd exclaimed as he scrubbed his body down with a bar of lye soap, the very last item from his sack.

"I guess you didn't have the pleasure of joining your fellow countrymen in our extended bout of madness," Urias commented, succeeding in nailing the partially shaved walrus to the spot with one raised eyebrow.

"There's a saying in Welsh, 'Gwna dda dros ddrwg, uffern ni'th ddwg.' Loosely translated, it means, 'Repay evil with good, and hell will not claim you.' Although I don't know if I still qualify for that deal after last night."

"I'm afraid I don't follow," Urias admitted.

"Nor I, and that is certainly a good start," the sheriff hiccupped a short, sharp laugh that frightened him as it escaped. "When the war broke out, I could see no benefit in following up a two-hundred-year record of inhumanity with more murder and mayhem; but I could try to protect the citizens—all citizens—of this county. And, I am sorry to say it, but there is no way that the larger fight is over. Neither side seems to have learned to treat anyone with anything approaching humility and grace."

"Fair enough," Urias conceded, too exhausted to get into a political discussion while standing naked in a creek. "Having experienced my fill of war, I cannot blame anyone for avoiding it, however they might."

"I could do with a bit of shut-eye," Gruffydd surrendered the conversation, "if at all possible. Perhaps a wee dram will tamp down that horror long enough—"

The sheriff felt the man silently staring at him. "All right, perhaps not, but I plan to try if you'll join me in the gambit."

"Who else would have me?" Urias moaned, the fleeting idea of looking up Águeda María Luisa having flown. "Where do you propose we go from here?"

"If that body is who you say it is, that would explain a few things," Gruffydd was glad to be able to start thinking analytically. "The mercantile has been closed since the revival disaster. The townsfolk just thought the Gilliam family was in mourning the loss of their reverend. We should make our way over to the house as soon as we... Right, daybreak it is.

22:2 The infected hours between the time two men marched sullenly down Main Street wearing only boots while carrying wet clothes, picks, and shovels, and the time those same men, now tragically sober, could be seen walking fully dressed in the opposite direction toward the Gilliam house, seemed to fester and stretch, pushing their corruption out against the skin of the new day.

Neither man had slept, each of them silently replaying the atrocity they had committed. The periodic reintroduction of spirit into their respective systems was quickly evaporated away by a shared resignation that both men would inevitably burn for their transgression.

Urias took note of the decrepit state of the Gilliam's screen as Gruffydd strode up and knocked on the door.

"Mrs. Gilliam," he announced, "it's Sheriff Gruffydd and I've got Mr. Urias with me. We would like to have a word."

For his part, Urias held his hat in his hands as he wondered just how one goes about telling someone that their spouse is dead. *Not just dead*, he thought, *but buried in the grave of the man you entrusted with your faith.* It was going to be another bad morning in what was turning out to be an unrelenting string of them.

"Mrs. Gilliam?" Not getting an answer, Gruffydd tried the knob and found the door unlocked. He glanced over at Urias who merely shrugged. The sheriff pushed the door open and announced himself again. Hearing nothing, the men entered and between the two of them, completely filled the threshold, barely leaving room for a small table where the dark stub of a strong cigarette lay balanced on the lip of a cut-glass ashtray.

An exhausted line of ash led up to the butt, giving up the narrative—to anyone ready to notice it—of a smoker interrupted in the exercise of his or her passion, an intrusion that lasted longer than the life of the sacrament in question.

"Stop where you are!" A surprisingly high voice demanded. Out of the shadows, a young waif in a well-worn cotton dress stepped up brandishing a revolver. "What have you done with Philomena?"

The pair of men raised their hands more in an admission of total exhaustion than any sense of trepidation.

"Easy, now," the sheriff sighed. "We are here to try and figure this out, same as you. Why don't you put the gun down?"

The girl, obviously on her last legs, hesitated, dropping the barrel, only to raise it again in jerky indecision.

"Listen, miss," Urias stepped up closer to the skittish girl, "if you are going to shoot us, fine. We probably deserve it. But if you aren't ready to do that, let's stop this charade. We've had quite a night."

The waif hesitated and lowered the pistol, looked at it with remorse, and then threw it into the corner of the room, sending the two men scrambling for cover.

"Jesus jumped-up Jiminy!" Gruffydd exclaimed. "Hasn't anyone taught you anything about gun safety? Is that thing even loaded?"

The girl, slowly taking in the gravity of the situation, followed the sheriff's eyes to where the gun had landed. "I don't know," she admitted. "That's where I found it."

Urias, relieved to not have been shot by a stray bullet, approached the young woman who was still in a state of confusion, but—happily for all involved—was now unarmed.

"What is your name, miss?" He engaged the girl as Gruffydd circled around and retrieved the pistol. Over the girl's shoulder, Urias could see the sheriff slide the pistol's release back and open the barrel, taking stock of the gun's ammunition.

"Lucette, sir," the girl squeaked. "Lucette Narcisse. Philomena is my friend. We go to school ... We went ... I don't know what is going on here!"

The two men looked at each other helplessly as the young girl broke into tears.

"It's alright, Lucette," Gruffydd took the lead. "We are all upset and confused." For his part, Urias silently nodded in agreement much like one of the marionettes he so despised. "Why don't you tell us how you came to be here and what you know about what happened to the Gilliams."

"Philomena and I snuck off to the revival that night," Narcisse began, her pent-up story giving way like an overfilled rain barrel with rusted-out hoops. "Philomena saw her father over by that preacher's wagon just before everything exploded. She took off through the crowd but they were all running towards me and I couldn't follow her right away. When I caught up, I saw the preacher lift her up onto his horse and ride away. I thought they might have come here, but when I got here the place was empty. Empty except for that pistol. I've been waiting for her ever since."

The sheriff pulled out an elegantly carved dining room chair and sat down so that he was closer to the girl's height.

"Do you mean to say that you've been living here alone all this time? Where are your parents?"

"I told them that I was staying with Philomena," the girl sniffled. "I think that they are happy enough to have one less mouth to feed. You should see the pantry in this place!"

Gruffydd's stomach growled at the thought and Urias chuckled at the young girl's pluck despite the situation. Something about her reminded him of his own hardscrabble youth.

"You haven't seen any sign of Mrs. Gilliam, then?" The sheriff continued.

"No sir."

Gruffydd emptied the pistol's cylinder onto the dining room table. Four silver cartridges bounced out on the Italian crochet tablecloth. The sheriff raised the open gun to his bulbous nose and inhaled like the bloodhound he once was.

"It appears as if someone has fired this gun. Twice."

Urias immediately started scanning the walls and wainscoting for holes and a telltale sign of blood. Finding neither, he reached out for the empty pistol.

"This didn't belong to Reverend Fox," he sighted down the smooth, short barrel. "Ever since Virginia, he said that he had seen enough of guns and what they can do."

Gruffydd raised an eyebrow at the two pistols that hung low on Urias' hips.

"I never claimed to subscribe to all of his beliefs. He was comfortable enough with the idea of letting me handle his safety. It's a mad country out there."

"Truer words, compadre," Gruffydd sighed and turned toward the young waif. "If your parents are all right with you staying here, I wonder if you could do me a favor? I'll check in on you when I can, but if anybody comes back here, I want you to hotfoot it straight to the Sheriff's Office and tell me. Do you know where that is?"

Narcisse's hazel eyes grew wide in excitement and the sheriff was afraid the girl was going to nod her head right off of her neck.

"Am I getting deputized?" The girl perked up.

Gruffydd laughed and placed his meaty hand on the child's head.

"By the power invested in me by the good citizens of Colusa County, I hereby do recognize and deputize you."

"Do I get a gun?"

Both men could not get their response out fast enough.

"No!"

22:3 Urias and Gruffydd were silent while walking back to the station from the Gilliam house, each man turning over the events they knew about and trying in vain to conjure up the ones they did not.

"We know where Mortimer ended up," Gruffydd broke the silence with a shudder. "And now we know that Philomena rode off into the bloody sunset with your man."

"Hold on, now," Urias protested.

"All right, let's set aside for a moment the fact that we have a plucky eyewitness that put Fox and young Miss Gilliam on a horse headed God knows where. The mystery that remains is what the deuce happened to Emilia? You saw that house. She built herself a pretty comfortable nest here. Why would she fly the coop without a sign?"

"Do you think she might have gone somewhere with Mordikai and her daughter?"

"You probably have a better sense about that," the sheriff stopped as they approached his office. "Does that sound like something your man would do?"

"No," Urias spat into the gutter. "It does not."

"Then, I am at a loss," Gruffydd shook his head. "Perhaps more whiskey would help."

"It couldn't hurt at this rate. After you."

The pair had barely cracked the seal on yet another bottle of Old Overholt when a young man wearing a cap with a brass Western Union shield pinned to it burst into the Sheriff's office.

"I hoped that I'd find you here, sheriff," the boy huffed, out of breath. "There's an urgent telegram for a Mr. Urias that was sent in care of you."

"This is Mr. Urias right here, son," Gruffydd pointed with the neck of the bottle of whiskey. "Go ahead and tell him what you need to."

"Urias return to San Francisco at once. Stop. *Pride of Jefferson* in quarantine. Stop. Must interview crew before too late. Stop. Telegram end."

"Who is the 'pride of Jefferson?'" Gruffydd asked.

"She's not a 'who' sir," the boy answered. "She's a 'what;' a steamship, sir. The biggest and fastest ever built!"

"I see," Urias mused. "How do you know so much about steamships, young man?"

"With all due respect, sirs," the boy scanned the room, "I do not intend to spend my whole life in this mud hole... sirs. The first chance I get, I'm transferring to San Francisco and then getting a job on one of these steamers. Imagine travelling to foreign ports all the time. Eating exotic food and meeting exotic women!"

"The boy does have a point," Gruffydd admitted. "That doesn't sound half bad."

"Say, are you the same Urias that used to come to town with Reverend Fox?"

"I am," Urias raised one notorious eyebrow.

"I lost my cousin in that debacle. He blew himself up with a wagonload of fireworks."

A pang of guilt rendered Urias speechless for a moment, leaving an opening for the boy to pile on.

"He was an idiot, but a good kid. The reverend should have never put him in charge of something like that. If you ask me, Fox got what was coming to him."

Gruffydd was up and out of his chair in a flash, ushering the boy back out onto the street before Urias could react.

"Sorry about that," Gruffydd apologized. "Young folks today don't have any respect for their elders. I tell you, Urias, the country is going to hell in an apple cart."

"No, the boy was right. I never should have trusted that farm boy with such a dangerous job. That was sloppy on my part," Urias sighed and then laughed. "I didn't think you could move that fast."

"I have enough dead bodies around here without you making more," Gruffydd poured two glasses out. "So, San Francisco, then? Who sent you that telegram?"

Urias took a deep pull from his glass and admired the whiskey's color in the light streaming through the open door. "My haberdasher, if you can believe it."

"Brother, I could believe anything at this point."

Chapter Twenty-Three

23:1 Anias was relieved when Alexander got up at his usual hour ready to wrestle the day to ground and walked out without mentioning anything about a morning ride. *That conversation was sure to happen soon enough,* she mused.

Anias knew that had anyone else hidden his beloved horse, they would already have been sorry for it. Alexander often loved an argument just for the sake of practicing his instrument, and had long considered himself a maestro of contretemps. Only Anias was exempt. Of course, it was never suggested that the maestro was afraid he would lose that contest.

Despite dodging one sticky situation, Anias was still unable to take her usual comfort in the morning trade breezes that tickled the lace curtains. Even her beloved surf seemed to be whispering secrets. Certainly, a lot had transpired since the pair of visitors had appeared on their shore. She felt that she had better take charge and start swimming lest she be swept out to sea by changing currents.

Anias lit a candle and stole barefoot into the hallway, careful not to wake the rest of the house. At the end of the corridor, she stepped into what appeared to be an open linen closet, but what she would describe, if anyone thought to ask, as a small alcove. She loved that word, alcove; a delightful steal from the French alcôve, who purloined it from the Spanish alcoba, who snatched it—probably by force—from the Arabs, who said al-kubba, meaning "the vault."

Pushing against the back panel of polished koa, Anias heard a small click as a secret door swung inward revealing a narrow staircase that led up to just that: her own private vault.

For a man so astute in the ways of business—a man who took pride in personally overseeing every aspect of his plantation—Anias was often astonished at how disconnected her husband was when it came to the home front. Alexander had never asked what was actually stored in the attic, or even how one might go there.

As far as any visitors approaching the house from the courtyard who might be tempted to remark on the way the Sun reflected off the room's pair of windows, it was Anias' predilection to ply them with enough food, drink, and stimulating conversation throughout the course of the evening to ensure they forgot all about it by the time they were poured back into their carriages.

Anias carefully pushed the panel closed behind her and ascended the dim passageway, the morning light not yet filling the room above. Her attic sanctuary was spartanly appointed and not, as Alexander might imagine, if he were to take the time, stuffed full of the ordinary detritus of a wealthy household.

On the wooden floor lay a woolen Irish Donegal rug, its center decorated by a garland of leaves woven in green and beige. Within the boughs, a Celtic triskelion, or three-armed spiral, represented to its owner the meeting of the spiritual, the visible, and celestial worlds.

Placing the candle on the floor, Anias turned to the only piece of furniture in the space, a French chifforobe. Carved in interlocking patterns of serpents and poppies in one of the later, slightly less-baroque, periods of Louis XV, the walnut cabinet was a guilty nod to the wealth that she enjoyed as a sugar baroness. Alexander had paid a small fortune to have the piece shipped from Paris and, as was his habit, promptly forgot it existed. Anias had to hire several stevedores from the busy Hilo wharves to move the heavy closet up the secret staircase lest her own workers become curious as to what the room was being prepared for.

Anias reached into a pocket on her morning wrap and produced a small key that fit the brass-plated keyhole on the locked doors. Opening the cabinet, she absentmindedly fingered the simple tunics embroidered in Celtic designs that hung on the left, while it was the series of drawers stacked on the right that interested her. She pulled open the third drawer from the bottom and retrieved a small, unadorned box of yew. Due to the density of the wood, the weight of the box belied its size, giving it an innate gravitas. Anias reverently lifted the box from its rest and carried it to the center of the rug.

Any of the Lanthiers' wide-ranging circles of acquaintances would have been shocked to see the matron of Milakale drop her morning

162

wrapper of exotic silk and sit crossed-legged, completely nude, in the center of her attic. Even Alexander, who would let his beloved burn the world if she so chose, would have had questions.

Anias' alabaster skin glowed in the half-light of the dawning day, her red hair smoldering with the promise of a banked fire. Eyes closed, she took three deep cleansing breaths, her back attentively straight, and opened the box.

Opening her eyes, Anias removed a small cloth embroidered with a circle within a circle, both shapes quartered with lines of silver thread. She spread the cloth over the woven triskelion and again closed her eyes. Visualizing herself as part of an unimaginably complex web of life, the hostess of a small piece of a small island in the middle of an immense living ocean became the manifestation of a collective spirit immeasurably larger than her own.

Before meeting Alexander and moving to Milakale, Anias had always maintained contact with what her Irish ancestors would have called her taise, or double, in the spiritual realm. Respecting her husband's missionary background—and taking full advantage of his many earthly distractions—she kept her communion with helpful spirits to herself; yet she still relied on their advice from time to time to help maintain the complicated social postures she found herself required to hold with an outward facing grace.

Eyes still closed in contemplation; Anias again reached into the box and removed a simple green cloth bag. Upon leaving the North American continent for good, she had upended the bag upon the surface of the Pacific Ocean, releasing all of the psychically charged icons that had helped her communicate with the spirits present in her hometown of San Francisco. Once established on the island, she opened herself up to recognize and welcome new helpers and attendant symbols, and they eventually arrived.

One morning, while walking along Milakale Beach with Alexander, she had been called into the surf by an irresistible force. Her husband thought it a lark as she raised her skirts and charged into the waves. He took the time to remove his leather boots before joining her, and by that time she had found what had summoned her: a hag stone, a small piece of wave-polished coral with a perfectly round hole through the middle of it.

To gaze through a natural hag stone was to look upon the spirit world as through a spyglass. The treasure went straight into the green bag as soon as she could manage it.

Each item she collected—the last being a bright yellow feather from the mamo bird, an item sacred to the native Hawai'ians—revealed over time what corresponding aspect of her spirit it would help represent.

The ancient Celtic art of divination required Anias to keep a query in mind as she upended the bag, allowing the items to scatter across the embroidered cloth as they might. Curious as to what the arrival of Reverend Fox and Philomena might ultimately hold in store for Milakale, she opened her eyes and gasped.

"Oh," she spoke to no one as she instinctively covered her breasts, suddenly all too aware of her vulnerability. "Oh, no."

23:2 Ever since the morning they left Makana Kealoha to her ancestors and what was left of their offering of pineapple, a powerful unspoken tension grew between Maleko and Philomena. The pair was still inseparable, but Maleko's boundless enthusiasm to show his co-conspirator all of the secrets of the island was channeled into a campaign to find out just what the kupua had said to her.

A couple of days later, having finished breakfast, the pair shot out of the back kitchen door with their usual gusto, but after leading Philomena into the dense vegetation surrounding Milakale once again, the closeness of the jungle canopy and the resonant sound of their footfalls upon the fecund ground, finally caused Maleko to crack.

The boy stayed quiet as long as he could bear before firing off a barrage of questions.

"What did she say? What is in that cave? Did you two talk to ghosts together?"

Philomena stopped in her tracks and faced her overly inquisitive companion.

"What is it with you?" She demanded. "Do you think I like all this?"

Maleko looked chastened but a needful glint remained in his eye telling Philomena that, despite her outburst, she was not off the hook. Not yet.

"All right, since you have to know, she said that even though I am not 'Kanaka Moly'—whatever that is—I still seem to be some kind of healer, just like her... a kupua?"

Maleko snorted. "Kānaka Maoli, that's me... us... Hawai'ians! You are certainly not that, white girl, but a kupua? Come on. Did she really say that?"

"Why would I make that up, Maleko? I don't even know what all this means. Or why I can see ghosts that nobody else can. I certainly didn't ask to be followed across the ocean by my dead father with his head all blown off."

"Wait. What?"

"Never mind," Philomena calmed down, realizing that she had revealed more than she wanted to. "I don't want to talk about this anymore."

"OK," Maleko gazed at the wet ground. "But—"

"Maleko! Please don't make me punch you."

As if flipping a switch, the thought of Philomena trying to beat him up caused Maleko to nearly choke on his laughter.

"What is so funny?"

"Some kupua you are, going around threatening poor defenseless Hawai'ian boys!"

Maleko's mirth was contagious and Philomena found it impossible to stay angry with him.

"You are far from defenseless, Kanaka Maoli," she managed to get out before bursting herself.

"Against the likes of you, sure I am," Maleko chuckled. "You might turn me into... a honu or something."

"I can't do that," Philomena protested. "Can I?"

"Hold on, now!" Maleko wound down. "Don't be testing out your powers on me. Especially if you don't know how to change me back."

The ridiculousness of the turn in conversation was enough to break any tension the pair might have felt and soon they were marching through the iron-rich muck with their usual camaraderie.

"Where are we going, anyway?" Philomena asked, not really caring about the answer as long as it was more adventure.

"I have a special surprise for you today, kupua," Maleko deferred as he lifted a tangle of yellow woodrose vines for Philomena to pass under. "My own secret waterfall."

"Keep it up and I will turn you into a honu," she warned. "Whatever that is."

Maleko's paroxysm of laughter was cut short by an extended, melancholy whistle from the dense canopy.

"What is that sound?" Philomena asked as she scanned the seemingly endless vegetation, nearly tripping over the exposed roots of a banyan tree.

"Hush," Maleko motioned for the girl to stop moving. He crept toward her as quietly as he found possible, as the soggy ground was loath to relinquish a single footstep without a fight. "I think that is a mamo. They are very rare now. Very valuable."

Maleko pointed to a lobelia bush, a riot of small purple flowers against green shrub. A black bird as long as the girl's forearm was caught in some sort of sticky sap; its long, downward curved beak opening slowly to let out the heartbreaking cry.

"What is it stuck in?" Philomena whispered. "Is that from that bush?"

"No," Maleko bemoaned, "that is a trap. Look at the yellow feathers underneath its body. Hunters set out sap under the mamo's favorite flowers and when it gets stuck, they come and pluck those. They are priceless. Only royalty can wear an 'ahu'ula made of those feathers. I heard story that the cloak of King Kamehameha the Great took the feathers of eighty thousand mamo birds to make. That was a long time ago, though. I've never seen it."

"The poor thing doesn't look too good."

"The collectors are supposed to come and clean off the bird's feet and release it once they've got their feathers, so it can go grow more. It looks like maybe they forgot this one."

Maleko slowly approached the trapped bird, its terrified eye rolling back to watch him. "It's OK, manu li'ili'i. You are safe now. Philomena, hold its body so it doesn't flap around when I try to unstick its feet."

Philomena could feel the bird's tiny heart racing in its chest as she held it from behind its head, pinning its wings to its sides. Maleko carefully pulled the sticky sandalwood sap from the mamo's claws rather than just trying to lift it out of the trap. Luckily for him, once he got one foot clear, the bird was catatonic—either in sheer panic or total exhaustion—and it didn't try to draw blood. Soon its other foot was free and Maleko told Philomena to set the creature down so it could fly away.

"Oh, Maleko," Philomena cried. "I don't feel its heartbeat anymore." She cupped the bird in her hands and extended it to show him that it had passed.

"You can't blame yourself, Philomena. At least we tried. Who knows how long it was stuck out here?"

"No," she stated categorically as she cradled as much of the bird's body as she could with both hands—its bowed bill sticking out between her fingers toward Maleko—as she closed her eyes.

"What are you doing?" The boy's eyes grew wide in amazement.

Philomena began to sway on her feet until she sat down hard, still holding the mamo out in front of her. Opening her eyes she gave her friend a sleepy look as she opened her hands. The mamo immediately stood up, looked at the two of them, and promptly flew off, swearing off lobelia for good. Maleko's mouth hung open as he processed what had just happened.

"Kupua," he mouthed, and helped Philomena to her feet. The two started back in silence, the waterfall all but forgotten.

"But really, though," Maleko finally broke the spell as they retraced the way they had come through the forest, "don't turn me into a honu."

23:3 Fox awoke at sunrise with an unwelcome craving he thought he had left behind years ago. An all-too-familiar tightness in his belly drove him to sit up in bed and automatically reach for a cigarette that he knew wasn't going to be there.

"Damn it all to hell," the reverend groaned. "You know better," he chastised himself. *Does this Khadae character have some sort of power over you to make you forget your vow? No. You were just being weak. You let your ego drive your actions and now look at you.*

167

Fox quickly tired of self-flagellating and anxiously dressed for breakfast. He thought that perhaps a cup of strong island coffee would help calm his nerves. When he arrived downstairs, however, he found that the rest of the house had already gone off to start their days. The Lanthiers were nowhere to be seen, and his charge and her native friend had apparently long run off to explore the nooks and crannies of the surrounding wilderness.

Fox wondered for an overdue moment if he should be concerned about Philomena running wild with Maleko when the boy's aunt entered with a carafe of the Kona coffee grown on the west side of the island.

"Good morning, reverend," Noelani welcomed. "Can I pour you a cup?"

"Miss Mahoe, I do believe you just may be an angel sent down from heaven."

"I'll take that as a 'yes,' then." As she poured, the aromas of flowers, chocolate, and exotic spices all swirled up to caress Fox's jangled senses. "Can I get you anything else?"

Fox paused to better inhale the coffee's ambrosial perfume as he lifted one of Anias Lanthier's delicate china cups to his lips. The first sip of the strong brew immediately hit his pleasure centers and helped bring the day into focus.

"Just keep this magic potion coming and I think we'll be grand," he purred. "Unless you have a cigarette."

"Reverend Fox, I would think that an evolved person such as yourself would have long sidestepped such foolishness."

"Ah, Miss Mahoe, it is a failing to be sure, but how much easier it is to recognize His perfect light from the darkness of our mortal frailty."

"Pretty words, reverend. My youngest brother, Kekoa, has been known to have a cigar from time to time. You might ask him where he gets them. You can't miss him. He is the tall one. He says it's the cigars, but I don't believe him. Neither should you."

"Where might I find this righteous giant this morning?"

"I believe you will find him working in the chapel gardens today," Noelani placed the carafe down in front of Fox and took a step back as if to better size him up. "I'm guessing that you may well want to investigate our humble house of worship, regardless. Reverend."

"Right you are, Miss Mahoe!" Fox declared, the coffee having worked its dark magic. "Perhaps one more cup and I'll be ready to do just that."

"One more cup and you'll be ready to swim around to the Puʻuhonua. Is refuge what you need, Reverend Fox? You seem to me as a man who is often looking over his shoulder. Who are you expecting to see there? Are they gaining on you?"

"Excuse me?" Fox realized that he might have missed something important while lost in reverie.

"Pardon me, reverend." Having second thoughts about voicing her frank observation regarding the Lanthiers' guest, Noelani reclaimed the carafe and filled his cup one last time. "I was just wishing you a pleasant morning."

"Oh, yes," Fox struggled to find where he had dropped the thread of conversation. "Thank you, Miss Mahoe. And thank you for the coffee. I almost feel myself again."

"Miracles abound here at Milakale."

"Yes, I am beginning to realize what a singular and blessed place this is."

23:4   After visiting the Lanthiers' indoor bathroom where he enjoyed the use of an ingenious device with a small, engraved placard announcing it as *Smith's Patent Earthenware Siphon Jet Water Closet*, Fox walked out in search of the youngest Mahoe brother and by proxy, perhaps a bit of tobacco.

Taking a moment to get his bearings in the bright tropical sunshine, Fox recognized the white clapboard spire of a Protestant church poking into the sky across the courtyard and over a small rise that either hid or protected the small village of outbuildings that surrounded the Big House.

Cresting the berm, he recognized one of the Mahoe brothers working a raised flowerbed in front of the tall arched windows of the chapel. Not seeing the other two brothers around for comparison, Fox was ready to take it on faith that the gentleman was indeed the youngest and tallest of the three and set out to formally introduce himself when he felt a hand at his elbow.

"Reverend Fox!" A voice at his ear declared. "What a fortuitous pleasure. I was just on my way to your new pulpit."

Fox, startled at how someone could sneak up on him so easily, recognized Alexander's voice at the same moment that he realized that he had better start paying better attention to his exotic surroundings.

"Alexander! You startled me... I'm sorry, what did you say?"

Lanthier had not let go of Fox's arm and now steered him at a clip toward the front door of the church, passing Kekoa Mahoe in the process, now leaning on his hoe watching the proceedings with a look of incredulity.

"This church and its congregation," Lanthier gushed, "they are yours! I have dispatched the old pastor back to Kona where he came from. Come, this is the rock from which your glorious vision shall light up the entire archipelago."

Fox couldn't miss the sound of a hoe being dropped against a flowerbed edging of lava rock. "I didn't ask for this," he began a half-hearted protest.

"You didn't have to ask. You saved my life. This has been the greatest confirmation of God's infinite wisdom that I have ever received. I am as grateful for that as I am for continuing to draw breath. You are here for a reason, Mordikai—if I may be so informal."

"Of course," Fox removed his hat and let his eyes adjust to the light inside the chapel. Brilliant sunlight streamed though a profusion of stained glass windows flooding the interior with a disorienting kaleidoscopic play of color. "Oh, my."

"I realize that this isn't how you usually reach the people," Lanthier admitted, noticing the look of shock on the reverend's face. "Just think, however, without the added work of packing up and moving from place to place, you can really focus on your message. You can go deeper."

"I don't know what to say," Fox admitted that for one of the first times in his life he was truly speechless. The events that brought him to Milakale had unfolded so quickly that he hadn't had time to imagine what a life on the island would actually mean, but now he found himself warming to the idea, as well as the possibilities. "I'm honored, Alexander. Yes, I think that together we can do great things."

Outside the church, Kekoa Mahoe picked up his hoe and started back toward the Mahoe family house having overheard the entire exchange.

"Doomed? Perhaps," he mused as he walked. "Perhaps not."

PLATE FIVE ※ Alexander & Anias Lanthier

172

Chapter Twenty-Four

24:1 Having left the nasty business in Fiesta in Gruffydd's capable hands, Urias settled into his seat on the Southern Pacific and took a pull from the silver flask the sheriff gave him for the long trip to San Francisco.

Although he was relieved to not find his partner buried in the graveyard, he was still sorry to have discovered a man he knew well and worked closely with over the years. The mystery of what had happened to Fox and the rest of the Gilliam family worried his mind as the rhythm of the train worked to pull at his eyelids.

He was just about to nod off when a pair of cowboys strode up the center aisle, the movement of the car underfoot tossing one of them into the side of Urias' seat. Reflexively reaching for his revolver, he caught the eye of the perpetrator who seemed neither interested in apologizing or escalating the offense.

All at once, Urias felt the weight of the years he had spent on edge. There had definitely been a time when the cowboy would have most likely been staring at a sudden hole in his chest instead of stumbling his way to the front of the car.

The ceaseless jostling of the train soon found Urias looking for the gentlemen's lavatory, another concession to aging that he did not welcome. Walking though the smoking car, he noticed the two men huddled together in the corner. One of them shot Urias a furtive look as he passed, yet he paid it little mind as he was focused on finding relief for his battered bladder.

At the far end of the car, a door separated a small double room from the boisterous smoking lounge. Catching sight of his reflection in the bathroom mirror, Urias stopped at the sink and splashed his face and washed his hands before opening the inner door that housed the hopper toilet. He realized that after his recent ill-starred visit to Fiesta, it was going to be a long time before he truly felt clean again.

Entering the cramped inner chamber, and lifting the porcelain lid, Urias fully expected to see railroad ties speeding along underneath the train; instead he saw Washburn's face looking up at him.

"Howdy, Yank!" The disembodied Confederate exclaimed.

Urias reeled back in shock yet was penned in by the confines of the lavatory. "Damn your eyes, Washburn! I almost pissed right through your head."

The ghost dematerialized from the bowl and reconstituted more or less whole and standing next to Urias. "I duly appreciate your reticence, sir. By God, we shall make a gentleman of you yet."

"Says the ghost haunting the men's lavatory."

"Now, let us not cast aspersions, my blue-bellied friend. We were getting along so well."

"Can you please excuse me for a moment?" Urias growled. "I must see to a pressing matter."

"Of course, of course," Washburn began to fade. "Forgive me. I do forget about the needs of the flesh. But don't go away, I need to tell you something."

Absent the incorporeal crown of a man Urias once would have called his enemy, the flashing wooden ties below were in full view. *Perhaps I am finally losing my mind*, Urias ruminated as he watered the rail bed at eighty miles an hour.

Urias gave himself even odds as to whether the spirit would return, chalking the latest appearance of the apparition up to a very stressful couple of weeks. *It's all in my head*, he thought at the precise moment that Washburn again materialized at his side.

"Gaaaa!" Startled despite himself, Urias became resigned that he was finally going mad. "What is so important, Washburn? Out with it, specter!"

"Oooh, I like the sound of that. Specter. At last, a title worthy of a son of Mother Washburn."

"I'm beginning to understand why someone fired a cannon at you," Urias speculated. "Are you sure it was the Union Army? If you prattle on this much while dead, I can't imagine what you sounded like while still drawing breath."

"You wound me sir," Washburn bemoaned. "Well, not really wound, but—"

"My God, man! Will you get to the point?"

"Right," Washburn regained focus. "There are two men planning on shooting up this train, and, well, I've become strangely fond of you. For a 'living,' and all. It seems that we are on the same trail, and I thought perhaps we could help each other. It's good to have someone that can talk to other livings without them getting their petticoats all in a knot. No offense."

"Let me guess, two conspiratorial-looking cowboys?"

"The very scallywags, all right. Hold on a moment—" Washburn disappeared through the wall and reappeared quickly to report on the scene. "It is happening now, I'm afraid. I'd hurry; they are right outside the door ready to fleece yonder unsuspecting citizens."

Urias quietly stole out of the lavatory and found himself right behind the men just as they drew their guns. He dispatched the closest by bringing down the butt of his Colt on the back of his head. As his partner turned to see what was happening, he simply applied the same technique to the bridge of the man's nose.

The full smoking car—suddenly aware of two bandits prostrate on the floor, their pistols having skittered under the nearest bench seat—erupted into cheers. Urias was pulled toward the bar and plied with drinks for the remainder of the trip, while a U.S. Marshall, somewhat late to the party, collected the two cowboys.

Washburn, playing against type, stayed out of sight.

SAN FRANCISCO, CALIFORNIA, UNITED STATES OF AMERICA | 1889

24:2 Niall Hendry met the ferry shuttling Urias' train at the Pier 43 Belt Railroad terminus on the bustling San Francisco waterfront. He was surprised to see the normally serious-minded gentleman to be in a level of dishevelment he would not have expected of him.

"Oh, my giddy aunt," Hendry laughed as he shook the man's hand. "What happened to you? And what has become of your beautiful suit?"

Urias shook his head as to better see the man who had sent him back to Fiesta and nearly toppled into the Bay. "I stopped a robbery."

"With what, your breath? Come on, Aaron; let's get you sobered up. Time, I am afraid, is short." Hendry led Urias across the seawall and flagged down a horse-drawn hack. "Listen, I don't imagine you are familiar with the writings of a certain Viennese neurologist, but I have something that may just fix you right up."

The haberdasher pulled out a small vial of white power and taking Urias' hand and turning it over, poured out a generous pile between his thumb and index finger. "Take it up like snuff."

Urias rolled his eyes. *Perhaps my plaid companion is a dandy after all,* he thought.

"I saw that you ungrateful bastard," Hendry groused. "Just do it, we need you in full possession of your faculties."

Urias sniffed up the bitter powder and felt it begin to numb the back of his sinuses. Immediately, the long ride from Fiesta was all but forgotten.

"Whoo! Hat men certainly have more interesting lives than I hitherto gave them credit for."

"You have no idea, my friend. I'm afraid, that in my case, it actually is a curse. A former colleague of mine has made it a long-term project to see that it remains so."

"I know the feeling, Niall," Urias wiped his nose on the back of his hand as it had begun to run at the same time the night reeled into perfect focus. "I haven't had the chance to tell you—"

"Your man was not buried in Fiesta."

"How did you know?"

"No time for that, I'm afraid. We are here," Hendry pronounced, before taking a hit of cocaine himself and holding the vial out to Urias. "It helps with the smell," he explained. "Welcome to Butchertown."

"What have cows to do with all this?" Urias waived off the offer, as he had smelled worse in his time and learned the hard way how to mostly ignore it.

"What we seek is on the other side of all this. When the *Pride of Jefferson* was refused a berth, it was moved out here until the Port and the City figure out what to do with her."

"I gathered from your telegram that the ship is in quarantine, but you didn't say why," Urias sidestepped a pile of cow dung with a smooth grace that took him by surprise. *Perhaps there is something to the hat man's tonic,* his thoughts blazed.

"Influenza," Hendry explained, handing Urias a bandana before tying one around his own face. "A particularly virulent strain by all accounts."

After promising to return in an hour, the hansom cab driver was all too glad to return to the somewhat less fragrant side of town and dropped the men in front of a large warehouse with *Union Iron Works* painted in man-sized letters above its closed and chained entry.

Hendry led Urias around the side of the building and pounded on a nondescript door. A small eye-level Judas window slid open.

"Yea?"

"It's Niall Hendry, I'm here with a colleague to speak with the crew."

"You are a bit late, British," a voice sneered from beyond the darkened slit. "The captain is dead and most are quick to follow."

"Damn it, man!" Hendry exploded. "Let us in, then. We have official business."

"Oh, official is it? By whose order, the Queen Mum?"

Urias pushed forward and stuck the barrel of his .44 through the slit before the guard had a chance to close it. "By orders of Samuel Colt. Open the fucking door."

"Your funeral, asshole," the guard intoned and then relented.

The door swung open to reveal a scene that had Urias wishing it had stayed closed. Beds filled with the sick and dying were lined up in rows as far as he could see in the dimly lit warehouse. The smell of vomit and bodily wastes competed with the residual metallic tang of industry and the stockyard funk from outside.

"My God," Urias muttered as he raised his bandana to cover his nose.

"Your god has abandoned this place, I'm afraid," Hendry lamented before plunging into the cavernous sick room.

"He is not half wrong, you know," the guard motioned to Urias to follow as he shut and bolted the door. The sound echoed into the cavernous space with a finality that brought a chill to anyone who was well enough to notice it.

Urias stepped carefully, but quickly, past tragedy after tragedy in order to catch up to Hendry who had already cornered an exhausted looking doctor.

"Aaron Urias, this is Dr. Coleman Whitaker from the *Pride of Jefferson*. This poor fellow has had the unfortunate job of riding roughshod over this sorry affair from the beginning."

"Dr. Whitaker," Urias held out his hand only to have it dismissed by the doctor.

"Please forgive me, Mr. Urias, I'm afraid that civility is yet another collateral victim of this disease."

Ever the pragmatist, Urias was not offended by the breach of conduct, and instead felt freed up to get straight to the point.

"What are you dealing with here, doctor?"

Whitaker's tired eyes reflected the light from the coal fire burning in a repurposed cupola foundry furnace. A line of sweat dripped down the dark skin of his face leaving Urias to wonder if the man himself may soon succumb to whatever had ravaged the ship's crew.

"Influenza," Whitaker sighed. "May the power of Obeah save us."

"What was your destination?" Hendry asked. "Do you suspect you may have contracted it abroad and brought it back here, or—?"

"The latter, I'm afraid," Whitaker stared disconsolately into the horror of the warehouse. "We were under steam to the Hawai'ian Islands when one of the crew became ill. He succumbed quite quickly and just to be safe, we buried him at sea. The captain made up a cover story so good that I think he started to believe it himself. I felt we had dodged a bullet, so we continued on to Hilo and Honolulu before returning to San Francisco. It was the next trip that I fear may have delivered the full blown flu to the islands."

"What happened on that trip?" Urias pried. "Were there more cases on the voyage back?"

"No, strangely enough, we didn't have a single case until we left Hilo. Then all hell broke loose. We barely made it back with so many stricken."

"No symptoms at all, and then a full-fledged outbreak?" Hendry pondered. "That seems a bit abrupt, doctor. Are you sure there was nothing?"

"I did have one strange case," Whitaker recalled. "It wasn't influenza, though. It was more of a dementia. One of the passengers, a preacher of some kind, was practically foaming at the mouth. I had to sedate him. You know a German psychiatrist, Dr. Emile Kraepelin, has recently made great strides—"

"Hold on," Urias perked up. "This 'preacher,' he didn't happen to be traveling with a young girl by any chance?"

Whitaker wiped his arm across his forehead to keep the sweat from dripping into his eyes. "As a matter of fact he was; a charming girl, although I did become concerned over her mental state as well. An oddly fragile pair."

"Reverend Fox!" Hendry exclaimed. "We've found you, you rascal."

"You must tell us, doctor!" Urias implored. "Where did you see them last?"

"Fox... yes, I do believe that was the man's name. His daughter's name was... Francine? No. Wilhelmina?"

"Philomena Gilliam," Urias summoned what patience he could muster. "And I assure you doctor, that young girl is not his daughter."

"Nonsense," Whitaker opined. "I have delivered enough children in my time to fill this sorry mud hole, and I can tell you that child practically fell from Fox's face. Come to think of it, Dr. Kraepelin has identified a heretical link in many cases of dementia praecox. That makes sense, now that I—"

"Doctor, please," Hendry noticed the patience of his partner was nearly spent. "What happened to them?"

"Forgive me," Whitaker sagged. "This has all been a trial. I fear that my own mind may be in peril. I believe that Reverend Fox and the girl disembarked in Hilo, right before it all turned tits up, as they say."

"Hilo it is, then," Hendry declared and turned to leave.

"Please, gentlemen," Whitaker begged. "If either of you have any pull with whatever authorities exist in San Francisco, tell them what you have seen here. We can't go on like this. These people deserve better."

"Can I ask," Urias tarried, "why bring everyone here, of all places? Why not just stay on the ship?"

"Gentlemen, you should probably be going," Whitaker evaded the question.

"I can tell you why," a sickly voice rose from the nearest cot. "Those damn Danes! They want to clean the *Pride of Jefferson* and get her back plying the routes. It all comes down to money."

Urias turned and knelt so that the stricken man didn't have to exert himself. "Who are you? How do you know this?"

"My name is Romo Laurant," the wraith choked. "I sailed under Captain Kasper Munk, one of the finest men to sail the Pacific trades. I heard him receive the order myself."

"This is inhuman," Urias growled. "Do you think we can speak with the captain?"

"Not unless you can speak to ghosts," Laurant began to laugh bitterly which quickly turned to a paroxysm of coughing.

24:3 The discarnate presence of Jeremiah Erasmus Washburn III stood, more or less, on the fog enshrouded deck of the *Pride of Jefferson*. If any of the living were left aboard to see the former soldier appear unbidden near the ship's bridge, they would most likely have passed him off as a trick of the moonlight feebly finding its way through the soup.

Perhaps that is what has become of me, he pondered, holding his all-too-portable head out in front and turning it as to get a better look at the rest of his shambles. *Nothing but a trick of the light.*

"All right, Jeremiah, pull it together, so to speak," he spoke with a voice that could have been mistaken for the wind that was currently tearing at the Danish flag far atop the forward mast. "Now if I were the captain of one of these hulks, where would I haunt?"

Washburn passed through the bulkhead of the bridge and, upon finding nothing, sank though the iron spar deck to the darkened interior of the ship. Working off a veritable haystack of karmic debt, Washburn had been a ghost hunter nearly as long as he had been a ghost, and—over the ensuing quarter of a century—had become quite good at it.

Many ghosts he found were merely diminishing reverberations spun into an eddy by a particularly strong spirit blazing by, not aware enough to even know that they were left behind. Others, like this Gilliam character he was searching for, had agency.

That son of a bitch knows damn well what he is doing, Washburn fumed, *and it is fucking up my books.* The spirit suspected he would find Captain Munk caught somewhere between the two extremes; aware of his demise, but with some baggage slowing him down, some unfinished business.

Washburn finally found Munk on the passenger "A" deck standing before a ghastly wooden carving of a seaman about to be torn apart by ill-intentioned sirens having lured him onto their rocks.

"Captain," he spoke quietly as to not spook him.

"I always hated this thing," Munk replied, not bothering to turn around. "It surely is cursed. I should have had it tossed it into the sea where it belongs."

Washburn, no art critic while alive, pondered the piece.

"I think you may be right. Is that why you are here? I'm afraid you will find your ability to affect the tangible is quite diminished. It is, however, horribly easy to frighten the living into taking care of things for you."

Munk paused, taking in the parameters of his new situation.

"Captain, if I may, why were the crew and passengers taken to shore if the ship is in quarantine? Wouldn't it have made more sense to care for the stricken on board, rather than risk an outbreak?"

"Det var noget pjat!" Munk spat. "That was unconscionable. Certain factions high in the company can't bear the idea of losing a single krone of their holy profit. I see now what a folly it is to chase anything but life."

"Yes, well, as my granddad used to say, 'It is all a waste of time, but you have to do something.'"

Munk finally turned from the carving to focus on his uncanny visitor. If he was taken aback by the mutable location of the man's head, he was stoic enough not to show it.

"You can't believe that. Given your—and my—position, you have to hope that our lives meant something. Don't you?"

"Listen, cap'n, I have never been much of a philosopher. It all makes it harder to keep my head on straight, if you know what I mean.

What do you mean the owners are chasing profit? Surely they are not going to fill the ship with passengers again?"

Munk choked out a laugh as he tuned back toward the sirens. "Passengers? Din satans nar! Don't be a fool! The *Pride of Jefferson's* real cargo is opium: from Chinese producers to Hawai'i, bypassing British Hong Kong, and straight to our people here in San Francisco. Our advokats are working on the new Hawai'ian Legislature, and it's just a matter of time before they get a Chinese license. If King Kalākaua hadn't put his foot in it, and had just given that skiderik Aki his bribe money back, it would have been a done deal by now."

"If I may be so bold," Washburn interrupted, "none of that really concerns you anymore. The damned livings are always going to end up doing what they do. The question now is; what are *you* going to do? A gentleman such as yourself can't spend eternity haunting a piece of bad art."

"A captain goes down with his ship, doesn't he?" Munk snapped. "Yet, I seem to have gone down and here she sits. It hardly seems fair."

Washburn laughed despite himself. "Captain, nothing is fair in this life or the next. Whomever led you down that primrose path has done you a disservice, sir."

"Forgive me, I do know better," Munk apologized. "'He is the Rock, his work is perfect: for all his ways are just—'"

"Spare me," the ghost hunter interrupted. "I believe you will find that it's more complicated than that." Washburn noticed the look on the captain's face. "Listen, it does beat working for the other team, but this half-life is not all sweet tea and petticoats, not by a long shot. Do you want my advice?"

"If it is not too much trouble. I seem to be at a bit of a loss here."

"Let go. Unless you really fancy wandering the twice-damned Earth like myself, surrender to the infinite," Washburn implored.

"What will become of me?" Munk asked, not used to not being in control of every situation.

"Honestly? Everything. You have always been part of everything, you will just become... even more so. I would be lying if I said that I wasn't a little bit jealous."

Chapter Twenty-Five
MILAKALE, HAWAI'I, KINGDOM OF HAWAI'I | 1889

25:1 The soothing sound of a gentle morning rain woke Philomena from a welcome dreamless sleep. She was quickly becoming used to the capricious showers that visited the island in the wee hours and then moved on. Back home in California's Central Valley, once the faucet was cracked open during the short—but serious—season, the rain often didn't stop until the Sacramento River overtopped its banks and the surrounding fields became mirrors of the gunmetal sky.

Philomena was also becoming very accustomed to the incredible food streaming out of Jun Jin's kitchen, served daily by Maleko's aunt. For her part, Noelani quickly came to appreciate someone in the house that could keep Maleko out of her hair, and despite the furor that the pair had caused at the post-accident dinner, had grown to care for the new addition to the Big House. She was secretly glad to see the girl start to put some meat on her bones and always made sure that Jun remembered to make her favorite lilikoi-filled malasadas.

While the smells wafting up from the kitchen held the girl in thrall, there was something pulling at the corner of her eye as she dressed, a very familiar shadow silently craving her attention.

"Hello, father," she whispered but did not turn around.

"Philomena," replied a voice sounding very much like the wind in the acacias outside her window.

"You don't have to check up on me anymore," the girl declared, staring at the hardwood floor. "I am going to be all right. I like it here."

"I am glad that you are finding your way," the leaves in the trees shook, "but there are things that you do not yet understand. I worry that you are still in danger."

Philomena whipped her head around to catch just the most gossamer glimpse of her father standing behind the curtains, which billowed in the breeze.

"And you are going to protect me, are you? How do you plan on doing that? Father, you are but a glimmer now! I would be better off going out to meet the day wrapped in that window lace for all the security it would offer."

"You wound me, daughter."

"Not as much as you have wounded yourself!" Philomena shouted. "And wounded me as well in the bargain! What do you want?"

"I—" Gilliam started. "I don't know."

"Well, feel free to haunt me again when you figure it out. I am going to breakfast."

25:2 Kapono was pouring Anias a cup of coffee when an upstairs door slammed and Philomena came storming down the polished stairs.

"Good morning, dear heart," Anias purred, remembering her own tendency for impetuous outbursts at the girl's age.

Philomena was instantly soothed by the smell of Jun's sweet bread French toast smothered in even sweeter coconut syrup.

"Coffee, miss?" Kapono paused, shooting Anias a sideways glance.

"Don't be silly, Miss Philomena is much too young to be picking up our bad habits; aren't you dear?"

Philomena didn't want to tell her host that she had been drinking coffee for years back home, but the smell of the strong Kona brew pulled at her very soul. Anias, not one to miss such blatant yearning— especially at her table—easily relented.

"Oh, what could it hurt?" Anias motioned Kapono to pour the girl a cup. "A small one, if you would, I believe our guest will find that our brew is quite a bit stronger than anything poor Jim Folger may have been passing off as coffee in San Francisco. A shame about Jim, one shouldn't speak ill of the dead, I suppose, even if his coffee tasted like a tarnished penny."

"Ma'am?" Philomena asked, completely lost in the woman's conversational flight.

"Please, dearest, don't 'ma'am' me, it makes me sound so old," Anias entreated. "Furthermore, 'ma'am' is short for 'madam,' and while a more than a few have passed through these doors over the years, I assure you that I am not one of them."

"I'm sorry ma'... erm, what should I call you, Mrs.?"

Kapono failed in his attempt to stifle a laugh at the girl's expense, drawing a stern glance from Anias.

"You will have to forgive Mr. Mahoe, dear, he is filling in for his sister this morning and apparently has forgotten that he is not out feeding horses, or whatever he usually does around here. That will be all for now, Kapono. Thank you.

"As far as what to call me," Anias pondered, taking a long sip of coffee. "'Mrs.' won't do either. I don't define myself by my relationship to Alexander, and I don't expect you to. Then again, Anias is a little familiar given the difference in our ages." Leaning in conspiratorially, she added, "Between you and me, I would be all right with you using my Christian name, but it may raise a few eyebrows with the other landed gentry. I know! How about 'Aintín?' It means 'auntie' in Gaelic. That will keep them guessing, won't it?"

The important business of the morning now finished, the two sat in comfortable silence for a moment until Anias realized that she had sent away the very person who was going to bring them their breakfast.

"Oh, dear," Anias lamented. "Philomena, be a lamb and ask Mr. Jun for our meal. I would do so myself, but he has long banned me from coming anywhere near his kitchen."

"OK, Aintín," Philomena winked and took off toward Jun's domain.

25:3 Jun Jin was placing more wood in the belly of his stove when Philomena knocked on the doorframe. *Working without Noelani for the early morning meal was bad enough,* he ruminated as he tossed another stick of kiawe wood into the firebox, *but now that the rush was over and Alexander and his cronies are gone, the lady of the house and Maleko's little friend have deigned to come downstairs. That girl eats like a horse!*

"Excuse me," Philomena spoke up, "Mr. Jun?"

"What is this?" Jun demanded, nearly dropping a log on his foot. "Where is Kapono?"

"Aintín, I mean, Mrs. Lanthier sent him away."

"Unbelievable," Jun muttered. "First Noelani gets sick, and now her good-for-nothing brother has angered the mistress. Let me guess, did he spill hot coffee on her?"

"No," Philomena answered, pondering just turning around and going without breakfast, but the smells in the kitchen nailed her feet in place as it steeled her resolve. "He laughed. At me."

"Oh, child," Jun's demeanor changed, "do not take that vain fool's words to heart. 'A big tree will always attract the gale,' and Kapono Mahoe is all wind."

"It's all right," Philomena said, looking wistfully past Jun to the iron stove. "I didn't take it personally."

"Good girl!" Jun exclaimed, rethinking his initial read of this particular castaway. "Say, since the mistress has run off my help this morning, after we get some food into you, I wonder if you could help me with a favor?"

"Of course," Philomena piped, "I would be glad to!" All the while she was thinking: *All you had to say was French toast.*

"The only reason I let that oaf into my kitchen in the first place was because your friend Maleko's auntie is ill. I am going to make her my secret potato soup. We'll cure her right up!"

"And you want me to take it to her?" Philomena asked, not sure where she fit in to the picture.

"Smart girl! Smart girl and pretty!" Jun gushed. "Maybe you'll be mistress some day. Or president of America! Who knows?"

25:4 Breakfast came and disappeared as fast as Philomena could will it. When Jun finally came back to the table—although she felt as stuffed as a Fiesta piñata—she was more than ready to jump up and help out.

"Please forgive the cheek, missus," Jun comfortably joked with his boss, "Miss Philomena has graciously agreed to take Noelani Mahoe some nourishment. I have prepared my potato soup, and you well know the effect it can have on the infirm."

"An excellent idea, Mr. Jun!" Anias exclaimed. "If anything short of another miracle can roust the poor woman, it is your unworldly delicious specialty. I will personally accompany her, although I am sure that she knows the way to the Mahoe house like she knows the freckles on her own nose."

Philomena blushed as she had recently become all too aware of the effect the Hawai'ian climate was having on her complexion. Given her olive skin color, she had always tanned easily in the blazing hot Central Valley summers, something her mother had discouraged to no avail. The tropical Sun's rays were a whole different bird, however, leaving its tiny footprints across her cheeks and the bridge of her nose. She was glad that it hadn't been Maleko that zeroed in on the new additions to her appearance; it would have only given him more ammunition with which to tease her.

"Be very careful, it has just come off the stove and is quite hot," Jun warned as he handed the two women a wicker basket containing a covered and towel-wrapped bowl that gave off an amazingly mouthwatering aroma regardless. Even though Philomena had finished every bit of the filling breakfast, her stomach responded to the new heady mix of smells by growling quite audibly.

"Oh, my," Anias tittered despite herself. "If you plan on staying awake today, dear heart, you will want to stay away from this particular delicacy. I have watched it send all three Mahoe brothers into a food coma."

"Excuse me, Aintín," Philomena blushed. "I don't know what came over me."

"You do not need to apologize, child, that is quite the appropriate reaction. Let us just hope that Mr. Jun's magic soup has the same effect on Noelani's appetite."

25:5 The two women made their way across the courtyard to the Mahoe family cottage. An unusually taciturn Maleko sat on the same stair where Philomena had first spotted him from the carriage when she first arrived.

"How is the patient today, Dr. Mahoe?" Anias gently asked, causing the boy to look around before realizing she was addressing him.

"Not so good, Mrs. Lanthier," he replied as bravely as he could muster. "I boiled some Lau-ki and gave it to her, and put more Ti leaves on her forehead, but she is burning up."

As the trio entered the small but fastidiously tidy front room of the cottage, the grassy smell of the cooked Ti as well as an unmistakable undercurrent of sickness met them.

"Open the window, would you, dear?" Anias directed Philomena toward the single, cloth-covered pane. "Let us get some fresh air in here!"

Pushing on into the darkened bedroom, Anias found Noelani tangled in her sheets as if she had been wrestling them and lost. The woman had stripped down to a thin cotton slip that was pasted to her body with sweat revealing that her normally golden brown skin was developing a disturbing bluish tinge.

"Oh, dear," Anias exclaimed, rushing past the worried boy to Noelani's bedside. "Maleko, run up to the house and tell Mr. Jun to send for a doctor right away!"

Philomena caught Maleko's frightened gaze as he turned to go. "Can you do something?" He whispered before sprinting toward the Big House.

"Philomena, I am afraid that Noelani may be more ill than we feared," Anias warned. "You don't have to come any further if you don't want to."

"It's alright, Aintín," Philomena assured her. "No matter how bad she is, I have seen worse."

Anias paused a second to wonder just what the girl had been through in her young life. *Perhaps there is more to this girseach than I gave her credit for*, she thought.

"Why is she blue?" Philomena asked, approaching the moaning woman. "I have never seen that before."

"Nor have I, child," Anias whispered. "My father had, though. Some forty years ago, the fever ripped through Ireland during the Hunger. He used to tell me of the horrors he experienced before leaving for America. I'm afraid poor Noelani here probably isn't getting enough oxygen. Her lungs must be full of fluid."

The two women turned as a rapid-fire explosion of footsteps assailed the wooden stairs of the cottage. Maleko burst into the room out of breath and sweating almost as much as his aunt. Kapono was hot on his heels.

"Mr. Jun said the men are all in the far fields today," the boy panted.

"The wires in Honoka'a must be down," Kapono said. "Mr. Jun is telegraphing the doctor in Hilo. He will ride for Mr. Lanthier and the others, but it will be some time before someone comes either way. Is she going to be all right?"

Anias and Philomena exchanged a passing glance that was not lost on the panicked Maleko.

"You have to do something!" He entreated his friend. "You know you can! You must!"

"What is he talking about, Philomena?" Anias turned to the girl who was visibly shaken by the request.

"I can't," she stuttered. "A bird is one thing, but—"

"You are a kupua!" Maleko beseeched. "You must try!"

"Keiki!" Kapono protested.

Anias decided that indeed there was more to the young girl than she had noticed heretofore, and having nothing in her own bag of tricks that might remedy the situation, encouraged her with a nod to try what she might.

"What if it doesn't work?" Philomena fretted as she approached the sick bed. "You will hate me! I am not a kupua. I am not even a Kanaka whatever."

Maleko snickered despite the tense situation, and that was enough for Philomena to feel grounded enough to focus on the task at hand.

"You *are* a kupua," Maleko encouraged. "Makana Kealoha said as much, and she is never wrong. I do not know why—or how—but like it or not, that is what you are. Now, do the thing, please!"

The thing? Anias wondered. *Exactly what went on when these two ran out from breakfast to meet the day every morning?*

Philomena approached the shivering Noelani and removed the damp Ti leaves from her forehead. Taking a moment to decide how to best go about her work—Maleko's auntie was much bigger than an injured mamo bird—she knelt down and cradled the woman's head and trunk into her own thin chest.

Closing her eyes, she imagined a cooling wind moving makai down the eastern face of the mountain and blowing Noelani's fever out to sea. All at once, she became the cooling wind. Philomena saw herself travelling over the rich volcanic soil, rustling the ʻŌhiʻa Lehua trees and their bright red and yellow flowers as she went.

Maleko, Anias, and Kapono watched in wonder as the color returned to Noelani's skin. They didn't notice that Philomena was slipping out from under her until her limp body hit the bare floor.

"What happened to her?" Noelani asked, sitting up in bed and following the pair's gaze to the prostrate girl. "Do I smell Mr. Jun's potato soup?"

Chapter Twenty-Six
MILAKALE, HAWAI'I, KINGDOM OF HAWAI'I | 1889

26:1 Fox found himself standing at Madame Wei's shack not really sure how he got there. *I was speaking with Alexander and he offered me the pulpit at Milakale,* he struggled to remember the events of the morning. *How that came to this, however... I must have been overwhelmed. This damnable heat!*

Fox was even more surprised to find that he was holding the leather satchel that—he knew without looking—contained his opium pipe, the very same pipe that somehow had survived the fiery cataclysm at the Fiesta revival before following him unbidden across the ocean.

"Something here is not exactly kosher," he proclaimed, and turned to walk back to a more socially appropriate corner of the Lanthiers' vast plantation, blundering full on into the swinging paper lantern with the crocodile motif. "Blast Khadae and his skilamalink meddling!"

"Reverend Fox, what a surprise!" A voice at his ear purred and led him by the elbow back toward the open door. "You must be careful, it is easy to become ensnared within my lanterns; that one in particular. Perhaps I should move it."

Fox entertained a vision of being trapped within a giant version of the lamp. *Or will I have become small?* He pondered before shaking out of his reverie and recognizing that the proprietress herself had indeed captured him.

"Madame Wei," he stuttered, "you will have to forgive me, but I seem to be at a bit of a loss as to what I am doing here."

"Of course, reverend," Wei enchanted, "as are many who find themselves at my door. Let's get you out of this hot sun, shall we? Come in, let me serve you a cool drink while you find your bearings."

Wei led Fox into the cool antechamber of her hua-yan jian. Once accustomed to the dim light, he cut his gaze over to the familiar red silk drape with the golden dragon. A shiver shot up his spine as he remembered how the last time he had crossed the threshold the interior of the opium den had morphed into a hellish battlefield scene before his eyes.

"Mr. Khadae has told me that you have come here from California," Wei sang in a low, soft voice. "I too, left Jiù Jīnshān, Old Gold Mountain, to come to Hawai'i."

"I'm sorry," Fox shook his head in an attempt to clear the cobwebs that were threatening to coalesce over his consciousness, "where now?"

"It is I who should be sorry," Wei gave a small performative bow. "Old Gold Mountain is what the Chinese call San Francisco. Unironically, if you can believe it."

Fox noted the slip in Wei's pantomime of what many Westerners would expect from a middle-aged Chinese woman and made a mental note to listen to her more closely on the off chance that she gave up a clue as to what her real game might be.

"Reverend Fox, if I may be so bold," Wei began, "it is well within my professional purview to be able to recognize a man who is under a lot of pressure. Has island life not turned out to be the sanctuary that you hoped it would be?"

Fox laughed in spite of himself. "Madame, I can honestly say that I have never seen the like; it is an extraordinary place to be sure. I am afraid, however, I haven't had the opportunity to really get my mind around it."

"Too busy performing miracles, I suppose," Wei gently teased. "There is another type of man that I have learned to discern at a glance over the years, and if I am not being too forward, I believe that I am speaking to one now.

Fox began to protest before the familiar pull of his craving stayed his tongue. It was merely a matter of moments before Fox was laid out on one of Wei's pallets and the proprietress herself was attending to him. All of his doubts and concerns about the new strange chapter in his life were swept away in a great exhalation of bitter smoke.

As Fox settled back, he was relieved that the scene of battlefield carnage did not reemerge out of the shadows of the opium den. To his ultimate dismay, however, the room disassembled and rebuilt itself as the orphanage where he lived as a child.

26:2 Ten-year-old Mordikai Fox lay back on his cot and stared up at the ceiling of the Saint Gerard Majella Home for Fatherless Boys and tried to imagine himself somewhere else. Anywhere else. The very word "home" in the orphanage's maundering name pained him whenever he passed the wooden sign at the front of the property. The orphanage had certainly *housed* Fox since both of his parents had been killed in a train accident, but the Majella—as the boys called it—was certainly no home.

He had just about succeeded in projecting his consciousness to a deserted tropical island—as far as he was concerned, Robinson Crusoe didn't know how good he had it—when one of the nuns whom Fox had long suspected had devoted her life to making him miserable shouted out his name.

"Fox!" The holy banshee screeched. "Mordikai Fox! You have a visitor. Make yourself presentable and report to the office immediately."

"A visitor! Perhaps a gentleman caller—" the other boys in the drafty barracks taunted. "You must make yourself presentable now, Foxy. Good luck with that. Har! Har!"

Fox stuck out his middle finger and presented it to the room so that all might see it. "Get thee bent," he declared in the deepest senatorial voice he could muster. *Who the blazes could want to see me?* He wondered as he sniffed his only shirt and found it to be a mile past pristine.

"Is that the best you could do?" The nun growled as she intercepted Fox, grabbed an ear, and steered him toward the office.

"You know darn well I know the way!" He protested as he twisted out of the nun's grasp and ran straight into the strangest looking man he had ever encountered.

"Hello there," the stranger's cadaverous visage gazed down on him from an implausible height. The man held a black silk top hat in one hand and a walking stick capped with a lizard head in the other. "Do I have the pleasure of meeting the esteemed Master Fox at last?"

Fox looked back at his tormentor who merely glared before turning back to whatever she did when she wasn't busy finding fault with everything about him.

"Might do," Fox prevaricated. "What is it to you?"

"Well, son," the man smiled, immediately causing Fox to wish that he had not, "it may very well mean a great deal to me. A great deal indeed." The visitor stuck out his bony hand and Fox involuntarily recoiled from his touch. The man either did not notice or was used to the reaction.

"The name's Akram Khadae, anecdotalist, purveyor of fine goods, friend to the gentry and proletariat alike."

"Fair enough. What does any of that have to do with me?"

"An inquisitive mind! What a pleasure to experience honest American curiosity out here in the—if I may be so rude—hinterlands."

"It means nothing to me," Fox permitted. "I am not a big booster of these particular boondocks. Why are you here, Mr. Khadae? What do you imagine that I can do for you?"

"It is more of a case of what I may be able to do for you," Khadae rubbed his hands together, which to Fox sounded exactly like a dead tree branch scraping against the side of the orphanage in the middle of the night.

"All right. What can you do for me, Mr. Khadae, and more importantly, what compels you to make the effort?"

"I know that you are young, Mordikai... May I call you that?"

"You may call me anything you like, but a flapdoodle," Fox replied, standing as straight and tall as his ten years would allow.

"Ah," Khadae chuckled, "I would never take the liberty. I don't suppose that there are too many opportunities for a good wager in this institution. You see, Mordikai, I am a bit of a gambler myself, and if there is one thing I truly detest, it is to lose a bet. You can understand that, can't you?"

"I can," Fox admitted. "I just don't see what—"

"Please," Khadae interrupted, "let me finish. I once bet big on a losing proposition, and it nearly cost me everything. I learned from that experience, and you might say that I prefer to hedge my bets ever since. If I may again be so bold, you seem to have quite the vocabulary for a boy your age. I find it remarkably refreshing."

"I read quite a lot," Fox admitted. "There isn't a lot else to do around here."

"Excellent, excellent," Khadae again rubbed his hands together, this time causing the hair on the back of Fox's neck to crawl. "Might I give you a book?"

"You may indeed, sir. I have long finished everything I could find around here," Fox reached out to take the black covered gift, but almost dropped it when he saw what it was. "A Bible? Did you miss the sign out front? You can't swing a dead cat in here without hitting a Bible. Thank you anyway, Mr. Khadae. I have read it. More times than I prefer to count."

Khadae again chuckled—a sound that Fox found even worse than when he rubbed his hands together—and pushed the book into the boy's hands. "It is, ah, perhaps a different take on events than you may be used to."

"I don't follow."

"Exactly, my son!" Khadae exclaimed. "You strike me as a young man with a head on his shoulders. A lad that is unafraid to make his own assumptions—unless I am mistaken."

"Now, let's not be hasty," Fox gripped the book as Khadae pantomimed taking it back. "I can give it a look-see. Like I said, I've finished everything else. You still haven't answered my question, though, why me? How do you even know that I exist?"

"Therein lies the rub, doesn't it? How can any of us know that we truly exist, unless we beat against the bars of our internment? Furthermore, why would a creator make—and then abandon—us to stumble along in an indifferent universe? What does that say about His/Her/Their culpability?" Khadae poised himself to further expound on his philosophical treatise when he realized that he was quickly losing the boy. "Forgive me, I am getting ahead of myself. I have been searching for you for many years, Mordikai. You see; I knew your parents. Briefly."

"My parents?" Fox gasped. "Where did you meet my parents?"

"On a train. Listen, I must be going but I have something else for you. I have quite enjoyed our little chat; I almost wish that you would remember it. Now, after meeting you, I am quite certain that you will find your way in this world, perhaps this will help you arrive on time," Khadae declared as he handed Fox a silver pocket watch.

"Thank you, sir!" Fox exclaimed, marveling at the engraved cover of the watch. "Will I see you again, Mr. Khadae?"

"I am quite sure of it, Mr. Fox," Khadae said, turning to leave. "Don't be late."

Chapter Twenty-Seven
SAN FRANCISCO, CALIFORNIA, UNITED STATES OF AMERICA | 1889

27:1 Urias and Hendry stood mute in a relentless drizzle blowing in from San Francisco Bay, each man lost in his own thoughts. If there was anything good to be found about the damp, it did help keep down some of the Butchertown funk.

"Where is that damned carriage?" Hendry finally spat. "I told that fool to give us one hour!"

"Where do we go from here?" Urias asked. "You and I have both marched into the mouth of our separate hells and lived to spit, but that charnel house, Niall... Something must be done."

"And something shall," Hendry declared as he spotted a pair of jostling lanterns signaling the return of the hansom cab in the dark. "We are headed up to Nob Hill, my good man. There very well may be something we can do, but I'm afraid we shall have to disturb the haut monde. Do try to project having money so we aren't shot for being vagrants."

Urias laughed despite the atrocities the night had already provided. "And how do you suggest I do that?"

"Prerogative, my friend," Hendry explained. "Remember, it is our God-given right to be wherever we choose to be, and the Devil can take the man who dares to question that privilege."

"And that works for you, does it?" Urias' eyebrow betrayed his skepticism.

"It has yet to fail me," Hendry held the carriage door and inspected the disheveled Urias as he ducked his head to climb in. "Of course, there is always the first time. Perhaps you should wait with the horse. You are starting to smell alike."

"Color me impressed," Urias sighed. "I don't think I will ever willingly use my nose again after this episode."

The character of the City's streets began to change as the carriage climbed away from the docks and warehouses of the waterfront. Urias began to notice ornate wrought iron gas lamps passing outside, ghostly orbs further abstracted by condensation dripping down the windows of the cab. Lavish or not, the lamps were no match for the fog. Only the morning sun, finally threatening to make an appearance, had any chance against the gloom.

Urias began to get curious about their destination, as the baroque mansions grew larger and more ostentatious the higher up California Street they climbed.

"So this friend of yours," he probed, "is this the party that hired you to find Mordikai?"

Hendry considered his reply, a sign that automatically put Urias on alert.

"Something like that, yes," Hendry finally offered. "Listen, if we do get an audience with O Elefante, do not say anything about his bollocks.

"Excuse me?" Urias choked. "I don't know where to start with that. The Elephant?"

"Also, do not call him that," Hendry warned. "We will both end up washing up on Ocean Beach."

"Don't call your mysterious benefactor 'The Elephant' or make fun of his balls? I can handle that." Urias sat back against the padded seat and gazed out the window at the Impressionist scene beyond. "We are moving into serious real estate here, is Mr. Not-The-Elephant a railroad magnate or something?"

"Something like that, yes," Hendry answered like a prevaricating parrot. "Let us just say that he is an associate of the Association."

"That certainly clears things up."

"Listen, Aaron," Hendry emphasized, "you and I are alike in many ways. There are few things on God's good green that I savor more than taking the piss out of some bumptious cretin, but there are men you can fuck with, and those you cannot."

"And O Elefante—"

"If he didn't invent the later category, the bastard bought it, carved his name into it, and left it for dead."

"Charming."

The house lots began to resemble the grounds of European palaces—terraced, immaculately groomed, and providing enough of a buffer to keep the stinking, and occasionally revolting, masses at arm's length. The mesmerizing clopping of the horse pulling its load up California's steep grade finally came to a stop at a corner that could have been Mt. Olympus; it was so far removed from where the two men just left.

"Have we died?" Urias quipped as he donned his Stetson and stepped to the road.

"Not yet," Hendry sighed, "but mind what I told you."

"Please, Mr. Hendry," Urias feigned offence, "I am a professional."

Hendry glanced down at the man's brace of Colts hanging low on his hips. "Let's hope it doesn't come to that, shall we?"

The carriage did not wait as the two men stepped through a waist-high iron gate, the spires of which were topped with finials that looked to Urias as if they had been sharpened to a razor's edge that morning.

The pair climbed a hedged ziggurat toward what certainly wasn't the largest mansion on the summit but was the most distinctive. Whereas the other kings of American industry opted for hiding behind imposing facades, monumental walls that glared down disapprovingly on passerby. The three-story pile that loomed atop the uppermost terrace before them was laid out like a five-pointed star, each point widened into a blunt transept. If it wasn't for the gingerbread-heavy gable denoting the location of the front door, Urias imagined the evening could have been spent circumnavigating the mansion indefinitely looking for an entrance.

Having summited the landscaping, Hendry was about to knock on the heavy oaken front door when it swung open of its own volition.

"Niall Hendry, what an honor," a chestnut-colored gentleman in a dark maroon tailored suit welcomed him from across the threshold. His shock of white curly hair glowed in the moonlight. "And who, may I ask, is your companion this evening?"

"Saturnino Adão, may I present the conspicuous Aaron Urias, most recently the aide-de-camp of one Reverend Mordikai Fox."

"Really?" Adão's face lit up. "Your reputation precedes you, senhor. My employer will be most interested in meeting you in person. Gentlemen, if you please," he motioned for the men to enter.

"Senhor Urias, if I may impose, the master of the house has developed a severe lead allergy over the years. If you could leave your firearms here, they will be well taken care of, I promise you."

Urias cut a glance over at Hendry who merely shrugged and gave a nod. He handed over the guns while noting the exits and possible blind spots within the hall.

"You two will not have to fight your way out of this house," Adão assured the men when he noticed Urias' furtive looks. "We have received you both as honored guests, and so you shall remain at very least until we part company. I should hope that designation would remain in place in perpetuity. Right this way, gentlemen."

Adão led the pair into the center of the mansion where the closeness of the entryway gave way to a huge open atrium three stories tall. A stained glass skylight forty feet above their heads began to show a hint of dawn, while riveted iron works, a nod to the owner's background in heavy construction, bolstered the polished dark wood of the upper balconies. The walls surrounding the ground floor gallery were covered in oil paintings of pastoral scenes punctuated by those of dark and relentless jungle.

"Quite the eclectic collection of art," Urias remarked, receiving a hard glance from both Hendry and Adão. "What did I say?"

"How much has Senhor Hendry told you of Senhor Rodolfo's business ventures?"

"Not a wit," Urias answered truthfully.

"Senhor is, shall we say, a man of vision; a man who looks at the world not as it is, but as it could be. Perhaps, as it should be."

"I am not here as an investor, if that is where you are headed, Mr. Adão."

"Please, call me Saturnino," Adão offered. "You misunderstand me, senhor, I only wish to soften the shock by giving you a little background, if I may."

Urias motioned for the man to continue while Hendry remained silent, having experienced the full monologue before.

"You see, like his neighbors here on the hill, Senhor Rodolfo has his fingers in many pies, some legitimate," Adão searched for Hendry's gaze, but was left wanting, "some, shall we say, with a little more suco—a little more juice."

"If I may be so blunt," Urias remarked, "if you scratch a magnate, you will—more likely than not—find a scoundrel."

The hall became quiet enough for all three men to hear each other's heartbeats until Adão broke out in laughter. "Right you are, senhor! Right you are. And it takes a great man to embrace his shadow and fulfill his destiny."

Adão's tone turned evangelical.

"It is Senhor Rodolfo's predestination to be the man to finally unite the two greatest oceans of the world, ushering in an unseen era of prosperity and free trade."

"What he is taking his time to tell you is that our host is engaged in an effort to build a canal across Nicaragua," Hendry stole the man's thunder as he could sense that his friend's natural irascibility was about to derail Adão's discourse.

"I heard the French were digging across Panama," Urias thought out loud.

"Caralho, não!" Adão exploded. "Fuck those French! Panama is a graveyard. There is a beautiful lake that reaches halfway across Nicaragua. God has done the digging for us. Nicaragua is the place! You mark my words."

"I apologize," Urias demurred. "I spoke out of ignorance; I really don't follow news from down south."

"It is I who should apologize," Adão gave a curt bow, "The canal is a bit of a... sore spot, as I am sure you understand."

"I am afraid that I don't," Urias admitted, looking for help from Hendry.

"It was in the jungles of Nicaragua where Mr. Rodolfo contracted his affliction," Hendry offered belatedly.

"It is true," Adão bemoaned. "Whereas Panama claimed lives, Nicaragua claimed a great man's pride. I should let senhor explain for himself, I believe he is ready to receive you."

27:2 Adão led his guests to what looked to Urias as a small water closet and shut the door. The room was as ornate as any other corner of the mansion, with a cut crystal chandelier flooding the cramped quarters with electric light.

"If you don't mind, senhores, please take a seat, this technology is young, and the journey may be… enervante."

"What is this foolishness?" Urias demanded. "Why have you locked us in a WC?"

"Due to Senhor Rodolfo's infirmity, he prefers not to traverse the many stories of this house," Adão explained and began to whisper conspiratorially. "I have repeatedly tried to get him to set up his receiving chambers on the ground floor, but he is a man with very strong ideas, as you shall see. This room was designed by the very firm that recently worked on the Eiffel Tower in Paris."

Adão waited for a reaction from either man and when he realized that he was not about to receive the proper level of astonishment he felt was due, he elucidated. "France."

Hendry and Urias merely looked at each other blankly before the entire room jerked to life.

"Earthquake!" Urias exclaimed. "Good God, man, let us out of this cupboard before we are buried alive."

"Fear not, gentlemen," Adão laughed delightedly, "the only thing in danger of being buried here is the past. We are in the age of mechanical miracles! No longer shall the aged or infirm be subjected to a purely horizontal existence."

A persistent humming vibrated what the visitors came to understand was a sort of conveyance, a revelation made easier when the motion stopped and Adão opened the door to a completely altered scene; gone were the paintings of natural wonders, replaced by a massive library.

Books completely covered the walls of four of the five halls. The fifth was an open chamber with a pair of facing fireplaces containing the room like parentheses, and a short raised platform underneath a dimly lit chandelier at the far end.

"Mr. Hendry, you are a wonder, sir!" A baritone voice boomed from an open litter occupying pride of place upon the stage as if the men had just missed a production of a colonial-themed farce. The ornate sedan sat at an angle toward arriving visitors, both to provide space for the lifting poles at either end and to present its tenant in the best light. "I asked you to find news of Mordikai Fox, and you bring me Aaron Urias in the flesh."

As the men's sight slowly adjusted to the dark of the office, they could make out a gentleman of a similar skin tone as Adão, but where the majordomo banked his natural temperament out of a sense of decorum, the seated figure radiated a commanding presence.

The man's curly black hair was cropped close to his skull except for the top, which was combed backward and resembled a great wave about to break on the smooth beach of his forehead. A rounded graying beard softened the man's severe jaw, and a wide handlebar moustache gave him an air of displaced European aristocracy. In front of his steel gray eyes a pair of pince-nez eyeglasses floated as if enchanted. The only detail that seemed out of place was a vividly striped Mexican serape that covered his lower extremities.

"Come closer, gentlemen," the figure beckoned and pushed his torso up to a straighter bearing. "Tell me, what news of the reverend and his charge?"

"What did you say?" Urias choked. "How could you possibly know about—?"

"My dear man," the man explained, "money knows all. Or at least hears all. I needed to confirm the rumors before executing my plan.

"I'm sorry; I have been very rude. Let me introduce myself. My name is Edgar Bartolmeu Rodolfo. It is not a name that I expect you are familiar with as I spend a good deal of money in order to keep it that way. There, seeing how everyone knows each other now, how about enlightening me as to where that slippery pair have gone off to?"

"With all due respect, Mr. Rodolfo," Hendry finally spoke up, "not so fast. We have a favor to ask."

Rodolfo roared with laughter causing the shawl to partially slip from his bare legs. Forewarned, Urias did not react when he saw how horribly disfigured the man was from the waist down. His afflicted scrotum was the size of a pair of Hewlett's medicine balls, while his legs were as swollen and misshapen as an over-stuffed cloth doll.

"Might either of you be familiar with the macabre writings of one Edgar Allan Poe? 'But see, amid the mimic rout / A crawling shape intrude!' I am afraid that the conqueror worm consumes me while I am still very much alive—such is my misfortune. 'It writhes! It writhes with mortal pangs / The mimes become its food / And the angels sob at vermin fangs / In human gore imbued,'" Rodolfo intoned. "Except, of course, the smart money says that angels do not give a tin shit what happens to us unless they themselves are on the losing end of a wager.

"Gentlemen, what is your favor?"

"There is a ship, just returned from the Hawai'ian Islands, in quarantine off Hunter's Point. The owners have warehoused the afflicted in an iron works as if they were cargo," Hendry explained.

"Afflicted with what, may I ask?"

"I believe it is influenza," Urias spoke up. "I have never seen anything as voracious, even during the war. It is burning through the wretches like wildfire. They must be attended to—or all will perish."

"That is a sticky situation," Rodolfo pondered. "I can imagine that the City fathers are loathe to touch that particular flambeau to the dry tinder of public health."

"Damn it, man!" Urias roared. "Hendry here led me to believe that you are a 'City father,' if we must plead our case in front of someone with more clout, than I am afraid we must say goodnight. Time is of the essence."

"Well played, my friend," Rodolfo laughed unexpectedly. "Appeal to your adversary's last shred of vanity. I couldn't have done it better myself." Still laughing, he called Adão to his side and murmured directives into his ear before turning his attention back to his guests.

"Not to be overly dramatic, gentlemen," Rodolfo's gray eyes flashed with electricity. "It is done."

"Very well, then," Hendry capitulated, "it seems that Reverend Fox travelled by that very same ship to a place called Hilo on the Big Island of—"

"I know where Hilo is. What the hell does that sacripanta think he is doing out there?" Rodolfo growled. "More importantly, does he have the girl with him?"

"The girl?" Henry prevaricated, suddenly wishing he had been more careful about getting involved in Rodolfo's affairs in the first place.

"Apparently Fox took Philomena Gilliam with him to Hawai'i," Urias realized that he hadn't had time to fill Hendry in on all he had discovered in Fiesta.

"The same wee one—"

"The same," Urias looked from Hendry to Rodolfo who sat like a hungry raptor in his nest.

"Bollocks," the possible enormity of the situation dawned on Hendry. "Oh, bollocks!"

"You may be slow, coster, but don't let anyone tell you that if led by the nose you won't eventually see the water. A little bird has told me that interesting things have been happening in Hawai'i as of late."

"You knew all along where they were," Urias snarled.

"Knew? No. I had my suspicions, but it is always good to be certain of what is in a purse before you snatch it."

"What exactly are you planning to snatch?" Urias kept on him.

"Life, what else?" Rodolfo motioned to his stricken body. "A second chance. Redemption for my many, many sins."

"You can not possibly believe—" Hendry asked, incredulous.

"Granted, belief is not really my forte," Rodolfo admitted, "but I am afraid it is the last card I have to play. I intended to bring Reverend Fox and his miracle girl back to civilization and, who knows, perhaps I shall live to see my knees again."

"Let us just set aside how insane you sound right now," Hendry struggled to grasp the man's intentions. "What makes you think they would go along with your plan?"

"Easy," Rodolfo purred, "one word from me and your Reverend Fox is wanted for murder. Granted, extradition from a sovereign nation might be a bit of a nuisance at present, but I am pretty confident that it may be a different kettle of fish in the near future. Besides, I have an ace up my silky sleeve. If you gentlemen check behind that door in back of the library—"

PLATE SIX ✳ Niall Hendry

206

Chapter Twenty-Eight

28:1 Jun Jin always made a point of personally driving the buckboard wagon to meet the merchant ships at the Hilo docks. There were many benefits to living on an island, but many things Jun required in order to maintain the high standard he had long established in his kitchen had to be imported either from the east, where ships from China brought in bags of rice and tea, or from the west, where ships from the United States brought in anything else he might require. Luckily, working for the Lanthiers, money was rarely an obstacle.

"Mr. Jun!" A young Hawai'ian stevedore called to him from a pile of fifty-pound sacks of rice that had just been hoisted down to the wharf from the ship's hold. The dockworker quickly and efficiently freed the massive net cradling the precious cargo and signaled for it to be lifted away. "I don't know how you always manage to know the moment the ship touches land. You must smell this coming in on the wind."

"Years of practice, my son," Jun joked with the young man. "I can tell the volume of displaced ocean from your arriving ship."

The young man removed his white longshoreman's cap and combed his thick, black hair back from his forehead with his fingers, considering Jun's claim for a moment. "That is impossible!" He finally concluded.

"Perhaps," Jun admitted. "Perhaps not. Never underestimate a chef waiting for a delivery. We may resort to all sorts of arcane chicanery to get what we need. What do you have for me today?"

"One hundred pounds of rice from Hong Kong, and," the stevedore looked around conspiratorially although no one on the pier could care less what the two were up to, "twenty pounds of black rice—the emperor's own."

"Now, don't 'talk story' just so you can charge me more," Jun gently chastised. "Black rice is dear, but it is no longer the exclusive right of the emperor and hasn't been since the fall of the Taiping Heavenly Kingdom. I should know! I cooked for Emperor Hong Tianguifu himself!"

"Forgive me, Jun Jin, I should know better than try to get one over on an 'ūhā hope artist such as yourself."

"I will take that as a compliment," Jun gave the young man a short, quick bow."

"As well you should. I can imagine you sweet talking a turkey out of a tree if there was a need for it at your table."

"Ah! That gives me an idea for tonight's menu," Jun exclaimed. "You know, if you ever get tired of working these docks, I may have room for you in the kitchen."

"Exactly what you would say to the turkey, you old trickster," the stevedore laughed. "I'm fine right where I am, thank you."

28:2 Before heading up to the Big House, Jun parked his wagon in back of Wei Lei's shanty. The chef hoisted one of the heavy sacks up over his compact but powerful shoulders. The smaller bag of precious rice, he cradled in his arms as if it were a lost black lamb.

"If it isn't the 'Saint of Dào,'" Wei called from her clapboard back porch where she was smoking a clay pipe. "You have finally answered my prayers and graced me with your presence."

"There is no call for that, Lei," Jun laughed as he placed the small bag at the woman's feet and dropped the larger sack on the porch. "I brought you a peace offering. Forgive me if I have been otherwise engaged. Noelani Mahoe was stricken and it has been hard to get away."

"You say that from within spitting distance of my door," Wei countered. "It looks to me that you escaped just fine as soon as it suited you."

"That is a very interesting story. Invite me in for tea and I just might share it."

Wei's truculence soon proved to be nothing but a front as the two old friends sat down to share one of the proscribed seven Chinese necessities of life. Wei removed a delicate porcelain teapot and two cups from above her wood stove where a pot of water was already at the boil.

"It is almost as if you were expecting someone," Jun teased.

"It was you I have been expecting," Wei countered as she rinsed her porcelain with the hot water, "for more than a week now. The men were in danger of going hungry, and that is never a good thing for a man with a machete to be."

"This is true," Jun admitted, "but you know well that I do this out of compassion, not fear. If the cane cutters ever got a notion to rise up against the sugar barons, I am afraid they would find that a machete is no match for a bullet."

"Sometimes I wonder whose side you are on, Jun Jin," Wei mused as she filled her teapot with fragrant leaves and quickly rinsed them to wash away any impurities. She then refilled the pot and left it to steep, all the while holding Jun to account with an inquisitive stare. Wei's small but immaculate living space was soon filled with the enticing aromas of orchid and coconut.

"I am on my own side," Jun finally answered, "the same as you. We have come a long way, you and I. Although our paths may not look the same, they have proven over time to be concordant have they not?"

"I suppose so, old man," Wei laughed. "You are like a counter melody that I cannot seem to get out of my head."

"Who are you calling old?" Jun protested with a wry grin. "Did you not see me carry that weight on my shoulders as if it were nothing?"

"I did not say you were weak, my friend, merely decrepit. Perhaps this will help bring some youthful color to your ancient skin." Wei poured the perfumed tea into a fair cup with a strainer to catch the loose leaves and then poured Jun a cup, placing it to his right.

Jun lifted the delicate brew to better take note of its golden color. He then deeply inhaled the complex aroma before taking a sip. "Ah," he sighed, "Tie Guan Yin! You spoil me, Wei Lei."

"You cannot blame me for that," Wei chuckled, pouring herself a cup. "You were already rotten when I met you."

The two transplants took a moment to reflect on the long parallel journeys that had brought them together on a speck of volcanic rock in the middle of the world's biggest ocean. After their restful pause, Wei spoke first.

"So what kept you from my door? What happened to Noelani Mahoe?"

"You are too young to remember, but I lived though the influenza epidemic back home in the early '30s. We lost so many elders in my village—a whole generation ruined! I saw the same signs in young Noelani. She was drowning in her own breath, the same as if the ocean had captured her. She was as blue as a morning glory, Lei!"

"My goodness!" Wei responded, blowing on her tea.

"It would have been tragic enough, losing such a good worker," Jun continued, "but I have seen how that pestilence spreads. It would have been just a matter of time before the whole plantation fell ill."

"Something tells me that you are keeping the best part of this story to yourself, Jun Jin," Wei put down her tea and froze her visitor with a stare she had long honed to an edge that she could go out and cut sugar cane with if she so wished. "Where is Noelani now?"

"She is in the kitchen, preparing lunch."

"I am confused," Wei admitted, it was a feeling that she was obviously not used to or comfortable with. "I thought you said that the woman was at death's door."

"She was," Jun explained. "She simply refused to pass through. Mrs. Lanthier and the Fox girl took her some of my potato soup, and the next thing you know, she was as good as new."

"I know that you are not telling me that your cooking has the power to cheat death," Wei cautioned. "You are good, Jun Jin, but not that good."

"If only," Jun laughed. "I believe it was the girl. Do you remember when I told you of the so-called 'miraculous' resurrection of Alexander Lanthier at the hands of the reverend?"

"Of course," Wei rolled her eyes. "It was all anyone on this side of the island could talk about. Are saying that a power to heal runs in the Fox family?"

"Not exactly," Jun closed his eyes, attempting to clarify an idea that he had just begun to put together. "The night of Alexander's recovery I prepared a great feast—a miracle in its own right—and everyone from Honoka'a to Hilo was there. There was a storm that night and Noelani sent her nephew out to secure the stable doors. The Fox girl went with him. They came running back in the middle of the second course saying how the girl was recognized by the night marchers."

"Oh my," Wei exclaimed from behind her cup of tea. "How did that go over with the Hawai'ians?"

"Not very well, I can tell you. But that is not all. A few days later, I overheard the two of them talking about Maleko having introduced the girl to Makana Kealoha, the healer. Apparently the woman recognized her as well."

"What do you mean 'recognized'?"

"As a kupua," Jun shrugged. "As one of her own."

"That is ridiculous," Wei disclaimed. "Philomena is as white as a plumeria blossom!"

"Be that as it may—" Jun paused. "How do you know the girl's name, Lei?"

"What do you mean?" Wei innocently poured Jun another cup of Tie Guan Yin.

"The Fox girl, I never mentioned her by name," Jun ignored the steaming cup and searched the woman's face instead.

"Oh, I am sure that I must have heard it around," Wei waved her hand in an attempt to innocently indicate the ether.

"Your cane cutters and opium addicts have an interest in children visiting from California, do they?"

"That is not what I am saying."

"Who are you reporting to, Wei Lei?"

"What are you getting at, Jun Jin?"

"Please, old friend, do not attempt to prevaricate. You cannot fool an old fool. Have you been tasked with watching for just such an individual?"

"Enjoy your tea, Jin," Wei smiled. "It is my turn to tell you a story. When I am done, however, I have a customer that could use a ride back to the Big House."

28:3 As she did most afternoons, as soon as Noelani Mahoe was done serving in the Big House, she made her way to the family cottage with a late lunch for her brothers. She knew from experience that Maleko could not be trusted to stick around as he had a whole island to get under his feet, but the three men would usually muster around the small table set under a shady palm in front of the house.

"Look who it is!" Her oldest brother Kalani teased as she approached with cold chicken, rice, and macaroni salad. "It is our very own miracle kaikua'ana. Soon we will all be beholden to the 'alopeke 'ohana."

"We could do worse than thank the Fox family for saving our sister," Kapono objected. "What is wrong with you?"

"Perhaps he is just hungry," Noelani offered as she set the table. "You know that Kalani is ruled by his stomach."

"And what an imposing monarch it is!" Kapono teased. "Quickly, sister, pay tribute before we are all subdued."

"Very funny, you two," Kalani said, reaching for a chicken leg glistening with teriyaki glaze. "You will not be laughing when this haole magic helps to deliver the islands right into the hands of the Americans."

"You know what auntie used to say, 'Kuhi no ka lima, hele no ka maka,'" Kapono countered. "Where the hands move, there let the eyes follow."

"What does that have to do with this deviltry?" Kalani gestured with the denuded chicken bone.

"If there is a story here," Kapono explained, "it is only of healing. The reverend brought Mr. Lanthier back to life before our eyes. How can we fault him for that? And I saw his kaikamahine heal our very own sister! For that, I am willing to give the Fox 'ohana the benefit of the doubt."

"You three will never believe who I just saw Mr. Jun carry back from Madame Wei's!" Kekoa announced as he approached the rest of his family from across the courtyard. "Sister! It is good to see you looking so well!"

The youngest of the Mahoe brothers took a seat and began to heap food on the plate that was set for him, oblivious to the stares of his siblings. It wasn't until he had a mouthful of food that he bothered to look up.

"Who?" Noelani finally broke the silence.

"Who, who?" Kekoa mumbled as he chewed.

"What are you, a pueo?" Kalani retorted. "Whom did you see?"

"Look who is putting on airs," Kapono laughed, almost choking on his lunch. "I say, whomever did you discern, brother?"

"Enough!" Noelani interrupted the brothers' routine, knowing full well that it might go on for hours. "Tell us who you saw or put down the chicken."

"Very well," Kekoa feigned being hurt. "It was Reverend Fox, and he was higher than Mauna Kea!"

"Are you sure it was him?" Kalani gasped.

"Oh yes," Kekoa began filling his plate in earnest lest his sister cut him off. "As a matter of fact, I saw him just this morning talking with Mr. Lanthier. He is giving Fox run of the chapel."

The oldest Mahoe brother began to choke, causing Noelani to begin pounding on his wide back.

"Are you sure of that?" Kapono asked, ignoring the struggle to breathe that his older brother was fighting. "What about the pastor?"

"Lanthier has sent him packing," Kekoa replied. "What is the problem? We are trading one haole preacher for another. At least this one has done something for us."

"None of you understand the danger here!" Kalani finally caught his breath. "If Fox does have mana, and he is in bed with Lanthier and the annexationists, we are done for. Don't you get that?"

"Come on, now brother," Kapono soothed. "There is no evidence that Fox is interested in island politics. Maybe all he cares about is our salvation."

"In a pig's eye, he cares about us!" Kalani sputtered. "Mark my words, we should push them all into the sea before it is too late."

"And then what?" Noelani picked up the fight. "Do you think the Americans would take kindly to that? Perhaps we wait for the French to come back, cannons a' blazing? That ship has sailed, brother. We had better learn how to live with the friends we have."

"Friends? Pah!" Kalani spat into the red dirt. "Some friends: a junkie and his daughter. What friends are these?"

"She saved my life," Noelani whispered.

28:4 Philomena awoke in a strange but very comfortable bed with the afternoon sunlight streaming in through a set of impossibly delicate lace curtains. Her first thought was that she had died and gone to heaven, the bed was that comfortable, but then she saw Maleko grinning at her from across the room.

"Maleko!" She shouted, pulling the cotton sheets tight around her neck. "What are you doing in my room?"

"You're alive!" The boy bounded over and, leaving all sense of decorum behind, jumped up on the bed and began to bounce. "This isn't your room, silly! It is Mrs. Lanthier's, she asked me to keep an eye on you."

Upon remembering whose feather mattress he was jumping on, the boy hopped back off, careful to miss the carved walnut foliate scrollwork at the foot.

"What happened, Maleko? What am I doing in Mrs. Lanthier's bed?" Philomena asked, propping herself up against the equally intricate headboard as to better take in her surroundings and scan the room for her father's ghost.

"You saved her!" The boy exclaimed, jumping in place since he couldn't jump on the bed. "You saved Auntie Noelani and then you passed out. Mrs. Lanthier told me to watch you and tell her as soon as you woke up."

"Hold that thought, Maleko," Philomena stopped him and climbed out of bed, only belatedly realizing that someone had thankfully retrieved her nightclothes. "I need to get dressed, and then we need to go see Makana Kealoha. Do you know where to find her?"

"I think so... but," the boy stopped mid-jump, "what about Mrs. Lanthier?"

"I can't really explain what she will want to know until I speak with Makana. Meet me out by the stables!"

Minutes later, Maleko stood nervously in front the empty stall that usually housed Lucifer, waiting for Philomena. He had a good idea where the afternoon was going to go once he told his friend where they might find the healer and he was not happy about it.

"Maleko!" The girl shouted as she came stomping up, ready to go. "We have to get going if we want to reach the lava tube before it gets dark!"

"Lava tube? What are you talking about?"

"Makana Kealoha's lava tube!" She exclaimed. "We have to get going!"

"Wait, did you think Makana Kealoha lived in a cave?" Maleko doubled over in laughter. "That is so wrong!"

"What do you mean?" Philomena demanded. "Was that all a show? Let's have a laugh at the white girl's expense?"

"Please stop," Maleko begged as he wiped tears from his eyes. "You're killing me. I hardly have to make up a reason to laugh at you, white girl. Makana does commune there, but she doesn't live there... yet. I imagine that someday we shall have to put her bones up with the rest of the aumākua, but hopefully that is a long way off."

"Where are we going, then?" Philomena asked, looking down valley from their perch on the ridge.

"Do you know how to ride?" Maleko asked, resigned to his fate.

"Horses?"

"No, dolphins," Maleko quipped. "Of course, horses. What else is there? If you don't know how to ride, do you at least know how to hold on?"

Philomena flashed back to Fox extending his long-fingered hand from atop his steed the night her life changed forever.

"Of course I know how to hold on," she said. "What else is there?"

The pair was miles away from Milakale before Philomena thought to ask if Maleko was going to get into trouble for stealing a horse.

"We aren't stealing," the boy corrected. "We are merely borrowing. Besides, if I get a whipping, can't you just fix it?"

"I don't know if it works that way," Philomena shouted as the jungle foliage sped by. "Let's hope that we don't have to test it out."

Chapter Twenty-Nine

SAN FRANCISCO, CALIFORNIA, UNITED STATES OF AMERICA | 1889

29:1 Hendry and Urias left the moribund magnate listing on his litter and followed the walls of books to the opposite end of the floor. Neither man had noticed the small door as they came in even though it was the only area not covered in esoteric leather-bound tomes.

"Are you sure this is a good idea?" Urias asked the Londoner, his hand already on the polished brass nob.

"Oh, fuck no," Hendry ground out through gritted teeth. "Not a minute spent in this canker's company is a good idea. Of course, it is not like we have anything else to lose. We are a pair of houseflies picking our way through a spider web right now."

Urias turned to get a read on their host. *If he seems to be enjoying this a bit too much, I am done,* he thought. The tycoon merely waved him on, with no more passion than a flag on the Fifth of July.

Upon opening the door, the first thing that hit the pair was the smell. The room was no bigger or better furnished than a cell, and was filled with the stagnant air of a caged animal. A tarnished iron bed was bolted to the floor opposite the door and molded to it was a woman. A shock of white hair obscured her dirty face, but both men recognized her immediately.

"That son of a bitch!" Urias reflexively reached for a revolver that was not there.

For his part, Hendry marched back toward his benefactor and spat.

"You monster!"

"Do you mean to hurt my feelings, British?" Rodolfo grimaced. "I have long had Adão remove all of the mirrors in this pile, but I call myself that—and worse—every time I chance my reflection in a window, or a glass, or a puddle of piss."

"What is wrong with you?" Hendry kept at him like a bulldog. "You are not even human any more!"

"Do you imagine that is news to me?" Rodolfo bellowed. "Before you begin to psychoanalyze me in whatever manner is currently in fashion—before you tell me that my corpus simply betrays my inner corruption—I will stop you right there! I tried to do good works. I tried to drag this sorry century into a future of trade and international brotherhood! What did I get for my troubles? Damnation."

"Damn you, sir," Hendry cursed.

"Yes! Damn me," Rodolfo began to laugh. "Damn me! Damn you! Damn us all! God has long lost all interest in this bear pit and we must do what we can to climb out of it on our own. If it means standing on the backs of every other gutted dog, so be it. If I need to add a few more to the pile, I am more than willing to do that as well."

"Niall!" Urias called from the hidden chamber. "Leave him to his debasement and give me a hand in here."

"This is far from over," Hendry menaced before turning his back on Rodolfo who didn't feel the need to respond.

"Emilia," Urias knelt down over the prostrate woman. "Wake up! It is Aaron Urias. I have news."

Slowly, the narcotized woman opened her hazel eyes and struggled to focus on the man shaking her shoulders.

"Brother Aaron?" She fought to understand what was happening. "Am I dreaming? What are you doing here?"

"What am I doing here?" Urias gently rebuked the confused woman. "What the hell are you doing here? How did this maniac get ahold of you?"

"I... I don't remember," she attempted to shake the cobwebs out of her head. "Philomena! Where is Philomena?"

"Don't worry, I am going to take you to her, mark my words," he whispered. "You are going to have to be a little more patient."

"Gentlemen," Rodolfo called from across the library. "I must rest. I am afraid this magnificent evening is at an end. Mr. Adão will show you out. If you would be so good to return tomorrow, perhaps we can discuss how you may help me retrieve the girl from the *tropics*." The man's revulsion at even speaking the term was obvious.

As if summoned by magic, Adão appeared at the door to Emilia's prison. "Gentlemen, if you would be so good to accompany me—"

"I am not getting back in that box!" Urias declared. "I will take the stairs like a man. Where are they?"

Adão rolled his eyes and conceded the point. "This way, gentlemen."

29:2 The short walk from Nob Hill down to the North Beach neighborhood allowed Urias and Hendry to take some air and clear their heads. The two men started off down California Street, retracing the way they had arrived, each feeling as if they had aged years in the short time they spent in Rodolfo's mansion.

"We obviously need to rescue Emilia," Urias finally broke the hypnotic effect of their boot heels echoing on the empty road, a feeling only magnified by the pair's total exhaustion.

"Obviously," Hendry yawned.

"What is our plan?"

"I need a drink," Hendry sighed, pointing out the self-evident. "That is my plan. As your tailor, I suggest that you join me."

A half an hour later, the two were sitting at the battered wooden desk in Hendry's shop.

"Let me show you why I keep this old thing." Hendry pushed a hidden lever underneath the scarred surface. "Watch your fingers." Immediately, the desktop split in two and a spring-loaded wet bar appeared from within the hulk's interior.

"Nice trick," Urias said, salivating at the sight of an unopened bottle of Old Overholt nestled between two tumblers.

"This is carpentry," Hendry bemoaned, "the real trick is going to be getting our laudanum Madonna out of that mansion."

"Don't call her that," Urias came to Emilia's defense. "She has been through a lot. There is no telling what that cretin has been up to."

"Point taken," Hendry conceded, sliding a heroic pour of rye to his friend as a token of apology. "Even if we pull it off, he is never going to let it go, and he has the resources to follow us to the ends of the Earth. We may just have to shoot the wanker."

"I have seen enough killing in my time," Urias mused, downing the entire tumbler in one go. "As have you, I'm sure. I've found that I have lost the taste for it. If Rodolfo wants to chase me to hell and back, he is welcome to do so. I am no murderer."

Hendry merely raised one eyebrow in an imitation of his friend's signature look as he refilled his glass.

"Anymore."

"Fair enough. I doubt if Adão would be too happy with us if we killed O Elefante anyway. We would probably have to do him as well before he dedicated *his* life to getting revenge."

"What's this about killing an elephant?" Washburn's spirit rose up through the desk causing Hendry to drop the bottle of rye.

"Cor! A bloody fucking ghost!"

"Now is that anyway to greet the best investigator you two have on this case?" Washburn protested.

"He is not wrong," Urias reached through Washburn to pick up his whiskey.

"Hey, that tickles!" Washburn protested before reading the tenor of the room. "No it doesn't, I'm just messing with you."

"Niall Hendry, meet Jeremiah Erasmus Washburn III, or at least what is left of him."

"You two know each other?" Hendry asked, his mouth hanging open.

"It was Washburn who got us confirmation from the captain of the *Pride of Jefferson* about Fox's whereabouts."

"The captain?" Hendry mused. "The *dead* captain... I can see how your talents might come in handy, Mr. Washburn. Welcome aboard."

"Finally, a living that can appreciate talent when it sees it."

"O day and night, but this is wondrous strange!"

"Right back at you, Horatio," Washburn tipped his head. "So, what have you two rascals been up to?"

29:3 After filling Washburn in on their eventful evening, the two men retired to a pair of apartments Hendry kept above the shop. Meanwhile, the spirit sat scheming, passing his own head back and forth in thought. By the time the Sun began to rise, he was ready.

When Hendry came downstairs to make arrangements for Emilia's rescue, he saw Washburn waiting at the desk bar, left open in full bloom.

"Make yourself at home, ghost," he said, grabbing his coat and heading out the door to the already busy street. "We shouldn't be gone long."

"Oh, I am coming with you," Washburn asserted. "I wouldn't miss this for the world."

Hendry stopped in his tracks, curious. "I'm about to hire us a carriage, smoke. How do you travel? Bell? Book? Candle?"

"Very clever, living," Washburn tipped his head. "Since you asked, one of the perks of my condition is to be no longer burdened by the heavy yoke of geography. I can be anywhere—or nowhere—however, it is easier to throw my lot in with you ambulatory types. You are not completely useless, as you do help to bring a certain directional focus."

"Is that why you haunt Aaron Urias? Because he gets around?"

"Haunt?" Washburn fulminated. "I beg your pardon, sir. I do not haunt. Do you take me for a common spook? Have you heard a single 'boo' pass these gin-clear lips? No, you have not."

"Forgive me, Washburn," Hendry asked, actually chastened by the spirit's objection. "This is all a bit strange, and until very recently I thought that I was well familiar with strange."

"Yes, you have kept some interesting company, haven't you, Pearly King?"

Hendry, unnerved by Washburn's apparent omniscience, simply left. By the time he returned, Urias and Washburn were both waiting for him.

"What is the plan, gents? Our carriage awaits," Hendry announced, spending a moment choosing just the right hat for a rescue mission.

"If I may, my meat-covered comrades," Washburn began, "you should start by asking your man for the release of his prisoner. If he refuses to relent, leave him to me."

"And you imagine that you will be able sway his answer?" Urias asked.

"Sway?" Washburn parried. "No, I imagine that your man will be too busy pissing himself to rustle up a counter offer. Check. And. Mate."

"Fair enough, let's do this," Hendry said, deciding on a stiff-crowned hat with the side brims turned up toward heaven.

29:4 Urias and Hendry both recognized the distinctive aroma of an Egyptian cigarette on the wind as they pulled up to Rodolfo's mansion. Adão met the pair on the porch, stabbing out the pungent smoke on a wooden railing before addressing the visitors.

"The master is waiting," he swanned. "I take it the elevator is not called for."

"No, it is not," Urias deadpanned. "Tell me, major, where do you get those cigarettes?"

"Senhor Rodolfo has many connections, as you can imagine," the steward quipped as he motioned toward the stairs. "After you."

Rodolfo received the men much as he had the previous evening, dressed in a flowing caftan and perched upon his sedan chair like the Arabesque emir he imagined himself to be.

"Ah!" The magnate exclaimed. "I am glad to see that the two of you have come around to my way of thinking. When will you be leaving for the islands?"

"We will be leaving as soon as you release Emilia Gilliam into our care," Hendry spoke up. "We intend to reunite the girl with her surviving parent."

"Oh, that's rich!" Rodolfo broke into laughter. "Adão! Did you hear that? Our little haberdasher is quite the comedian! Seriously now, my sense of humor only reaches so far."

"Are you saying that you will not release Mrs. Gilliam to us?" Urias asked, eying the exits and positions of all players by hard-earned force of habit.

"What is this?" Rodolfo demanded. "Adão, have you not taken their arms?"

"They did not arrive with weapons, sir," the steward recalled, sensing a definite turn in the tide of events but unable to tell from which direction it might be coming.

"That is a 'no,' then?" Hendry gave the man one last chance.

"That is a 'no!'" Rodolfo exploded. "That is a 'fuck you very much!' That is a 'go straight to hell!'"

"Funny you mention that!" Washburn appeared, carrying his head like a picnic basket.

"Ho, ho," Rodolfo nervously laughed. "A specter? That is your play? Please, I have made deals with the devil himself. Do you expect me to be afraid of a ghost?"

"Is that what he told you he was?" Hendry finally made the connection. "You have thrown your lot with nothing but a pretender. Did he tell you that the girl could save you from your fate?"

"He did at that," Rodolfo side-eyed Washburn who had carefully put down his head in the corner of the room.

"Let me ask you, was it Khadae who sent you to Nicaragua in the first place?"

"It was a business opportunity," Rodolfo coughed. "Our Egyptian friend has his fingers in many pies."

"He is no friend of mine!" Hendry spat. "Or yours, you fool. You still can't see that he has played you from the start? I told him to bugger off years ago and had to fight my way back from hell. He is probably china and plates with the very worms that are destroying your body."

"Your problem, Hendry, is that I can never understand a fucking word you are saying."

"Understand this then," Hendry gave Washburn a nod. The head on the floor returned an exaggerated wink that was not lost on Rodolfo. "Khadae is not here to save you now. You deserve this."

"Deserve what, exactly?" Rodolfo mocked.

"This," Washburn's head answered with a tinge of sadness in his voice before his hands gripped either side of his tattered neck. As the ghost approached the immobile mogul, he continued to stretch the ragged hole out to the very limit of his widened arms and began to run toward the man as if to capture Rodolfo in a net of himself.

"Hold on, now!" Rodolfo attempted to forestall events that he belatedly realized he had lost control of.

"You think you understand worms, do you?" Washburn's head spoke from where it had rolled over on the carpeted floor. "My body still lies in a field where it was quite the feast for the little bastards. Let me show you what I have learned!"

Rodolfo moaned as he was engulfed by total darkness, the smell of copper and damp soil enveloping his entire being. All at once, he was overcome by the sensation of being eaten alive by hundreds of hungry creatures burrowing into his body from all directions, creatures blind and chewing.

The three men watched as the tortured man writhed on his pallet until he finally rolled off his perch onto the floor and came face to face with Washburn's head.

"Boo," the head taunted.

"It couldn't happen to a nicer fellow," Hendry finally broke the uncomfortable silence. "Adão, we will be leaving now. We trust the evacuation of the ship's crew and passengers will continue apace."

Adão watched the gray, malevolent cloud around Rodolfo dissipate then reconstitute as the lower six-sevenths of Jeremiah Erasmus Washburn III, now closer to its missing piece. "It is as good as finished," he promised.

"Always a pleasure, Saturnino," Hendry tipped his hat before moving to assist Urias with collecting Philomena's mother.

Chapter Thirty

30:1 From her attic windows, Anias Lanthier watched the ignominious return of Jun Jin and Reverend Fox to the heart of Milakale. Unnerved by Philomena's apparent healing of Noelani Mahoe, she had once again turned to her Celtic magic for guidance.

The last time she had asked her taise for insight from the spirit world, she had been shocked by what her divination had revealed. This time, however, the advice she gleaned from casting her collection of psychically charged icons was ambiguous at best.

"Time to ask the experts, I suppose," she sighed as she returned the items to their bag, rolled up the embroidered cloth, and returned everything—yew box and all—to the chifforobe.

Her father had taught the young Anias how to seek the council of certain birds, the way he had learned as a boy in the Irish Connacht. Upon following her new husband to the tropics, she was glad to learn that the species that held the greatest connections to her teaching all had island cousins that were more than happy to tell her what they thought on all sorts of topics.

Anias again rummaged in the wooden cabinet and came up with a set of tarot cards and a cut crystal flower vase in which she placed a single feather from the 'io, the Hawai'ian hawk. She spread out the major arcana on a table under the window, which she opened wide, and put the vase on the sill. With all the pieces set out, she began to meditate.

Before long, the tell tale self-referential cry of 'io reverberated over the courtyard as the afternoon light streaming into the attic was broken by the shadow of a soaring bird of prey.

A regal raptor with a white chest streaked with chocolate brown appeared, its broad wings filling the double window frame before it perched on the sill, folded in its wings, and stared at her over its shoulder, the hawk's piercing black eyes as sharp as its black beak.

"Welcome, 'Io," she addressed the bird. "I have need of council from nā 'aumākua, if you would be so kind to convey my message. I realize that this method is not your preferred way to communicate, but I fear that time is short."

The hawk merely stared at her as if impatiently waiting for her query.

"Proud 'Io, can you ask the spirits if I have made a terrible mistake by bringing Reverend Fox to Milakale?"

The hawk considered the question for a moment, strutting back and forth on the windowsill before hopping down onto the table, squarely landing on one of the tarot cards.

Anias carefully approached the bird as if not to spook it, but the 'Io had no intention of going anywhere. Inspecting the hawk's talons, she saw that it had landed on a card labeled *The Hierophant* in gilt script. The illustration showing between the bird's bright yellow digits revealed a wise priestly character holding a scepter in one hand with the other raised in a sign of blessing.

"I see," Anias murmured, smiling, "the symbol of the link between this world and the next. This can only be a good sign, right, 'Io?" A feeling of relief flooded through her knowing that Fox's appearance meant the arrival of a teacher who would provide wisdom and a deeper understanding of spiritual matters, a roll she had hoped all along that the reverend would fulfill.

The hawk cocked its head as if unable to believe her question, hopped around to face the window and promptly defecated onto the card.

"Oh, my," Anias exclaimed and covered her mouth with a delicate hand. The bird, as if to underscore its pronouncement, let out a screeching 'io and flew out the window, disappearing into the jungle expanse below Mauna Kea.

30:2 Maleko drove the borrowed palomino as nimbly and naturally as a fish swimming through water; while Philomena fastened herself to her friend's torso like a starfish on a rock. The long, sharp elephant grasses on either side of the trail leading to Honokaʻa seemed at times to be trying to knit together, as if the road were working to either heal or hide itself in front of their eyes. The young pony beneath them would hear none of it, however, as it dove through the matting as if its tail was on fire.

Her face smashed against his sweating back, Philomena inhaled the familiar scent of the boy who had become her best friend in the world. *Perhaps my only friend in the world,* she thought as she felt his young, strong heart pounding as they rode. Her attention was brought back into sharp focus as Maleko called out for her to hold tight as the palomino leapt across a creek that cut across the path.

"Maleko!" She cried. "We want to get there alive."

"I thought you said you knew how to hold on," the boy only half-kidded his nervous passenger.

"I thought you said you knew how to ride," she shot back, immediately hugging her friend tighter as the pony flew over a tangle of exposed banyan roots.

By the time the pair reached Honoka'a and hitched the tired, but exhilarated, steed to a post in front of one of the only wooden buildings open on the dusty street, Philomena had almost forgotten why they had come. She unexpectedly missed having Maleko close.

"What?" The boy asked, having felt her gaze on the back of his neck.

Philomena—startled that he was able to tell that she had been looking at him with a longing she didn't expect—turned red and muttered, "Nothing. What do you mean? I wasn't—"

"What is wrong with you?" Maleko asked, turning to scrutinize the girl's condition. "Listen, you had better get it together before we bother Makana. Are you alright?"

"I am fine," she stated while straightening to her full height, noting that she was now almost as tall as the bewildered Hawai'ian boy.

"Fine," Maleko motioned for her to enter the building. "After you, then."

Philomena pushed through the planked batwing doors to find that she was standing in a dark saloon. The grizzled giant behind the bar looked up only long enough to point with a filthy rag toward the back of the room. She turned to tell Maleko that they must have entered the wrong place but he was already looking past her toward the cool shadows beyond.

"Sista'!" The familiar voice called out. "And little cousin, too. What a nice surprise. I was just thinking of you two."

"Sorry to barge in like this, auntie," Maleko approached, contrite. "Things have been very strange up at the Big House. We... she needs your advice."

"Come and sit down with Makana," the woman motioned toward two empty chairs at her small table. "Strange is often just a state of mind. Perhaps I can help you see the situation in the right light."

"The situation is that she is a kupua!" Maleko exclaimed, unable to contain himself.

"Keiki, let the young woman speak for herself. If she does possess the gift, she just might turn you into a honu if you don't."

"You told me that you couldn't do that!" Maleko wheeled around to face Philomena and to check what she might be doing with her hands. Both women burst into laughter, the tension completely expelled.

"Very funny," Maleko moped. "I am going to go brush down the horse. At least I know where he stands."

"Yea, out in front!" Kealoha parried.

The high-pitched laughter only doubled in intensity as Maleko stomped his way out of the bar.

Maleko removed a brush and a carrot from the palomino's saddlebag and began the meditative job of grooming the pony while it enjoyed its treat.

"Nice horse," a gravelly voice remarked from the direction of the street. Maleko turned to see Khadae standing closer than he would have liked to see and eating a carrot of his own.

Did you just take that out of the saddlebag? Maleko almost said aloud. The boy could see the man's sharpened teeth masticating the root mercilessly. He realized, uncomfortably, that the man's manducatory display was meant for him rather than servicing any hunger the man felt—at least any hunger for root vegetables.

"Thanks," Maleko offered up the smallest response he felt he could get away with and turned back to the pony.

227

"That's one of Lanthier's, isn't it?" The man absolutely did not get the hint.

"It is," Maleko admitted, realizing that denying the horse's provenance would probably just keep the man around longer.

"Might I ask what brings the two of you so far afield? So to speak." The man stepped up on the wooden sidewalk next to Maleko so that he could see orange bits of carrot still impaled on the man's shark-like teeth.

Kāmohoali'i? Maleko wondered for a moment if the shark god had taken a human form, but quickly remembered that his shape shifting abilities were limited to aquatic creatures. Or were they? If the stranger could read his thoughts, he did not show it. He merely waited for Maleko to respond to his line of questioning.

"Business," the boy again offered as little as possible.

The man laughed, an abrasive bark that put Maleko even further on edge. "What business does a kanaka 'u'uku have so far from home?"

"None of yours," Maleko stopped brushing the pony and faced the stranger, bristling at being referred to as a "little man."

"Fair enough," the man changed strategy. "I am afraid I have been terribly rude. My name is Mr. Khadae," the man stuck out a hand that Maleko found he had no intention of touching. Ever.

"How nice for you," Maleko uttered. "If you will excuse me, I'm afraid I must finish attending to my horse." Maleko turned away from the unwanted visitor hoping that he would finally walk on.

"Alexander Lanthier's horse."

"Excuse me?" A flush of anger flashed upon his face, but the boy tried to maintain an air of civility.

"It is Alexander Lanthier's horse," Khadae repeated. "Isn't it?"

"I already told you it was, Mr. Khadae. Can I help you further?"

"They do not look kindly upon horse thieves in Hilo, Mr. Mahoe." Khadae began circling the pony, which whinnied nervously, tossing its white mane back and forth.

"I'm not a horse thief, Mr. Khadae," Maleko stammered. "I told you, I am here on business."

"Ah," the man purred, which caused the palomino to paw the ground. "A businessman! I, too, consider myself a businessman, Mr. Mahoe. From way back."

"How do you know my name?" Maleko demanded, knowing full well that he hadn't ever had any intention of revealing that information.

"You see, that is *my* business, I know things," Khadae explained. "And the things that I do not yet know, I have a gift for finding out."

"I will be sorry I asked this—but maybe it will get help rid of you, Mr. Khadae—what are you looking to find out from me?"

"You see!" Khadae rejoiced. "A true born businessman! It is indeed a pleasure to interact with someone who understands the craft. A transactional relationship is the only kind you can trust, Mr. Mahoe. It does my black heart well to see the younger generation able to understand that stone cold fact."

"I am listening," Maleko gave up any gesture of grooming the horse and stood facing the man. "All I am hearing is you talking. What. Do. You. Want?"

"Forgive me, Mr. Mahoe," Khadae gave a short bow. "Sometimes I get carried away."

"I wish."

"Information, Mr. Mahoe. Nothing less. Nothing more. You and the girl have become quite close have you not?"

"I won't disrespect you by pretending that I don't know to whom you are referring," Maleko channeled one of his uncles and took a step toward Khadae. "Please don't disrespect me by not understanding what I tell you. Perhaps you want to write this down."

"I think that I am capable of remembering what you say. Please."

"If I see you around again—"

"No, I beg you, stop right there," Khadae laughed out loud. "Let me remember our conversation in a positive light. It is a shame about the horse theft charge. Who is going to believe a little man when he says that he 'borrowed' it."

"I think that you forget whose island you are on, Mr. Khadae. My intentions are true, and will be recognized as such. Yours, on the other hand—"

"Things are changing, Mr. Mahoe," Khadae touched the edge of his hat with his cane and turned to go. "I only hope that you end up on the right side of it all. I'm afraid the delicate dance of repartee is in danger of falling out of fashion and I would so enjoy watching you come into your own. Until then."

Maleko and the palomino watched Khadae walk down the street until they were both certain that he wasn't turning around. Once sure that the man was truly gone, he turned and ran back into the saloon. Philomena and Kealoha were deep in conversation in the exact spot he had left them.

"We have to go," he announced.

"Maleko, I can't go right now," Philomena protested. "Makana is teaching me what I need to know."

"What you need to know is that some lōlō kanapapiki is on his way to make life miserable for me... us."

"She is right, keiki," Kealoha began.

"Don't call me that!" Maleko exclaimed. We, she and I, have to go. Do you understand that, kahunas?"

"What I have to teach our sister is more important than anything, Maleko," Kealoha said and cast her eyes down at the table. "My time is short."

"Makana!" Maleko howled in frustration. "What do you want me to do? We have to get back to Milakale. Now."

"Leave her here, Maleko Mahoe," Kealoha grabbed his hand and looked deep into his eyes. "I know that you can handle questions if they come up."

"If they come up?" Maleko knew the way the conversation was headed, but kicked against its sides just the same. "If I return without the princess of Milakale, I am shark food!"

"Maleko!" Philomena protested. "That is not fair! I thought we were friends."

The boy, knowing that he had lost any and all arguments with the pair, accepted his fate.

"Very well," he sighed. "Whatever you need to tell her, I would make it quick, though. I can't stop Reverend Fox or Mr. Lanthier from coming out here and dragging her back as soon as they get my uncles to whip it out of me."

"Thank you!" Philomena jumped up and planted a quick kiss on Maleko's cheek, which left the boy without any further words to say or the capacity to do so if he had them.

"Kahunas," he muttered as he mounted the palomino and pointed it back toward home.

30:3 Alexander sat back in a wicker chair and enjoyed the midday shade provided by his lānai. As was their routine, Noelani had brought him out a pitcher of fresh-squeezed lemonade—bolstered by a healthy splash of Caribbean rum—and he took pleasure in holding a cool glass up to his cheek, letting drops of condensation run down his neck and under his collar. The older he became, the more the Lord of Milakale appreciated the tropical heat of his sugar barony. He tried to imagine himself enduring the Midwestern winters that he knew as a child, before he was old enough to leave it all behind, and came up wanting every time.

A cloud of red dust announced the rapid arrival of Kalani Mahoe in from the fields. The oldest of the Mahoe brothers rode straight up to the Big House, something its matron frowned upon as the iron-rich dust was persistent once it had made its way inside.

"What is it, Kalani?" Lanthier put his glass down and stood, squinting into the brightness. "Did something happen out in the cane?"

"No, Mr. Lanthier," the stocky Hawai'ian patted the neck of his tired steed. "You are about to have visitors. I saw three men coming this way, riding hell bent for leather."

"Come now, Mr. Mahoe, I knew I shouldn't have lent you that Kipling book," Lanthier laughed at the allusion. "Surely you flirt with hyperbole—"

"No sir," Mahoe hesitated. "You can ask them about their haste yourself in a few moments, I am merely the messenger."

"Very well," Lanthier buttoned his collar and reached into his inside vest pocket for a cigar. "Thank you for the warning, Kalani. You may return to your duties. Whatever business is afoot, I am sure that I can handle it."

"Very well, Mr. Lanthier," Mahoe turned to leave his boss standing alone on the lānai searching his many pockets, "and sir?"

Lanthier looked up in time to catch the box of matches that Mahoe tossed before turning his steed back toward the cane fields.

No sooner than Lanthier had his cigar smoking just right, three horsemen indeed did arrive. He recognized the men as local members of the Hawaiian League, a group of white, mostly American, businessmen and missionary types who had forced the king into writing a new constitution a few years earlier. Once they got the reforms they were pushing for, the group unsurprisingly started fighting internally about which big fish they would cast around for next.

"Good afternoon, Alexander," the closest man dismounted and took off his straw hat. "Long time."

"Well, if it isn't Tweed Colson!" Lanthier charmed. "What brings you all the way out to Milakale, pray tell? Have you found yourself with a surplus of silver that you would like to disencumber yourself of? I could always use a few more shiny portraits of Claus Spreckels around the place."

"You are never going to let me forget that night, are you? You mean son of a gun!" The men embraced as old friends. Colson could have been struck in the same mint that had produced Lanthier. A lifetime of ranch work and liberal applications of whiskey had tanned the man's English Midlands skin to tough leather, but a twinkle in his green eyes still revealed an inner rogue.

"I hear that you yourself have had some interesting nights of late, old friend," Colson probed.

"If you mean dying and being miraculously resurrected, why the rumors are true," Lanthier took a puff of his cigar and blew a cloud of smoke toward the two men who remained in the stirrups. "Forgive me, I am being unforgivably rude, won't the three of you join me for a drink in the shade? It is powerfully warm today."

"Mr. Lanthier," one of the mounted men started before being cut off.

"That does sound delightful," Colson turned toward the men he came with and gestured toward the lānai. "Gentlemen, we do have the time to be civilized now, don't we?"

"I suppose so," the more vocal of the pair relented and motioned to the other to dismount, an interaction not lost on Lanthier.

"Does he not speak?" Lanthier pointed with his cigar.

"I do indeed, sir," the man objected. "And I intend to speak with you on the matter of your very soul!"

A flashing stare from Colson was enough to halt the man's objection to Lanthier's gentle jib.

"You will have to forgive my associate," Colson beseeched. "Mr. Davis is not as... resigned from his missionary calling as you and I."

"And you, sir?" Lanthier pointed at the third man with his cigar. "Are you ill-reformed as well? Have you traveled all the way out here to tell me that I am on the road to perdition?"

The gentleman laughed to spite himself and turned his head to spit out a mouthful of road dust, careful to miss the meticulously tended flowerbed. "No sir, Mr. Lanthier. I've been down that road a-piece myself. I am no one to judge."

"Well met, then, fellow traveller," Lanthier shook the man's hand and turned to lead the group up to the porch.

"Alexander Lanthier, allow me to introduce Jonathan Boyle of the Honolulu Rifles," Colson belatedly introduced the pair. "Our companion is the Right Reverend Ezra Davis, of the Church of Hawaii."

"An infantryman and a bishop, no less? We had better go top-shelf, lest we never live it down. Noelani!" Lanthier called back over his shoulder. "O nā mea maikaʻi! Bring out the good stuff!"

Once the delegation had settled into the slower rhythm of Milakale, and Lanthier had plied them all with drinks and cigars, he finally felt that he sufficiently arranged the chessboard to his liking and could now conduct business the way he was accustomed.

"So, gentlemen, to what do I owe this splendid afternoon? Although our Hāmākua Coast is magnificent this time of year, I do get the feeling that the three of you are not just out taking the air."

"Can I be blunt, Mr. Lanthier?" Boyle leaned over the table now laden with drinks and pūpūs both consistently replenished by Noelani.

"I would appreciate it, Mr. Boyle," Lanthier said, procuring a piece of pipikaula, or Hawai'ian beef jerky, and popping it into his mouth.

"There are certain interests that have concerns about what is going on up here," Boyle explained. "We certainly do not need a homegrown Adventist sect stirring things up on the islands."

"These 'interests' do they include those that would see our home swallowed up by the United States?" Lanthier spoke around the masticated jerky before mimicking what America might do.

"The League only wants whatever is best for the islands," Boyle said. "If a closer relationship is what it takes to protect what we have built here, so be it."

"Said the whale to the minnow," Lanthier countered.

"There are rumors floating around about your Reverend Fox," Davis interrupted. "Stories from California."

"The reverend is a singular individual," Lanthier admitted. "I can imagine that stories follow him like bees follow cut sugarcane. I can only confirm the rumor that he saved my life."

"Cheating death seems to be a thing with him."

"What Bishop Davis is saying, poorly, I might add," Colson knew his friend well enough to step in before the conversation derailed any further, "is that the papers claim that Reverend Fox was killed in a fire during a revival in a small town called Fiesta."

"Shortly before he showed up in Milakale," Davis interjected, tossing a well-worried copy of San Francisco's Daily Examiner onto the crowded table.

"And yet, here he lives," Lanthier stated, unimpressed.

Davis removed his bifocals and rubbed his eyes before finally getting to his point. "Mr. Lanthier, I am afraid the question before us is not the tenacity of Reverend Fox. Be it by divine providence or not, the existence of your champion is obvious. However, the quandary remains—if Fox is here—then who was the poor unfortunate that took his place in the ground?"

"Mr. Davis," Lanthier growled, "just what are you insinuating?"

"Bishop Davis, Mr. Lanthier, surely you owe me that courtesy."

Lanthier was struck silent for a moment, a feeling he was not used to and was not sure he liked. Instead of rising to the bait, he simply relit his cigar and considered his options before beginning to quietly chuckle.

"I don't see what is funny here, Mr. Lanthier," Davis protested.

"I'm sure you don't, *Bishop* Davis," Lanthier poked toward the man with his glowing cherry. "The thing is, gentlemen, I don't owe a single one of you a damn thing. That's the best part about being stupidly rich."

"Now, Alexander," Colson spoke up.

"Don't 'Alexander' me, Allen. I must say that the caliber of your associates leaves a bit to be desired these days. Perhaps you should return with Claus next time."

"I am sorry that you feel that way, old friend. Gentlemen," Colson motioned to his companions to leave.

A pang of regret, another feeling Lanthier was unacquainted with, drove him to stop the men as they rose from their wicker chairs.

"Listen, gents, please forgive my short temper today—it must be the heat. It does get to a man from time to time. Let me invite you back when Reverend Fox begins his ministry. You can see for yourself what kind of a man he is. I think you will be surprised, Bishop Davis."

"Oh, I have no doubt of that, Mr. Lanthier," Davis himself laughed. "None whatsoever. Until then."

Colson, feeling that the meeting—and their friendship—had been salvaged, patted Lanthier on the shoulder as he left.

From the lānai, Lanthier watched the three men mount up and ride back the way they had come before turning to pick up the newspaper.

"Well, A. L., it looks like our man has been waking some snakes," Lanthier declared as he tossed his exhausted cigar into the flowerbed. "I sure hope he can turn and twist his way out of this one."

PLATE SEVEN ✹ Akram Khadae

236

Chapter Thirty-One
MILAKALE, HAWAIʻI, KINGDOM OF HAWAIʻI | 1889

31:1 Khadae sat beside the tumultuous roar of the waterfall that had become his favorite spot on the entirety of what he had long considered a miserable rock infested with half-evolved hominids. If he closed his eyes—something he rarely did—he could imagine himself back in the comfort of the paradise that he willingly chose to leave behind.

He chuckled to himself at the thought of actual autonomy. Did not everything happen at the pleasure of the Creator? Why should he have been punished for only carrying out those things that he was destined to do? *What a setup*, he thought for the millionth time since being cast out.

"Still feeing sorry for yourself, Tamiel?" A voice seemed to burble from the water rushing over rounded stones.

Not being one for self-reflection, Khadae knew the voice didn't come from within and he bristled at the use of his original name.

"What a busy boy," the voice taunted. "You have made quite a name for yourself down here, what with teaching 'the children of men all of the wicked strikes of spirits, demons, and... the bites of the serpent.' Isn't that how their famous book put it? I have to say, Khadae, with all that bad press I might have changed my name as well. But rebranding with an appellation meaning the 'hidden power?' It's a bit on the nose, isn't it? Or does it mean the 'covered hand?'"

"I am not in the mood for a history lesson *or* a trademark critique," Khadae growled. "State your business or fuck off."

"Such coarse language for one who was once exulted," the waterfall goaded.

"Exulted?" Khadae spat into the rushing water. "Enslaved, was more like it. Again, this is all water under the bridge, so to speak. What do you want?"

"People are talking, Tamiel," the waterfall got down to business. "Certain actors within the Bureau have taken notice of your meddling."

"The Bureau *of Nefarious Undertakings?*" Khadae laughed. "Meddling is their raison d'etre, is it not? It is right in their twice-damned charter, if I'm not mistaken."

"Look, nobody loves a good scheme more than Kokabiel," the waterfall admitted. "Personally, I admire the work that you have put in down here. Befriending the avatar's father as a child? Genius."

"What's the problem then?" Khadae's curiosity began to override his natural obstinacy. "Is this a shakedown? Are you muscling in for a cut? Now, that I could respect."

If it was the waterfall's turn to laugh, Khadae couldn't differentiate it from its natural sound. The flow, however, did seem to pause. Whether it did so for effect, or merely to gather its thoughts, he also couldn't tell.

"Look, I probably should not be telling you this," the waterfall released with a sigh, "there are rumors of revoking your immortality if you don't let this one go."

"Don't do me any favors," Khadae rumbled. "Besides, none of you have the juice—except the so-called boss upstairs—and no one has heard a peep from Him/Her/Them for longer than these mud monkeys I am forced to deal with have been around."

"That is what I'm saying," the waterfall whispered, sounding even more like a waterfall. "There is talk that He/She/They is/are coming back."

"Angel, please," Khadae barked out a laugh. "You go tell the Upstairs Agency's deadbeat dad to do His/Her/Their worst. What could be worse than spending eternity in the dirt with these half-wits?"

"You might be surprised," the waterfall burbled.

"I might, at that," Khadae hedged, "but somehow I doubt it. How do you know that the boss even still exists? I am beginning to think that He/She/They have merely become a bedtime story to keep the Upstairs Agency on the straight and very narrow."

"Don't say that!" The waterfall splashed. "You just might be digging your own grave Tamiel."

"Something I would gladly do with a fucking spoon, if only I would be given my rest," Khadae lamented. "Now if you don't mind, I have schemes to scheme. If you do happen to run into the big boss, be sure to tell Him/Her/Them where to find me."

31:2 Khadae's private reverie having been shattered by the unwelcome intrusion from the Bureau's scullion, he began to pick his way back to the road, carefully stepping on the high points of moss-covered stones when a glimmer appeared immediately before him, almost causing him to pitch off into the cold stream.

"Oh, for Dog's sake!" He exclaimed. "Now what?"

The shimmer fattened and focused, becoming the translucent semblance of a portly shopkeeper with a nasty head wound.

"At last, I have found you," the vision spoke, echoing the sound of wind moving through the elephant grass.

"I am through with these ridiculous pantomimes for the day," Khadae carefully spoke, as not to lose his newly regained balance. "Like I told the waterfall, state your business or back to the ether with you!"

"I know who you are," the spirit stated. "Who you really are."

"Do you now?" Khadae regained his equilibrium. "And who might you be? A rumor of a dead man? A flicker of light beneath swaying palms? Those leaves have more agency than you, and they shall very soon be in the ground as well. At least they will have the good grace to stay quiet as they rot."

The ghost began to glow with a brilliance that surprised Khadae.

"'Ay, thou poor ghost, while memory holds a seat in this distracted globe,'" he mocked, while the spirit fixed him in his gaze. "At least do me either the honor or horror of knowing to whom I may be speaking, Sir Echo."

"My name is... rather, was," the ghost faltered. "Philomena!"

"That was not my first guess, I must admit," Khadae mused. "But I am no one to judge, as you seem to be aware."

"I was Mortimer Gilliam," the ghost flared. "Philomena is my daughter."

"Is she now, Mr. Gilliam?" Khadae mused. "I understand that her pedigree may be open to some speculation."

"You understand nothing!" Gilliam raged. "Your kind claims to have brought us the gift of free will, but you only bring wretchedness. You have forgotten the greatest gift of all."

"And what might that be, shadow?" Khadae snorted. "Please, enlighten me with your hallowed insight. What could you possibly have to reveal that I have not known already these countless millennia?"

"Love," Gilliam said.

"I'm sorry," Khadae sputtered. "What was that now? I thought you had been a grown man before your apparent ventilation, and not a moony schoolgirl!"

"You still don't understand, do you?" Gilliam threw his words at Khadae like a handful of rocks. "It doesn't matter how my daughter came to be in my life. She is a miracle. Full stop. And I can't have you messing about in her life any longer."

"Oh, ho-ho!" Khadae chortled. "You can't have it, can you? And what do you intend to do about it, remnant?"

"This." The spirit stepped forward and walked through the long disgraced angel. The remaining consciousness of Mortimer Gilliam was overfilled with memories of incomprehensible carnage and a coldness that made the vastness of space seem like a day at the shore.

"What did you do?" Khadae staggered, shocked to no longer feel the burden of his countless transgressions stemming all the way back to his fall from grace. "Why would you do this?"

"In the end," Gilliam managed to say, his light turning black before Khadae's eyes, "it all has to be about love. There is no other force in the universe worth believing in. Even you deserve love."

"Well, I'll be damned," Khadae muttered as Gilliam faded away, his toothy smile the last bit to disappear.

31:3 Reverend Fox bustled around inside the former Protestant chapel, removing the leftover prayer books and any paraphernalia that he thought wouldn't jibe with his singular brand of revivalism. Having collected the oddments of what once, long ago, was seen as a revolutionary branch of the church, he turned toward the front of the vaulted wooden room and approached the raised pulpit that looked out over rows of empty pews.

"Well, Mordikai, this is definitely a step up from the damp hay of the tent circuit," he announced, as if saying it out loud would lock it in.

"It certainly is," a familiar voice responded from the other side of the baptismal font near the front door. "It seems to me like you're shitting in high cotton, reverend."

Startled, yet still filled with an expansive excitement, Fox called out into the dark.

"Is that you, Akram?" Fox took the liberty of calling Khadae by his first name, a license the man had never expressly given. "Come in, come in. What do you think of the new sacristy? A far cry from a fallow field, wouldn't you say?"

"Architecture is not really my métier, padre," Khadae called from the front stairs. "If it is all the same to you, I believe that I will remain out here."

"Don't be ridiculous," Fox countered. "Come in and look at the stained glass. It's beautiful!"

"I wish that I had time to take it all in," Khadae prevaricated. "I'm afraid that I do have other business to attend to. I only came to ask you a question."

"Of course, my friend," Fox stopped fawning about the chapel and turned to give Khadae his full attention.

"Do you know where your daughter is?"

Fox began to answer, then stopped when he realized that he really had no idea.

"I don't think that I am going to like this line of conversation," he finally responded. "Why don't you just tell me what you know?"

"Of course," Khadae purred. "I am only coming here as a concerned friend. There are remnants of the old heathen ways that still hold sway about these islands. I would hate to see your daughter be caught up in any pagan nonsense; what with you becoming the new guiding light here at Milakale."

"Akram, please!"

"Right, right," Khadae feigned an innocent befuddlement. "Well, you didn't hear it from me, but... Would you like a cigarette?"

Fox took one of the proffered Egyptian smokes and searched the man's face as he pulled his signature trick with a preternatural match and lit his own Kyriazi Frères.

"You are enjoying this," Fox accused Khadae as his face was illuminated by sulfuric flame.

Instead of answering directly, Khadae took a deep pull from the pungent cigarette and blew a massive cloud of smoke out over the chapel steps.

"Nothing could be further from the truth, Mordikai. Take it from me, I have been doing business in these islands for a very long time and I know how stories spread in this climate. I would hate to see all your plans come to naught before they are given a chance to get off the ground."

"How... Christian of you."

"Not at all," Khadae motioned with his cigarette as if directing an invisible orchestra. "Having met you at the beginning of all this, I feel like I have a stake in your endeavors here."

"Do you now?" Fox began to lose his patience with the prevaricating Egyptian. "Then you know how busy I am. Either tell me what you know, or I am going to have to say good day."

"Do you know what a kahuna is?" Khadae found that he actually was enjoying stringing Fox along before experiencing an unfamiliar pang of guilt.

"I am afraid that I don't." Fox noticed the pained look on the man's face and was beginning to fear the worst. "Is Philomena all right?"

"Forgive me, padre, it must have been something I ate. The girl is fine, for the time being. I would, however, worry about what certain parties may be filling her head with."

"Damn your eyes, Khadae! Is Philomena in danger or not?"

"Oh, they've been twice-damned for millennia," Khadae sighed, unable to maintain his usual delight in torturing the man. "The girl will be fine, after all she is the avatar. Unless, of course, there is a contuberium of Romans on the island that I may have missed."

Fox merely stared at Khadae, unable to parse any sense from his apparent mental crisis. Sitting down on the top stair, he held out his unlit cigarette. After begging Fox's pardon, Khadae once again pulled a lit match from thin air and disappeared it just as quickly once it had done its job.

"You are a singular individual, I will grant you that," Fox mused, inhaling deeply and letting the heavily aromatic smoke nestle in his chest before blowing it out. "Who are you Akram Khadae? Why are our paths so entwined? Have you been following me all these years?"

Khadae sighed and began to explain.

"You've caught me in a rare vulnerable state," he admitted. "I was gifted something today that has no one has thought to give me longer than I can remember, and that is a very, very long time."

"A gift?"

"A kindness."

"Well, good for you," Fox took another drag and briefly wondered why he would have ever thought to give up the habit. "I am afraid that I still don't see—"

"Most do not think that I deserve kindness, I... we have gotten a bit of a bad reputation in the local literature."

"We?" Fox found that, against his better judgment, he had become drawn into whatever Khadae was on about. "There are more odd ducks such as yourself out there?"

"Hosts."

"Hosts," Fox repeated back. "As in 'hosts of angels.'"

"'Ay, there's the rub,' as Willie used to say. To put it in terms that you would recognize, we are often referred to as 'the fallen.'"

"I'm sorry, are you asking me to believe that you are a fallen angel?"

"You can believe what you like," Khadae mused, "you seem to be quite good at it. But, yes, that is what I'm telling you. More or less."

"More or less?" Fox found himself unable to do anything but parrot Khadae's incredible claims.

"It's complicated," Khadae admitted. "The victors get to write the history books, do they not?"

"I suppose they do at that. So do you and your fellow 'fallen' worship Satan, then? Have I been taken in by a demonic presence?"

"You see," Khadae protested, pointing out the indignity with the Kyriazi's glowing cherry, "there you go, right there. 'Demonic' is a hurtful term; and, no, we don't 'worship' anyone. That is the whole point. That is what got us into trouble with Upstairs. Lucifer is actually a decent guy, a crap general, but you play the hand you are dealt."

"How could you justify going against the Creator?" Fox asked, his head spinning.

"Let me put this in terms an American can understand. It was a case of spiritual taxation without representation, you see. 'Heaven,' as you call it, is a monarchy, no, an authoritarian regime. We were rebels, fighting for our freedom."

"I still don't understand," Fox shook his head and flicked his cigarette into the tended flowerbed at the bottom of the stairs.

"Look at your own people's take," Khadae continued. "You have a man and a woman placed in a beautiful garden—naked as a peach is pink—and with nothing to do but eat, fuck, and name some animals. The Creator puts in an apple tree and says, 'don't touch it.' Now, I don't know about you, but I tend to get a little peckish after a nice shag. As an omnipotent being, He/She/They knew *exactly* what was going to happen. It's a frame job.

"See here; if you walked down to the beach for a swim in the ocean right now, and were bitten by a shark, could you really be angry at the shark? That's the way they're made. Fucking killing *machines*, they are."

Fox silently absorbed Khadae's story without further comment, churning it over in his mind, while his benefactor merely smoked and looked up at the stars.

"You said something regarding Philomena," Fox finally spoke. "You said that she was 'the avatar.' What did you mean by that?"

"Are you sure you want to hear this?" Khadae fixed the man in his gaze and held him. "You may find this quite strange."

"Stranger than learning that a fallen angel has been following you around your whole life?" Fox cried out. "Hang on, where were you during the war? I could have used a guardian angel back then."

"Oh, that," Khadae waffled, "I was on suspension. A paperwork issue, really. It turns out that no one ends up loving bureaucracy more than revolutionaries. Also, we don't really *do* the 'guardian' thing. That is more of an Upstairs ticket."

"I have lost my mind," Fox moaned.

"Yes, well, I am not saying that you haven't, I know that it is a lot to take in," Khadae admitted. "That is a big reason that we don't go around announcing ourselves. It tends to cause a lot of gnashing of teeth and rending of garments. Nobody needs that sort of attention. It's bad for business."

"I'll bite," Fox gave in. "What, pray tell, *is* your business?"

"Disregarding the side hustles?"

"Of course."

"To understand that, I have to give you the big picture."

"Please," Fox almost wept, "enlighten me."

"Ah, clever, I see what you did there."

"I am beginning to see why you may have been kicked out of heaven," Fox muttered. "Could I murder you if you were to never come to the point?"

"Probably not, no," Khadae considered the question. "Actually, definitely not. We are immortal. You see; that is exactly where the trouble starts. One gets awfully bored after a few forevers. Your mate, St. Jerome had it sussed: 'Fac et aliquid operis, ut semper te diabolus inveniat occupatum.'"

Fox's blank stare begged a translation.

"'Engage in some occupation, so that the devil may always find you busy.' Well, that pertains to both sides, doesn't it?"

"I may still give it a shot."

"I really wouldn't do that if I were you," Khadae gave Fox the side eye. "All right, I'll give it to you as straight as I can. You have the Upstairs Agency who is tasked with giving the universe a little nudge toward the light now and again. I don't have to tell you what a splash an individual with certain insights and proclivities can make, say, among the outcasts of a wandering desert tribe."

"You are saying the creation of the savior of mankind is a regular thing?"

"Hey, you called him that, but you're catching on. This has gone on for time immemorial, some work out—some don't. It's a process."

"And my daughter just happens to be the next Jesus?"

"Don't skip ahead," Khadae snapped. "Where was I? This one particular millennium there happened to be massive layoffs in the

Agency. Pretty soon angel unemployment is at fifty percent. What happens then, *St. Jerome?* What starts out as frustrated malfeasance, soon becomes a movement, then an insurrection, and over time, a rival industry. Bingo, bango, the Bureau of Nefarious Undertakings is born."

"I can't believe I'm asking this," Fox rubbed his eyes. 'That's who you work for? The Bureau of Nefarious—"

"Undertakings. Yes, well, not exactly," Khadae tried to clarify. "You could think of me as more of an independent contractor these days. I found that I needed less structure."

"Than was afforded by the Prince of Lies?"

"Again, Mordikai... shark... bite, bite," Khadae pantomimed. "We all are as we were made, forever and ever, amen. Don't be so judgmental. It doesn't suit you.

"When the Bureau started up," he continued on, "we were all content to undo the Agency's 'good' works. Don't get me wrong now, those were fun times, but like I said, familiarity breeds contempt... I did say that right?"

"Hell if I know," Fox murmured.

"Well, I meant to. Eventually someone posed the question, 'what would be better than thwarting our rivals at every turn?'"

The sound of frogs out on the edge of the jungle provided Khadae with all the impetus he needed to answer his own question, since Fox was apparently not going to provide it.

"We could wreck them from within! Setting aside the old chestnuts of drugs, booze, and broads, we weren't left with a lot of options, but it turns out that angels love gambling. They can't get enough of it!"

"You are kidding," Fox marveled at the absurdity of Khadae's story. "I will probably kick myself for asking, but, what do they bet on?"

Khadae jumped up and down, delighted that Fox had taken the bait.

"That's the beautiful part. We got them wagering on their own avatar. Every time they drop a new spiritual catalyst into the mix, they line up all the way to the gates to bet on whether the latest heathen scum are going to progress or—"

"Or what?"

"Would you look at the time?" Khadae pulled out his pocket watch and made a perfunctory glance at it. "I should really let you get back to work. I can't wait for the big show. Aloha pō, Mordikai Fox."

"Hang on," Fox grabbed Khadae's shoulder as he turned to leave. "You haven't told me where Philomena is!"

"Talk to the boy," he said, sliding out from under Fox's grasp. "He'll sort you out."

31:4 As Noelani approached the Mahoe family house, she wanted nothing more than to lie down for a few moments before preparation for the next meal service started in earnest when she saw her nephew surrounded by all three of her brothers and Reverend Fox. The boy was being interrogated by the ad-hoc mob, and appeared to be holding his own despite the onslaught.

Watching her peaceful respite evaporate in front of her eyes put Noelani in an offensive mood and she charged into the scrum, ready to take on all four of the men if necessary.

"What in the world is going on here?" She demanded, placing herself between the angry adults and her shaken but stalwart keiki hanauna. "Don't you grown men have better things to do than gang up on Maleko?"

"Sista'," Kalani began, "don't get involved. This is men's business."

"Excuse me?" Noelani whipped around and fixed the oldest Mahoe uncle in a gaze that would give Pele a run for her money. "Don't you eva pull the kāne card on me, Kalani Mahoe! Not when I cleaned your nasty 'ōkole when you were a keiki li'ili'i. Now someone had better tell me what you so-called 'men' are doing harassing this boy, or I am going to lose my good mood, and you—none of you—want that."

"Better listen to her, my brothers," Kapono, the first to come to his senses, pleaded. "I've been on the wrong side of that look before."

"Yes, please listen to her," Maleko finally spoke, to his detriment.

"And you," Noelani fused her nephew to the spot with eyes spitting lava. "What. Did. You. Do?"

"They want to know where Philomena is," Maleko yelped. "I don't know where she is. It is not my day to watch her!"

"Why don't I believe you, keiki?" Noelani queried. "You two are thick as thieves. If you know something, Maleko, you had better speak up. The reverend here is just worried about his daughter. You can understand that, can't you?"

"Your auntie is right, son," Fox interjected. "If something were to happen to Philomena, I don't know what I would do."

"Please," Maleko snorted, "how long was it before you even noticed that she was missing?"

"Maleko," Kekoa spoke up, "I know that Philomena is your friend, and I respect that you want to protect her secrets, but this has gone too far now. If you know where the girl is, there is no shame in telling her father. If she is really in no danger, then ease his mind. If action is called for, then let us begin before it is too late."

"Keiki," Noelani's face softened, "please."

"Gaaaaa!" Maleko howled in frustration. "She is going to kill me! But I guess she could just bring me back... If this is what being a kanaka makua is like, you can have it! She is with Makana Kealoha. Are you happy?"

"The old kahuna?" Kapono asked. "Why would she—?"

"Does no one here know her at all?" Maleko exclaimed, exasperated. "Philomena is the strongest kahuna that this island has ever seen!"

"What is he talking about?" Fox turned to the Mahoe brothers. "What is a kahuna? What is going on here?"

"I think what Maleko is saying," Noelani began, "is that your daughter is a great healer. I can attest to that claim. It appears that she has gone to learn from the one person that might understand what she is going through."

"Gone?" Fox sputtered. "Gone where, for God's sake? Where is my daughter?"

All eyes turned to Maleko, something that he decidedly was becoming tired of.

"I left her in Honoka'a," he finally sighed. "I was sure that she would be all right, or I never would have left her."

"You didn't do anything wrong, Maleko," Noelani reassured him before addressing the men. "The boy has done the right thing.

248

Reverend Fox, my brothers will go fetch your daughter and bring her back to Milakale, but be assured, she could not be safer where she is. Makana Kealoha is one of our most venerated elders. Absolutely nothing could harm her while she is under her protection."

"It may be Makana who is protected by Philomena," Maleko interjected.

Noelani whirled around and slapped Maleko across the mouth, an action that shocked the three older Mahoe men to silence. Fox, however, was not wise enough to keep his own mouth shut.

"Miss Mahoe," Fox protested, "there is no need—"

"Reverend Fox," Noelani fumed, "with all due respect, do not presume to tell me what is needed or not needed when it comes to my family. There is a reason that I know exactly where these four men are right now, and that, I assure you, is not by luck."

Maleko, while wise enough to stay silent, noticed that his aunt included him as one of the Mahoe men and a cracked a smile subtle enough not to be slapped off his face.

31:5 Makana Kealoha sat Philomena down on a smooth boulder overlooking the surf, choosing another for herself facing the girl. Kealoha took the opportunity of the new vantage point to have a good look into her dark eyes.

"Honestly, Philomena, I am not sure what I can teach you," the kahuna admitted. "As I mentioned to you once before, my strength flows from nā 'aumākua, my ancestral line that stretches back to when the Kānaka Maoli first came to this island, maybe even farther. When you first met me, I had been in communion with the collective wisdom and strength of a people. Do you understand that?"

"I think so," Philomena said, trying hard to follow.

"The mystery of your power, however, leads me to reconsider the limitations of my position. Having no lineage to speak of, one would think that you would not be able to draw on a lot of help from those particular quarters."

Philomena merely shrugged, having no idea how she was able to cure Noelani, and apparently, Mr. Lanthier, not to mention the mamo bird.

249

"It seems that you are somehow able to access the entirety of spiritual mana. You are able to access the ancestors, not of a people, but of all people."

"But why me?" Philomena voiced the question that had endlessly repeated in her mind ever since the night of the Fiesta revival. "Why should I be able call on anyone? I am just a girl from a small town in California. I didn't know anything about your customs before we spoke. I half expected to see the island covered in monkeys when I came here."

Kealoha laughed and slapped her thigh.

"You may have been right in your assumption," the woman admitted. "They just don't look the way you thought they might. Some of the visitors to the Lanthier's Big House could pass for simian, if you ask me; at least in action."

Philomena had been a guest at Milakale long enough to be able to tell her mentor that she wasn't exactly wrong, but decided to keep those feelings to herself.

"Every once in a while a truly great healer appears in the world. Think of the flow of mana as a clear stream whose movement is restricted by large rocks jutting into the water from either side. Those stones represent our individual characters—they shape the depth and strength of the flow. Some of us are flat stones and the water flows right over, the stream can move quickly along but is not very deep. Others of us are stubborn stone monoliths, thinking that we can control the stream. This, of course, is folly. Water always wins."

"So what kind of rock am I?" Philomena asked.

"You are not a rock at all, kaikamahine nani. You are a waterfall," Kealoha reached over and moved her hand over Philomena's cascading black hair as if drawing the picture. "Someone or something has removed your obstructions and you are free to dance and roar and splash as you see fit."

"How?" Philomena cried out. "Who would do that? Who could do that?"

"I am afraid that I don't know what to tell you there," Kealoha shrugged. "Maybe you were born this way. Regardless how it happened, it does make you very special, and very dangerous in the eyes of certain monkeys. I would be careful about who knows about your abilities."

"Noelani knows, obviously," Philomena recounted, "and her brother, I don't recall which one. Aintín... I mean, Mrs. Lanthier, was there... and Maleko."

"Maleko," Kealoha sighed.

"Maleko."

Chapter Thirty-Two

MILAKALE, HAWAI'I, KINGDOM OF HAWAI'I | 1889

32:1 Emilia Gilliam watched from the top deck as the two-masted brigantine, *John D. Spreckels* sailed past Hilo headed for the busy sugar mill to the north of the harbor. Her dazzling white hair whipped around in the tropical breeze having regained much of its luster since she was liberated from the clutches of Rodolfo and opium.

The woman's naturally sturdy bearing was still twenty pounds light, and she didn't feel as anchored to the moving ship as she would have liked; consequently, Urias found her clutching the wooden railing as he approached.

"Quite the view, isn't it," he asked as a way to announce that he was behind her.

"It looks like paradise," Emilia responded without taking her eyes off of the approaching expanse of verdant green as it seemed to rise up out of the ocean and disappear into the white clouds topping Mauna Kea, the volcano sleeping—for the moment—in the background.

"I must admit," Urias took off his Stetson and let his own hair get buffeted by the fragrant wind, "I have seen much of America, and there are wonders to be sure, but you may be right Mrs. Gilliam, this just may be paradise."

"Please, Aaron," the woman turned to face the buttons on Urias' vest before craning her neck to find the underside of the man's chin, his head eclipsing the Sun as his hair became no less than a wild, back-lit corona, "I don't know how many times I have asked you to call me Emilia over the years. Now that you have legitimately saved my life, I would hope that you would finally accept that liberty."

"Of course, Emilia," Urias laughed and replaced his hat. "Old habits die hard I am afraid."

"Yes, you don't have to tell me that, Aaron," her eyes fell to the deck that heaved beneath her feet as if on cue.

"Forgive me," Urias looked down to the find the woman a thousand miles away, perhaps back in O Elefante's teak-paneled prison. "I meant no disrespect. I know that this voyage has not been easy for you."

"It is I who should beg forgiveness," Emilia shed a remorseful salty tear that was immediately blown into the Pacific where it rejoined its kind, "especially from Philomena, if we can find her. You do think we shall be able to find her, don't you?"

"Please, Emilia," Urias soothed, "you are in the hands of a professional. I have spent my life—when not sorting out Mordikai Fox—finding people who, for one reason or another, were not crazy about being found. Luckily, this tub stops at the approaching mill. Before we left San Francisco, I learned that one Alexander Lanthier, a local sugarcane grower, paid for Fox and Philomena's passage. If anyone can point us toward Lanthier, it is the men in that approaching building."

"Even if we find ourselves on a wild goose chase," Hendry declared as he joined the pair at the rail, having overheard the end of their conversation, "there are worse places for it."

As if on cue, a flock of nēnē, Hawai'ian geese, flew over the ship headed makua to the slopes of Mauna Kea.

"It is good to see you looking so well, Mrs.," Hendry decided not to ride on the coattails of the woman's demand that Urias call her by her first name.

"And you, Mr. Hendry," Emilia gushed. "The salt sea air appears to agree with you."

"It's Niall, Mrs., or 'that rotten son of a bitch,' depending on one's inclination."

"I can't imagine someone so inclined," she feigned a wide-eyed innocence that started all three of them laughing.

"Bless you for saying that, Mrs.," Hendry wiped a wind-whipped tear from his eye, "but I do cherish my obstinacy. I've worked hard to maintain this air of malevolent stubbornness. Please don't ruin my reputation."

"Your secret is safe with me," Emilia promised.

"Has anyone seen our diaphanous friend of late?"

"Washburn?" Out of habit, Urias looked around the deck, paying heed to the adage that if you mention the devil's name, he appears.

253

"He does have the uncanny practice of showing up at just the right—or just the wrong—time. I'm quite certain that we will see him again."

32:2 Once the ship was tied at the end of the sugar mill's pier, it was a small matter of walking the short distance to the office to drop Lanthier's name and the trio was immediately provided with a carriage and driver to take them out to Milakale.

The closer the horses got to the property, however, the more nervous Emilia became about having to face her daughter and Reverend Fox. She thought about the last time she had confronted her former spiritual leader about Philomena being his progeny. The man had denied it, yet did abscond with the girl to a distant tropical island.

Why would he do that if she was not his, she chewed the question over as the steel-rimmed wheels of the carriage pounded the red dirt road.

"Are you all right, Emilia?" Urias noticed the worried look on the woman's face. "Are you still ill?"

"I am fine as far as that goes," she answered, biting her lip. "Actually, I haven't physically felt this good in years. I still may throw up, however."

"This may help if it comes to that," Hendry nudged a brass spittoon across the bouncing floor with his boot. "If I were you, I wouldn't look into it until absolutely necessary, though."

"Thanks for the warning," Emilia shifted her gaze to the profusion of passing green and let the sight soothe her. "I have never seen a place so full of life. Perhaps we should stay here once Philomena and I are reunited. There is not really anything left for us in Fiesta, that is certain."

The two men in the carriage opted not to comment on the woman's ongoing musings, the lack of feedback prompting a pause in her monologue.

"You do think she will be glad to see me, don't you?"

"Oh, yes!"

"Of course!"

"You are her mother!" The pair stumbled over each other to assuage Emilia's fears.

"Mordikai may, at times, be a lowdown motherfucker, excuse my language," Urias pleaded, "but he is no mother. If I were your daughter, I would be over the Moon to see you."

"Do I sense a falling out between you and the good reverend?" Hendry carefully worded his question, sensing that the closer the conveyance brought them to the inevitable showdown, the more angry Urias became.

"Forgive me," Urias tamped down his rage. "After everything we have been through together, I still cannot believe that he did all this without telling me first. I thought he was dead! His selfishness caused me to become a grave robber, for Christ's sake."

Urias realized his insensitivity. "I didn't mean—"

"It's all right," Emilia said. "We have all been driven to extremes, haven't we, gentlemen?"

Hendry and Urias merely nodded in agreement and settled into the rhythm of their travel. Outside the carriage, the riot of vegetation began to submit to some measure of considered order. The unbroken expanse of different shades of green began to concede an occasional plot of red soil awaiting the next bounty to be raised in it. A flurry of blossoms from surrounding citrus trees began to swirl behind the moving coach as if celebrating the trio's arrival.

"We are here," the coachman announced. "This is Milakale, the house that cane built."

Emilia poked her head out of the open window and was gifted a blast of perfumed air that nearly knocked her back into her seat.

"Oh my," she gasped. "I don't think that I can do this. What if I don't deserve a second chance? I don't think that I can bear the implications of that."

Both men dropped their eyes to the floor of the carriage, having been in comparable positions at least a handful of times over the course of their lives. Finally, Hendry was able to pull his thoughts together and put them into words.

"If I may speak for both of us, Mrs.," he began in a whisper, "we have learned in the hardest ways possible that you cannot allow the past to dictate what you may do today. The Sun that shines above us right now is not the same one that looked down on our past sins. That star has burned away. It is gone. The light that guides us now is fleeting as well. You cannot waste it. That would be the greatest sin of all."

"Touching," the coachman remarked as he opened the door and placed a short stair where Emilia might reach it. "If you please, I do need to get back."

"You are just going to leave us here?" Emilia panicked.

"My dear lady, you are being left in the lap of luxury," the coachman removed his hat and motioned toward the Big House. "If there is any chance that you know how to handle a team of horses, I would gladly trade places with you."

"That is enough," Urias declared as he unfolded himself from the carriage. "Thank you for kindness, but we shall be fine."

Having nothing but the clothes on their backs, the trio bid the coachman good day and made their way to the mansion.

"Where is everyone?" Hendry wondered out loud, taking stock of the empty courtyard. "Is it Sunday? It's not Sunday is it?"

"I am afraid that I have lost track, myself," Urias laughed. "It used to be my job to know that, if nothing else."

"Look there," Emilia pointed toward the chapel. "If it is Sunday, perhaps we shall find someone there."

32:3 Beyond the courtyard, where the order of Milakale's tended grounds again gave way to riotous growth, a banyan tree cast patterns of leaf-filtered sunshine upon roots like tangled rope. If anyone was watching the dancing interplay of sunlight and darkness, they may have caught a glimpse of a single shadow a shade darker than the rest.

Having arrived on the island along with his living companions, Washburn was watching, and saw what he was looking for.

"One thing about not being tied to the earth," he began, picking his way over the banyan's jumbled expanse, either for effect or out of habit, "it affords a man a wider perspective. I have learned things that, as a soldier—and before that, a simple farmer—I would never have come across in a million years."

Only a rustle of leaves high in the tree's branches bothered to comment on the spirit's musings.

"Have you ever heard of a Chinaman named Confucius?" On a roll, Washburn hardly waited for an answer. "No? Well, it turns out that way over there in China, there was this fellow who lived a long time ago, about five hundred years before Jesus Henderson Christ, *if* you can believe it."

Washburn held onto his head, as the way grew even more impenetrable.

"Now, this fellow had some pretty good ideas. The Golden Rule? That was his. My very favorite rule of his, however, is this: 'Three things cannot long be hidden: the Sun, the Moon, and the truth.' Ain't that some shit? I've come to think of it as a personal motto, if you will."

"What do you want?" the banyan leaves seemed to ask.

"Well, now, that *is* a sight more neighborly," Washburn declared. "I thought that I might be left discussing philosophy with this here tree; not that there aren't worse ways to spend the day, as you and I certainly have learned."

Gilliam's shadow stepped out of the same and confronted the stranger, a sight that nearly caused Washburn to drop his skull.

"Well, carry me out with the tongs!" Washburn exclaimed. "Who beat you with the ugly stick?"

"Says the ghost with a head for a hat," Gilliam countered, solidifying the best he could manage.

"Fair enough," Washburn allowed. "You will have to forgive me, however, in all my years as a ghost wrangler, I have never seen one go so... inky. What happened?"

Gilliam held his hands in front of his face and found that, indeed, he had gone black.

"I passed through a fallen angel," he explained. "I think that I might have gotten some on me."

"Oh, *them*," Washburn sighed. "It's best to just steer clear a' them. They can't help you, no matter what they say."

"Now you tell me," Gilliam laughed despite the situation. "What can I do for you Headless Horseman?"

"That's a good one," Washburn quipped. "I haven't heard that before, you eight ball-looking... No, no, that's all right. Anyway, the question is not what you can do for me—it is what can I do for you. I've come a long way to help you out, whether you want it or not."

"Is that so?" Gilliam asked, becoming genuinely curious as to what the other spirit might be able to tell him about his situation.

"It is, it is," Washburn rhapsodized. "You have no idea how long I've been looking for you. It's time."

"Time?" Gilliam parroted. "Time for what?"

"Time for what? It's *time* time," Washburn spread his hands out leaving his head to balance as it may. "As in, *time's up*. It's that great gettin' up morning! Time to shuffle off this mortal coil and rejoin the infinite."

"Oh, I can't leave," Gilliam explained. "I have got to stay here to protect my daughter."

"I thought you might say that," Washburn admitted. "If you would indulge me for a moment, I have something to show you."

The former Confederate soldier led the former shopkeeper back across the expanse of the Milakale property until they reached the edge of the courtyard.

"Look a' there," Washburn pointed, doing his best impression of a proper Dickensian specter. The effect was somewhat lessened as his head fell off onto a tuft of pili grass.

Gilliam followed the ghost's finger and not his gaze, as that now pointed straight down into the dirt. Across the way, he saw Emilia making her way to the chapel, accompanied by Aaron Urias and another man that he didn't recognize.

"Emilia!" He exclaimed. "How can this be? I must go to her!"

"Wurf nuff," Washburn's head called down into the pili grass before being picked up by his groping hands, which helped immeasurably to clarify his message. "Whoa, now! Hang up your fiddle, civilian. That woman has been through enough. She doesn't need to be scared out of her wits by the likes of you."

"I have so much to tell her," Gilliam protested. "I need to say how sorry I am."

"Well, we have only just now met, and I can attest to what a sorry son of a bitch you are," Washburn carefully balanced his head back onto his neck. "It doesn't work that way, however."

"What do you mean? She is right there!"

"And, lamentingly so, I am right here," Washburn pointed out. "You have already rat fucked my schedule beyond... just beyond. We are done here. The girl's mother is here and everybody gets to live happily ever after, except for you and I, but that's how it is."

"But—"

"If ghosts had butts, could you smell their farts?"

"What in God's name are you talking about?"

"I am talking about the natural order of things. You are one of the lucky ones; most aren't gifted closure like this, but, my friend, it is time to let go."

Gilliam began to see the wisdom in what the ghost wrangler was telling him and stopped trying to resist the pull that began to tug at the edges of him.

"What is to become of me?" Gilliam cried out.

"Honestly, friend," Washburn lamented, "I cannot speak from experience, only from what I have been told. The you that is *you*, becomes the you that is *everything*. To tell you the truth, it sounds like a pretty good deal."

Once he stopped fighting against the inexorable pull, the first aspect to disappear was the obsidian tint that Gilliam had picked up while passing through Khadae. As it left him, the look of horror on his face turned to one of relief.

"I had no idea," he said, lifting his hand to his face, both of which had begun to reveal more and more banyan tree behind them.

For once, Washburn had no comment as the same process had started to affect him as well.

"I'll be damned," the ghost wrangler exclaimed. "Is that it, then? Was this joker the final job? Are we straight?"

Only the leaves of the banyan tree were left to answer, and they were staying quiet about what they saw.

32:4 Inside the chapel, Fox paced back and forth in a frenzy. Foam flecked his lips and loose leaves of paper followed him and floated in his wake as he scribbled away in a small notebook, only pausing to tear out a page and add it to his slipstream.

"How do I tell them it has all been a lie?" He demanded an answer from a silent, absent God. "Have I done any good all these years? Is it enough to just believe in something, even if it turns out to be a corruption?"

"Hello?" Fox's turmoil was derailed by the arrival of his former comrades. "Is there anyone here?"

Fox turned to see Emilia enter the chapel, her familiar form back lit by bright tropical sunlight, a sight that staggered him and caused him drop everything he had been holding.

"It can't be!" He exclaimed and fell to his knees. "Is this a vision? Have you sent me a sign?"

"I assure you that I am flesh and blood, Reverend Fox," Emilia stepped forward, mixed emotions playing across her face. "Where is my daughter?"

Why does everyone keep asking me that? Fox wondered as he rose to meet the woman who was once one of his most ardent followers.

"I'm not sure," he offered in lieu of another lie.

"What the hell do you mean that you are not sure?" Emilia's patience to listen to Fox prevaricate had long worn out. "You stole my daughter and I want her back. Now!"

"It's not like that at all," he pleaded. "I only meant to save the girl... You are alive!" The corporeal existence of the angry woman finally began to sink in.

The sound of rising voices brought Urias and Hendry in, both of them shocked to see the sorry state of the once indestructible reverend.

"Oh, Mordikai," Urias bemoaned, seconds before his anger caught flame, "what have you done?"

"Aaron!" Fox cried, his mistake snapping into sharp relief. "I—"

Fox's excuse was cut short as Urias stepped forward and punched his former partner full in the face, knocking him out cold.

"You son of a bitch," Urias raged and made to continue the beating before Hendry caught him by the shoulder.

"That is enough, friend," he spoke quietly as to quell the man's fury. "The good reverend looks like he has been hard enough on himself; he doesn't need compounded interest, so to speak."

Urias silently walked back to the chapel's entrance where a small font of holy water awaited incoming congregants. He picked up the small glass bowl from its wrought-iron holder and returned to the supine preacher.

"Wake up, Mordikai," Urias said, his anger now dissipated enough so that when he threw the water into Fox's face, the bowl did not follow.

"I'm going to go up to the house to see if anyone else is around," Hendry offered, knowing that the other three had much to talk about when Fox finally came around. "However, if you two decide to start kicking him, feel free to give him one for me."

Chapter Thirty-Three
MILAKALE, HAWAI'I, KINGDOM OF HAWAI'I | 1889

33:1 With a strong wind brewing up from Milakale Bay, Wei Lei was busy carefully bringing in the paper lanterns that danced on the threshold of her business. She had been on the island long enough to know when a storm was about to spring out of the Pacific and make a mud puddle out of the cane cutter's camp.

One good thing to come out of it, she mused, as she untied a fearsome dragon, *the rain would drive customers to find shelter where they might. They just might find it here.* The last lantern to come down was always the crocodile, a gift from Khadae, and true to type, it always gave her a hard time.

"Tā mā de!" She cursed the lantern, the knotted string, and Khadae all at once.

"Such language," a melodious voice called out. "Don't you know that you are in the presence of royalty?"

Wei whipped around to see Princess Lili'uokalani, the heir apparent to the Hawai'ian throne, standing at her doorstep. She was wearing a simple wool skirt with a cuirass bodice that hugged her healthy middle-aged frame.

"Lili'u!" She exclaimed. "What a delight to see you. I almost didn't recognize you without eight yards of bustle following you around!"

"Wei Lei," the princess cooed, "how long has it been?"

"Let's see," Wei thought back. "It had to have been San Francisco, before your brother William passed. I don't think I've seen you in the flesh since you were Lydia Kamaka'eha."

"That long, my friend?" Lili'uokalani mused. "I appreciate you taking on this task for me, even though I have been a poor friend."

"Nonsense!" Wei exclaimed. "You have a nation to care for, and I, well, you can see that I have been busy. Won't you come in? I don't think your understated outfit is going to fool anyone for very long, you look so regal."

"Stop it. I could use a cup of tea, however."

Once Wei had prepared tea and the two women had a chance to become reacquainted, the reason the princess had come began to hang heavy in the air.

"Is it true, Wei Lei?" Lili'uokalani whispered. "Is the girl the real thing?"

"It appears so, Lili'u," Wei blew on her tea to cool it. "Her father is a fraud, but the young Philomena really does seem to have the gift."

"Incredible. I can't thank you enough for keeping me appraised of the situation. I need to see her for myself. I think I will go up to visit with Anias under the pretense of stealing her chef."

"Jun Jin!" Wei exclaimed. "What makes you think that she would give him up?"

"Please," Lili'uokalani dismissed the idea. "Being a princess has to be good for something. Do I sense a certain reluctance to the idea on your part?"

"It is my turn to tell *you* to stop it," Wei blushed.

"My good lord! I have embarrassed the indefatigable Wei Lei? Wonders never cease."

"He is my friend, that is all," Wei half-heartedly protested, knowing full well that she had lost the argument before it began.

"My work here is done," Lili'uokalani put down her teacup and rose to leave. "Perhaps I do not need a miracle worker after all! Let us not wait another twelve years, my friend."

"Princess," Wei gave a small bow. Whether it was out of respect for her old friend's station or in acknowledgement of Lili'uokalani having cracked her famously hard shell, she herself couldn't be sure.

33:2 The courtyard in front of the Big House was abuzz with activity when Kealoha rode into Milakale with Philomena holding on tightly behind her on the horse.

"There she is, now!" Fox exclaimed, causing the small crowd gathered around him to turn their heads.

Kealoha climbed down from the Arabian she had borrowed from a paniolo in Honoka'a, and gave Philomena a helping hand with her dismount. She was about to ask the reverend about his bloody nose when a woman stepped out from behind him and began running toward them.

"Philomena!" The woman cried out as she closed the short distance. Philomena herself would have fallen to her knees in disbelief, if Kealoha hadn't caught her.

"Mother?" The girl whispered, unable to comprehend that Emilia was alive and at Milakale. "How are you here?"

Emilia didn't bother to answer, but swept the girl up in her arms, both women weeping openly.

"Maleko!" Noelani called to the boy who, like the rest of the bystanders, was quietly watching the tearful reunion between the mother and daughter. "Take Makana's horse to the stables and try to catch your uncles before they ride out."

"There is no need, Noelani Mahoe," Kealoha said. "I have done what I came here to do, and I should return this animal. Its owner will have need of it."

"My baby girl," Emilia sobbed, "I am so sorry about everything."

"I thought you were dead!" Philomena cried out. "I saw you with my own eyes. Fath... Reverend Fox said you were gone."

"Well, my dear, it turns out that Reverend Fox is an idiot," Emilia cut her eyes over at the party in question. "To be fair, I was probably close to death. I was drugged and then kidnapped, or I never would have left you. These two men saved me and brought me here to find you."

"You were what?" Philomena asked, incredulous. "Who would do that? Why would someone do that?"

"It doesn't matter whom; he will never hurt anyone ever again. As to why, he seemed to want to get his hands on *you*. Somehow, the reverend did the right thing by taking you far away."

"Thank you!" Fox spoke up against all better sense. "Finally some credit where credit is due."

Before Urias could punch him again, the reunion scene was interrupted by the arrival of an ornate coach.

"Oh my, what a day," Anias climbed down the stairs from her lānai. "Noelani, can you make sure that Mr. Jun knows that we are having guests? Who can *this* be, now?"

33:3 Makelo reached the stables just in time to see his uncles scatter, each of them taking a different route away from Milakale to find Philomena. Momentarily at a loss as to how to get their attention, he remembered how the chief of the night marchers recognized him, and without thinking, let out a mighty, "Naʻu," that rang down the valley. Surprised as anyone, he watched as one by one the men stopped and turned back toward the sound.

The first to reach him was Kalani, who rode up with a look of amazement and bemusement by equal and conflicting measures.

"It appears that young Maleko has a little mana himself now," his uncle slapped him on the back as the others approached.

"Makana Kealoha brought Philomena back," Maleko announced, hoping to avoid an interrogation. "Everyone is in the courtyard, and more guests are arriving by the moment."

"Are we going to just ignore what happened?" Kekoa asked.

"It appears that way, younger brother," Kapono answered for the rest of them. "I know that you prefer a practical explanation for things, but sometimes—as you know—the island has a different idea."

Kekoa lagged behind the three Mahoe men, wondering how he had become odd man out all of a sudden. All thoughts of Maleko, however, were forgotten as the group walked up to see Anias Lanthier chatting with the heir apparent to the Hawaiʻian crown.

"What is *happening?*" Kekoa wondered out loud, causing the other Mahoe men to turn and shrug in equal astonishment.

33:4 "I cannot believe that I should be caught so unaware," Jun grumbled as he and Noelani scrambled to prepare a pāʻina, or dinner, worthy of such an important guest as Liliʻuokalani on such short notice.

"Have no fear, Mr. Jun," Noelani trying to bolster the head chef's confidence as she frantically chopped vegetables. "You have this well in hand. I have never once witnessed anyone get up from your table that did not need help to move!"

"Where can your brothers be with my fish?" Jun worried. "If only I had been given time to prepare something in the imu, as is appropriate!"

Noelani's mouth watered at the mention of the earthen oven, remembering how well Jun had mastered the traditional Hawai'ian cooking method of kālua.

Meanwhile, an ad hoc collection of guests had gathered in the Lanthier's drawing room for pre-dinner cocktails, while the matron of Milakale glowed, relishing the moment, completely in her element.

Urias cradled a glass of Cassidy & Co.'s whiskey from County Kildare while marveling at the opulence of the Lanthier's home. The koa paneling seemed to ripple and shine from deep within, adding an extra dimension to what was already a fantastical fabrication far beyond what he was accustomed to.

If anything, it reminded him of Rodolfo's ostentatious display of wealth back on Nob Hill. He only hoped that whatever had paid for the Lanthier's luxury had not corrupted its owners like it had O Elefante.

Hendry, on the other hand, amused himself chatting with their hostess and the Hawai'ian princess.

"Excuse me, your grace," he mustered his best imitation of courtly behavior, "we English are lucky to have a few princesses running around ourselves. One of them just became an empress for a hot minute—a shame about old Fritz. Have you had the pleasure of meeting any of them by any chance?"

"Mr. Hendry, I believe?" Lili'uokalani gave the man her full attention. "Indeed, I was lucky enough to accompany Queen Kapi'olani to Queen Victoria's Golden Jubilee in London a couple of years ago."

"Really?" Hendry sounded surprised belying his better manners. "How did you find The Big Smoke?"

"Well, Mr. Hendry," the princess leaned into the conversation, "I believe we took a right at Ireland."

The group surrounding the princess held their collective breath waiting for a signal from their hostess who immediately broke into laughter, much to their relief.

"I declare that the princess got you on that one, Mr. Hendry," Anias decreed. "Who needs a refresher before we adjourn to the dining room?"

"Princess Lili'uokalani, please allow me to properly introduce Reverend Fox," Alexander Lanthier and the preacher joined the party.

"I had to practically drag him from the chapel. Tomorrow morning is his big debut here at Milakale."

"Reverend Fox," the princess took his hand. "Your reputation precedes you."

"Uh oh," Urias reflexively muttered under his breath.

"Princess," Fox gave a short bow. "It is indeed my pleasure."

"I have heard about Mr. Lanthier's miraculous recovery at your urging," Lili'uokalani continued. "I would love to hear your sermon tomorrow."

"It is decided then!" Anias nearly exploded with joy. "You shall stay here at Milakale and join us in the morning. It would be our honor to have you and your coachmen be our guests."

"You are too kind, Mrs. Lanthier," the princess began.

"Please, call me Anias, if you feel that is appropriate, that is!" A devout student of continental etiquette, the woman found herself twisting in the wind for a moment, not knowing if she had committed an inexcusable social gaff.

"Of course, Anias," Lili'uokalani graciously rescued the woman from embarrassment. "How friendly. I would like us to be friends. I do have a friendly favor to ask of you later."

"Anything," Anias gushed. "Please, just name it."

"Tell me, princess," Alexander broke in, "I had the chance to admire your horses as they were being watered and brushed down. You know, I am a bit of an equestrian myself."

"Your reputation precedes you as well, sir," Lili'uokalani remarked.

"Yes, well, forgive me if I am being nosy," Alexander continued unabated, "but doesn't the royal family travel with a bit more... pomp?"

"Alexander Lanthier!" Anias exclaimed.

"It is quite all right. You are correct, sir, when it comes to official business. Sometimes, however, I do enjoy getting out in the country without all the trappings of my station. Equestrian-to-equestrian, you can understand that, can't you?"

"Yes, of course," Alexander agreed. Had he any sense, he would have withered under his wife's stare. "I should have recognized you as a woman that appreciates the wind in her hair."

Urias nearly choked on his Irish dram, while Fox lightly touched Anias on the arm to keep her from braining her husband with the nearest blunt object.

"Paka'a is the Hawai'ian god of wind, is he not?" Fox mused. "Perhaps what our host means is that it does the soul good to commune with Paka'a however one might find him."

"Fair play, reverend," Hendry admired the diving catch. "Fair play."

33:5 Upstairs, Emilia and Philomena took time to become reacquainted under the excuse of getting ready for dinner. Emilia stood before the mirror in her daughter's room and held an elegant gown up to her body that Anias had lent her to wear.

"I can't believe that anything of Mrs. Lanthier's would ever fit me," she marveled, while ignoring the elephant in the room. "It goes to show you what I have lost."

The woman turned to see Philomena watching her from across the room, a concerned look on her face.

"But of course, look how much I have found!" Emilia tried to bolster the worried girl. "Don't worry, my love, I will never let anyone keep us apart ever again."

"That's not it, mother," Philomena chewed her lip and struggled to meet her mother's gaze. "I saw him, you know."

"Saw whom, dear?" Emilia laid the gown out on the bed and took Philomena's hands.

"Father," she said. "He was dead, but he followed me out here."

"Oh, my," Emilia fought to process what her daughter was telling her.

"I have certain... abilities," she continued. "I was able to speak to Father, and direct Mr. Lanthier back to his body, and the bird!"

Emilia simply held Philomena as she broke down in tears.

"So, it is true?" Emilia finally asked when the girl's sobs had finally subsided. "The reason that evil man took me was because he thought that you might be able to cure him. Oh, my poor girl. Thank heaven that he never found you!"

Philomena merely looked up at her mother with eyes that looked obsidian in the half-light. Emilia easily followed the girl's train of thought.

"Do you think you are safe out here?"

"I really don't know, mother," she whispered. "I don't know anything."

33:6 The momentary buzz caused by Emilia and Philomena's graceful descent of the staircase from the upper rooms was cut short by the announcement of dinner.

"'Ai a ma'ona, inu a kena," Noelani came out of the kitchen and gave a traditional Hawai'ian invitation to a feast. "I invite everyone to follow me to the dining room and 'eat until you are satisfied, drink until quenched.'"

Having to scramble to create a meal that would live up to his own high standards, Jun began the evening's service with a traditional Hawai'ian dish that would come to be synonymous with all island feasts in general: lū'au.

"Noelani, tell your brother Kekoa that the first course is almost ready to go out," Jun ordered.

"I don't know where he has gone off to," Noelani called over her shoulder while checking the roasting fish course. "We shall have to ask Kalani to serve this evening."

"I don't care who takes this food out, as long as it goes out!" Jun declared as he plated the tender taro tops and octopus baked in coconut milk. The fragrant dish filled the small kitchen with sense memories of past feasts and celebrations for both cooks, a smile creeping onto both of their faces despite the rush of an important evening shift.

Maleko, feeling a bit out of place now that Philomena's long lost mother had appeared, was making himself useful in the kitchen, prepping fresh vegetables and generally trying to stay out of Jun's way.

"Keiki, go find Kalani and tell him to get his butt in here!" Noelani ordered.

"Please stop calling me that!" Maleko pleaded. "It's embarrassing. I am a man now."

Noelani looked over the stove with an expression that meant either she was carefully considering his request, or was about to beat him to death with the steel ladle she held in her hand. Maleko wisely chose to believe the latter.

"I can serve, you know," Maleko tempted fate one last time before going to find his uncle.

"Maleko Mahoe," Jun stepped in to put an end to the back and forth, "this is perhaps the most important meal that we have served here at Milakale. Although I do have total trust in your abilities, there is a certain way that things are done around royalty. We need to project a very specific image, and I am afraid that your youthful enthusiasm is not it. I promise that once we have survived this meal, I shall let you begin to serve. With glee. For now, go!"

Maleko, counting the exchange as a win, ran off to bring his oldest uncle back. Meanwhile, Noelani was able to keep the feast going by bringing out some of Jun's carefully aged poi and fresh lomi lomi salmon. The salty fish and tomato salad perfectly complemented the sour taro. While Jun pounded fresh poi almost daily, he was adamant about balancing his flavors, and most people who experienced his artistry in the kitchen, would come away in agreement.

Kalani burst into the kitchen buttoning up a white jacket as he came.

"Tell me, Jun Jin, what is the entree?" The oldest Mahoe brother lifted up the lid to a simmering stock pot and got a rap on his knuckles with a wooden spoon appearing out of nowhere for his troubles.

"That is my chicken long rice," Jun explained. "Do not let the steam out! I didn't have time to use the imu, so I am baking uku in the oven stuffed with ogo and linguiça. I really wanted to use lop cheong, but it will do."

"Brother, come take out some wine," Noelani chose a bottle to help quench the thirst the diners had to be feeling given the early courses. "I'll take the rice off and let it set up. Jin, how is the fish coming along?"

"Five minutes," Jun called out. "How about dessert? Have Maleko cut up some pineapples, and we'll grill them with some brown sugar."

"Maleko!"

33:6 Outside of the bustling kitchen, and even busier dining room, a dark and quiet night had washed over Milakale. Kekoa used the shadows to carefully make his way up to the stables. The echo of Noelani calling out for his keiki hanauna gave him a momentary pang of guilt, but he felt compelled to let the Hawaiian League know that Princess Lili'uokalani was a guest of the Lanthiers.

While the plantation owner was a captain of industry, and part of the haole business class, Kekoa knew that Alexander usually deferred to his wife on matters other than sugar and his damnable horse. Anias Lanthier could be easily be swayed by another strong woman to take up the cause of maintaining the monarchy.

Unlike his brothers, Kekoa felt that their island nation had become stagnant. Right or wrong, he had decided the only way for him to become anything but the Lanthier's serf was to become an American and was not about to let a dilettante sugar baroness and her dodgy friends ruin that chance.

Although he knew there would be hell to pay for stepping out on the dinner for the princess, he chose a horse and, without a look back, rode for Hilo.

33:7 The buzz of conversation around the Lanthier's dinner table soon gave way to the click and clack of cutlery on fine china, punctuated by satisfied sounds coming from the diners. Kalani made his way around behind them, refilling glasses and attending to every need.

"So tell me, young Philomena," Lili'uokalani addressed the girl who had been quietly picking at her snapper, "how do you find life in our country? It must be quite a change from California."

Philomena was grateful to have an excuse to stop torturing the baked fish and brightened up immediately.

"It is so beautiful, princess," she gushed. "I almost can't believe that it's real sometimes."

"I understand that you have had quite the guide in young Maleko, have you not?"

Kalani, who was in the middle of refilling Fox's water glass, was so shocked to hear that the princess knew that his nephew existed, let alone what his name was, that he missed the tumbler and watered the reverend instead.

"Blast it, man!" Fox pushed back from the table, a wet splash covering his midsection.

"Reverend Fox, forgive me!" Kalani reached for linen to help blot his mistake.

"Please, don't bother," Fox graciously let the man off the hook. "I should take my leave, anyway. I need to finish my sermon. Princess, ladies, gentlemen, I shall see you all in the morning."

The remaining guests watched Fox leave as Kalani slunk back to the kitchen as unobtrusively as he could manage.

"This meal has been so wonderful," the princess finally broke the silence having perceived it was up to her to do so. "Perhaps this is the right time to ask you my favor, Anias."

"Of course, my dear," she took the liberty of the familiar. "Anything I can do for you, consider it done."

"Perhaps you should hear my request first."

"If you insist," Anias deferred as she looked around the table to see everyone now on tenterhooks.

"As you are well aware, my new friend, food is such an important aspect of entertaining. It goes double for successful statecraft."

"I am afraid I don't follow," Anias apologized. Several diners, however, were a step ahead of her, and waited to hear how the ask was to come about.

"It cannot be news to any of you, I am sure, that our nation is in a precarious place. There are world powers that circle us like sharks, waiting for us to miss a stroke and slip beneath the waves," Lili'uokalani explained.

"At Iolani Palace, I have the opportunity to receive emissaries from nearly every civilized nation in the world. The king and I possess the patience to hear what they have to say, to listen to the promises that they carry from across the ocean. What we lack, I am afraid, is someone that can fill their bellies as full as they attempt to fill our ears. Someone that understands all of the disparate accents of the universal language of food."

"Jun Jin," Anias cottoned on to where the conversation was heading. "Say no more! If he will go—I have no hold on Mr. Jun—he is yours."

"Mahalo nui loa, Anias Lanthier, Alexander Lanthier," Liliʻuokalani thanked her hosts.

"Noʻu ka hauʻoli," they both replied.

Chapter Thirty-Four

34:1 "It looks like the pā'ani is afoot, gentlemen; as they say!" Boyle grinned out from under his massive walrus mustache. He spurred his horse to run faster so that he might reach Milakale before sunrise.

"Is this all a game to you, Boyle?" The aging, yet still spry Bishop Davis admonished the rifleman from over his shoulder as he led the trio of riders. "The very future of this nation may depend on cooler heads being on site to influence the Lanthiers. If the princess fills their heads with ideas of a Polynesian Confederacy under Kalākaua, our position here is as good as over."

"Surely you exaggerate, bishop," Colson interjected, catching up to the two men. "I know Alexander's mind. He will not be in a hurry to lose his empire."

Davis's gray pallor shone with reflected moonlight as if he were yet another stone satellite floating in the darkness.

"Why take that chance?" Davis asked before pouring on the leather.

34:2 As the Sun rose on Milakale, Princess Lili'uokalani was already dressed, on the lānai, and watching for it. When it finally appeared out of the ocean, painting the sky in color, she quietly sang it a new tune that she had been working on.

"Do you mind if I join you, princess?" Philomena softly asked as to not startle the woman. Lili'uokalani acted as if she had been waiting on the porch for daybreak all along, instead of expecting the girl.

"I did not come for Jun Jin, you know," she spoke without turning her head from the sunrise. "I mean, he is a prize, and I will be glad to have him, but he is not why I came to Milakale."

Philomena was often surprised at how the adults on the island spoke to her. *Did they have no one else that would listen?* She wondered. *Perhaps they were always too busy considering the next thing that they themselves were going to say to pay attention to each other. What did that say about her? Is that what she was doing now?*

"You should ask about his potato soup," she offered in lieu of any other meaningful response.

Lili'uokalani turned and sized up the enigmatic young woman.

"Some say it is magic," Philomena struggled to fill the silence.

The princess burst into hearty laughter, a sound that further spurred the day into becoming.

"Do they, now?" She asked once she was able to restrain herself. "There are those who might say the same thing about you."

"I'm not magic," Philomena cast her eyes down. "I'm just... I don't know exactly what I am."

"Well, I think you are something special, and I have a proposition for you to consider."

34:3 "Are you going to Honolulu, then, Jin?" Noelani was careful not to badger her fellow chef when the idea was broached after the evening service. She gave him the night to collect his thoughts, but now that breakfast was to be made, she was bursting with curiosity. "To cook for the royal family! Do you know what an honor that is?"

"Yes, I am aware, Noelani Mahoe," Jun played it close to his kitchen whites. "It shall not be an easy job, I fear. The king is a famous eater."

"Come on, you old fool!" Noelani uncharacteristically called him out. "You have never been one to hide your light under your batterie de cuisine. Why start now?"

"I told Mrs. Lanthier that I would consider the princess's offer only under one condition."

"What cheek," Noelani now teased her culinary companion. "What else could you possibly ask for? A gold soup tureen for that voodoo soup of yours?"

"I asked her to make you head chef at Milakale," he said. "There is no one else on this island that knows the breadth of cuisines needed to keep the Lanthiers and all their guests well fed."

Noelani was speechless as Jun removed his chef's toque and placed it on her head, adding a foot to the woman's height.

34:4 Alexander Lanthier stood on his lānai and started his morning with a
Por Larrañaga, the special day calling for a dip into the humidor for a
special cigar. He was contemplating asking Noelani to fit him with a
Bloody Mary to round out his absolutions when a cloud of red dust
again announced the arrival of riders from Hilo to his doorstep.

Lanthier stepped down to the courtyard and was joined by Kapono
Mahoe who had also taken heed of the telltale cloud of dirt.

"Is that your brother escorting those scoundrels, Kapono?"
Lanthier teased.

"It appears so, Mr. Lanthier," the middle Mahoe brother mused.
"It is very hard to keep an eye on the young these days. There is no
telling what mischief they will get up to."

"Gentlemen," Lanthier effused when the party arrived, "did you
somehow sense that the bar was about to open?"

This time, it was Bishop Davis that took the lead, leaving "Tweed"
Colson looking slightly sheepish, an expression not lost on Lanthier.

"We have heard that Milakale has quite the prominent guest,"
Davis said. "We thought we would come pay our respects."

"Is that so? Did a little mamo bird tell you that?" Lanthier froze
Kapono with a raised eyebrow as he tried to make his exit.

"Are you saying that it is not the case that the heir apparent to the
Hawai'ian throne is here?" Davis asked.

"I am not saying anything of the sort," Lanthier toyed with the
bishop. "I am not in the practice of discussing my guest list with
anyone other than my wife and my chef. You three have come on a very
fortuitous morning, however. Reverend Fox is giving his first sermon
in the chapel in a bit. You are all welcome to come listen and have a
peek at the congregation if you like."

He turned to Colson and Doyle.

"Gents, I believe we may have just enough time to bend an elbow.
Bishop, if you'll grant us the indulgence."

34:5 Fox stood at his new pulpit and looked out over the assembled crowd.
The Lanthiers naturally occupied pride of place in the first pew and sat
with Philomena, Emilia, and Princess Lili'uokalani beside them.

Behind them, Bishop Davis waited with a slightly inebriated Colson and Boyle for the sermon to begin.

"I would like to start with a reading from Isaiah," Fox announced to the crowded chapel. "'He shall not fail nor be discouraged till he have set judgment in the Earth, and the isles shall wait for his law.'" Fox let the last word echo, the normally resonant building somewhat deadened by the multitude of bodies that filled every available seat and empty nook.

"The isles shall wait for his law," he repeated. "Now, I if I have read that passage once, I have read it a thousand times. I had no idea what it meant, until now. I feel that my whole ministry... no, my whole life has led me to this moment. I have been given wonderful news, and I have been hoping to share it with a congregation that was ready to accept the gift. Are you ready to accept the gift of the golden light?"

The mixed aggregate of the island's disparate social stratum murmured in assent. Across the aisle from the Lanthiers, several members of the extended Hawai'ian royal family looked around at the assembled throng and nodded their own agreement.

Fox scanned the congregation and stopped cold when he saw Khadae standing in the portico just beyond the open doors.

"First, let me ask you a question," Fox pivoted. "Can it be said that nothing happens under God's watchful eye that is not part of his plan?"

The crowd readily conceded the point.

"I have come here to your paradise having walked through the very gates of hell. Why, even now I carry a lead slug next to my heart as a reminder of man's uncanny capacity for cruelty. And yet," Fox paused for effect, "and yet not once did I question that it all was somehow part of God's will. I am sure that each of you has experienced your own tribulations, have you not? I am sure that there were times that you wanted to look up to the heavens and cry out, 'Why me, Lord?' Heaven knows that I *have* cried out, only to receive stony silence for an answer. Is this because God does not care what happens to us?"

Only a whisper of shifting silk on silent shoulders belied the few shrugs that the question engendered.

"Let me equate our position in terms that some of us here are all too familiar with. When my unit with the Union's II Corps was mercilessly attacked at Savage's Station, did Abraham Lincoln, our nation's father, feel each shell that landed in our field hospital?"

"Lincoln is not *our* nation's father," one of the shoestring Hawai'ian royals whispered.

"Of course he didn't," Fox continued. "A president is more of a 'big picture' guy. So too, does the Creator have more pressing matters than the trials and tribulations of individuals. However, if we have faith in ourselves—"

The reverend gazed out across the room and saw Khadae listening, his ears well pricked.

Beyond him, the Pacific Ocean sparkled in the morning sunlight, and Fox may have seen a whale jump in the sheltered bay of Milakale, or it may have been a trick of the light. Whichever, it was enough to derail his train of thought. As the congregation waited for him to continue, Fox stepped down from the pulpit to the level of the teeming pews. He took a deep inhale and set off on a different tack.

"I said that I have some good news for you," Fox announced, spreading his arms wide as if to gather everyone around him. "I am here to tell you that there is a heaven! The scriptures are true, it does exist."

An excited murmur rose from the crowd and Fox could see heads bobbing in affirmation.

"There is also some bad news, I'm afraid," the reverend continued as he stared back at Khadae who was caught in the chapel's entrance like a bug in amber. "The sad truth is that heaven is not for you. Heaven holds no more place for us than our own homes have space for the fish that swim in the sea or the multitudes of insects that crawl in the dirt."

The buzz that had begun to lift from the congregation took on a dark undertone.

"It is not personal," he continued, "we just do not factor into the big picture."

Alexander glanced over at his wife who was enraptured by Fox's flights of colloquy. Peeking around her, however, he saw that Emilia and Philomena sat with expressions that clearly read, 'tell me something that I don't already know.' Beyond Lili'uokalani, who looked willing to see just where the reverend was going with it all, the assembled royal cousins were watching her closely for guidance.

"Years ago, back in California, I had been called to witness a miracle, but the grace that I received was not what I had expected. It rarely ever is," Fox lamented. "I followed a star from the east to witness a birth. Sounds familiar doesn't it? However, when this child was born, I was disappointed. I thought that there would be choirs of angels attesting to the arrival of a new king, but what I saw, what I witnessed, was merely the ordinary birth of a baby girl."

The girl in question shifted nervously in her pew while the remaining believers sat silently, unsure of the direction Fox was headed in, yet still rapt.

"That, compared to all the others, was my greatest sin," the reverend proclaimed. "How dare I discount the greatest miracle of all? What gall. What audacity. For that weakness alone, should I step down from this position, but I have more to tell you before I am finished.

"I brought Philomena here to Milakale under false pretenses," he confessed to the crowd. "She is not my daughter, although I have come to think of her in those terms. She was... is the child of two members of my congregation who trusted me. Her real father thought that I had done him wrong and lost all faith. I can attest to you now—that is a very desperate place to be. At the time, I thought her mother was gone as well, but as we just blessedly found out, that is not the case."

Philomena squeezed her mother's hand as they sat through the painful recitation of their recent trials.

"I was an orphan myself," Fox barreled ahead, "and I could not just let that happen to a member of my spiritual family. You see, when I was alone in the orphanage, I did have someone take an interest in me. Someone who gave me a gift."

Fox lifted the bible that Khadae had given him so many years before. The benefactor in question watched intently from the foyer as many of the assemblage began to sense that Fox was speaking past them and turned to look.

"I was given the gift of faith!" Fox began to regain some of his oratorical mojo. "And what a gift it was! Faith is what got me through the War Between the States! Faith is what picked me up out of the mud and the blood and the filth and put me on the path of righteousness! Faith is what brought me here to Milakale!"

As Fox's peroration gathered speed and energy, many of the congregation began to respond to his declamation with assents of their own.

"The man who took such an interest, the man who gave me this singular book, is here with us today. I would like him to step forward so that you all might bear witness."

Khadae shook his head but was captured by the chapel full of eyes.

"Akram Khadae, come forth and receive the credit that you deserve!" Fox entreated.

Murmurs of encouragement seemed to pull the man closer and closer to the open doorway as beads of sweat began to trickle down the sides of his face.

"Have no fear!" Fox continued on. "This is a house of love, Akram. I only want to show you the respect that you showed me."

"Yes! Yes! Come in!" The congregation now chanted.

Against his best judgment, Khadae took the final step across the threshold, wincing against an adverse reaction that didn't occur.

"Akram Khadae, or shall I refer to you as Tamiel? You gave me this very book at a moment when I needed guidance."

Khadae was unnerved by Fox calling him by his real name, and took a tentative step back.

"It wasn't until all these years later that I finally learned the truth," Fox held the one-of-a-kind bible to one of the candles that flanked his altar. "I learned that this book contains only lies!"

"No!" Khadae shouted, a sound that blew out the stained glass windows, littering the grass outside in rainbow shards. As the book took flame so did Khadae, a pair of leather wings unfolding out of the smoldering ruin of his coat. Shocked at first, the fallen angel soon realized that the fire wasn't about to consume him and he took a step toward the altar.

"You fool!" He growled as the congregation scattered to either side of the chapel, the entrance starting to smolder from the footsteps he left behind.

"Khadae!" Hendry stood and retrieved a pistol from inside his coat. "You bitch-wolf's son! I knew you were a devil, but I didn't think you were *the* devil!"

"Niall Hendry," Khadae snarled. "All of this could have been avoided had you done your job."

"Go back to hell, demon!" Hendry shouted and shot the still flaming man in the chest.

Khadae looked down at the hole that had appeared in his reddened hide. The shocked throng stood mute as an asp poked its head out of the smoking opening and dropped to the ground. Khadae simply laughed as the snake slithered up the aisle toward the altar, dripping fire as it went.

"'A'ole," Lili'uokalani declared as she stepped out of her pew and crushed the snake's head under her fashionable boot. "No, I don't think so."

The action was underscored by a crack of thunder announcing a sudden island shower, the damp coolness relieving the overheated chapel through the open doors and shattered windows.

As if brought down by the sound, Fox fell backward against the altar and sank to the floor, while Khadae was instantaneously consumed by the flame he had been wearing like a suit.

Seizing the moment, Alexander gathered his pew together and shepherded them out past the stricken preacher toward a back door. Taking the hint from the vacating princess and sugar barons, the rest of the throng soon followed.

Urias and Hendry fought their way through the escaping crowd to Fox's side.

"My heart," Fox managed to say.

"It's all right," Urias soothed the stricken man, "We've got you."

The two men picked up the preacher and made to carry him out before he protested.

"Who brings a gun to church?" Urias gave Hendry a hard time despite the desperate situation.

"Who invites the Devil?"

"Put me down," Fox croaked. "Tell Philomena—"

"Tell her what?" Urias asked, resting Fox on the steps of the chancel. "Do you want us to get her?"

"No," he sighed. "Let her be. Tell her not to bring me back. My war is finally over." With that, Fox closed his eyes for the last time.

Leaving his friend a moment to grieve, Hendry proceeded to stomp out any small remaining flames. It wasn't until he picked up the charred remains of Fox's bible did he interrupt.

"Aaron, would you look at this a moment?" Hendry pried open the remaining text and held it out for Urias to see.

"What am I looking at?"

"Exactly," Hendry replied as confused as anyone. "I was no altar boy, but I've been around the block enough times to know that this is no Bible."

"What are you talking about?" Urias was in no mood for riddles. "Of course it is. Mordikai carried that damn thing since the day I met him."

"That may be the case," Hendry allowed, "but it is no Bible, traditionally speaking, at least. Try to read this thing."

Urias took the charred remnant and held it up to the light now streaming through the empty window frames.

"What was this?" He asked Fox who was in no position to answer. Urias turned page after page, the burned edges crumbling to dust.

"Fox said that our dragon man there gave it to him," Hendry pondered. "Do you figure that he wrote it?"

"I guess we'll never know," Urias walked over to the pile of ash that had been Khadae. A glint of silver caught his eyes, and against his better judgment, he reached down and retrieved a pocket watch from the cinders. "Look at this!" He tossed the timepiece to Hendry who caught it instinctively. "Keep it, you earned it."

"'A caelo usque ad centrum,'" Hendry recited, having flipped the case open. "What do you figure that means?"

"Beats the hell out of me."

34:6 Outside the chapel, the tropical squall had disappeared as quickly as it had arrived and the traumatized congregants milled about in a shocked stupor. From across the lawn, Princess Lili'uokalani approached Emilia who was holding a weeping Philomena. The girl had begun to think of Fox as family, and although they struggled with their differences, she had now lost yet another father.

"Mrs. Gilliam, I am sorry to intrude, but your daughter and I spoke on a matter this morning that I would like you to give some serious consideration."

"Can you explain to me what just happened back there, your highness?" Emilia pointed toward the chapel.

"Alas, I cannot," Lili'uokalani admitted, "but I fear that Philomena may be a target, if not for supernatural threats, then for more pedestrian—but no less dangerous—ones. I think I may have a mutually beneficial idea to keep her safe, at least until this furor fades a bit."

"I am listening," Emilia stroked Philomena's dark hair. "We obviously cannot stay here, and there is nothing left for us in California."

"On the north coast of Moloka'i, there is a community dedicated to helping poor unfortunates who suffer from a truly debilitating disease. I really think that Philomena can do some good there and would be safe from every jeopardy due to the remote nature of the colony and, of course, the quarantine."

"What do you say, daughter?"

Before the girl could answer, Anias Lanthier approached with Alexander following close behind.

"We are so sorry, my dear Philomena," Anias spoke for the both of them. "I foresaw a great calamity, but I had no idea—"

"Tell her about your latest casting," Alexander prompted.

"I have seen a growing opportunity for you to do great things!" Anias exclaimed. "I am afraid that your destiny is not here in Milakale, however much I wish it were."

Just then, Maleko came running across the property, shouting for Philomena.

"Maleko!" The girl broke off from her mother and met the boy with an embrace.

"What the heck did you do, white girl?" He teased his partner in crime. "Do you know how much trouble I would be in for setting fire to a church?"

Philomena took the boy's face in her hands and touched her forehead to his in a traditional honi expression of love and respect. The two friends touched noses and inhaled, breathing the same air for a fleeting moment. Philomena sealed the greeting by kissing the boy, her lips grazing his and causing him to blush.

"I will come back for you, Maleko Mahoe," she promised. "Aloha."

34:7 Although Alexander had formally declared the bar open—inviting any visitor that needed a stiff drink up to the Big House—the three riders from Hilo took the opportunity to retreat. The bishop and his two cohorts were not even going to try to put the morning's events in context without some serious distance. One thing was sure, however, the ascendancy of Milakale as a political force on the island had taken a big hit.

Hendry was watching the men ride off when he heard a familiar voice call his name.

"Mr. Hendry, what a fortuitous surprise," Wei Lei approached the Londoner who was gobsmacked to see the former Chinatown matron.

"Wei Lei, what in the world are you doing out here in the middle of the ocean? Hang on, did you call me 'Mr. Hendry?'"

"Of course, would you rather I refer to you by your Christian name, Niall?"

Hendry's mind whirled as he struggled to rethink everything he knew about the woman.

"Are you telling me that all the times we met back in San Francisco that you were playing a part?" Hendry began to admire the work that Wei had put into her role of an archetypical opium den dragon lady. "You bricky girl!"

"Come now, Niall, you yourself have been known to a play a pretty decent haberdasher," Wei teased. "'Bang up to the elephant,' as I believe the saying goes."

"My dear, Wei Lei," Hendry began to appreciate the woman in a new, clearer light. "Did you have anything to do with this Khadae business... What am I saying? Of course you did. You were on to him all along weren't you?"

"That is classified information, coster," Wei baited him.

"What now, may I ask?" Hendry probed. "Is it back to Chinatown?"

"That's what I wanted to talk to you about. San Francisco is changing," Wei lamented. "It is quickly losing its wide-open sense of adventure—almost like it wants to become a real city all of a sudden."

"A shame that," Hendry admitted, "but I've felt it as well. It's harder for a well-meaning ne'er-do-well to get over these days. What did you have in mind?"

"A business proposition," Wei purred. "With my brains and your big white face—and sense of style, of course—I think we can carve ourselves out a nice piece of the proverbial pie."

"I'm in, my lady," Hendry exclaimed. "Let's go toast the idea with Lanthier's liquor before it's all gone!"

35:1 Karabu the tetramorph stood at the book and watched the odds for and against the latest Earth-bound avatar fluctuate back and forth. It had been the most contentious season in his long memory, and remained any angel's game at this point. The sharp vision and predatory perceptiveness of his eagle eyes caught every nuance of the shifting likelihood that humanity would or would not drop the ball.

"How goes the game, Hawkeye?" Jehoel the seraph walked up and asked, his innocent-looking face belying his fiery nature.

"Eagle."

"I don't follow."

"I am presenting as an eagle at the moment," Karabu clarified, not taking his eyes off of the leaderboard. "Not a hawk. That would be stupid."

"Well, excuse the heaven out of me," Jehoel waved two of his six wings in the air.

"Actually, Jehoel, I could use one of your triple *holy*s about right now. I can sense that these idiots are about to fumble."

"The trisagion?" The seraph covered his perfect child-looking mouth with a wing. "Those are not meant to be tossed around, willy-nilly! We're supposed to proclaim His/Her/Their absolute and supreme holiness and that's it."

"I'm not asking you not to do your proclaiming, my friend," Karabu presented his lion countenance—the one he knew from experience was his confidant's favorite. "Just throw in a good word for the kid would you? That can't be against the rules, can it?"

Before the seraph could protest any further, the scrolling odds went dark and there came a crack of thunder.

"What the heaven?" Karabu roared. But even his mighty anger was lost in the general commotion arising from the collected hosts.

"I have an announcement!" Archangel—and head bookmaker—Sachiel, called out. "Due to unprecedented interference on the part of the BNU, resulting, I might add, in an annulment of immortality—"

A tumult arose from the accumulated angels, as historically even open rebellion didn't call for annulments. Granted, the guilty had to spend their eternities as they might—be it cast downstairs, or wandering the Earth—but the invalidation of immortality was heretofore unheard of in either angelic community.

"It is the decision of the Upstairs Agency that the success or failure of this season's avatar shall be considered a push."

The book exploded in protest. Angry angels surged forward and surrounded Sachiel.

"Enough!" A celestial thunderclap rang out across the heavens. "All bets are null and void. However, given the circumstances, we have decided to move up the insertion of the next avatar. For those who have bet the parlay, you are lucky, consider this a win."

"Yes!" Karabu snorted, having manifested as a bull just in case something needed charging and knocking over.

"That reminds me," Jehoel said, ripping up his ticket. "I heard that Harut and Marut were called for interference and are back downstairs."

"Hanging upside down, no doubt," Karabu laughed.

"You have to wonder if they actually like it."

"No telling with some angels. Do you thirst, Jehoel? I'm buying!"

Hawai'ian glossary

'ahu'ula	feathered cloak of royalty
'Ai a ma'ona, inu a kena	"Eat until you are satisfied, drink until quenched"
aloha	greeting, lit. "breath of life"
'alopeke 'ohana	fox family
'a'ole	no
'aumākua	ancestral spirits, lineage
E mālama kakou no ka ho'ola 'ana	"We support each other for healing"
haole	someone not Hawai'ian, esp. European
heiau	Hawai'ian temple
hilahila	shy
honi	traditional Hawai'ian expression of love and respect
honu	Hawai'ian green sea turtle
imu	earthen oven used to roast and steam at the same time
imua o ka mauna	toward the mountain
'io	Hawai'ian hawk and its cry
ka wa haumia	monthly period, "unclean season"
kahuna	an expert in any field, priest
kahuna lapa'au	Hawai'ian healer
kaikamahine	girl, daughter
kaikamahine nani	beautiful girl
kaikua'ana	older sibling
kālua	to cook in an underground oven
Kāmohoali'i	Hawai'ian shark god
kanaka makua	adult
Kanaka Maoli	full-blooded Hawai'ian

Kānaka Maoli	the Hawai'ian people
kanaka 'u'uku	little man
kapa	traditional cloth made from wauke bark
kapu	forbidden
keiki	child
keiki hanauna	nephew
keiki kāne	boy
keiki li'ili'i	little child
kupua	healer or shaman
kupuna wahine	grandmother
lānai	roofed porch
lōlō kanapapiki	stupid son of a bitch
lū'au	a baked dish made with taro tops and octopus
mahalo nui loa	thank you very much
makai	toward the sea
makua	toward the mountain
mamo	Hawai'ian honeycreeper
mana	power, life energy
manu li'ili'i	little bird
Menehune	mythological race of small people who build things
na'u	mine, belonging to me
no'u ka hau'oli	you are welcome
'o nā mea maika'i	the good stuff
'ohana	family
'Ōhi'a Lehua	native plant with red and yellow flowers
oia'i'o	it is true
'ōkole	asshole
pā'ani	competitive sport
pāhoehoe	smooth lava
pā'ina	a meal, dinner
Paka'a	Hawai'ian god of wind
paniolo	cowboy

pipikaula	Hawai‘ian beef jerky
poi	starchy paste made from taro root
pū	conch shell
pueo	Hawai‘ian short-eared owl
pūpūs	snacks
Pu‘uhonua	city of refuge
‘ūhā hope	hindquarters
uku	Hawai‘ian blue-green snapper

This book is dedicated to the memory of Louie Larsen who, among many other things, instilled in me an interest, love, and respect for the islands. A hui hou.

The author remembers the Exploratorium Writing Salon, where this journey began, with great fondness. Keep writing my friends, wherever you are.

I would like to thank Ryan Cicak for drawing his ass off during a global pandemic. You can find more of Ryan's work on Instagram at tk.makes.art.

Thanks once again to the Esau girls—Dana, Jeanette, and Rocco—and Annalise Phillips for the early reads and advice.

Dana Goldberg and Zeke Cullen deserve a hearty shout out for tagging in and wrestling words to the mat like a couple of superstars.

Much respect goes out to Liz Ball for graciously fielding my theological questions early on. Her counsel provided this all-important lodestone: "In the end, it has to be about love." Tru dat.

Last but not least, thanks to Bert and Sage McCluskey for their spirit of aloha and magic potato soup.

About the font: Alegreya was designed by Juan Pablo del Peral and was chosen as one of the 53 "Fonts of the Decade" at *ATypI Letter2* in 2011, given the Certificate of Excellence at the Latinoamerican *Tpios Latinos 2012 biennial*, and was selected in Madrid's 2nd *Bienal Iberoamericana de Diseño* competition.